LIGHT

&

TRUTH

Volume One

The Field Is White

A Historical Novel
Based on a True Story

Visit us at www.harrispublishing.com.

Library of Congress Control Number 2004105179
ISBN: 0-9747376-0-7

First printing May 2004.

Printed in the U.S.A.

Dedicated to my wife, Chris,
and to my ancestors who sacrificed so much.

For behold the field is white already to harvest...

Doctrine and Covenants 4:4

"The whole of that mission to England, from the beginning to the end, placed the apostles in such a position that they had to walk by faith from first to last...[as] we prepared to go on our mission to England...the devil undertook to kill us...I never had the ague in my life until called to go upon that mission...there was not one solitary soul in the quorum of the twelve but what the devil undertook to destroy; ...two hundred cents would have bought me every pound of provision I left with my family when I left home...I was called by revelation to go to John Benbow's and preach the gospel...I went there and found over six hundred people, called United Brethren, and among them were eighty-three preachers, and they, as a people, were in the gospel net. I found that they were praying for *light and truth* and that they had gone about as far as they could go. Out of the [1800 people] we baptized there [in Herefordshire, Gloucestershire, and Worcestershire] in seven months, I hardly know one that has turned against this Church. There has been less apostasy out of that branch of the church and kingdom of God than out of the same number from any part of the world that I am acquainted with."

Wilford Woodruff
Journal of Discourses 15:345, 18:122-125, and 21:315.

"It seemed to me that we had come to a precipice and could go no further until Brother Woodruff placed a bridge over the precipice and we went on with glad hearts rejoicing."

Edward Phillips
Former United Brethren preacher

Foreword

Light and Truth is a historical novel based on a true story. It chronicles the greatest missionary event in the modern history of The Church of Jesus Christ of Latter-day Saints – how Wilford Woodruff converted all six hundred members of the United Brethren congregation in England within just a few months. To give the novel human interest appeal, the missionary event is mingled with two love stories – how our main characters meet, fall in love, deal with their parents and their religious biases, marry, and subsequently align themselves with the United Brethren. That decision placed them in a unique religious group that truly sought additional light and truth.

To understand how and why this modern miracle took place, this first volume, *The Field is White*, will take you through three important steps. The first part introduces you to the main characters – two couples – who represent the typical English people Elder Woodruff met, taught, converted and baptized. Through these main characters, you will learn about the highly stratified British society in the mid 1800s – its traditions, social rituals, and economy. And details about three religions that trace their genesis to England – the Anglicans, the Methodists, and the Quakers.

In the second part of this volume, and somewhat woven through the first, you will learn about the United Brethren congregation – how it got started, its philosophy and teachings, and about the two men who started it, Thomas Kington and John Benbow.

The third part tells of Wilford Woodruff's arrival in England in 1840, his instructions from the Lord to "go south," how he met Kington and Benbow, and the process of converting the United Brethren members during that spring and summer.

The second volume, to be entitled *The Gathering*, will tell how our main characters make the decision to emigrate to America, their trip across the treacherous Atlantic to New Orleans, hardships of the riverboat trip up the Mississippi River, and their first years in Nauvoo. It will detail how these English immigrants strengthened the church, strengthened one another, helped build the temple, and dealt with the challenges of Mormon life on the Illinois frontier. Subsequent volumes will tell the story of how they were exterminated from Illinois, journeyed to Winter Quarters, and what happened when the two main male characters enlisted into the Mormon Battalion.

The process of writing this novel began shortly after I returned in the summer of 2000 from serving as mission president in the Korea Seoul Mission. I began in earnest to study and write the history of Robert Harris, Jr., the first member of my family to join the church. I desired to know everything about him, in as much detail as possible. I became somewhat fascinated with church history in England because I discovered that I had not one, but two sets of grandparents that were part of the United Brethren, plus two aunts and two uncles.

The four main characters in this novel – Bobby (Robert), Hannah, Daniel, and Elizabeth – were real people. They lived in Gloucestershire when Wilford Woodruff arrived. Bobby and Hannah were my great-great-great grandparents. Elizabeth was Bobby's sister, who married Daniel Browett. My other set of grandparents, John Hyrum Green, and his wife, Susannah, are also characters in the book. So is the other set of aunts and uncles, Thomas and Dianah Bloxham. Dianah was Bobby's sister.

If your genealogy can be traced to people who, in the 1840s, lived in

Herefordshire, Worcestershire, or Gloucestershire, chances are that this is the story of your ancestors as well. That might be true, especially, if your last name is one of the following (family names of United Brethren converts): Badham, Bailey, Bayliss, Benbow, Birch, Bishop, Bloxham, Brooks, Browett, Burns, Burrup, Clark, Clift, Cole, Coleman, Curtis, Davis, Dutson, Evans, Gailey, Gibbs, Green, Halard, Hall, Hardwich, Harris, Hayes, Hill, Holmes, James, Jenkins, Jones, Kington, Lambert, Lord, Lucy, Meeks, Morgan, Oakey, Palmer, Parry, Parsons, Perkins, Phillips, Pitt, Powell, Preece, Price, Prichard, Pullen, Roberts, Rowberry, Rowley, Simmons, Smith, Spires, Steed, Tompkins, Tyler, Wall, Watts, Williams – just to name a few.

To write the life history of Robert Harris, Jr., I found myself gathering research from the Family History Center, LDS Church Archives, the BYU Library, Nauvoo Land and Records, and other resources, I became more and more fascinated with his life. Eventually, I decided to take the process one step further. Thus, the idea for this novel was born. I then took a trip to England to do additional research. The lives of Robert, Hannah, Daniel and Elizabeth took on a new dimension.

I realize that it is unusual to write a novel about real people. But they were long deceased and that became the beauty of it. I could recreate them as my feelings dictated. I could shape my characters not only based on their suspected physical attributes but also their sociological and psychological dimensions.

Based on actual events in his life, I felt Robert (Bobby) was a hardheaded butcher and an egotistical pugilist (boxer), although certainly not to the extreme he is portrayed in the book. Hannah seemed to be submissive, quiet, and had the makings of a wonderful wife and mother. Daniel really was a carpenter who eventually became a trusted church leader after his conversion. Elizabeth seemed the type who was giddy in her personality but devoted to serving others.

Every good novel has to have a villain, so I created Henry, Hannah's brother. He fills every expectation of a bad guy: mean, insensitive, dual personality, and full of surprises.

Writing this novel turned out to be challenging, educational, fun, interesting – and one that took an extraordinarily amount of time. The trip to England in 2001 with my wife, Chris, and my sister, Lyla, found us visiting every significant historical spot there such as John Benbow's farm and the pond where many of the United Brethren converts were baptized. Our guide was a cousin that until earlier that year I never knew I had, Dr. Ben V. Bloxham, a man who had taught English history at BYU for many years. He led us to quaint hamlets and parishes such as Apperley and Deerhurst, portions of which are largely untouched by the passage of time. We visited the old Methodist and Anglican churches where my ancestors were married. We stepped inside the restored Gadfield-Elm chapel, at one time the only chapel in the world owned by the Church of Jesus Christ of Latter-day Saints.

Light and Truth will be a four-part saga. Like all stories, it will have an ending. In this case, it will have both a happy and a tragic ending.

The fun for me is in the telling. I hope the fun for you will be in the reading.

Acknowledgements

First and foremost I wish to acknowledge my wife, Chris, who patiently endured me as I acted out my passion to write this book. I thank her for not only her love and devotion, but for accompanying me on trips; reading trial sentences, paragraphs, pages and chapters; and going to bed without me on nights I couldn't stay away from the research or the computer.

Second, I thank my newly discovered cousin, Dr. Ben V. Bloxham. A retired Brigham Young University professor who taught English history, Ben not only spent several days with us in England but made his vast library and previous research available to me. Now a professional genealogist, Ben spends three or four months in England every year. He is considered the church's foremost authority on LDS church history in England. He even loaned me Wilford Woodruff's Journal, an out-of-print priceless set of books that details the apostles' mission in England and the names of all the people he baptized.

Dr. Bloxham's ancestors are Thomas and Dianah Bloxham. Dianah was a sister to Robert Harris, Jr. Obviously, Thomas and Dianah are characters in this novel.

Providing additional valuable information on the United Brethren, especially about its founder, Thomas Kington, was Dr. Don Smith, an orthodontist living in Pullman, Washington. He grew up in Hyrum, Utah, but spent many of his summers as a youth working in McCammon, Idaho, where I was raised. His children are descendants of James G. Willie, captain of the ill-fated 1856 handcart company. Nearly half of that company came from the same area in England where the United Brethren were organized.

Several dedicated people provided valuable assistance by reading or proof-reading my manuscript and giving me support and encouragement. Of course that would include my daughter, Stephanie, and my four sons, Chuck, Mike, Jason and Ryan – and their spouses. It also includes my sisters, Lyla Epperson, who accompanied me on my trip to England; Renae Burton, who read and commented on the manuscript, and my brother, Alan. Also: Nola Kay Harris Duncan, a first cousin who is a retired English teacher living in West Jordan, Utah; A. Dean Wengreen, an uncle who is a retired CES employee having taught at BYU and at the Utah State University Institute of Religion; my former home teacher in Korea, Brent Stanger, now of Boise; my former stake president, Reed Moss, now of Ririe, Idaho; my current stake president, Gary Wight; my former next-door neighbor in Idaho Falls, Sandy Bybee, an English teacher; our good friend Ilene Stolworthy of Idaho Falls; Dell Van Orden, former editor of the *Church News,* a distant cousin; and professional proofreaders Elaine Lindstrom and Kathryn Martin.

THE THOMAS EAGLES FAMILY

Thomas Eagles
b. 22 October 1775
Apperley, Gloucestershire

=

Ann Sparks Eagles
b. 26 July 1783
Corse, Gloucestershire

George_____
b. 6 July 1805
Apperley, Gloucester

Henry_____
b. 8 April 1807
Apperley, Gloucester

William_____
b. 26 March 1811
Apperley, Gloucester

Hannah Maria
b. 10 June 1815
Apperley, Gloucester

Nancy_____
b. 2 July 1817
Apperley, Gloucester

Elias_____
11 February 1822
Apperley, Gloucester

Jane_____
b. 14 March 1830
Apperley, Gloucester

THE ROBERT HARRIS, SR. FAMILY

Robert Harris, Sr.
b. 17 March 1777
Badgeworth, Gloucestershire

=

Sarah Oakey Harris
b. 27 October 1781
Twigworth, Gloucestershire

William_____
b. 17 March 1805
Deerhurst, Gloucester

John_____
b. 6 April 1806
Huccle-cot, Gloucester

Dianah_____
b. 27 September 1809
Apperley, Gloucester

Bobby_____
b. 16 December 1810
Huccle-cot, Gloucester

Zacharias_____
b. 7 July 1812
Churchtown, Gloucester
d. 9 October 1812

Elizabeth_____
6 June 1813
Sandhurst, Gloucester

Ellinor_____
10 February 1815
Sandhurst, Gloucester
d. 15 February 1815

Caroline_____
10 February 1815
Sandhurst, Gloucester
d. 15 February 1815

THE MARTHA BROWETT FAMILY

Thomas Browett
b. 1787
Tewkesbury, Gloucester

=

Martha Browett
b. 4 June 1779
Southam, BC, G, England

Daniel_____
b. 18 December 1810
Tewkesbury, Gloucester

Thomas_____
b. 26 March 1815
Tewkesbury, Gloucester

Rebecca_____
15 June 1817
Tewkesbury, Gloucester

John_____
11 December 1819
Tewkesbury, Gloucester

William_____
b. 25 May 1820
Tewkesbury, Gloucester

NOTE: These names and dates are contrived to fit the purposes of the novel, and may not reflect actual Family Group Sheets

XII Light and Truth

PRINCIPAL CHARACTERS

All characters are real except those indicated with an asterisk. Bold face indicates main characters. Ages are as the book opens in 1834.

THE EAGLES FAMILY

Thomas, 58, the father.
Ann, 51, the mother.
George, 29.
Edward, 26.
*Henry, 25.
William, 23.
Hannah, 21.
*Nancy, 19.
Elias, 12.
Jane, 10.

THE HARRIS FAMILY

Robert, 57, the father.
Sarah, 53, the mother.
William, 29.
John, 27.
Bobby, 24.
Dianah, 22.
Elizabeth, 21.

THE BROWETT FAMILY

Martha Pulham Browett, 50.
Daniel, 23.
Tommy, 19.
Rebecca, 16.
Johnny, 15.
Willie, 13.

OTHERS

John Benbow, 34.
Jane Benbow, 41.
John Cox, 23.
John Davis, 21.
John Hyrum Green, 33.
Susannah Phillips Green, 28.
Joseph Hill, 27.
Thomas Kington, 40.
William Pitt, 21.
Edward Phillips, 21.
*James Pulham, 22.
Levi Roberts, 23
Mary Ann Weston, 17.
Wilford Woodruff, 27.

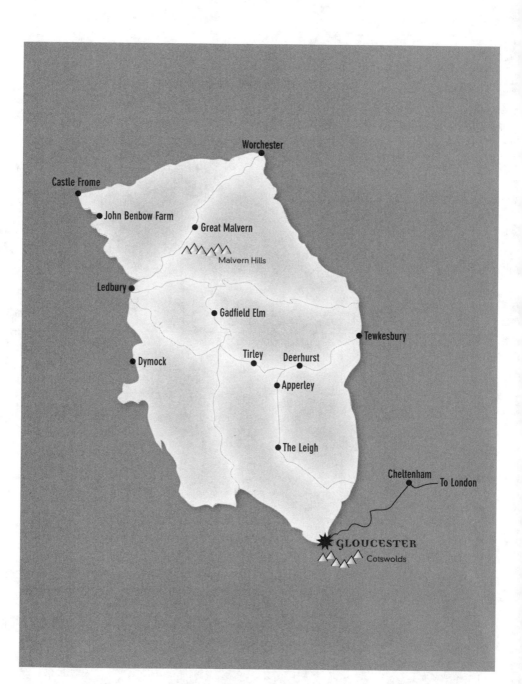

PART ONE

Anglicans
Methodists
Quakers

1

Hamlet of Apperley, Gloucestershire, England, June 1840

A HEAVY WOODEN DOOR creaked on its rusty hinges as three men barged into the Ferret's Folly. Henry Eagles, a swarthy man with greasy black hair hanging over his eyes, and a devilish smile on his face, stormed through the pub toward his brother-in-law's table.

"I'll bet you have no idea what's going on at your home, do you?"

Revulsion crossed the face of a man named Bobby as his eyes shot up at Henry and his two ruffian friends. "What do you mean?" he asked, taking stock of his old enemy.

"I just came from there," Henry said with a smirk. "There's a Mormon missionary in your parlor preaching to Hannah. Daniel and Elizabeth are there. There's so many people that some are sitting on the floor."

Bobby's eyes narrowed. Suddenly his plate full of sliced ham, boiled vegetables, baked apples, and hot bread lost its appeal. So did the ale.

"Are you certain it's my house?"

Thirty pairs of eyes locked on Bobby. Thirty pairs of ears had been listening to the blow-by-blow account of his last fight in London – for the hundredth time.

Henry nodded. Yes.

A snicker came from a man seated at Bobby's table, a lanky, sandy-haired cobbler named Geoffrey. "I wonder if my wife is there, too. She likes religious meetings. I never know what she's doing when I'm at the pub."

Low laughter was heard for a few moments. It stopped when the leading contender for the British heavyweight championship glared at the thirty sets of eyes, one by one.

Bobby burned at the inference. "Shut up, Geoffrey. Henry's not telling the truth. Hannah wouldn't dare have a meeting like that in my house without telling me." His suspicions forced him to stand up. Without realizing it, his back straightened and his fists went into a ball.

"Go see for yourself," Henry said with a curt nod in the direction of Bobby's home. An audible gasp could be heard from the pub patrons.

Bobby grabbed Henry by the shirt, and shook an index finger in his face. "If you're wrong, I'll break every bone in your body." He shoved Henry into Alex and Richie, the two wild-eyed ruffians.

"I'm not wrong," Henry replied, wilting.

Numb with anguish and embarrassment, a controlled rage was visible in Bobby's walk as he left the Ferret's Folly. He broke into a run, regretting that he didn't have a horse tied to the hitching post. One of Squire Hasting's servants had dropped him off at the pub, following his workout at the training camp in Gloucester.

He covered the half-mile in just over two minutes. Bright lantern lights gleamed from his stone cottage. The sight of carriages and gigs, and horses tied to posts, shocked him. His chest heaving, he looked through the parlor window. It was just as Henry said. Hannah was beaming.

A short man dressed in a dark suit was gesturing, talking. He looked confident. Bobby quickly concluded the man must be Wilford Woodruff.

With tiny beads of perspiration trickling down his forehead, Bobby crept to the back door. In stealth, he opened it. *How could Hannah do this to me? Doesn't she respect me anymore? I'll grab Woodruff by the neck and throw him from here to Deerhurst.*

Without warning, a feeling of dizziness bordering on nausea struck Bobby. He paused to brace himself, dumbfounded. *What's happening to me? I only ran a half-mile!*

All eyes swept to him as he stumbled into the parlor.

"Bobby!" Hannah exclaimed. She cupped her hand over her mouth to muffle her surprise.

Stopping in mid-sentence, Wilford took a step backward. An eerie silence fell into the room.

Bobby pulled his face into a twisted contortion. The failure of his body to respond to his brain stunned him. Words would not come from his constricted throat. *Why can't I move? Why can't I talk? What unseen power is protecting this man?*

The American missionary remained motionless, waiting for Hannah to introduce him to her husband.

"Bobby?" Hannah said, puzzled. "Are you all right?"

A groan hissed from Bobby's mouth. He turned around and vanished in the direction he had appeared. The back door slammed.

Hannah licked her dry lips. "That was my husband," she said to Elder Woodruff. "He didn't expect this tonight. I'm afraid he may be a little upset."

Tears welled up in her eyes, and her shoulders sagged in disappointment.

"He'll be back," Wilford said in a confident tone. "Let's continue."

Before Bobby barged into the room, Elder Woodruff had been relating one of the most unusual experiences of his life. Three months ago, in a church meeting in Hanley, the Lord's voice had come to him. *Go south.* Until then, he had been a finding, teaching, baptizing Mormon missionary in the Potteries area of England. Obedient to the voice, he made a two-day trip south and found John Benbow, Thomas Kington, and the United Brethren congregation. To date, he had baptized nearly all six hundred members of the United Brethren.

Wilford Woodruff was confident Bobby Harris would be added to the fold. That, despite the strange behavior he had just witnessed.

Bobby slogged back to the Ferret's Folly, his strength returning. A dark feeling engulfed him and a devious plan came into his racing mind. The American would pay for the embarrassment he had just suffered. He dashed into the pub, sweating, cursing, and pointing.

"John, give me all the eggs you have. Rotten ones if you have them."

Caught off guard, the manager of the Ferret's Folly considered his brother's erratic behavior. "Why?" John asked, "What are you going to do?"

"We're going to rotten egg an American preacher," Bobby yelled, gasping for breath. He pointed a finger at Geoffrey the cobbler. "Untie your team. You and you, help John with the eggs. Let's go. Hurry!"

An amused Henry Eagles rose to his feet.

"Not you Henry," Bobby said, glaring. "You and your friends are not invited."

Bobby pulled four other men to their feet. "Come with me," he ordered.

Within seconds Bobby's mob had boxes of eggs loaded into Geoffrey's wagon. Bobby ripped the lines from Geoffrey's hands and whipped the horses into a gallop. With white knuckles, the mob clung to the wagon as it bounced toward Bobby's home.

Bobby's orders continued in sharp clips. "When we get there, hide outside. I'll go in alone. They'll think everything's fine. When I raise my arm, storm the house. We'll take the American outside and rough him up. Use up all the eggs, every one of them. Then we'll dump him outside of town. He'll never come back, that's for sure."

Bobby spied a whip. He used it the on the terrified horses. "Hyaa! Hyaa!"

With the cool evening air swirling by as the wagon made a mad dash toward Bobby's house, John wondered why the next British pugilist champion needed help to rotten-egg and rough up a preacher. True, it would give customers of the Ferret's Folly something to laugh about for weeks and months ahead, but John thought it was curious. He also thought it was curious how easily a group of drinking men could be coaxed into organizing themselves into a mad mob.

2

Six years previous, September 1834

HANNAH MARIA EAGLES woke in the small upstairs bedchamber she shared with her two younger sisters, Nancy and Jane, and washed her face and hands in a basin of cold water. She looked out the small window. A rainy September night had ushered in a misty morning. Water drizzled off the steep thatched roof of their stone cottage in the small hamlet of Apperley. Hannah glanced at the stained ceiling that sometimes leaked during hard rains, and at the cracking plaster walls.

Nancy stirred.

"Better get up," Hannah said, taking off her cream-colored linen shift and replacing it with a blue daydress, her favorite. She had carefully hung it on a hook outside the armoire so it would not be wrinkled. She wished her mother would let her have a warm bath in the kitchen tub, just this once, but that was an event reserved for Saturday evenings.

Nancy winced and rolled over, preferring the warmth of her straw-filled mattress bed to the chill of the morning air. "I know," she muttered, without opening her eyes. "Did you jolly well dream about him again?" she asked in her southwestern English accent.

"Wouldn't you like to know?" Hannah sang out as she began brushing her silken auburn hair with long strokes. A rooster crowed as she walked to the bed and shook her eleven-year-old sister, Jane. "Up, up, up! You'll be late for Bible reading."

Jane moaned, wondering why her sister was in such a rosy mood.

Descending the narrow, steep stairs into the parlor, Hannah sat in the same oak chair she had sat in a thousand times and waited for her parents, brothers, and sisters. When everyone was there, Thomas and Ann Eagles, seated on a well-worn sofa, surveyed their large family and calmed the joking, the sibling rivalries, the arguing, and took turns reading to their children from the Gospel of John for fifteen minutes. Hannah tried to hide her yawning, and the fact that her stomach was twisting in anticipation of the day's events. It was just past six in the morning. Ann played a song on the upright piano; Thomas led the family prayer and blessing on the food.

Then followed Hannah's usual breakfast of cheese, milk, butter, and rye bread. Picking at the food as she sat at the wooden table covered with a red and white checkered oilcloth, unable to eat much, she soon got up. She donned her ankle jacks, a simple white bonnet, and a nearly worn-out, dark-blue, woolen mantle to protect her from the rain. She dashed to the dairy with Nancy to the music of dozens of bellowing cows to begin her day's work. She could see just a little blue sky breaking through the low, slate-gray clouds that hung over the rolling Cotswold hills to the south, hinting that the light rain would soon cease.

"Do you think he will be here early?" Nancy asked as they opened the planked wooden door to the redbrick Nightingale Dairy. Next door, they could see their father and brothers going into the barn to start milking the red and white cows.

Staring at the copper milk vats, butter churns, and cheese moulds, Hannah sighed and broke into her usual shy smile. "You heard father. The appointment is for eight o'clock."

Bobby slammed the back door so hard that the two-story shop shook on its foundation. The sound startled Duke, the family dog. In a foul mood, Bobby marched to the barn where he jerked Old Earl toward the wagon and tossed a heavy leather harness onto the gelding's back.

"Don't say a word, Duke," Bobby told the dog. "I've had it up to here with being told what to do." He gestured a hand to the top of his head, where drops of rain were splattering from a passing squall.

The door opened and Bobby's father emerged. Squarely built like his son, gray-haired, wrinkled but stern-faced, the old butcher saddled Queenie in silence. He swung into the saddle and walked the red roan mare past his son, pointing a bony finger. "Remember what I told you," he said in his crusty English brogue. "No courting that Methodist milkmaid." With those words of finality, the father kicked the mare in the flank and galloped off to the Tewkesbury cattle market.

Bobby shrugged his shoulders in defiance as he threaded the leather lines through the harness rings, and back to the driver's box. He hoped his father choked on the tea he would be drinking at the cattle sale. If he bought a few steers, he could brand them on one horn himself. In Bobby's opinion, his father ought to change his brand to read, "R. Harris, bigot," instead of just plain "R. Harris."

Pointing, mimicking his father, Bobby said to the dog, "Go gnaw on your bone, Duke, and remember — no sassing. We'll be cracking off soon enough."

Biting down on his father's last words put Bobby into an even nastier mood. If Hannah Maria Eagles were so off limits, why had his father assigned him and his brother to slaughter a steer at the dairy Hannah's father managed?

The door to the shop opened again, and twenty-one-year-old Elizabeth stood in the doorframe, her blonde hair halloed by the first rays of sunshine peeking through the clouds. "Come, Duke." She tossed a meat scrap into the air that the dog snapped up before it hit the ground. Amused, she tossed another, and another.

Bobby watched his younger sister and the dog for a moment then asked, "I don't suppose you've seen John. He's late. He's always late. I guess I'll have to barge in on the way by, and get the lazy chap out of bed again."

"*I knew* Papa wouldn't give in," Elizabeth commented, rubbing salt in Bobby's wounded pride.

"What happens, happens," Bobby retorted. He threw two bloody leather aprons, a sharp knife, a hatchet, and an axe into the wagon. "Come, Duke." Sniffing the mud where a meat scrap had lain, the brown dog whined and jumped into the wagon.

Bobby had named the mongrel dog "Duke" and the horse "Old Earl" as a symbol of his disrespect of England's stuffy privileged class – the nobility. In his mind there was no difference between an English aristocrat and a dog, or a beast of burden like a horse. The aristocrats were a burden to Bobby and all lower-class people. He took great pleasure in giving the dog orders, and putting a bit in the mouth of an Earl.

"Well, if you just *happen* to see Hannah, tell her hello for me." Elizabeth winked and gave her brother a comic look.

The comment did not change Bobby's mood.

"Stay away from Daniel Browett, the Quaker," he told his sister. "Or you'll be in just as much trouble."

"Don't tell *me* what to do," she said, narrowing her eyes.

"Get up here, Duke," Bobby said to the dog. "Right now! Up in the wagon. No chasing the barnyard cats or the cows at the dairy. You got that?"

Elizabeth watched as the creaky old wagon lumbered down the narrow muddy lane trimmed with hedges. It stopped in front of John's cottage, where lazy smoke curled from the chimney. Bobby whistled, and whistled again. John finally crawled into the wagon, wedging himself into the narrow seat with his brother. Then the wagon bounced out of sight.

Bobby did little to acknowledge John's presence. He slapped the lines on Old Earl's back. "Get on with it, Earl! Liven it up, mate!" Mud from the gelding's hooves splattered the two men.

"Slow down," John complained. "We've got all day to butcher one bloody steer." Dressed in well worn black wool trousers and a green woolen coat over a dirty-white cotton shirt just like Bobby, John flicked at the pieces of mud that seemed to cling to him like glue. "Let's just get our job done and get out of there as fast as we can. I don't want trouble with any of the Eagles family, especially Henry."

Bobby glared at John.

"Oh, I get it. It's the pretty milkmaid, isn't it?"

Bobby returned his eyes to the road.

"Face it," John said, chewing on a toothpick he had carved that morning. "Father's going to find you a plump little Anglican girl from right here in Deerhurst parish, just like he did for me. So get your mind off Hannah. It's miserably unfair, but that's life."

"Lots of rot to you, too," Bobby said in a sharp voice. "Your problem is that you have no backbone. Never had, never will. That's the difference between you and me."

"And the problem with you is that you never back off from a ruddy fight, even if it's with your own father," John shot back. He hoped Bobby would not interpret his remarks as too malicious. Bobby's independence was one of the qualities John admired in his brother.

John was right, Bobby thought to himself. He was determined to marry the girl of his choice, not his father's, not his mother's. He didn't care if she were Anglican, Methodist, or Quaker. His father's warning at breakfast grated on him. *Just because Mr. and Mrs. Eagles have announced the coming out of their daughter doesn't mean that you can court her. And you don't need to ask why.*

It was the why that irritated Bobby Harris.

Stepping with Nancy into the redbrick dairy, sheltered by rows of heavily laden apple trees, Hannah donned her apron and in a dreamy manner began turning last night's cheeses in their moulds, pressing out the leftover liquid in them. They smelled clean and nutty as she removed them, wrapped the cheeses in linen bandages, and placed them on the dairy shelves for storage. However, her mind was not on her work. It was on the butcher's son from the parish of Deerhurst. She loved his enchanting smile, especially the way it curled up on one side of his mouth more than the other. He had the longest eyelashes she had ever seen on a boy. He always wore a cap over his dark brown wavy hair. She would like to see him without his cap, just once, and gaze into his deep blue-gray eyes.

Henry Eagles, with his wide face, broad shoulders, thick chest and hairy arms, barged into the dairy. He carried two wooden pails full of the morning milk, interrupted Hannah's daydreaming, and then left for the barn again without speaking.

"Henry must have sucked on a pickle this morning," Nancy commented with an unpleasant look.

"He's sucked on a pickle all his life," Hannah said, her voice sharp. "The abysmal donkey."

For reasons she never understood, Henry was different from any of her brothers. He was arrogant, self-serving, defiant, inconsiderate, a promoter of turmoil, and a control freak. She could make quite a list if she set her mind to it. Strong as an ox, he could crush a rock in either hand. His hands were made stronger every day from milking cows. Five-foot ten-inches tall, broad-shouldered and muscular, he could swath more hay in a day than his brothers, or any of the farm servants. He spent nearly every night at a pub, filling his belly with ale, picking fights. He was a boorish bully even at home, chasing away every suitor that had shown interest in her. Sometimes she wished she could put Henry's head in the cheese press and give it an extra turn or two.

"Hannah, you're getting behind," Nancy said as she poured the pails of milk into copper vats so the cream could come to the top. Henry never poured the milk for them like her other brothers did. "You haven't even churned your butter yet."

"Don't fret," Hannah answered, pulling a face. "I'll catch up."

"You're dreaming about him again, aren't you?"

"Wouldn't you like to know."

"I just know."

Hannah's heart jumped. She wondered what Bobby would think of her in her work clothes. She worried that she smelled like spoiled milk. She wished she were back in the house, standing in front of a mirror, changing into her crimson Sunday dress.

"Don't get your hopes up dear sister," Nancy taunted. "Papa would never let an Anglican like Bobby court you."

Nancy's frankness sank Hannah's heart. Until her attraction to Bobby, Hannah had not paid too much attention to the continuing conflict between the Anglican Church and her own Methodist faith. Why couldn't all Christians get along better? Why did her father view Anglicans with such suspicion? True, there were stories from the past about how Anglicans persecuted Wesleyan Methodists as their movement spread from Bristol into other shires and parishes. But that was yesterday, not today.

Hannah wished her father was not so biased, but everything about the Anglicans seemed to rankle him: There were more Anglicans in the hamlet of Apperley than Methodists. The smug Anglicans regarded themselves as the only official religion in England. Anglicans had a storied history tied to King Henry VIII and the Roman Church. Anglicans regarded Methodists as dissenters. The building her father had helped construct for the Methodists, by Anglican rule, had to be referred to as a chapel, not a church. Methodists had not been able to hold public office.

And on and on and on.

"There's a couple of plump Anglican girls with crooked teeth going into the church right now," John teased, pointing as the wagon bounced past the Deerhurst Parish Church, enclosed by a thick, well-trimmed hedge. "Want me to whistle for you?"

"You do, and I'll toss you off in the mud," Bobby threatened.

John pursed his lips.

"I'm not kidding."

Years back in his memory Bobby could hear himself reciting Anglican catechisms inside the rain-glistened Gothic stone building with those two chubby girls and other parish children in sleepy, droning voices. Even back then, he disliked religion. After today's argument with his father, he hated it. Besides, why so many religions? How many did God need? How could his parents belong to a church that was started by a king who had broken away from the Roman Church just because he couldn't get an annulment? And how could anyone belong to a church in Rome that had such a controversial history? Did the pope who had commissioned Michelangelo to paint the ceiling of the Sistine Chapel really have four illegitimate children? Did popes really forgive sins for money?

"Don't get so testy," John said.

"Then leave me alone."

"You're testy every morning. One would think you hate your life as a butcher."

You're right, I do, Bobby thought.

Bobby's hatred of his work wasn't much different than that of his brother. John's dream was to manage a pub. Bobby's dream was to be a famous pugilist. A lowly butcher's life did nothing more than symbolize the nothingness of working-class life in England. There was only one way out as far as he was concerned, and that was to become the British heavyweight champion.

Ever since he'd seen a championship fight in Worcester between Tom Springs and Jack Langan, way back when he was only twelve years old, he was hooked on the idea of becoming a pugilist. Even though it was a brutal barefisted fight, ending after seventy-two rounds with both men bleeding badly, he had been fascinated. Thousands had watched the fight. In Bobby's eyes, both fighters had been heroes, famous throughout the British Isles. They had not exactly been upper-class aristocrats, but they had certainly escaped the boredom of the lower working class.

Robert Harris, Sr. had never allowed Bobby to participate in the fights at the county fair, but he fancied it anyway. There had to be more to life than being the son of a butcher. Fame. Fortune. And a beautiful wife.

Footsteps. Nancy opened the door and let William in, carrying two more pails of milk. He smiled, poured their contents into the settling pan, and gathered his pails with the two Henry had left.

"Thank you for the empties," William said.

Thinking about her two older brothers as she pumped the butter churn, further depressed Hannah. She remembered as a young girl that they had expressed interest in courting local Anglican maidens, but her father would have nothing to do with it. George had finally found an acceptable Methodist and was now happily married and still working for Farmer Nightingale in the dairy Hannah's father managed. William was courting a Methodist girl. *If I fall in love with an Anglican, I'll marry an Anglican. I'll elope if I have to.*

Hannah had a vivid imagination. For the past two years she had used it freely to think what her life would be as a married woman, having a handsome husband and becoming the mother of many children. She had caught herself hundreds of times wishing that English tradition allowed girls to be courted at age sixteen or seventeen. It seemed to her that marriage was the only practical escape from her dreary life at the dairy.

In some respects Hannah didn't mind working for her father because he was certainly the best dairy manager in the world. His shorthorn cows were fatter, more content, and gave more milk than any she'd ever seen or heard of, but lately her work attitude had plunged into sheer monotony: Grain the cows. Scrub the floors. Heat the milk. Add rennet. Make curds. Stir and cut the curds. Heat the mixture again to separate the curds from the whey. Add salt. Spoon the curds into wooden cheese moulds. Press excess whey out of the moulds. Wrap the cheeses in bandages. Turn the cheeses every day.

In her mind, Hannah could hear her father's commanding voice: *Don't forget, quality is important.*

But Papa, life here is so boring.

3

THE CUSTOMER in the dairy was a pigeon-faced lady in a red flowered dress. "I need two gallons of milk and some cheese."

Hannah appeared frozen to her butter churn, deep in thought.

Nancy grimaced at her sister and tended to the customer's needs, dipping milk from the counter pan. The woman watched carefully, making certain she received her fair share of cream.

"I hear a wagon," Hannah said, rising suddenly. She rushed to the window and peered out. Her heart fluttered as she watched Bobby tie his leather apron around his muscular neck and waist, and command his dog to stay in the wagon. He gathered his knives, hatchets, and other tools, and disappeared into the barnyard with his brother John and one of the farm servants.

Nancy chuckled at her sister. The lady in the red dress began her weekly exam of every block of cheese in the dairy.

"I'll be right back," Hannah said. She made a mad dash to the house to wash the smell of the dairy off her hands and change clothes.

Bobby, John, and the servant roped a large red ox and tied it snugly to a post. John turned an axe to its blunt end. He raised it high over his head, and then paused.

"Bobby, move him over a little," John said, focusing on a spot between the animal's eyes. "If he falls into the mud, we'll have more of a mess on our hands."

Bobby placed his shoulder against the ox and with an audible grunt pushed with all his strength, digging his boots into the mud.

The ox did not move.

"Get over you stubborn mate," Bobby said to the animal. He thought about giving the ox an aristocrat's name before he slit its throat, like Baron, or Viscount. He punched the steer in its wide gut. Still, it did not move.

"Need some help, tough guy? I don't think you can break the ribs of that ox."

Bobby whirled to face Henry Eagles. His twisted cocky grin, circled by long black whiskers, revealed a gap where two front teeth were missing. His voice had a distinct lisp.

"Not from you, old sod," Bobby said, his tone tinged with contempt.

"That ox won't move if he doesn't want to. You're not man enough to do the job."

"Looks like you're man enough to get your front teeth knocked out of your head," Bobby said with a smirk.

Henry took a menacing step toward the butcher.

John stepped between the two men, trying to deflect the confrontation.

"I'll help you push, Bobby," John said.

Bobby shook his head. "Get out of my way. I'll give the ox a tail twist."

As he stepped to the rear of the animal, two other persons made their appearance. It was Hannah and Nancy.

"Good morning, Mr. Harris," Hannah said in a musical voice, directed to Bobby.

With a melting appeal, Bobby returned the greeting. "Good morning to you, Miss Eagles." His words were laced with a musical tone, matching Hannah's.

Bobby was struck by Hannah's sinewy female shape, her dimpled smile, and her dark brown eyes. As their eyes met, Bobby took a blind step and reached for the steer's tail.

Thud!

There was a deadening sound as the steer's powerful and muscular hind leg caught Bobby squarely in the stomach. The force of the kick knocked his cap off. He crumbled to the muddy, manure-infested ground, gasping for breath.

Henry pointed at the fallen butcher and laughed. "Harrh, harrh, harrh!"

Hannah cupped her hands over her mouth in disbelief. She rushed to Bobby's side, kneeling.

Sucking air, groaning, Bobby suddenly became aware of Hannah. He caught a faint hint of perfume, and the smell of aged cheese. He rolled over, letting his head settle into her lap. He gazed into her face. She had dark, narrow eyebrows, a cute pug nose, deep-set brown eyes gleaming with bold intelligence, and full lips circled by an oval chin. Hannah's look was satiric, as though she had already concluded that he was a fool for so carelessly stepping in the way of the steer's hind leg.

"Are you hurt, Mr. Harris?" she asked, stroking Bobby's forehead. She wanted to touch his long eyelashes. She liked his long, straight nose. It looked more Jewish than Roman.

"Of course, he's hurt," Henry said, laughing. "He's a baby. He can't stand pain."

"Shut your mouth, Henry," Hannah warned. "Or I'll stuff it full of cheese wrap myself."

John stood with his fists balled, ready to protect his brother.

"I'll be fine," Bobby said, enjoying his position. Hannah was running her fingers through his hair. "I just have a question."

Eyes twinkling, Hannah said, "Go ahead. What?"

"When can I come calling on you?"

"Never," Henry hissed.

Hannah glared at her brother. "I told you to shut up, Henry."

Henry returned the glare.

She returned her gaze to Bobby and cleared a lump in her throat. "You can come calling anytime. How about tomorrow, for our church services?"

"What time?"

"Ten o'clock."

Bobby smiled. For a chance to sit at Hannah's side, he would attend any church service, Methodist, Anglican, or even in a Jewish synagogue.

"Can we seal this with a kiss?"

Hannah turned away, her face beet red. In nineteenth century England, kissing was strictly forbidden among courting couples, and barely within consent of the engaged. *Not here in the barnyard. Not with everyone staring at us.*

Henry erupted. "You are not going to be courted by any bloody butcher Anglican from Deerhurst!"

With a powerful grip sure to leave her arm bruised, Henry jerked Hannah to her feet. He tossed her aside like a rag doll, and stood over Bobby.

Hannah flew into a rage. She placed her face against her brother's and thumped him in the chest with her forefinger. "Henry, this is none of your business!"

"Bah! Get out of my way." This time, Henry shoved his sister to the ground. Her clean dress soiled by mud and manure, she began to cry.

It was Bobby's turn to erupt. He lunged at Henry, crashing his shoulder into Henry's sternum. He lifted the bully brother off his feet and slammed him to the ground, near the ox. The animal kicked at them.

Leaping, growling, Duke attacked. The dog bit at Henry's leg and pulled on his trousers.

"Get that bloody dog away from me or I'll kill him!" Henry screamed.

An imposing figure suddenly stood over Henry and Bobby. It was Thomas Eagles. "Henry! Get up from there. You too, Mr. Harris."

Thick white hair, ruddy skin, composed brown eyes, a square jaw, and only a slightly overweight waistline, the fifty-eight-year-old dairyman grabbed Henry by the leg. Using the strength of an athletic body warped only slightly by the passage of time, he pulled him away from Bobby.

"What is the cause of all this?" he asked in a gruff voice as Henry and Bobby rose to their feet.

Pointing at his dog, Bobby gave a quick command. "Back off, Duke. Good boy. Now git, git back in the wagon."

Whining, Duke skulked away.

"It's Henry's fault," cried Hannah, swiping at the mud that clung to her once-clean dress.

Thomas Eagles ignored his daughter. "If you two want to fight, do it at the fair."

"Fine," Bobby replied, his fists still balled. "Unless Henry's afraid of me."

"Well strike me blind," Henry countered. "What do you mean, afraid? I'm not afraid of you or anyone." He took a threatening step toward Bobby.

"Splendid," Thomas said, pushing his son back. "A fight at the fair it is. But for right now, end it. Henry, go to the fields and get your work done. Mr. Harris, that ox won't slaughter itself. Get busy."

Henry gritted his teeth and backed off.

"Can I get that tail twist now?" John said, motioning to his brother. His words broke the tension. He couldn't wait until the Gloucestershire fair. He wanted to watch Bobby tear Henry's head off with an uppercut.

Dejected, Hannah returned to the dairy. Henry had ruined everything. She knew there was no chance Bobby would come calling tomorrow. But there would be another time, another place. She had not answered Bobby's question about the kiss.

Right now, that's all Hannah could think about.

4

THE PARISH OF DEERHURST, in the shire of Gloucester, is located on the east bank of the River Severn. Only a few shops were scattered along the main road: Cobbler, saddler, wheelwright, blacksmith, etc. The Harris Butcher Shop was located in a two-story stone cottage not far from the parish church. Like most shops, the structure doubled as living quarters.

A gray-haired, delicate woman opened the door to the butcher shop and yelled to her son. "Bobby! Come to supper. You hear me?"

Still in a foul mood, Bobby kicked the red and white skin that had just fallen from the carcass of the beef. It settled in a crumpled pile in the corner of the shed. "I hear you. I'll be right there." He scraped more hair from the carcass, pegged his knife into a wooden block, discarded his bloody apron, and started for the house.

"You wash up good before you come in here," Sarah Harris said, pointing to a wooden tub.

Bobby discarded his shirt and obeyed his mother, splashing water over his head and shoulders. He didn't look forward to sitting at the table with his father. He suspected he already knew about the fracas at the Eagle Dairy. John undoubtedly had told him. He no sooner stepped into the house than his father began to ask questions, almost forgetting to ask grace over the food.

"Fat steer from the dairy?" his father asked.

"Yes, sir," he said, fighting the temptation to sneer. "The meat's well marbled." *You picked it out yourself. Why do you have to ask?*

Bobby plunked down a ladle full of thick stew, made of throwaway meat cuts and garden vegetables. His mother had cooked it in an iron pot over an open fire in the hearth. She was an expert at using everything edible from an animal carcass, leaving the rest to sell to the stream of women who frequented their shop.

The line of questioning continued. "Messy job? Your clothes are filthy, quite."

Elizabeth flinched for her brother. She toyed with her stew while it cooled, and munched on fresh carrots.

Bobby slumped in his chair, swiping at moths that had been drawn by the light of the kerosene lamp. While his father stared at him, waiting for an answer, he began eating, sucking air as his tongue touched the first hot wooden spoonful of stew. "It rained all last night, especially hard in Apperley."

"Tush! Foolery!" the senior butcher harped. "Appears to me that you let that Eagles boy roll you in the mud."

Bobby grimaced as the words pierced the room. Outside, lightning flashed, followed by a thunderclap. He watched his father sop a biscuit in his stew and plop it into his mouth. "That's not what happened."

The old butcher knit his brow fiercely. "And now you're fighting the Eagles boy at the fair next week? Is that right?"

"I can't back down, Father."

"I told you stay away from the girl."

"She just showed up. It wasn't my fault."

Robert reached for another ladle of stew, keeping the same coarse expression. "I should have sent William with John. I warned you about that girl."

Bobby pushed himself away from the table and stood up. "Father, I didn't do anything ruddy wrong." With those words he opened the door, slammed it, and retreated into the darkness. Thick rain hissed down from a black sky.

Robert stood as though he were going to follow his son.

"Let him go," Sarah said, raising her hand, warning her husband with gestures. "Sit back up to the table and eat."

Elizabeth tried to hide her smile at the sight of her father meekly sitting again, and filling his mouth with food. She knew her mother would give her wrong-headed father a genuine curtain lecture later on, upstairs, when they retired for bed. Robert had crossed an imaginary line, prying, digging, and venting at his son.

There was silence for a period of time, until the gray-haired butcher rose from the table, sat on a bench near the hearth, and opened his King James Version of the Bible. He lit another lantern to facilitate his reading.

"Going to join me, Mrs. Harris?"

Sarah was bent over wiping a spill off the wooden-planked floor. "Oh, hush. You know I will when I'm done here. This mess shan't clean itself up, will it?"

Elizabeth silently giggled, holding a hand over her mouth.

Robert grunted, and pretended to read as he thought about his son and Henry Eagles. He knew of Bobby's dream to become a pugilist, but had never permitted him to actually fight at the fairs or at the pubs. Henry's reputation as a pub brawler concerned him, but there were aspects of the fight that began to intrigue him. *Bobby my butcher son will skin the dairyman. The Anglican will crucify the Methodist.*

Robert made no attempt to hide his smile.

The smile on her husband's face puzzled her as Sarah took her time to finish her housework. An adroit homemaker, providing a house where the tea was always hot, the food appetizing, the rooms well furnished and clean, fresh flowers in sight, Sarah had not made up her mind to support her husband's insistence that Bobby marry an Anglican just as William, John, and Dianah had done. As far as she could determine, Hannah Eagles would make a good wife for Bobby, in spite of her religion. She sat on the bench with Robert and gave him a cold look.

"I guess I'm ready now," Sarah said.

The smile disappeared from Robert's face. He turned to the Gospel of Mark, chapter eight, and began to read aloud in a monotonous tone.

Sarah pretended to listen, but thought of Robert's bone-headed narrow-mindedness about religion. He was perhaps the most die-hard Anglican she had ever met. He constantly ranted about his allegiance to the Church of England, that it should remain the "official" state religion forever. King Henry VIII was his hero. It gave her husband great pleasure to testify to dissenters that he totally and unequivocally supported the king's break from the Roman Church. He was proud of the fact that the Church of England had confiscated not only the monasteries but also vast tracts of land back in the 1500s. On the other hand, her husband cringed at the stories linking Queen Mary – Henry and Catherine's daughter – with efforts to destroy the Reformation and the Church of England, and restore Catholicism. Robert had always called Mary "that wicked lady" who had abolished Henry VIII's prayer book, and reversed the changes Henry and his son King Edward had made in worship policies. In Robert's opinion, Mary deserved the title "Bloody Mary." Robert had long worn out the phrase that Bloody Mary was undoubtedly suffering in hell for her part in killing Anglican "heretics."

Sarah was tired of hearing it.

On the other hand, her husband seemed to love the story of how Elizabeth – also a daughter of Henry VIII – came to the throne and restored the royal supremacy of the Church of England. Robert had insisted to Sarah that they name one of their daughters after the stately queen. Queen Elizabeth had done a lot, but she could have done more, in his opinion. She should have banned more of the Roman Church images and crucifixes, using the power of the monarchy. To Robert, those things were nothing but a mixture of Christianity and paganism. The idea of "holy water" was a little too much for him. And in his opinion, priests should not be celibate. They should be married like all normal men.

But even with those deficiencies in his church, Robert was born Anglican, christened Anglican, and would die Anglican. That was a fact that Sarah could not deny. When this life was over he wanted his remains to be buried in the churchyard of the Deerhurst parish church, not far from their cottage. It was built by the Catholics but it was Anglican now. He already had the spot picked out where he and his wife would be laid to rest. At fifty-seven years old, he hoped to live to the ripe old age of sixty or better.

When Bobby came ambling up to the house, having spent an hour trying to work in anger trimming the beef carcass by the dim light of a lantern, Elizabeth met him at the door. She took him into the shop, making certain he ate the remainder of the meal he had left behind. He was still dressed in his muddy pants and shirt. She reflected on the many times Bobby and she had spent together as the only two children left at home, on occasion whiling away the hours together in the shop, sharpening knives, arranging the cuts of meat, and just talking. Sometimes, however, she recognized that Bobby liked to be alone and take walks at night, sniff the breeze, and let the countryside talk. The country talked quietly. If he were far enough away, the sound of the crickets and birds and the farm animals could drown out the voice of his father. If there were a disagreement, Bobby found it best to get out of range of his father's voice so that he could think on his own.

Bobby greeted his sister with a grim but accepting look. He usually liked to listen to his sister, whom he often described to his friends as sort of a lioness type, a girl who does as she pleases and you just have to get out of her way. When they were together, Elizabeth did most of the talking. She must have got that gift from her father, but Elizabeth was more sensible than Robert, even if a little giddy. Bobby figured that he was more like his mother, quiet, but when he said something he made it count. He was glad he had walked out on his father during dinner. Otherwise he may have said something to cause a rift between them, a rift that might have lingered for several weeks.

Brushing locks of blonde hair from her green eyes, Elizabeth talked in a low voice so their parents would not hear them. They were upstairs, still reading and discussing the Bible. So far, Elizabeth had not heard her mother take up a conversation with her father. When she did, Elizabeth reckoned it would be short and to the point. Her father would grunt and try to ignore her mother, but the words would penetrate and they would go to bed without speaking further.

"Are you *really* going to fight Henry Eagles at the fair?" Elizabeth asked in a cockney brogue, over-emphasizing certain words, a habit she had acquired from her mother. "You do look *ghastly*, you know."

Eating voraciously, Bobby answered between bites. "I have to. I challenged him, right in front of Mr. Eagles."

He studied his sister, admiring her concern. Slight of build, with her mother's skin and a pert figure, she oddly resembled her father in the deep-set green eyes, long straight nose, and the determined air, always expressing her opinion, right or wrong. She sat poised on her elbows, staring at him.

"Well, you *always* wanted to fight at the fair," Elizabeth said. "Now's your chance. Are you sure you didn't do this on *purpose*? Because you want to be this famous pugilist or something?"

She had long recognized that her brother was more of an athlete than a butcher. He was agile, sturdy, bull-headed but fun to be around, trusting, disliked the regimen of his work, but had developed a remarkable capacity for doing it anyway.

Bobby let her words float off. Henry Eagles was not the kind of opponent a man would choose the first time. Henry had destroyed everyone he had previously fought, whether it was a fight at one of the fairs or outside one of the pubs after a few too many drinks, with raucous men looking on and betting on who would eventually win.

"Anyway, since you're going to the fair, I want you to do me a *favor*. Are you listening?" Elizabeth paused, waiting for an answer.

Bobby nodded his head.

"I want you to *arrange* it so I can spend some *time* with you and Daniel. You mustn't fail me."

Elizabeth had never been in the presence of Daniel Browett without her father imposing his dominant personality. It was her one aim, to be with Daniel on her own terms.

With a mischievous smile Bobby said, "I think you want to be with Daniel more than you want to watch me fight."

Elizabeth shrugged her shoulders and blushed ever so slightly. "So?"

"If you're thinking about me asking Father for permission for Daniel to court you, forget it. That's Daniel's job."

Elizabeth waved a frantic hand in front of her face. "No! No! No! Don't do that!"

Bobby returned an abstracted stare.

"Think of some way we can be together *without* Papa and Mama either knowing or caring."

Bobby twisted in his chair while he contemplated her request, still gulping down his stew. Lightning flashed through a small window. Another thunderclap shook the cottage.

Impatient at her brother's silence, Elizabeth pressed on. "How about *after* the fights? I'll hang around with you and some of your friends, and Daniel will just *happen* to be there. There'll be so many people Papa and Mama won't care."

"Aren't you the sly one? There's nothing to arrange. You've got it all thought out."

"You don't mind me tagging along with you and your friends?"

"Even if I did, you'd be there anyway. Wouldn't you?" Bobby wiped his mouth, got out of his chair, and took a step toward the door. "I've had these muddy, stinking clothes on all day. I'm going to bed."

Elizabeth stayed downstairs for another ten minutes, thinking about her simple but ingenious plan. She had never believed in love at first sight, but when twenty-three-year-old Daniel Browett, the carpenter with the cute square jaw and blonde hair, moved into a nearby cottage just a month ago, she felt that God had answered her prayers and sent a living angel.

The problem was that the angel was a Quaker.

To her father, a Quaker was just as nonconformist and unacceptable as a Methodist. All her life, through childhood and her teen years, Elizabeth had considered herself to be obedient and well behaved in every respect. But if her feelings about Daniel remained the same, and she was certain they would, she had to respond to those feelings and find a way for Daniel to feel comfortable to ask permission to court her and – more than that – ask for her hand in marriage.

She thought about what she would do if her parents objected to any effort by Daniel to court her. When she had her coming out party in June, they didn't say anything about restricting potential suitors then, and still hadn't. But her father had said some awful things to Bobby the past couple of days about Hannah Eagles and her Methodist background, so she was sure it would come up if Daniel asked to court her. Gritting her teeth as she thought about the potential problem, she wondered what her parents would say if she told them that if she couldn't have Daniel she would "go back in."

So far her father seemed to ignore Daniel and the entire Browett family with a segregationist attitude. So did virtually all the other Anglicans in Deerhurst. Anglicans tended to do business with other Anglicans. Daniel's business was struggling here, just like it was in Tewkesbury. Elizabeth wished the Browetts would convert to Anglicanism. That would solve everything. But she guessed that Daniel's mother, Martha, a widow for the past ten years, was just as much Quaker as her parents were Anglican.

Taking off her shoes and rubbing her tired feet, Elizabeth congratulated herself on being so crafty despite the odds against her. She might be the only girl at the "after-the-fights party," following the fair, but she didn't care.

Upstairs, Elizabeth could hear her mother giving her father his well-deserved tongue-lashing. It was short, and then there was quiet. She could hear Bobby washing in the kitchen, tossing his filthy trousers outside, and then bounding up the stairs. Outside, the rain began to come in torrents with more thunder and lightning. She laughed at herself and her determination to court Daniel Browett, comparing it to Bobby's determination to court Hannah Eagles. *Poor Papa. Youthfulness will win out every time against age.*

5

WHEN THOMAS EAGLES finished his evening chores at the dairy he took a slow stroll through the barnyard and down the lane leading to the River Severn, which formed the western boundary of Yeoman Nightingale's farm. He stopped for a moment on a knoll overlooking the river. The evening was as quiet as sleep, except for the lowing of the cows. All day long he had thought about the incident with Henry and the young butcher from Deerhurst. Too bad Bobby came from an Anglican family. Otherwise, he would make a good husband for Hannah.

Thomas knew that he knew he was stubborn and pig-headed about religion, freely admitting it if someone cared to ask. A man had to have passion about the things he believed in. And a man had to have his heroes. The only hero he had in his life was John Wesley, even though he was long dead and gone. Wesley was the man whom he believed took the Reformation to a higher level. Yes, he knew Wesley never intended to form a separate church and always claimed to be a loyal son of the Church of England. Yes, Wesley's followers actually separated from the Church of England after his death in 1791 and organized the Methodist Church. But Thomas looked upon John Wesley as a man who was rowing the boat in the right direction although looking in another. It irked Thomas that the Anglicans continued to severely persecute the Methodists by breaking up their meetings. Years ago they had even killed one of Wesley's preachers and stoned Wesley himself. It irked him further that the Anglicans thought of themselves as the "official" church in England and regarded Methodists, Quakers, and other groups as nothing more than "dissenters" and "nonconformists." Methodists were required to call their buildings chapels, not churches. Anglicans did not recognize Methodist baptisms, ordinations, funerals, or marriages. That's okay. He reciprocated by not recognizing their established rites either.

Looking at the sky again as he walked back toward the dairy, Thomas sensed that there was enough time to walk to his Methodist chapel, less than a half mile away. Rounding the corner, he could see it in the distance. He wondered if anyone were inside praying tonight. As he approached, he found it empty. He stepped inside where there was barely enough light for him to find a pew, and knelt down. In his simple prayer, he asked God to bless his family and the cows, every one of them by name. He blessed Hannah, that she would marry a worthy Methodist. Then he arose, reflecting on the time that he had helped build the humble thirty by forty redbrick building. Not only had he helped in the construction, but he had helped acquire the building lot, too. To Thomas, all the old Anglican churches in England – now Anglican but originally Catholic – were out-of-date abominations full of images, crucifixes and tombs. If land had been available – but it was practically all owned by the detested Squire Hastings, an Anglican – he and his friends would have built the little Methodist chapel right next to the parish church in Deerhurst, so that it might be a tool to help convert more Anglicans to Methodism. But at least he had a place to worship and a place for his children to be married. His daughter Hannah would be married there, that's for certain, as would Nancy,

Elias, and Jane. His oldest son, George, was married there. So was his oldest daughter Editha, just last year. Sadly, she was buried nearby. She had died shortly after her marriage to William Ody.

Thinking of Henry, Thomas reflected on Bobby as well. Despite Bobby's Anglican upbringing, there was something that he liked about the brash young butcher. He knew Henry would whip Bobby at their match at the fair – it was the superiority of the Eagles blood. Nevertheless, he admired the tenacity he saw in the Harris lad. No matter. After Henry whipped him, he would certainly stay away from his daughter.

Thomas reached his home just in time. The first large drops of rain began pelting the thatched roof as he walked inside his cottage.

The amazing thing about Daniel Browett, in Bobby's view, was that he always seemed to be in a happy mood. Almost as amazing was the fact that Daniel actually liked his work. Bobby had only known Daniel for four weeks, ever since he set up the Browett Furniture and Cooper Shop near his father's butcher shop. Already they had found out they were almost exactly the same age. Only two days separated their December birthdays.

Opening the door to Daniel's shop in mid-morning, with a chilly breeze gusting from the north, Bobby stepped inside and let the smell of sawdust and glue assault his nostrils. Daniel and his helpers, James Pulham and John Davis, were bent over barrel staves. "Good morning, lads," Bobby said.

"Ah, good morning, neighbor," Daniel said, his blue eyes fixed on his work. "We've already heard about you and Henry Eagles. Jolly good. Do we get to watch the fight?"

"Can you afford to take the time off?"

Charismatic, thoughtful with always a hint of shrewdness, Daniel pondered a moment and said, "Make it worth my while."

"I'll arrange it so that you can be with Elizabeth after the fights."

Daniel dropped a barrel stave. Eyes wide open, breaking into a wide smile that revealed white but uneven teeth, he quickly replied, "Promise?"

Picking up the stave, James, a medium-sized dark-haired fellow with a square face marred by boils, said, "See how nervous the poor fellow gets just at the mention of your sister's name?"

Bobby laughed with the hearty guffaw of a man who loves to laugh when he has a reason. "I promise. On one condition."

"And what might that be?" Daniel asked, his brow wrinkling.

"You participate in the impromptu fights too, and be my sparring partner to help me train for Henry."

Daniel's face turned serious. "No way. I don't want a bloody lip or a black eye. What if I hurt my hands? A broken knuckle wouldn't do my business any good. It's miserably unfair."

"We'll use mufflers to practice."

"No."

"No to Elizabeth?"

Daniel's answer was instant. From his bony ramshackle frame he uttered a committal grunt. "You win."

After spending several more minutes in Daniel's shop, making detailed plans to practice, attend the fair, and appear at the impromptu fights, Bobby left to attend to his own duties.

Daniel's mind wandered as he resumed his efforts to teach his two assistants how to make a good barrel. He was already in love with Elizabeth, although he had told no one, not even Bobby, and he relished the chance to be with her during the fair. He wondered how Bobby and Elizabeth, who seemed so fun and normal, could have parents – especially a father – that were so "abnormal." To Daniel, they seemed almost in the category of religious zealots when it came to their Anglican faith.

Right from the day he and his family moved to Deerhurst, he felt the elder Harris looked down on the Browetts just because they were members of the Society of Friends, or "Quakers." Daniel could just barely remember his father, Thomas Browett – an ironmonger or hardware dealer – who had died ten years earlier. Daniel assumed that his father must have been a zealous Quaker, because it had rubbed off on his mother. They had never missed a Sunday while they lived in Tewkesbury, and for the past four weeks Martha Browett had insisted that her five children travel with her back to Tewkesbury – seven miles away – every Sunday to attend Quaker services.

Daniel had not told his mother, or anyone else, but as he grew older there were some things about his religion he did not like and was ready to tell his mother that they ought to quit going to Tewkesbury, and find another religion. He would be willing to become an Anglican if that were the only way to gain permission to marry Elizabeth. However, he did not particularly like the history of the Church of England, or even the original Church of Rome. Nor did he feel inclined to align himself with any of the other dissenting churches, whether Methodist or Baptist.

Daniel thought that his mother might object to any proposal on his part to change religions, because she felt that the members of her religion treated men and women equally. Plus, she did not have to pay tithes, take oaths, or see any of her loved ones fight in war. In fact, Quakers refused to doff their hats to any man, including old William IV, the current king of England. Their beliefs and practices had resulted in persecution over the years, causing his mother to harbor bad feelings about other religions, especially the Anglicans.

He would have to approach her carefully.

CHAPTER NOTES

In real life, the Eagles family members were Methodists; the Harris's were Anglican, and the Browetts were Quakers, just as portrayed in the story. It is doubtful, however, that Thomas Eagles and Robert Harris, Sr., were so narrow-minded as fictionalized.

6

WHEN BOBBY AND DANIEL met John Benbow and Thomas Kington the day of the Gloucestershire Fair, they had no idea of the dramatic impact the two men would have in their lives. Almost as dramatic as Wilford Woodruff, years later.

The fair was located in an area known as the commons, land not owned by the gentry, where small farmers known as husbandmen could graze their animals without fee. It was a pleasantly beautiful spot, tucked between the Malvern Hills to the north and the Cotswolds to the south.

Bobby and Daniel were in an exceptional mood by the time they met Robert at the cattle and sheep sale, an important part of the fair. A late September sun was drenching the shire. The rich oak, maple, elm, and birch trees were all showing a tinge of their fall colors. Flags promoting the fair flew from every steeple in the shire. The largest rippled from atop the huge Gloucester Cathedral, in the distance. Bunting hung along every major thoroughfare. Inns and alehouses near the fair booths and stalls were crammed with patrons. The pleasant odors of oxen and pigs roasting outside public houses beckoned all, as landlords sought to profit from the large festive crowds. Rings of new redbrick houses, spread throughout the countryside, added to the colorful atmosphere.

Despite being twenty-four years old, Daniel had never been in Gloucester.

Located in southwestern England, Gloucester had a rich history dating back to the time Romans built the town at a point where the River Severn could be crossed easily. The last Romans left Britain in 407 AD. Gloucester was largely abandoned except for farmers. In the late Seventh Century the Saxons founded a monastery and the town began to revive. William the Conqueror came here in 1085, and during that time he ordered that the Doomesday Book be written. During the Middle Ages, the population of Gloucester swelled to more than three thousand. In the Eleventh Century Normans built a castle here, because of Gloucester's strategic location. It rapidly became a market town. Wool became the main industry. Later, the leather industry thrived. Cloth and grain became exports. A community of Jews lived here in the twelfth century. Friars arrived a century later, preaching and helping the poor. In 1541, the town was given a bishop and the abbey church was made the new cathedral. Now, in 1834, gas lit the streets at night, old gates had been demolished to make it easy for traffic enter and leave, and the cathedral had been rebuilt into a large and impressive structure. Vessels were repaired at the Gloucester dry dock. Warehouses surrounded the docks. Thousands were employed in the flour and timber mills, in the hand pin factories, and in the farm machinery industry.

These were the main reasons the fair thrived each fall in Gloucester.

When Bobby and Daniel arrived at the cattle and sheep sale, they found Bobby's father engaged in a friendly but businesslike conversation with two strangers, both smartly dressed.

Robert looked pleased. "Bobby, perhaps you've heard me talk about

Yeoman John Benbow and Thomas Kington from near Ledbury. I've just purchased a few of their prime steers."

"Pleased to know you, lad," Benbow said, a warm smile gracing his face. Bobby found himself shaking hands with a man in his mid thirties, of medium height, stocky, square-shouldered, moustache, long sideburns, an aura of dignity about him. "Your father tells me you two chaps are participating in the impromptu fights today."

"That we are, sir," Bobby said, grinning with confidence. "This is my good friend, Daniel Browett."

"And this is Mr. Kington, my farm manager."

Kington was taller than Benbow, stood ramrod straight and possessed thoughtful brown eyes and sandy hair. He dressed as though he were on his way to a Sunday meeting rather than to a fair, but had the rough, callused hands of a hard worker.

"Mr. Benbow operates the Hill Farm near Castle Frome," Bobby's father said.

"And what do you do, Mr. Browett?" Benbow asked with a pondering look.

"I'm a cooper," Daniel answered, his blue eyes gleaming. "My shop is in Deerhurst, near their butcher shop."

Daniel quickly took stock of Benbow and Kington. Both looked confident, encasing blasts of willpower tempered with a generous amount of spirituality. Daniel perceived Benbow to have an unselfish loving heart, and Kington to possess strong leadership qualities.

Benbow's face lit up. He stood in thought for a moment. "A cooper, you say? How fortunate. One of my tasks here at the fair is to find a reliable supplier of barrels. Interested?"

"Yes, sir. Very much so," Daniel said, dancing his fingertips together. "Superior quality, too. Guaranteed."

Benbow rubbed the side of his nose, sizing up the young cooper. "Can you fill an order right away?"

"Certainly, sir. No problem. I just took on extra help." Daniel's heart thumped, hoping for the first big break in his life.

"Bring me a full wagon load as early next week as you can. Fall harvest is on, you know. Can you find our farm?

Daniel took a deep breath, sighing in relief. His face was lit with happiness. "Just give me directions."

As Daniel and Benbow talked, Thomas Kington appeared restless, curiously remote. He constantly glanced at his pocket watch. He gave the impression of a man late for a meeting. But right on cue he stepped forward.

"The Hill Farm is easy to find," Kington said, taking off his cap. He brushed his fingers along the side of his head where the sandy hair was thinning. "Take the road north to Ledbury. You'll go past Staplow and Stanley Hill. We're located six miles this side of Castle Frome. When you get close, just ask anyone for directions. They'll help you."

"Thanks awfully, I dare say," Daniel said, thrusting his right hand toward Kington and Benbow again. Their handshakes bound the agreement.

"You'll have to excuse me now," Kington said. "I have some business to attend to in the city. Sorry I can't stay and watch your matches."

"No problem," Daniel said. "Thanks again."

"Good luck anyway."

Robert touched Bobby and Daniel on the shoulder. "I have some sheep I want you to look at. Then you two can have some free time before the matches."

Thomas Kington mounted the black horse he called Beggar and rode off in the direction of Gloucester, an old leather saddle making muffled creaking noises as the horse walked through the fairgrounds. There was a lot on his mind.

Kington was on his way to the magistrate's office to license additional houses of worship for his religious organization known as the United Brethren. He would follow that with a visit to the Bishop of the each diocese to properly register with them. At first his group had used a large hall attached to John Benbow's farmhouse at Castle Frome. But with additional converts being added in the many parishes throughout the three counties of Gloucestershire, Herefordshire, and Worcestershire, it was necessary to license homes of members as meeting houses, and to license several members as lay preachers.

He was dotting every "i" and crossing every "t."

He wanted no trouble with the Archbishop of Canterbury or any of the Anglican vicars or rectors in his area.

As an adult, Kington had attended the worship services of all of the major religions in England, and had studied their doctrines in depth. However, he was frustrated with the substantially different doctrines taught by all the churches and, more especially, ashamed of the legacy of both the Protestant and Roman religions. He was a man who viewed the world as a web of profoundly intertwined histories and events, especially within the framework of religion.

Born in Bodenham, Herefordshire, in 1794, he was self-educated and loved to study and read when he was not busy making a living – first as a lowly farm laborer and later as the trusted farm manager for John Benbow.

He had carefully studied Christianity all the way back to New Testament times using every available resource, and had quickly become disenchanted with the Roman Church. He freely admitted that the literature and books he'd read, documenting corruption in the church and raising questions about the church's claim of authority back to Peter, were occasionally biased. He didn't know for sure. But his studies had been enough to convince him that the original church and the church in Rome were not the same.

The story of King Henry VIII was also laughable, in his opinion. For the King to set himself up as the head of a newly formed "Church of England" was ludicrous. To Kington, the Anglican Church was a mixture of convenience and theology that begged a full understanding, full of egotistic, willful, romantic people who, it seemed, were always poised to strike down competing philosophies. He doubted that even the first Protestant Archbishop of Canterbury, Thomas Cranmer, had fully understood Anglican theology, and would have admitted it if he'd been honest. If Cranmer were still alive he would ask him, but Cranmer had lived more than two hundred years before.

For much of his adult life, Kington had been a Methodist, and so had his original followers. This religion had brought a new standard of morality to the English lower classes. John Wesley's new religion had taught its followers to strive "methodically" for Christian morality, and for a perfection that Wesley doggedly believed was possible for some, but probably not for himself. Wesley's genius lay in his ability to organize groups. In keeping with his belief in good works, he had systematically explored the social evils of England, taking a stand against the enclosure act that hurt farmers, against child labor, and against the sale of liquor, which deprived the poor of their money. Kington also agreed with Wesley's opposition to the Calvinist concept of predestination.

Kington had aligned himself with the "primitive" Methodists, those who preferred to meet out-of-doors or in the homes of members whenever the weather was bad – a concept introduced to England in 1806 by an American Methodist preacher by the name of Lorenzo Dow. Dow, in fact, had been "cut off" from the Methodists for his stubborn insistence that Christians could worship out-of-doors, just as well as in doors, like members of the original Christian church had done in the time of Christ.

As for Kington, the more he studied John Wesley, the more he had become convinced that John Wesley was not satisfied with his own life, let alone with the religion he created. If Wesley weren't satisfied, Kington would not be either. There had to be something better. Because of his zealous quest for something better, the Methodists had recently "cut off" Kington as well.

If there was one thing Kington had learned during his years of devotion to religious study, it was how to pray. He began to ask God what he should do. While there was no voice from heaven, there was a feeling – a definite feeling. That feeling told him he should wait. Pray for more light and truth. Be patient.

When he had shared this feeling with his employer, John Benbow, Benbow had agreed that he had similar feelings, and together, with approximately five hundred other "primitive" Methodists who felt the same way, they had decided the best thing to do was to keep sharing the feeling with others.

If others were also disenchanted with their current religions and wanted to worship with them on Sundays, they'd be welcome to join them. They did not want to start a "church," but they did want to be organized. They decided to call their organization the "United Brethren." They would merely unite and wait for further light and truth. What would they do while they waited? Study the scriptures. Preach right from wrong. Keep the Sabbath day holy. Keep all the Commandments.

As he reached the edge of the commons, Kington turned in the saddle and looked back at the Gloucestershire fair. The mass of confusion reminded him of the world he lived in. He had something better to offer.

He was impressed with Daniel Browett and his deep sense of purpose.

Someday soon, he resolved, he would offer Daniel and his friends a chance to learn about the United Brethren.

Twenty-seven-year-old Wilford Woodruff seldom took such pains to draft a letter.

But he had started over on this one five different times.

With a stern face he read it again in his room in the Lyman Wight home in Liberty, Missouri. A wind moaned through the surrounding oak and maple trees and through the small log home itself. He skimmed through the words, the sentences, and the pages, contemplating his thoughts and all his meaning.

As soon as he had received the letter only a week earlier from his father and stepmother in Connecticut, he had been thinking of how to respond to their unrealistic demands that he renounce his new religion and return home. As he read his own words this time, he felt a little better about the way he had said everything. In carefully chosen words, he had expressed sorrow over the cleft that separated him and his family, but wrote that he was convinced he had taken the right course. He testified to his parents that God had restored the "new and everlasting covenant," explaining it the best he could, and that the purpose of his new church was to prepare the earth for the Second Coming of Jesus Christ.

He said that the kingdom, which God had established on the earth through the Prophet Joseph Smith, was the very kingdom that Daniel of Old Testament times had prophesied would eventually fill the whole earth. He was convinced – through the Spirit, the Holy Ghost – that this "restored" church, the Church of Jesus Christ of Latter-day Saints, was indeed the only true and living church on the earth.

As Wilford walked over a dirt road, littered with the first drop of late summer leaves, to the Liberty Post Office and posted the letter, he made himself a promise: From this day on he would keep a personal journal and write in it every day, reflecting his commitment to his new life.

On his way back to the Wight home, he stopped at the General Store and purchased a journal. As soon as he returned to his room he wrote on the first page: *The First Book of Wilford.*

7

AS THE SHEEP SALE ended, Bobby held a hand out toward his father. "Do you have a few more shillings? We're going to meet some of my friends and get something to eat."

Robert's brow furrowed, but he surrendered a few coins. "Fighting on a full stomach wouldn't be too smart."

Bobby smiled in appreciation. "Thanks, Father. See you at the fight stage later."

A growing concern was plaguing Daniel as he and Bobby walked away. "Aren't you nervous? You don't act like it. I think everyone in the entire shire knows you and Henry are fighting."

"No. Why should I be?"

"What if you lose?"

"I won't lose, I assure you," Bobby promised.

"But what if I lose?" Daniel said, the thought haunting him. His ego would suffer a setback, losing in front of Elizabeth and her family. He wished he had not given in to Bobby's demand.

"Just remember what I told you, and how we trained," Bobby said, feeling a pulse of excitement.

Daniel grimaced, trying to remember: *When you make a fist, keep your thumb tucked in, otherwise you risk dislocating it. Keep your guard up at all times. Lead with your left. Keep your left foot forward. Circle to your right, away from your opponent's power. Keep your chin tucked in. Guard your ribs with your elbows. Slide with your feet, don't step. Jab with your left to keep your opponent off balance. When you hit, hit hard, as though your life depends on it. Be on guard at all times. Some opponents will gouge at your eyes, grab your legs and try to throw you down, grab you by the throat and try to choke you. Some fighters will throw sucker punches. Some will bite you, try to hit your midsection where your liver is, then keep hitting you there.*

Daniel fought an unfamiliar undertow. "I still don't know. I'd hate to lose."

"Nonsense," Bobby said. "Get all negative thoughts out of your mind."

Daniel flashed his friend a doubtful glare.

"Remember to take advantage of the rules," Bobby said, ignoring Daniel's concerns. "Whenever you get hit, if it hurts, if it makes you dizzy, drop to your knees. Take the thirty seconds to recover. That's the way fighters win. Use your head by clearing your head. Then get up and attack, clench your fists tight and attack."

"How do you expect me to remember all that?"

"Instinct. Pure instinct. Do you remember Broughton's rules?"

"I think so," Daniel answered, pulling a piece of paper out of his pocket and looking at it for the hundredth time. The rules had been devised in 1743 after an opponent of Jack Broughton died from injuries sustained in a brutal match.

A puzzled look came over Daniel as he scanned the wording. "If I win," he asked, "how much will two-thirds of the money amount to?"

"Absolutely nothing," Bobby chuckled, raising his hands to block the blinding son. "We're amateurs, so we won't win any money."

Staring at his balled up fists, Daniel asked, "And what if I hurt these hands? How will I do my work? I'm fighting for nothing. I might lose in front of a lot of people. I don't know if it's worth it."

Bobby shook his head in disgust.

"Just watch how you throw your punches. Hit your man on the arms. That will bruise him. Hit him in the stomach. Those blows won't hurt your hands. Knuckles are broken mostly by blows to the head. Pick your shots carefully. A bare knuckle to the head is bone on bone. Your knuckles will break before a man's head will. The jaw will give a little, but not a man's head."

With a worried expression on his face, Daniel opened and closed his fists, certain he had made a mistake.

They came to the first booths: The shortest man alive. The silver-haired female child. The torso without arms or legs. The waxworks.

Next were booths where agricultural products were sold – butter, cheese, wheat, barley, oats, rye, pumpkins, squash, and woolen cloth. And booths where English wool and iron were traded for furs and falcons from Norway, wine from France and Italy, cloth from the low countries, and spices and other exotic items from the eastern Mediterranean. These were all clues that England was still the world's leading maritime power, controlling, in fact, forty-five percent of the world's trade.

Just past the glass blowing booth they came to the flying trapeze. About thirty feet off the ground promoters had installed a thick wire about forty yards long. A handle with wheels was attached to the wire that, with slight pressure, ran swiftly down the wire. Bobby took hold of the handle, and threw himself off the platform, laughing out loud as he flew through the air, high above the safety net below. His speed was slowed enough that he hit the padded board at the end of wire with barely an impact.

He saw a sign that said "No Females Allowed" and wondered if his two sisters, Dianah and Elizabeth, would be upset. He descended from the landing and waited for Daniel to have his turn. Daniel hit the padded board and laughed.

The merry-go-round fascinated Daniel. The carousel spun slowly in a circle, propelled by a single man in the center who cranked a handle, which in turn powered a system of gears. Daniel wished he were standing in the long line with Elizabeth.

Ignoring cheapjacks that tried to sell them watch chains and carving knives, they finally arrived at the food stalls. The aroma of boiled pork and peas pudding struck them. Bobby scanned the crowd for his friends, William Pitt, Levi Roberts, John Cox, and Joseph Hill. He was too hungry to look for them. Soon he and Daniel were swallowing the pleasant mixture of pork, peas, carrots, onions, cabbage, and celery.

Daniel's next words caught Bobby completely off guard. Still staring at his fists, he said, "What would you think if I proposed to your sister?"

"Proposed?" Bobby said, nearly choking on his food. "Wow, that's jolly fast, you haven't even courted her yet."

Daniel took off his cap, letting the midday sun glisten off his golden hair. "I know, but I really like her."

When he'd turned twenty, Daniel had begun to envision what his future wife would look like – dark brown hair, olive skin, blue eyes, and medium build. However, Elizabeth was none of that. She had long blonde hair that showed just a hint of red when the sunlight hit it just right, green eyes, a slender body and a determined, cheerful personality. The light of her eyes and warm smile had attracted him from the beginning, from the day he moved to Deerhurst. Her constant optimism and concern for the welfare of others caught him in a net of emotions that wouldn't let go of his thoughts.

Everything about this girl interested him, even gripped him.

Bobby stopped eating, tilted his head, and raised his eyebrows. "Like her? My brothers told me that they loved their wives before they got married."

Daniel began to look a little sheepish, regretting he had changed the subject. "If I loved her, I would tell her, not you."

"Come on, Daniel, you can tell me. Say the words. I...love...Elizabeth."

"Oh, cut it out. You're wearing me a bit thin."

Bobby smiled, examining his friend's depth of commitment. "Do you dream about her every night?"

"What if I did?"

"I didn't realize you were so serious about my sister. But I knew you were sweet on her. You go a little cross-eyed when you're around her. Did you know that?"

Daniel was aghast at the size of the spoonful of pudding that went into his friend's mouth at the end of his statement. He was more aghast at the thought of talking to Bobby's parents about Elizabeth, especially his father.

Robert Harris, Sr. had intimidated Daniel from the first day they'd met. Certainly, he hoped, all gray haired old people were not as opinionated as Robert Harris, Sr. The old butcher knew everything there was to know about anything. Take cattle for instance. He knew every breed: the longhaired Galloway, the red-haired Hereford, the Belgian Blue, the British Blonde, the British White, and the Welsh Black. He knew when a steer was ready to slaughter, which cuts made the best steaks or roasts. He knew all about sheep: Hampshires, Border Leicesters, and Suffolk. He knew everything about meat. Everything about English politics. Everything about religion. He even purported to be an expert in carpentry, and already he had given Daniel advice on making cabinets and barrels. The advice was worthless, but Daniel had politely tolerated it.

If he were to ask for Elizabeth's hand in marriage, Daniel feared the traditional interview he would have with her parents. Was he worthy of her? Could he provide for her? Would they live nearby? Would he be a faithful Anglican? Would he have their children christened?

"Tell me honestly," Daniel said, his tone serious. "Do you think your parents would approve?"

Bobby smiled and swallowed again before making his words. "Of course I do. They like you and that's a smashing fact. Shall we order a second round of pudding?"

"No thanks." Pressing for an answer, he touched Bobby on the arm. "Do you think Elizabeth would say 'yes'?"

This time Bobby broke into a grin and laughed. "Well, I don't know. You wear your cap a little cockeyed. You have a mouthful of crooked teeth. You have blonde hair and she prefers dark brown. You're a carpenter and we're butchers; you're a French Huguenot instead of a British Saxon. Not to mention the most serious problem of all: you're a Quaker and she is Anglican. Besides, you'll probably die young and leave her a widow with a house full of children."

"Be serious old chap. Would she say 'yes'?"

"Ask her after the fights."

8

HANNAH EAGLES HAD been raised not to complain, but her patience was wearing thin. She had already endured an hour at the adjacent hiring fair while her father had helped Mr. Nightingale talk with prospective farm workers, and she was feeling resentful, even critical of the whole thing. Nevertheless, she had always thought it clever how carters and waggoners advertised their skills by having a piece of whip-cord twisted around their hats, how thatchers wore a fragment of woven straw, and how shepherds held sheep-crooks in their hands. But she had seen it all before. Farmers desiring to hire a worker could tell at a glance what he was qualified to do. Today she had stood on one foot and then the other as Mr. Nightingale and her father sealed an agreement with a handshake and a fastening penny, a token sum as an act of good faith, an agreement to employ workers.

Hannah had no desire at all to sit at a food booth. She wasn't hungry, and she didn't like being around Henry, so she languished into a period of total silence.

"Here is your clotted cream," her father said to her, handing a dish each to her, Nancy, and Jane.

Jane quickly pushed hers away, asking for Yorkshire cream cheese. Twelve-year-old Elias and twenty-three-year-old William ordered blood pudding. Thomas and Ann Eagles settled on a dish of beistyn, made from the thick milk of a cow that had just given birth to a calf. Saying he needed the energy for the fight, Henry ate a blood pudding and two clotted creams.

Henry's two obnoxious friends, Alex and Richie, who had been tagging along, were another source of irritation to Hannah. At least they paid for their own desserts. It wasn't the fact that Alex had been brought up as an orphan, that he was illiterate, or that his face was severely pitted by smallpox, that Hannah didn't like him. Or that Richie was overweight, bowlegged, had unruly red hair, and was subject to violent sweating that she didn't like him.

It was because both of them had bad manners, just like Henry.

"Thank you, Papa," Hannah responded, with a heavy emphasis on the second syllable, breaking her silence.

The dessert was good but her mind was elsewhere, so she just picked at it. She had worn her prettiest day dress – she had only four – a bright yellow one with a high bodice and matching bonnet.

Where was Bobby? She hoped to see him at the fair before the fights and give him a chance to ask about sitting together in church. She thought he was still too afraid of her father, but it might not get better after the fight. She slapped at a fly that flew from dessert to dessert. She wanted to squash the fly, and mash it into the ground just like she wanted Bobby to squash her brother and mash his face into the ground.

Ever since Bobby placed his head in her lap last week, Hannah could not quit thinking about him, especially those long eyelashes and his athletic body – the body that had slammed Henry into the mud. She guessed Bobby to be almost six feet tall and weigh fourteen stones, maybe a little more. She would find out for certain today when his weight was announced at the matches. But amid a crowd so large she thought it hopeless that she would see him. Gloucestershire was home to thousands, and it seemed that every one of them was at the fair today.

"Are you going to eat all your clotted cream, Hannah?" Henry asked, poking her in the ribs. "Give it to me if you're not."

She shoved the dish at him without speaking, and watched in astonishment as he gulped it down. She wanted to shrink from view, certain that everyone at the fair was watching her big-mouthed, piggy brother.

"What if Bobby hits you in the stomach, Henry?" Nancy asked in disgust. "You've eaten so much today you'll throw up in front of everyone. You're always such an unscrupulous old horror."

Her words struck Henry as odd. "Ha! Don't fret your pretty little eyelids on that. Not a chance. Last year I knocked my man silly. Bobby is nothing. I'll knock him silly, too. No mercy."

"You might be surprised," Hannah hissed, clearly riled. "You could be the one knocked silly. It might do you some good."

Emitting a loud belch as he stood up, Henry had to snort at that remark. "Watch your tongue, sister. You'll wind up being an old maid. Nobody likes a smart mouth."

The crude jibe caused momentary silence, broken by Hannah's mother who clearly was disgusted with Henry's burp and his caustic words. "Henry, that will be enough," Ann Eagles said. "Go do something with your friends for awhile and leave your sister alone."

"See you at the fights, little sister," Henry muttered. "It'll be the end of Bobby the butcher."

Hannah watched with disdain as her brother disappeared into the crowd with his two boisterous friends. In her mind, it was a wonder Henry had any friends at all, the way he treated others. The more he could humiliate and demean others the happier he seemed. He even took out his frustrations on animals. She recalled the day he kicked the neighbor's sheep dog so hard it broke the poor animal's ribs. If a cow stepped in the milk bucket or kicked it over he flew into a rage. He seemed to have a fascination for violence yet, at other times seemed normal, especially around the family if her father was present. Maybe Henry's violent nature was because her father disciplined Henry harshly as a child, even resorting to beating him at times.

She was glad to be rid of him, at least for a while.

CHAPTER NOTES

Beistyn is made from the first milk taken from a cow after calving, thinned with plain milk, sweetened with sugar and flavored with a cinnamon stick or vanilla. It was usually topped with damp sugar and set under a grill until a crust was formed.

The British used the stone as a unit of weight. Eight stones constituted a hundredweight. Thus one stone equaled fourteen pounds. According to Hannah's estimate, Bobby weighed about a hundred and eighty-six pounds.

The author's descriptions of characters in this novel are fictional. A photograph of John Benbow as an elderly gentleman was available in a family history, for example, but details of his physical description were lacking.

IT SEEMED TO William Pitt that he was nearly as cursed as Job when it came to shooting rifles. Laying the gallery rifle on the counter, he gave up. He had only hit nine targets out of twenty. Levi Roberts had not missed once. John Cox had missed only two and Joseph Hill only five. Despite his poor shooting, he was having a good time.

"Oh, rot," William laughed, "I guess I'll never make the Carver Shooting Team." Poking fun at himself, he added, "I guess musicians never were very good at shooting."

On their way to the gallery William and his friends had watched Carver's marksmen splatter apples over a woman's head. The woman had never even so much as flinched.

Levi took his pocket watch out and looked at the time. "Best we move toward the fights, they'll start in a half hour."

"Let's not get there too early," William said, shaking his head. "Bobby'll probably make us sign up, too. I don't want to fight nobody, never."

"No matter what Bobby says?" Levi asked, silently disagreeing with

William.

"Right. Let him and Daniel do it, but not me."

"Where did John and Joseph go?" Edward asked, examining the seemingly never-ending rows of booths clogged with curious visitors. He had not seen John Cox and Joseph Hill since he had started shooting.

"Two booths down," Levi answered, pointing, "watching the free juggling show."

Edward waved his arms at them, calling their names. "Come on! It's time for the fights."

John and Joseph were not the only ones who could see William's arms waving in the crowded walkways of the Gloucestershire fair.

"Look," Henry Eagles said to his group of ruffians. "There's some of Bobby's friends. "Let's fetch ourselves over there and have some fun with them."

Alex and Richie merely nodded, knowing they didn't have a choice in the matter. They wore bright-checkered trousers, the mark of a con man or loafer in England. Whatever Henry wanted to do, they meekly followed.

William Pitt stopped in his tracks. "Uh, oh! Isn't that Henry Eagles and his friends?"

The name struck John Cox like a blow, so much had he heard about Henry. Of all the young men their age in Gloucestershire, Henry Eagles was the last person you would want to run into.

Henry quickened his pace until he stood directly in front of William, the smallest man in the group. "Two and six I beat Bobby to a bloody pulp." His voice was intimidating, low and guttural.

A creeping numbness overcame William, a scant ten stones in weight and only a lean five-foot eight. Goliath Henry was at least four or five stones heavier and four inches taller.

"I just spent all my money on the rifle range," William gasped, backing away. Henry's breath reminded him of spoiled milk.

Henry turned on Joseph Hill. Reaching out with a long, powerful arm, he pulled Joseph to his face.

"You heard me," Henry repeated. Eyes of flecked cold steel poured out of his half-evil face. "Two and six. Fork over the money."

Silence.

"Two and six! What's the matter, you rotten blokes? No faith in your friend?"

John Cox had always believed the only way to handle a bully was to stand up to him. Stepping toward Henry, his words came tumbling out, reckless, filled with a fire that startled Joseph, Levi, and William.

"Leave us alone, Henry," John said. "Back off. If we had that much money we would take your bet. But we're all broke."

Henry narrowed his dark eyes and growled with a terrible intensity. Cocking his fist, he punched John on the right cheek. John went down, the red welt already showing.

Levi jumped on Henry's back. Alex reacted immediately, pulling on Levi's legs until Levi fell to the ground. Henry pounced on Levi, choking him, and then delivering a powerful punch to the eye.

William, Joseph, and John found themselves held by Henry's other ruffian friends.

Squatting over his injured foe, Henry screamed, "Two and six, Levi! Or I shall do you more mischief?"

John Cox had seen enough. "All right, Henry. We'll give you two and six. If you beat Bobby we'll put our money together and pay you."

Rising to his feet with an evil smile, Henry said, "Give it to me now. I'll give it back if I lose."

"Come on, Henry, that's no way to make a bet," Levi stammered, rolling his eyes in pain. He rose to his feet. "You're nothing more than a white-livered thief."

Henry hit Levi again, this time to the stomach. Levi doubled over in pain.

John gave in. "Let's put our money together. Maybe we can come up with two and six." Within seconds, he had collected the money. "Here, Henry. Now go away and leave us alone."

"Thanks Mr. Cox, rum dog that you are," Henry said, grabbing the money with a sweep of his arm. "I knew you'd see it my way."

Henry led his jeering, chuckling friends away.

10

AT THE SOUTHERN edge of Gloucester Commons, nearest the city, stood a four-foot-high fair booth with wooden planks for a floor, surrounded by wooden stakes through which ropes had been strung to form a stage for the pugilist matches. Clamoring near the stage was a crowd of several hundred spectators, mostly men, through which great flagons of ale were passing along with cakes and bread.

Legendary stories about British pugilist personalities and their fights dominated the conversation: The time George Stevenson was killed by Jack Broughton in the vicious bout that brought about "Broughton's Rules." How earlier in his life Stevenson had single-handedly thwarted three highwaymen who attempted to rob the stage he was driving, smashing one highwayman in the face with the butt of his pistol, knocking another out with one punch, and shooting the third. How Tom Cribb defeated an American black fighter by the name of Molineaux by fouling shamelessly, even biting his opponent's finger to the bone. The time Tom Spring took eighty-nine minutes to beat Ned Painter in thirty-one rounds, winning when he slammed Painter into a ring stake, causing a knot the size of an egg to appear, then later cutting his eye and dealing crippling blows to the ear. The time Jem Ward took a dive against a man named Abbot, letting his friends win crooked bets. And the time an Irishman by the name of Simon Byrne died after being knocked out by James Burke in a horrid fight that lasted ninety-eight rounds, and extended for more than three hours.

It was in this raucous atmosphere, just after the first match had begun, with two young amateurs waling at each other, that Daniel attempted to introduce his mother to John Benbow.

"This is my mother, Mrs. Martha Pulham Browett," Daniel said in a loud voice, over the cheers, screams, taunts, and jeers of the spectators."

Daniel also introduced his three brothers, Tommy, Johnny, and Willie, and his sister, Rebecca.

"Pleased to meet you, ma'am," Benbow said, cupping a hand over an ear. "I have an agreement with your son for him to supply me with a barrel order."

Fifty-six-year-old Martha had hazel eyes, gray hair, and a thin face. She wore a dark green dress with a yellow mantle over her yet slim figure. She curtsied and smiled deeply. "You won't be disappointed, Mr. Benbow," she said. "Daniel does good work. Of course I'm a little prejudiced, but I think you will find that it's true."

Martha Pulham Browett was more appreciative of Benbow's barrel order than she let on. Little did he know of the Browett family's struggles. Her husband had passed away ten years earlier. That forced her into the poor house. Martha hated its loneliness, its mustiness, and its boring food that tasted like boiled, sweaty clothing. Charity came from her husband's previous Quaker friends. Daniel had to quit school at age twelve and go to work as an apprentice carpenter. She had to pay Daniel's apprentice fee to a master craftworker who treated Daniel cruelly, and kept him indentured until age eighteen. Martha had to home school Daniel after that. He was a good learner and developed excellent penmanship. The move to Deerhurst was a desperate gamble. What little savings they had been able to accumulate was invested i

Daniel's tools, and the first month's rent in the small building that served as his shop and their home. Their living quarters in the upstairs portion of the building were small and crowded, barely survivable for her and her five children.

As Benbow and his mother talked, Daniel scanned the fairgrounds.

"Has anyone seen John and James?"

Pointing, Bobby said, "Over there, watching the match."

Daniel attracted their attention. Eyes still glued to the fight, they stumbled to Daniel's side.

"I want you to meet someone," Daniel said. He introduced them to John Benbow. "They work at my cooper shop."

John Davis – of medium height but big-boned, brown hair, broad face, and clear complexion – wrapped a big hand around Benbow's hand.

"Pleased to meet you, sir," John said. "Are you here to watch Bobby and Daniel fight?"

Daniel interrupted. "I've decided not to fight. One might break a knuckle. If I injured my hands, I couldn't work."

"Smart decision," said James Pulham, Daniel's cousin, also employed in the cooper shop.

"What?" Bobby said, his eyes opened wide in disbelief. "But I thought..."

"Not today," Daniel said, his voice firm.

John Benbow smiled. "I see I'm dealing with a smart man. Excuse me now. I see some people I want to visit with." He stepped away.

Bobby was about to express his disappointment when he saw Levi, William, Joseph, and John Cox approaching. Levi's eye was swollen shut, black and purple in its color, still bleeding. Bobby's jaw dropped in shock.

"What happened to you?"

"Henry Eagles found us," Levi said, dabbing at his eye with a handkerchief. He hunched his shoulders.

Bobby's face reddened. "Henry Eagles did this to you?" A resentful anger coursed through his soul, festering.

Speaking in terse clipped sentences, as though he were out of breath, John Cox related the entire incident. He showed Bobby the welt on his cheek.

"I'd like to get one of them rum creatures alone," John said, his face scored with hate. "Believe you me. I'd black their eyes just like they did Levi's."

"Where's Henry now?" Bobby asked, clenching his fists. His eyes darted through the crowd.

"Calm down," Elizabeth said, reaching out to hold onto her brother's arm. "He's right over there. See? On the other side. I think your names will be called out next."

Bobby fumed. *You'll regret roughing up my friends, Henry. You have no business forcing a bet and taking their money.* He took off his shirt and cap.

From her vantagepoint on the opposite side of the ring, Hannah Eagles gasped as the current fight ended and handlers carried the loser away. Both eyes were closed and bleeding, and blood oozed from the young man's nose. She wondered if the loser of every fight looked so beaten and mournful, and quickly concluded that pugilism was stupid and cruel.

"You're up next," one of Hannah's brothers told Henry.

As Henry took off his shirt, Hannah gazed across the ring and watched Bobby strip to the waist. She blinked and blinked again. Henry was big-boned, raw, and had a crazy look about him, but Bobby had the kind of sculptured body that Hannah imagined Roman artists used as models for their statues. He had a thick neck, broad muscular shoulders, developed pectoral muscles and a tight, rippling stomach. No wonder he had slammed her brother to the ground so easily that day. If Henry were going to "butcher the butcher" as he had bragged all week, he had his work cut out for him.

Nancy elbowed Hannah and coyly pointed in Bobby's direction. "Look at that," she said.

Hannah smiled.

Thomas Eagles folded his arms tightly, deep in thought. *Henry's strength and fighting ability comes from the Eagles blood coursing through his veins. His meanness comes from the Sparks side of the family. If that were me in the ring at that age, I would easily beat the butcher.*

A mutton-chopped, heavily mustached, sandy-haired man came to the center of the plank-floored stage, wearing a striped shirt, a bow tie, and a bowler hat.

"And now we turn our attention to our next featured fight. From the hamlet of Apperley we introduce a young man by the name of Mr. Henry Eagles, twenty-six years of age, who weighs in at fourteen stones. We hear he has had several previous fights and has never been defeated."

Reluctantly, Hannah put her hands together and clapped politely for Henry with the rest of her family. She shuddered with embarrassment at the sight of Alex and Richie as they waved their fists, chanting loathsome depravations. She concluded that their bulging stomachs were full of ale and their brains empty.

The announcer turned and pointed to Bobby.

"And from the parish of Deerhurst but born in the hamlet of Huccle-cot, in the parish of Churchdown, may I introduce his opponent, twenty-four years old, Bobby Harris. He weighs thirteen and one quarter stones."

Robert Harris, wearing his butcher's hat, applauded stiffly. A sense of inward pride swelled through him. To him, the fight was simple. Anglican against Methodist. Butcher against dairyman. Harris blood against Eagles blood. The sooner Bobby's cracked Henry's jaw, the better. The sight of Alex and Richie was repugnant to him.

"Bobby's got to win, don't you think, Mrs. Harris?"

Sarah's look was indignant, and her reply snappy. "You don't doubt that he will, do you? Certainly you don't, Mr. Harris."

Levi Roberts massaged Bobby's back muscles. His eye still throbbed. Levi and John Cox were Bobby's handlers.

"Remember, Bobby," Levi said, "Henry has our money. We can't afford to lose it."

Bobby, Levi, and John walked to center stage, met there by the referee and Henry, Alex, and Richie, Henry's handlers. The stage was twenty-four feet square, bordered by two ropes loosely threaded between wooden stakes.

The referee, in a black-and-white striped shirt, chuckled at Alex and Richie's glassy-eyed look as he began explaining Broughton's rules. He pointed to a three-foot square in the center of the ring.

"If there is a knockdown, it is the handler's responsibility to bring you man back to scratch," he said, pointing to the square. "If my count exceeds thirty seconds, the match is over. Kicking, gouging, butting with the head, biting, and low blows are fouls."

"You're going to be sorry you roughed up my friends," Bobby said as the referee motioned the two fighters to their corners.

"Wrong, Bobby," Henry said, sticking out his jaw and spitting on the planked floor. "I'm gonna tear your heart out."

Henry turned away, pounding his fists against his chest.

Alex and Richie laughed a drunken laugh.

"He'll fight like a wild bull, Bobby," Levi counseled. "Just pop 'im in the gut when he charges. I think he's been drinking just about as much as his two friends, or more."

"I think Bobby knows how to handle a charging bull, Levi," John said, staring at Henry. "Think of all those bulls and steers he's slaughtered over the years."

The referee, short, paunchy, with beads of sweat dripping off his bald head, gave a signal. A bell clanged. The fight began.

Just as Levi predicted, Henry charged, grabbing Bobby's thigh. Bobby retaliated with a bear hug. The crowd groaned as they crashed to the floor. The four handlers rushed to assist the two fighters.

"No wrestling, gentlemen," the referee said, angrily. "Remember the rules. Round two!"

His eyes wide as saucers, mouth open, pawing aimlessly with his left hand, Henry cocked his right fist and charged again, throwing a wild right. Bobby sidestepped the blow, dancing away to his left. Henry pursued, trapping Bobby in a corner, giving him a bear hug and slamming him against the corner wooden stake. Again they grappled, again they toppled to the floor.

"I told you, no wrestling. Come to scratch. Round three!"

Henry charged again, throwing another wild right, naturally shifting his weight from his left foot to his right. The blow grazed Bobby's chin, barely missing its deadly target. When Henry charged this time, Bobby struck with three quick and hard left jabs. The third brought blood to Henry's nose.

"I won't miss the next time, by Jove!" Henry hissed, dropping to one knee to recover. Richie and Alex rushed to him.

"Round four!"

Lunging, Henry threw another wild right haymaker. Bobby was much too quick for him. The blow missed. Bobby danced away, laughing.

"I thought you were a coward," Henry taunted, wiping at his nose. He spat on the floor, the spittle reddened with blood.

This time, Bobby charged. A right cross landed on Henry's forehead. Stunned, Henry swung with his right. It missed. Leveraging all his weight, Bobby dug an uppercut into Henry's rib cage. Henry dropped, gasping.

Stunned to silence, Alex and Richie rushed to the fallen fighter.

"Get your breath, Henry. You've got thirty seconds."

No movement. The referee counted.

"Are you hurt?"

The count reached twenty before Henry could talk.

"I'm bloody fine, Alex. Get out of my way."

"Round five!"

"How did that feel, Henry?" Bobby asked, jabbing at Henry's bloody nose. "Like an ox's hind leg? Still think I'm a coward?"

Glassy eyed, but still with a wild look, Henry tried a left hook. It missed. A right cross. It missed. Bobby countered with stinging jabs to the nose, aggravating the bleeding.

Elizabeth cupped her hands over her mouth.

"At 'im again Bobby, hit 'im again," she yelled. "Pop it to 'im. It's the Harris blood a croppin' out in ya, it is!"

Her sister, Dianah, cupped her hands, too, yelling.

Sarah stole a look at Robert. He had a pleased look on his face.

Henry frog-stepped toward Bobby cautiously, leading with his left, placing a well-aimed punch that rocked Bobby. Bobby countered with more jabs to the nose. Henry cocked his right fist behind his back, and swung with all his might. He missed again. This time he fell into the ropes. Bobby attacked, driving a blow to the side of his head. Henry crumpled to the floor again.

"He's playing with you, Henry," Richie whispered. "You want to continue?"

"Get out of my way," Henry responded in anger, almost breathless. He scampered to the scratch line.

"Round six!"

A thirst for revenge stirring in him, Henry circled Bobby carefully this time. He tried a series of jabs. Bobby blocked them.

"That all you got, Henry?" Bobby taunted.

The fire returned to Henry's eyes. He threw a wild right again, the punch that had been used all his life to knock other men senseless in street fights.

Bobby was no ordinary street fighter. He ducked under the punch and countered with another wicked right to Henry's ribs.

Thud!

Henry made a terrible groaning sound, air hissing out of his mouth. He fell to the floor, limp, clutching his midsection.

Hannah cringed as she watched her brother fall. She knew he could not get up. He lay in a crumpled ball, holding his ribs, bleeding from the nose and mouth, moaning.

Hannah turned her gaze to Bobby. He winked at her.

At Henry's side, Alex and Richie rolled their eyes at each other. Alex gave a modest tug at Henry's right arm.

"Do you want up?"

There was only muttering as the count neared thirty.

"What's that again?"

More muttering.

Alex signaled the referee. "He says his ribs are broken."

As the referee signaled the end of the fight, and as spectators surrounding the stage exchanged money, many in shock over the quick ending of the fight, Daniel flew into the ring and jumped onto Bobby's back.

"You hardly worked up a sweat," Daniel said, throwing a defiant fist in the air.

Levi thrust Bobby's right arm upward in a victory salute: "Let it be recorded that on this day, Saturday, September twenty-sixth, eighteen hundred thirty-four, Bobby Harris defeated the wild bull, Henry Eagles!"

Alex and Richie pulled Henry off the ring apron. He cried in pain.

Thomas approached, studying his once-proud but defeated son. Henry's black hair was plastered to his head. Sweat ran in small rivulets down his pale face. His chest heaved.

"Are you all right?" Thomas asked.

"No," Henry groaned. "I feel sick."

"I'm sure you do," his father said, shaking his head. "Do you need a bucket?"

Henry faintly nodded.

Thomas motioned to his other sons. George brought a wooden bucket.

Kneeling in the bright September afternoon sunlight, still so near the stage that several spectators could see, Henry disgorged the day's generous helpings of food and desserts. Thomas and his sons turned away, grimacing.

An ominous shadow darkened Henry's crumpled body.

"Two and six, Henry," Bobby said, his fists still clenched. "If you refuse, I'll pull you to your feet and knock you down again."

Henry's eyes shot up at Bobby, filled with fear. Alex and Richie had disappeared.

Without argument, Henry meekly reached into his pocket and surrendered the money.

"Another two and six, Henry," William Pitt said, hovering over Henry with Levi, John, and Edward. "You lost the bet. So give as another two and six. And good riddance."

Reluctantly, Henry handed over another two pounds six shillings.

Anxiety swept over Bobby as Thomas Eagles approached.

"Congratulations, Mr. Harris," Thomas began, assessing his feelings. "You beat my son fair and square. I apologize for the way Henry acted the other day."

Bobby breathed a sigh of relief as he shook hands with the old dairyman. Out of the corner of his eye, Bobby could see Hannah ambling about close by, listening to the conversation, feigning her own conversation with her sisters. He exchanged a warm knowing look with her.

A scripture came to Bobby's mind. *Ask and ye shall receive.*

"Thank you very much," Bobby responded. "I hope Henry will be all right." He glanced at Henry, who was vomiting again, hunched over the bucket. *Pity the bully.*

"He'll be fine, thank you. I don't think his ribs are really broken. He just thinks they are."

"I have a question concerning your daughter," Bobby said, drawing on his courage.

"I take it you think rather well of Hannah."

Bobby cleared his throat. "Mr. Eagles, I have a favor to ask of you. I would like permission to attend Sunday services with your daughter this week in Apperley."

"At our Methodist service, not Anglican, correct?"

Bobby kicked himself and dropped his eyes. He had meant to specify the Methodist church so there would be no room for doubt, no reason for Thomas to say no. He felt stupid.

"Correct, sir. Methodist it will be."

Thomas nodded. "Permission granted."

Flushed with relief, Bobby said, "I'll be there to pick her up at half past nine. I will have my sister and my friend, Daniel Browett, with me. How do you feel about that?"

"No objection."

Hannah overheard every word of the exchange. Her emotions filled with elation and amazement. As she left with her family, she wanted to run back and give Bobby the kiss he had asked for the day she held his head in her lap.

CHAPTER NOTES

The reader is here reminded that of Daniel Browett's two employees mentioned in this book, one (James Pulham) is fictional and the other (John Davis) is real. Although it is known that Browett was actually a carpenter by trade, he may or may not have owned his own business. Daniel Browett and John Davis probably knew each other well, but it is doubtful that Davis, also a carpenter, worked for Browett.

Pugilism was a popular sport in England during the nineteenth century. According to the recorded family history, Robert "Bobby" Harris was a participant in matches held at county fairs, just as portrayed.

11

THE VICTORY party was festive. Casks of ale, set on stands and tilted at a slight angle, surrounded the booth where Bobby, Daniel, Elizabeth, and their friends sat celebrating. A cheery September sun, sinking lower in the western sky, cast a warm light over everyone. Lazy white clouds drifted overhead. A cool breeze swept over the commons.

"Here's to Bobby – conqueror of the wild bull from Apperley," Levi said, raising his mug high in the air. His eye had grown purple and yellow, still swelling. "Winner of the easiest fight in the history of the Gloucestershire Fair. May you always have the wisdom to sidestep when danger is near, and the strength to break the ribs of your adversary." Laughter erupted.

William Pitt raised his mug: "Thanks for doubling our money, Bobby."

John Cox: "Here's to Alex and Richie, the biggest chickens in Gloucestershire."

Daniel: "Here's to Henry Eagles, who will be hiding in the barn when you go to Apperley next Sunday." Rib tickling laughter.

"Daniel," Bobby said with disappointing eyes, "I was going to toast you, but you didn't even fight."

"I'll toast Daniel," John Davis said. "He's the smartest employer I've ever had. His eye is okay, his ribs are okay. He can work tomorrow."

The statement brought to mind Daniel's barrel agreement with John Benbow and Thomas Kington. He could not shake the special feeling that had captivated him when he stood by them.

"We're going to work twelve-hour days to get Mr. Benbow's order filled on time," Daniel said, smiling in anticipation.

"Need some extra help?" Elizabeth asked. "Sounds more fun than selling mutton roasts to little old ladies."

Bobby assessed the coziness between his sister and Daniel. "Now is a good time to ask her, Daniel."

Daniel placed a hand over his disbelieving face and glanced at Bobby. He felt uncomfortable about discussing courtship with Elizabeth among so many curious friends. His mouth froze shut, and he put his hands in his face, resting his elbows on the table.

"Something's up," Levi said. "I can tell."

Bathed in the late afternoon light, Elizabeth's blonde hair glistened in a gentle breeze. "Ask me what?" she probed, alternatively staring at her brother and at Daniel.

Daniel remained paralyzed during this awkward moment.

A smile flickered on Bobby's face, knowing how his sister thrived on adventure and spontaneity. "He's going to court you, little sister," Bobby said. "You and Daniel and I are going to attend church services in Apperley next Sunday with Hannah and her parents."

"Eeeee! My gracious goodness heavens!"

Daniel's response was one of confusion. "I thought I was supposed to ask your father for permission first."

Bobby gave a nonchalant shoulder shrug.

Elizabeth remained ecstatic. "The answer is yes, Daniel! Yes! Yes! Yes!"

Walking toward Daniel's shop under a purple sky at sunset, Bobby wished the pending double date with Hannah and himself and Daniel and Elizabeth were somewhere other than a Sunday worship service. Courtship tradition in England did not allow him to pick up Hannah in a carriage and whisk her off unchaperoned to some secluded shady nook on the banks of the River Severn for a picnic. He wished it did.

Other than the difference in religion and the fact that she had an obstinate brother, Hannah Eagles was a refreshing change from the snobbish, immature girls in Deerhurst that he had grown up with. Every time a daughter of one of the parish families had become of age and was considered to be "on the marriage market," his parents had forced him to be at home when the mothers came calling with their daughters. It was almost as though the mothers wanted to "arrange" a marriage. It was too old-fashioned. If he were going to be old-fashioned, he'd rather just go back a few hundred years more, pick out a club, hit the girl of his choice over the head, grab her by the hair, and haul her off to his cave.

As he entered Daniel's shop, Bobby's nostrils were again filled with the aroma of sawdust, wood shavings, and glue. Compared to animal pens, blood, entrails, and aging meat, it was a heavenly smell.

"Let's go get it over with," Bobby blurted. "It's time to face the music."

"Why don't you handle the whole thing?" Daniel said without looking up, working feverishly to fill Benbow's order. "Just tell me what time we're leaving for Apperley Sunday morning."

"Take him away, Bobby," James said, setting down his saw. "He hasn't been worth his salt all day. All he does is mope and swoon about Elizabeth."

Daniel's face reddened. "Hush, hush. Careful. One would hate to fire you now. We've too much work to do."

"My dear Daniel," John said, his arms full of barrel staves, "if you fire him, I'll quit. Get out of here, Daniel. Bobby can't do it for you. You've got to get on your knees in front of Bobby's father and beg to court Elizabeth."

"I want to go and watch," Daniel's brother, Tommy added. "Just in case I have to do it someday, I want to see how it's done."

"You're outnumbered, Daniel," Bobby said, jerking his friend to his feet. "Bad odds. Father's waiting. He knows we're coming."

To the snicker of his fellow workers, Bobby ushered Daniel out the door.

In faltering daylight, Daniel stared at the Harris Butcher Shop sign hanging on the redbrick building and peered through the window. Inside was a crusty, opinionated, preachy Anglican carving up a hog carcass with a big sharp knife. Daniel knew that if he and Bobby did not handle this correctly, the old man would carve him up as well. Slowly, one piece at a time.

Daniel cringed as the wooden door creaked on its rusty iron hinges.

"What do you two want?" Robert said in a gruff voice, not looking up.

Bobby cast Daniel a furtive glance. *Ask him.*

Daniel shrugged his shoulders, returning a blank look. *He's your father. You ask him. Besides, you need to ask permission to court Hannah.*

"Well?" The old butcher's watery eyes bored into Daniel as he sliced red ribs covered with white fat from the carcass and laid them on the table.

Daniel's voice did not work well. "I, uh..." he stammered.

Robert wiped a sleeve across his forehead and examined Daniel with a shade of curiosity. *This young cooper would make a fine Anglican.* "What does he want, Bobby? Be quick about it."

"Cat got your tongue, Daniel?" Bobby quipped. "Speak up."

Heart pounding, Daniel dropped his eyes and studied the floor.

The old butcher began to chuckle in a sinister way, and a certain recognition flashed in his old eyes. He pointed the knife. "Let me guess," Robert said, rubbing his chin. "Bobby, you want to take the horse and carriage Sunday. Daniel, you want permission to court Elizabeth. Bobby, you want permission to court the Methodist girl, Hannah Eagles. You want to attend church in Apperley. In the Methodist chapel, no less. And you want me to say 'yes' to all that?"

Bobby and Daniel's collective jaws dropped.

A few seconds passed as Robert waited, fondling his knife.

How did he know all that? Bobby wondered.

"Is that right?" Robert asked.

"Yes, sir," Bobby stammered, his fallen dry mouth still open.

The old butcher spun the knife in his hands, and chuckled again.

"Well," he said, "I see you two squirming around so I'll make this easy on you. Elizabeth already softened me up. She's been working on me all day. I've never heard of a daughter in all England who could pester her father for so long. All I can say is that she must really like you, Daniel."

"You mean we have your permission to attend church in Apperley?" Bobby asked. He was careful not to use the word Methodist.

Pointing his sharp, glistening knife straight at Bobby and Daniel, Robert said emphatically, "I told Elizabeth one time, and one time only. Next time – if there is a next time – you'll have to attend church with your own family here in Deerhurst. Do you understand? That means Elizabeth too, Daniel."

"Yes, sir!" Bobby responded, stepping toward the door before his father changed his mind.

"How about you, Daniel? Do you understand?"

"Oh, yes. Perfectly." Daniel's voice was meek, barely discernable.

"One other thing, Daniel," the senior Harris cautioned, flashing the knife again. "I can see where this thing is going. If there is to be a marriage, it will be Anglican."

With that last warning, Robert resumed carving the ribs.

12

USING THOMAS KINGTON'S directions and following fingerposts along the way, Daniel and John Davis traveled north toward Castle Frome in a wagon borrowed from Bobby's father, pulled by Old Earl and Queenie. Under a heavy load of barrels stacked three high, the horses lathered quickly in the brisk Saturday morning air. Steam spewed out their nostrils as the horses labored along the road to Ledbury then north past Staplow, Bowley Lane and Stanley Hill, dodging a few loose milk cows and sheep that were grazing on lush grass skirting the roads.

There was no rain today. The sky was bright with only scattered clouds. Most of the fields Daniel could see were bare, already shorn of their fall harvest of hops, hay, and varieties of corn – wheat, barley and oats. Wheat was a precious high-priced commodity in England, used for making bread and beer.

Herds of pigs roamed the fields, fattening up for slaughter. Barns were full of the fall harvest. At some farms, Daniel saw workers separating wheat from the stalks, making "perry" from pears and cider from apples. Now and again the barrel wagon passed carts filled with fall produce – apples, pears, cabbages, carrots, turnips, pumpkins, squash – on their way to the market towns of Ledbury and Gloucester.

In a happy mood, Daniel wondered if it were sheer luck or providence that he had met John Benbow and Thomas Kington at the Gloucestershire Fair. One thing he had already learned from Elizabeth was that she believed "lady luck" was always on her side, so maybe it was rubbing off on him. He may never have met Benbow and Kington if he had not moved from Tewkesbury to Deerhurst. If he hadn't become Bobby's friend, he would not have been at the sheep and cattle sale. He reckoned he was in the right place at the right time. He guessed that this was the beginning of a good relationship. Because of his penchant for detail, Daniel was confident that his barrels were better than those of his competition, and fairly prices. He hoped Benbow would give him another order.

Thinking about Elizabeth made Daniel even more elated that "lady luck" appeared to be smiling down on him. The more barrels he could make for people like Benbow the more money he would make and the sooner he could get married. He was tired of being single. Taking care of his widowed mother and younger sister and brothers had always been a source of pride but nothing could be equivalent to having a home of his own and a wife to take care of. If he were to marry and leave the house, it wouldn't hurt anything. They were old enough to take care of themselves. Financially he would continue to care for them, of course. One more mouth to feed also wouldn't make that much of a difference, especially if Farmer Benbow gave him more barrel orders and he received orders from other sources. He could foresee the day when he would own his own wagon and team of horses.

While he had no hope of rising into England's privileged class – the nobility and gentry – he knew he wanted to at least rise to the middle class. Those were the common workers who, despite the odds against them, rose above the ordinary working class people.

In Daniel's observation, most working class people couldn't see the end of their noses. They had no goals, no vision, and no purpose in their lives. He perceived himself as a person who saw life as a serious endeavor, something that gave him a deep sense of purpose, and a reason to achieve, to get ahead, and to help others. He wanted a beautiful wife who would bear him beautiful children. He wanted to be a better-than-average provider. Most carpenters and coopers worked for the squires doing simple jobs that required only simple minds.

To rise above his competition Daniel had also become an expert in dovetail joinery, making coffered ceilings, building handsome wainscoted walls using vertical boards set in tongue and groove. He knew which wood was best for every job – alder, ash, beech, birch, cheery, chestnut, cypress, fir, and on down the alphabetical list. He knew all the glue and paint recipes. Slowly, using every means necessary except dishonesty or theft, he had all the required tools – axes to shape and fit timbers, axes to fell trees, chisels, gouges, planes, saws, mallets, hammers, augers, gimlets, and braces.

Passing a large pond filled with ducks and geese, Daniel thought of his favorite Old Testament story – Noah and the ark. He would like to have helped Noah build the ark, because of the commitment and discipline it would have required, the patience, creative thinking, sacrifice, organization, and motivation.

A few nights ago he'd dreamed of sailing on his own ark with Elizabeth: He was a man of title instead of a workingman. Everywhere he docked the ark, people addressed them as the Duke and Duchess of Deerhurst. His pockets were lined with pounds and sovereigns instead of farthings, pence, and shillings. On their ark he had a small army of servants, a house steward, valet, butler, cook, lady's maid, kitchen maid, scullery maid – maids of every description. Instead of canvas trousers, he had plenty of black, double-breasted frock coats, wool trousers, and white shirts. No caps, but plenty of bowlers and top hats. He shaved every day instead of once a week. He pictured Elizabeth in a ball dress of tulle over white satin. In her private trousseau she had a huge selection of morning dresses, riding dresses, all made of rich silks or crepe; mantles, cashmere shawls, knit gloves, and both silk and fancy leather shoes.

The pond caused Daniel to think about another dream, one that had occurred over and over again. In this dream, he was alone in a canoe. He was gently rowing across a river in a mist of great darkness. The waters cast him about until he came to a fork in the river. He had to choose which way to go. He kept choosing the right fork and as he did so the mist became a little lighter but the waters rougher. His goal was to reach the light he could occasionally see through the mist. When he could see the light, it was bright, inviting, and peaceful. But every time he paddled hard to reach it, he woke up.

Nearing the Benbow farm, Daniel could see farm servants picking apples and pears from heavily laden trees. In another area, children were gathering acorns and collecting twigs from hedgerows. One child was tending a flock of domestic geese with a long stick. Orchards and neat farm cottages lined the rutty road on both sides; one new cottage was under construction. A crew of thatchers was busy at work, laying bundles of straw in horizontal layers on the steep roof, one upon the other so that they overlapped tightly.

Two black and white shaggy sheep dogs barked as the wagon passed a sign that read "Hill Farm." Daniel wondered how the dogs could see with all that long hair drooping over their eyes. The dogs and shepherds pushed a herd of eighty or ninety Suffolk sheep across the road.

Bringing the team of horses to a stop, Daniel caught the attention of one of the shepherds. "Where will I find Thomas Kington?"

The shepherd, an older man in a broad hat and a staff in his right hand, pointed to the north. "Make the next right and you'll see Farmer Benbow's big white house. Not more than a half-mile from here."

Urging the team of horses past the sheep, Daniel turned them to the right. Kington was standing in the lane wearing brown pants, a yellow shirt with a green vest and black boots, talking to three farm servants, gesturing, pointing. Noticing the load of barrels, Kington immediately summoned for Daniel to pull the load near one of the out buildings in front of the white-stucco farm mansion.

"Jolly good, lads," Kington said with a keen eye on the barrels. "You are a prompt young man, Mr. Browett. These are just what we need. You are to be complimented on the quality."

"Thank you heaps, sir," Daniel beamed as he jumped out of the wagon and hitched the horses to a post. His insides were taking a happy grip over his good fortunes.

Putting the unshaven, grizzled farm servants to work helping John Davis unload the barrels, Kington said, "We'll need another wagon load as soon as possible."

Daniel was elated. "One must say, your apple and pear crop appears to be awfully good."

"Yes, and thankfully there's a big demand."

In fact, Kington said, the demand for food from England's growing population, now numbering around fifteen million, was so great that it could not be met by farm production in England alone. Ships laden with cargo from America were being unloaded daily in both Liverpool and London. He also mentioned that the ports were busy with the increasing number of British citizens who were emigrating to America. Because of high food prices and a depressed economy, people were leaving Great Britain in record numbers.

Daniel scanned the farm horizon. "Just how large is Benbow's Hill Farm?"

"Three hundred acres," Kington answered as he finished the barrel count and handed Daniel his money. "As you can see, it takes a small army of farm servants to get everything done around here. Summers are busy getting the hay crop in, then the corn crop and the hops. Now we're harvesting apples, pears, and threshing the corn. And you can see cattle grazing in our stubble fields."

Kington explained that Benbow leased two hundred acres from a relative of his wife, Mrs. Ann Freeman, widow of Francis Freeman, who held gentry status, and thus able to own land in England. The other hundred acres were part of the Castle Frome parish glebe, owned by the Anglican Church.

Mounting the wagon box again and gathering the leather lines in his hands, Daniel was about to leave when he saw Benbow coming out of the house and walking toward them. Smiling sort of a paternal smile as he approached, Benbow waved his hand in the air, and then thrust it toward Daniel, who jumped out of the wagon again.

"Welcome to the Hill Farm," Benbow said. "How are you?"

"Oh, splendid, sir." Daniel shook his hand, grateful for the attention. "Mr. Kington just gave me another order."

"They look like excellent barrels, just as you promised," Benbow acknowledged, keeping the cunning smile on his face. "Keep them coming. You struck me as a chap who could pull this off. I'm sure there are a couple of other farmers near here who will also need barrels. I've taken the liberty to write their names on a piece of paper."

Daniel accepted the paper, smiling broadly.

"Be sure to contact these farmers," Yeoman Benbow said. "Tell them I sent you. You can sell them more barrels – if you can make them fast enough. See you again sometime soon."

"Yes, sir. I will," Daniel said, gaining the sense that Benbow was a busy man.

Kington reached out and touched Daniel on the arm. "One final question, lad. What religion are you?"

Surprised by the sudden change in topic, Daniel wondered if there were a possible wrong answer. He studied Kington, who stared at him.

"Quaker," he sputtered, hoping that Kington would not end their business relationship. If both he and Benbow were strict Anglicans like Bobby's father, it could be over.

"And you, apprentice Davis?"

"Anglican, sir," John answered, his brown eyes quizzical, not telling Kington that his widowed mother was one of the most zealous members of the Church of England in Tirley. The hamlet of Tirley was just a mile or two west of Apperley.

"Sometime in the future when I'm not so busy, we'll talk about religion," Kington said with a warm, radiant smile. "I'll tell you about the United Brethren. Thanks again and goodbye."

Turning the wagon around and clucking the two horses into motion, Daniel breathed a sigh of relief and wondered what the words "United Brethren" meant. He had never heard of that religion. He wondered if it might be affiliated in some way with the Anglicans or the Methodists.

As he drove back to Deerhurst, Daniel began to admire John Benbow and Thomas Kington and men like them for their aggressiveness and foresight. They were two examples of men who had achieved middle class status. Benbow didn't own any land himself – and would never be permitted to – but he obviously learned how to make connections to lease land and thereby achieve the status of a yeoman. Three hundred acres was a large farm in nineteenth century England. No wonder it took so many servants. No wonder Benbow needed Thomas Kington. No wonder Benbow lived in a white mansion.

Daniel wondered where Mrs. Freeman lived. Her mansion would be five or ten times as large, similar to the mansion owned by Squire Hastings in the parish of Deerhurst.

It was a case of the rich getting richer, pure and simple, Daniel thought, and totally unfair. Landowners like Mrs. Freeman received a pound-per-acre-per-year rent for doing nothing, and she probably owned thousands of acres. She was so wealthy, Daniel had learned, that she also owned a large mansion in London. From her status of power in Castle Frome she had the right to appoint the rector of the local parish church.

Daniel wondered how John Benbow got along with Mrs. Freeman. He probably gave her a birthday gift every year, maybe even a Christmas gift. He wondered what happened when a yeoman died – who would be next in line to take over the farm lease? His son? His wife? His nephews? Friends? Connections. Daniel wondered about connections. It would be worth giving up a cabinet and cooper shop for the chance to become a yeoman. A farmer of that status was definitely a middle class Englishman.

13

NEVER IN HER life had Hannah taken a bath both on Saturday evening and again on Sunday morning.

It was a family tradition that everyone bathed on Saturday. It began when the children were little. Ann Eagles personally supervised the kettle on the kitchen stove, "topping up" the tub each time someone new got in. From the time Hannah was a little girl, she hated using someone else's water. That's why she begged for permission to have another bath this morning. Plus, she didn't want to smell like the dairy. The cows never took Sunday off. She had to be in the dairy every Sunday morning, rain or shine.

Stepping out of the tub and drying herself, she thought of last evening's conversation in the parlor, and how nearly everyone teased her about Bobby courting her today. Even during her father's traditional Saturday night sermon with an open Bible, Nancy had rolled her eyes at her, making Jane giggle, and causing her father to get angry. He had tried to preach to the family about good ethical behavior and living the Golden Rule. Hannah felt her father was preaching mostly to Henry anyway. Henry had done nothing but stare daggers at her since their father had given Bobby permission to court Hannah. During her father's family prayer, he made a few unique requests of God: That Henry would give up his hatred of Bobby. That if she and Bobby were married, that it would be a Methodist wedding. Of course he always blessed the cows that they would give more milk.

Now she stood in front of her mirror in the upstairs bedchamber trying on a crimson dress under the watchful and jealous eyes of her two sisters. She broke into a girlish grin, flooded with thankful feelings for just being alive. Thrusting out a hip she asked, "What do you think? Will Bobby like this one best? Or my navy blue?"

Nancy gave a stiff nod. "Crimson. It goes best with your brown eyes."

All morning, Nancy's tone revealed her jealousy. She strongly resembled her sister in her fair skin, brown eyes, and dark auburn hair. If she were twenty-one, like Hannah, she reasoned, it would be her having a Sunday morning bath and trying to decide which dress to wear.

"Are you sure?" Hannah asked, glancing at the clock. Her patience was wearing thin. It was only half past eight. She decided to try on the navy dress. Trying to relax, she closed her eyes and wondered which dress Bobby would like best.

"I vote navy," Jane said, handing it to her older sister, wishing she were ten years older.

"Tush! Foolery! Crimson!" Nancy countered.

After settling on the crimson dress, checking herself in the mirror again, finishing her makeup and dabbing on another layer of perfume, Hannah went downstairs and listened to another lecture from her father during breakfast. It centered on the importance of British people being able to worship as Methodists if they so pleased. There should not be an "official" state religion.

The lecture depressed her. She wished he would talk about something else. *Preach brotherly love to Henry.*

Amidst the chat of her sisters, the lowing of cows out the widow, frogs croaking in a nearby pond, and the sounds of branches sweeping against the house from mild breezes that were blowing, Hannah finally could hear a horse whinny and a carriage pulling up in front. She put her right hand to her chest as though it would calm her rapidly beating heart, stretched her facial muscles, and then patiently waited for her father to escort her out the door.

Thomas Eagles extended Hannah's hand to Bobby. "We'll see you at the chapel in a few minutes. Don't get lost."

"Don't worry, Mr. Eagles," Bobby said with a wry smile, wondering how one could get lost in the small hamlet of Apperley. The alluring whiff of Hannah's perfume filled his nostrils, and he realized how much he cherished this moment.

Hannah scoffed inwardly. It was less than a fifteen-minute walk to the chapel. She hoped Bobby would take her, Daniel, and Elizabeth the long, long, way around, perhaps to Gloucester and back.

Out of the corner of his eye, Bobby could see the figure of Henry Eagles standing at an open upstairs window. A devious thought crossed his mind. As Thomas disappeared into the house, Bobby made a low bow to Hannah. He spoke in a loud voice, audible to Henry. "Welcome, Princess Hannah. May I present Prince Daniel and Princess Elizabeth."

Daniel chuckled in surprise. *Prince Daniel?*

"Welcome to the Royal Carriage," Elizabeth said, catching onto the charade quickly. She stood and curtsied.

"Thank you," Hannah said, with shy diverted eyes.

"How does it feel to be sitting by Bobby the 'Wild Bull Killer'?" Daniel asked, his voice full of mischief.

Bobby cast his eyes to the cottage. "Hang on tightly, Princess Hannah. We'll whisk you away from the evil toady dragon on the second floor."

An angry voice pierced the calm Sabbath air. "I hope all of you choke on your hymn books!"

Another voice, low and angry, could be heard from within the house. "Henry!" Thomas Eagles said, "Come down here."

Henry disappeared from the window.

Bobby tapped the lines, urging the horse into a fast trot. Minutes later, he pulled the gelding into a slow walk, turning away from the Methodist chapel. His commands to the horse were aristocratic. "Easy, Old Earl. Let's take a little tour of the hamlet." The horse threw its head at buzzing flies.

The carriage was winding past shops, pubs, quaint cottages where Squire Hastings' laborers lived, and the village green. There was less than a half-hour until the Methodist church services started, precious little time to be alone without the menacing stares of Thomas and Ann Eagles, Robert and Sarah Harris, and Martha Browett.

"Let's see now," Bobby said, gesturing to the girls, "if you two beautiful maidens are to be Princesses, and Daniel is to be a Prince, why do I have to be Bobby the Wild Bull Killer?"

Daniel laughed. "Because you nearly killed the wild bull in your fight."

"How about something like Bobby the Noble Knight?"

Hannah was quick to recover from her initial shyness. "I like that. Sir Bobby the Noble Knight. Henry is the big bad dragon and he has been dreadful to live with since the fight. I make the motion that we banish him to Australia."

Bobby chuckled, relieved at Hannah's dislike for her own brother. Never at a loss of words, he was puzzled that he didn't know what to talk about next.

Detecting Bobby's temporary silence, Hannah asked him to tell her about his family.

"Not much to tell," he said. "My father is a butcher because my grandfather and great-grandfather were butchers. I'm surprised my name isn't Bobby Butcher."

Hannah laughed, staring at his long eyelashes.

Bobby continued: His father was fifty-seven but in fair health. Someday Bobby's oldest brother, William, would own the butcher shop and he would have to work for him or do something on his own. His other brother, John, wanted to manage a pub.

"Do you like religion?" Hannah asked, bluntly.

"I have my reservations."

"Why?"

"I asked a lot of questions about my deceased twin sisters and little brother, who died as babies. Our reverend didn't answer them very well. I think families ought to be together in the next life. He seemed to have no idea about that."

Hannah nodded. *I wonder about that, too.*

Bobby grimaced in remembrance. He was only six years old when the twin girls died on a cold winter day. He recalled how his mother wept for days.

"I hope you don't judge my family prematurely because of Henry," Hannah said wistfully. "Or my father. He's very devoted to his faith. I admit, Henry is different. But everyone else in my family is quite normal, I can assure you."

Bobby grunted.

"We've had our share of death, too," Hannah said with a mournful sigh. "You won't believe this, but our family lost twin girls, too. One died at age eight, the other, nine. My sister, Editha, died a year ago, just a few months after she was married. That was really sad."

As the chapel came into view, Elizabeth tapped Hannah on the shoulder. "What will your minister be talking about today? At our Anglican Church in Deerhurst parish, the reverend *always* posts a bulletin that announces the topic of the next Sunday's sermon."

"Reverend Stephen Crooks is talking about predestination," Hannah answered without hesitation.

"Predestination?" Bobby choked in disbelief. "Again? Reverend Hobhouse in Deerhurst beats that subject to death."

"It's a worthy topic," Hannah said, irritated.

"Why is that?" Elizabeth asked.

"I like to think I have a destiny of importance," Hannah answered.

"You mean like a dream of what you want to be?" Bobby asked as he guided the gelding to a hitching post where other horses were tied. Several persons, all dressed in their Sunday best, were walking into the chapel.

"Sort of, but maybe not in a religious sense," Hannah continued. "John Calvin himself said that the discussion of predestination was very intricate and perplexed. But I think we are put here on this earth to accomplish something, and we need to find out what it is."

"So what are you going to accomplish?" Daniel asked, caught up in the possibilities.

Hannah's reply was instant. "Maybe something simple but noble, like raising a large family, like my parents are doing."

"You'll need a husband first," Elizabeth giggled, catching a glimpse of Thomas Eagles leading his family toward the chapel. "How about you, Prince Daniel, what are *you* destined for?"

Daniel uttered a short baritone laugh. "I just want to be a humble carpenter. I want more customers like John Benbow." He jumped out of the carriage and offered his hand to Elizabeth.

Accepting Daniel's hand, Elizabeth responded, "Nothing wrong with that. Jesus was a carpenter and he ended up all right."

Daniel paused for five or six seconds in a sort of reverent silence. "He was crucified."

"In the end, you will die, too, you know," Elizabeth said, raising her eyebrows.

Daniel nodded. "Yes, one would hope that would be later, not sooner."

"Are you afraid to die, Prince Daniel?" Hannah asked.

"No, are you?"

Hannah shrugged. "Never thought about it much before. What about you, Prince Bobby?"

Bobby paused to gather his thoughts as he began walking toward the chapel. "Only because I don't understand death. Like I told you, I have a lot of questions that I have asked my minister and others about, and I get a lot of theological gibberish. No straight answers."

Hannah's eyes brightened. "You brought up the predestination idea. Are you destined for something? What are your goals in life?" Hannah hoped for an answer that would be compatible with hers – a large family, secure home, a slow-paced life, and a marriage of mutual support and consideration.

Bobby wiped dust from his eyes but answered quickly. "Professional fighter. I want to be heavyweight champion of England."

"Is that all?" Hannah pressed. "One fight and you are ready to be champion of all England?"

"Henry was supposed to be one of the toughest around and I beat him easily."

Elizabeth touched her brother on the elbow, and came right to the point: "But what about *marriage*, dear brother?"

"Fighters can be married," he said with a shoulder shrug.

Thomas Eagles motioned for the foursome to sit near his family. Bobby cringed, but walked toward the old dairyman.

Hannah smiled in relief as she followed Bobby, Elizabeth, and Daniel to a pew directly behind the Eagles family. She was falling in love with Bobby. A husband who was a fighter would do for now.

She could mold him into a father and family man later.

14

Spring 1835

THE LITTLE REDBRICK Methodist chapel stood under a hazy blue sky. New bright green leaves were barely making their appearance to a collection of oak, elm, and birch trees. Birds chirped from the branches. The River Severn loomed across the horizon. Midday sunshine bathed horses and carriages. It was a scene of tranquil peace. A wedding. Men in bowler hats and women in shawls were standing in lines, congratulating the bride and groom, William Eagles and his new wife, Margaret. Others were visiting in clusters, eating lemon-flavored wedding cake.

The scene put Daniel Browett in a reflective, romantic mood. He tapped on Bobby's shoulder and motioned him several paces away from the crowd, rubbing his palms together as though it would help him think. The words that came out of his mouth startled Bobby. "I'm going to ask Miss Elizabeth to marry me today."

For a moment Bobby studied his friend. "That's no surprise. But why today?"

"Because it's spring," Daniel replied. "Because I feel like it. Because I've courted her long enough. Because I'm a man and she's a woman. Anything else you want to know?"

Daniel's bright blue eyes were full of light. He stood with his spine erect, his shoulders thrown back, like a soldier ready to do battle. He was deeply in love. In recent weeks he had done things that he had never done before, like stealing a little pale blue handkerchief that belonged to Elizabeth, taking it to his room, sniffing it. Once he ate half a cake she had left on her plate when he had dined at her house, because it bore the mark of her teeth.

Bobby's curiosity was aroused. "What are your plans? Are you going to have an Anglican wedding, or make your mother happy and have a Quaker wedding? You're in a tough spot, you know. Maybe you best just jump over the broomstick and call it good."

Jumping over the broomstick was an old English tradition followed by poor common people who could not afford to purchase a proper marriage license or take the time to have banns read in church on three successive Sundays. Daniel knew about the tradition, because that's exactly what his parents had done. They didn't have an official marriage until Daniel was two years old.

Daniel tipped his head down and grinned.

"You don't need my permission, by the way," Bobby added with reluctant admiration.

"That's not why I'm telling you," Daniel answered, extending his hands in a friendly, relaxed gesture. "I'm telling you because I have this terrific idea."

A perplexed feeling came over Bobby. "What idea?"

"Why don't you ask Miss Hannah to marry you?" Daniel blurted out. "Today. Right now."

The words hit Bobby like a thunderbolt. He blinked and felt his tongue roll through his mouth. "Right now? You must be crazy. Just because you want to propose to Elizabeth today doesn't mean that I need to. Can't I do it on my own timetable? You don't need to lean on someone else's courage."

Daniel stared at Bobby, aware of his shock. "Just listen. Here's the rest of my terrific idea. Let's both propose today, right now, ask their fathers for their hands in marriage the same day, give them their rings the same day, then get married the same day in a double wedding."

Bobby doubled over in disbelief, sucking air.

"Come on, old chap," Daniel said, sounding quite formal. "You look absolutely drained. Think about it. It's a marvelous idea. The girls will love it."

Bobby stiffened and shook his head with concern. Despite his brusque behavior as a fighter, he shuddered at the thought of asking Thomas Eagles for permission to marry Hannah.

Daniel ignored Bobby's reaction. "Let's get married in two months, in June. One should certainly think that would give enough time for the three families involved to help us make all the necessary arrangements. We'll get married on one of their birthdays — Miss Hannah's is June tenth, right? And Miss Elizabeth's is June eleventh. Think of it. A double wedding. It will be one of the biggest events of the spring in our community."

It was Daniel's normal habit to let conversations and ideas run their course, to let them sink in, and have patience while waiting for a reaction. Not on this important matter. He waved his hand across his friend's face. "Bobby — are you there? Hello. You look ghastly, by the way."

Bobby raised a reluctant gaze to his friend. "I'm here. You know as well as I do that Mr. Eagles will put pressure on me to become a Methodist. They'll want a wedding right here in this little redbrick chapel. My father will insist that it to be an Anglican wedding. You haven't thought this out too well. And what about your mother?"

"Oh, fiddle. Let's just do it. We can work all that out later."

Daniel took two rigid steps toward the chapel, expecting Bobby to snap out of his stupor of thought and follow him. "Come on. I'm going to find Elizabeth and ask her right now."

"You want me to be there when you ask her? That's not normal."

"No, stupid. Get off your high horse and go find Hannah. I can handle Elizabeth all by myself."

Daniel danced toward the chapel.

"But I didn't say yes."

"You didn't say no. Get it done."

Daniel found Elizabeth talking with friends. He whisked her away from the crowd, pulling on her elbow, striding into the trees for privacy. Hannah was still inside the chapel, visiting with her family.

"I need to talk to you," he said.

"What about?" Elizabeth shot Daniel a curious look.

"Bobby has this great idea. At any second he is going to escort Miss Hannah outside and propose to her. I thought you would like to know."

Elizabeth exploded with delight. She began to babble, again accentuating far too many of her words. "That's *soooo* exciting, Mr. Browett. That is a *great* idea. It must be the spring weather, or it must be the wedding today. *Something* must have inspired Bobby. Hannah loves him so much. Bobby doesn't talk too much to me about their romance, but I *know* he loves her too. They'll be *so* happy together. When is the wedding?"

With confirmation that he'd hit the right nerve with Elizabeth, Daniel said, "In June."

Elizabeth pressed her hands together and drew them up. "Oh, June is so perfect. The weather is so *perfect* then. My parents will be so pleased; it's the first marriage in our family since Dianah got married three and a half years ago. This is *soooo* exciting! I don't know what could be *more* exciting!"

"What could be more exciting, you ask?" Daniel said, placing his hand over Elizabeth's mouth. "Hush, and I'll tell you."

Elizabeth stared at Daniel.

"We're going to have a double wedding."

There was a few seconds of rapid blinking as Elizabeth comprehended the meaning, her mind whirling. She removed Daniel's hand. The blood left her face, her mouth dropped, closed, and opened again. "*Double?* Mr. Browett, Daniel, do you mean..." She felt herself staggering backward in amazement.

Daniel drew Elizabeth close to him. Looking directly into her green eyes, taking in her astonishment, he said, "Double as in you and me and Bobby and Hannah." He liked watching her reaction, the excitement, as it built inside her, the changing of her color from normal flesh tones to flush pink.

"We're going to be married in a double ceremony on the *same* day in June?" Elizabeth placed her hand over her mouth to muffle a scream. "Eeeee!"

Unaware that her scream brought prying eyes, Daniel continued: "Not only that, but one would want to schedule the wedding on either June tenth or eleventh, on either your birthday or Hannah's. I daresay that's exactly what I want to happen. But you have to tell me first that you will marry me."

"How romantic," she said, her voice tremulous with excitement. "Oh, Bobby is so *clever* to think of that. But wait, Mr. Browett. You have to *ask* me first, down on your knees."

Daniel glanced back toward the church, made a funny face, then knelt. "Miss Elizabeth, will you marry this humble carpenter, Daniel Browett? You must, you know. Because I love you so dearly."

Elizabeth scanned Daniel with her happy green eyes, a wide smile lighting her face. "Yes, humble carpenter, Mr. Daniel Browett, I will! Most *definitely* I will. You'll have to *promise* to give me all the pin money I want – you'll obviously be a rich and humble carpenter, won't you?"

"Probably neither humble nor rich. Just in love with you. And please call me Daniel from now on – now that we are officially engaged. No more Mr. Browett."

He rose to her arms, boomed a laugh, and they kissed. He swept her off the ground, twirled her around and kissed her again. She smelled sweet and alluring, and her face was rosier than he'd ever seen it.

"I love you, Princess Elizabeth."

"I love you, too, Prince Daniel."

As they stood in the trees, wrapped in a warm embrace, kissing, saying broken foolish sentences, whispering, laughing, kissing and kissing again, they happened to look back toward the chapel. A few gawking, pointing, laughing Methodists were applauding.

Inwardly cursing at the pressure, Bobby put off finding Hannah until he saw Daniel kissing his sister. Chewing on his lip, head spinning, hands sweating, he found Hannah talking with Susannah Phillips Green, the newlywed wife of John Hyrum Green. He pulled Hannah behind the hedge that surrounded the chapel.

"What were you two talking about?" he asked.

"Oh, the usual. Marriage," she said, giving away a mushy charm that had come upon her because of the ceremony. "After all, it was a long winter." Hannah's only setback of the day had been the wedding bouquet. Her little sister Jane, only eleven, caught it. Hannah considered it a bad omen.

Hannah hated how the winter had dragged: Working inside the cold dairy. Freezing inside the Eagles cottage, even with a fire going in the hearth. Wearing several layers of clothes. Trudging to the "necessary house" at the end of the garden in freezing rain. Putting up with Henry.

The only bright spot had been her slow-blossoming romance with Bobby: Ice skating two times on the frozen River Severn. Once convincing Bobby to ditch the chaperons her parents had sent with them, Nancy and

Jane, and stealing a kiss. Attending church occasionally together, but always caught in a tug-of-war between both sets of parents.

Bobby flinched. "Marriage?"

"You know, setting up housekeeping, getting used to each other, having enough money to live on, getting along with each other's parents. All that stuff. Why?"

"It's Daniel. He has this funny idea. It affects all four of us."

Hannah froze for a few seconds, and then gave Bobby a slow and shy female blink. "What kind of idea?"

Bobby eyes had always seemed to have an eager, aroused sparkle. Right now, however, he appeared to be stupefied, unsure of himself. She took his hand and squeezed it, as an act of encouragement. "You have something to tell me, so say it."

"Well," he said, still tense, "he's proposing to Elizabeth right now."

Hannah broke into a big smile, her eyes gleaming. She went off, sounding a little bit like Elizabeth.

"Oh, Mr. Harris, that sounds so wonderful. They will make a perfect couple, have lots of children. That's splendid good news, isn't it? When is he going to ask your parents? When will the wedding be? Did he just decide to do this at William's wedding today? Weddings make you that way, don't you think? Are they getting married right away? Maybe in June. A June wedding would be just right, don't you think? Did he tell you? Did he tell you when? Where are they? Let's go back. I want to congratulate them right now."

"Wait, Miss Hannah," Bobby said, holding up a hand. "Remember I told you Daniel has this funny idea."

"You mean there's more?" She caught her breath as her brown eyes held him firmly. There was a devious smile on her face.

Bobby took a deep breath. "Lots more."

"I'm all ears."

Bobby paused, mustering courage. He could hear the drone of the wedding guests in the background, birds chirping in the trees above their heads, the rattle of a carriage as it rolled by. He shifted his weight from one foot to another and tucked in his shirt. He peered through the leafy canopy to see Elizabeth and Daniel still happily engaged in conversation. "It's Daniel's idea that we have a double wedding."

Hannah's stomach did a dance as her face lit up. "Meaning?"

Irritated that he had to explain himself further, he muttered the answer. "You know – a double wedding."

"Mr. Harris, are you proposing?"

"It's Daniel's idea."

"Come on, say it. Out with it, dear boy."

Bobby let his breath out and relaxed. "Hannah, will you marry me?"

Hannah passionately pressed her face to his and gave him a warm kiss. "Yes, Bobby, I will. I love you so much."

They whirled, and she kissed him again.

"Now tell me more about Daniel's plans," she said with her most radiant smile.

"I love you, too. If you had kissed me like that before I would have asked you to marry me a long time ago."

She blushed. "Oh shhhh! Now tell me what's going on."

15

ARRIVING IN MEMPHIS, Tennessee, on a breezy, rainy late March afternoon, twenty-eight-year-old Wilford Woodruff was penniless, hungry, dirty, footsore, and in a low mood. His missionary companion, Henry Brown, had left him a few days earlier to return to his family in Kirtland, Ohio. Elder Woodruff, having traveled without purse or scrip for more than three months, had long ago lost any sense of hesitancy or embarrassment about asking strangers for food or lodging.

Choosing the best inn, an elegant brick structure with an oak-trimmed lobby, and ignoring stares from a mustached man richly dressed in a black frock coat and white shirt, Wilford approached the owner, Josiah Jackson. He was a hook-nosed, plump man with heavy gray hair, a big belly, and a huge brown moustache with flecks of gray. Without delay, Wilford asked to be accommodated for the evening – no charge because he was a "preacher." Appetizing dinner fragrances permeated the inn. Wilford hoped Mr. Jackson would be hospitable. His stomach gurgled as he waited for an answer.

Noting Wilford's shabby appearance, Jackson asked a question in a suspicious tone. "What is your business in Memphis?" He had accommodated preachers before. But they were all older, better dressed, and obviously better qualified. He doubted the word of this short, stern-faced, weather-beaten, analytical-eyed, squarely built, but otherwise handsome young man.

Wilford tried to look as presentable as he could in his wrinkled brown suit. He ran a hand through a mop of unruly dark hair, conscious of his unshaven face. Then he flashed a wide indulgent smile. "I am a preacher of the gospel."

Indeed, he was. At the end of December he had consecrated all his worldly belongings, valued at two hundred and forty dollars, to the Church of Jesus Christ of Latter-day Saints and had departed January thirteenth with his companion from Lyman Wight's home near Liberty, Missouri – called to serve in the Southern States Mission. Between Missouri and Tennessee he had camped in the woods, walked as many as sixty miles in a day, come face-to-face with a bear, evaded a pack of wild wolves, endured snow, rain, and wind, suffered from rheumatism, and literally had no money on his person. He had been humbled. However, he was always ready to preach the gospel.

Jackson returned a skeptical smile and laughed. "You don't look much like a preacher to me."

Wilford threw his shoulders back, stood erect, exchanged an appraising glance at his hoped-to-be host, and smiled politely. "Well, sir," he said," I don't blame you for doubting me. I'm certain that most preachers you have been acquainted with rode into this city on fine horses or in fine carriages, dressed in broadcloth, have large salaries, and would likely see our whole world sink in perdition before they would wade through one hundred and seventy miles of mud to try to save people."

The bold statement caused Josiah to take on an immediate puzzled look. He blinked his eyes and pulled at his handlebar moustache, then blinked again. Then a thought came to his mind, a thought that would make him popular with the guests of the inn and some of the leading citizens of Memphis. "I'll make you a deal, young man," he said with a mischievous smile, taking Wilford's valise, "I'll give you a room and a dinner if you will preach here at my inn. I'll have a roomful of guests presently."

In the back of Josiah's mind he could picture the learned men and women of Memphis poking fun at this pretended preacher. It would be better than the rehash of old politics and old religious ideas that tended to dominate the daily evening conversations in the inn's great hall.

At first, it seemed to Wilford a seemingly innocuous request. But as he thought about it, he sensed a setup. He decided to play along. He didn't mind. Let Mr. Jackson think he was going to embarrass him. He had been a member of the church for more than a year. He was a set-apart missionary. He had actual experience being a missionary. He had preaching experience. He had confidence. He could teach the gospel to the president of the United States if given a chance. Wilford was ready for anything.

"Well," he feigned, his eyes dancing around the room, standing on one foot and then the other, "I have never preached in such a formal setting. I don't know..."

Jackson lit a pipe stuffed with rum-flavored tobacco and took a few puffs. "A free night's lodging with all the food you can eat in exchange for preaching – what did you say your name was?"

Wilford straightened his tie. "Elder Wilford Woodruff."

Jackson repeated his proposal. "So you will preach to an audience in our lobby this evening?" His tone stayed mischievous.

Wilford nodded his head. "I came here without purse or scrip, Mr. Jackson. You leave me no choice. I will preach here at your inn if you want me to."

In a few minutes Wilford was seated at a table in the large hall that doubled as a dining room and lobby, and the landlady set before him a supper of roast meat and vegetables. As he ate, the room filled with a collection of people whom Wilford deemed to be the rich and fashionable of Memphis: doctors, lawyers, educators, and businessmen. Wilford tried to hide the fact that he felt sheepish and out of place in his muddy, soiled suit. As he finished eating, the table he was eating on was suddenly removed from the room, carried out over the heads of the people. Josiah pointed to a little stand placed in the corner, having a Bible, hymn book, and a candle placed upon it, hemmed in by Josiah and some of his closest friends. To Wilford's amazement, the hall had filled up with approximately five hundred persons. No one drank cheap applejack; rather they consumed expensive wines and champagne.

"This is Elder Wilford Woodruff," Josiah began, his voice besmirched. "He is a preacher. He is going to preach to you."

Sizing up the young man who had appeared out of the wilderness, the audience had its first laugh. Josiah was pleased. He anticipated an evening full of laughs.

Wilford surveyed his makeshift congregation, feeling a little awkward. He took a deep breath and opened his hymnbook. He read a hymn.

"Now let's sing the hymn," he said. He made a motion with his arm, like a choir leader. However, no one sang with him. Except for a few snickers, there was total silence. "Well, excuse me then, but I don't have the gift of singing and I shan't sing you a solo. But with the help of the Lord I will both pray and preach."

Quickly kneeling, Wilford paused. He refused to begin the prayer until others in the room followed his lead. His patience eventually paid off. A few at first, then others, and soon everyone followed his example and knelt on their knees. Wilford closed his eyes, folded his arms, and began a vocal prayer, uttering it loud enough for everyone in the hall to hear. He asked the Lord to give him the Spirit, and to show him the hearts of the people. He promised the Lord that he would deliver to that congregation whatever thoughts the Lord would put in his mind. When he was done, he arose from his knees and began speaking in bold, direct tones, quoting scripture, preaching basic principles of the gospel, holding his audience spellbound for an hour and a half.

When he was done, he had given a sermon that surprised even himself. The Lord had opened Wilford's mind to a vision of the wicked deeds done by every man and woman in the audience, and the reward they would obtain if they did not repent. What was even more amazing to Wilford was that within three minutes after he had closed, he stood alone in the room. There was no jeering, no laughter, and no heckling.

In a few minutes a bespectacled, wrinkled, slightly bent over landlady appeared with Wilford's valise and showed him to a room. Stepping into it and closing the door, he could hear voices in a large adjoining room. The voices were evidently those of people who had been in the audience. One shaky voice said, "I would sure like to know how that Mormon boy knew everything about everyone's past lives." Listening to another respond, then another, Wilford smiled and got ready for bed. As he settled in his bed they were still conversing and wondering about various points of Mormon doctrine.

A voice remarked, "We could find Elder Woodruff – he's staying here in the inn. We could ask him."

Another voice answered, "No, we have had enough for one night."

Wilford Woodruff chuckled, and slowly fell into a deep sleep.

After a breakfast of eggs and bacon the next morning, Wilford bid Josiah Jackson goodbye. To which Jackson said, "Young man, if you ever pass this way again you are welcome to stay at my inn for as long as you wish."

CHAPTER NOTES

The incident about Wilford Woodruff at the inn is true, documented in his journal and written in several books about the apostle.

16

THE CHILL OF THE March evening air washed over Bobby as he rode Old Earl toward Apperley, fretting about his appointment with Hannah's parents. Duke trailed behind, occasionally distracted by the scent of a hare. Wisps of fog hung over the trees and birds chirped their final lullabies of the day, undisturbed by the clip-clop of the horse and the creaking of the saddle. Faint lantern lights began to appear from the cottage windows along the road as the sun disappeared into a reddened sky. Smoke curled from cottage chimneys.

He had known for days, even weeks, that sooner or later he would have to sit in front of Thomas and Ann Eagles and talk about Daniel's idea for a double wedding. It could not be put off any longer. Aside from Henry, Bobby had found the rest of the Eagles family disconcertingly normal, though he had been prepared to detest them. Earlier in the day he and Hannah had attended Methodist services in Apperley again, sitting with the Eagles family. He had suffered through Reverend Stephen Crook's sermon about piety. To Bobby, Crook's sermons were more boring than those of Reverend Hobhouse in

Deerhurst.

Frightened at the prospect that Hannah's parents might balk at the request that the wedding be held in Deerhurst, Bobby talked to the dog along the way. "What do you think, Duke, old boy? Jolly promise to bite Mr. Eagles' leg off if he says no?" Duke looked up as though he understood, and then darted into the trees, whining, following another scent.

Two sights struck Bobby as he entered a long-beamed parlor inside the Eagles farm cottage. The first was the appalling presence of a small-framed, tall, thin man with a protruding Adam's apple. Bobby's worrisome mood turned foul as he immediately recognized the man to be the Reverend Stephen Crooks. The old preacher stood there in his black suit, deep creases in his wrinkled face, large vivid eyes, a wide forehead that gave way to a narrow foxy nose, salt-and-pepper thin hair, and a small chin that matched his frail frame.

The second was that Hannah had been removed to the kitchen. A single chair, obviously intended for Bobby, sat facing three others, obviously intended for the reverend and Hannah's parents. He had the uneasy sense that the evening would be a waste of time.

A large fire crackled in the hearth. It failed to warm Bobby. He had the perception that Hannah was under strict orders to remain silent, under threat of being taken to the dairy, bound and gagged.

Ann Eagles greeted him with a feigned smile. She took his coat, congratulating him on his pugilism career. He had won two matches recently. She wore the same black dress that she had worn to church, matching the black of both her husband and the reverend. Bobby felt like he had stepped into a funeral. He wished he had worn a bright yellow shirt and red britches, instead of his own black Sunday suit.

Reverend Crooks extended a withered dry paw. "I hear congratulations are in order, Mr. Harris. You are a very lucky man." He spoke in the same high-pitched voice he used to deliver his Sunday sermons. His Adam's apple bounced.

Bobby shorthanded the man of God, squeezing the ends of his fingers. "Thank you," he said, looking past the reverend to Hannah. A yellow cat in her lap, she managed a grim smile.

Wincing, trying to ignore the bungled handshake, the reverend said, "Miss Eagles will make you a fine wife."

"I invited our reverend to be here with us," Thomas Eagles said. "I hope you don't mind."

I certainly do.

Buoyed up by the reverend's presence, Thomas pointed to the chair. "Please sit. I know you have something important to talk to us about."

Bobby sat on the edge of the chair and surveyed his odds. Three against two. Three to one, not counting Hannah. If Thomas and his reverend were younger, he would challenge them to a fistfight. He preferred it to the verbal assault that he knew was coming. There was a moment of silence while Ann poured goblets of wine.

"I don't exactly know where to begin," Bobby said in a weak voice, turning down the wine. "My friend, Daniel Browett, put me in an awkward position. To come to the point, he and my sister want to have a double wedding with your daughter and me. I'm sure Hannah has explained it to you."

Thomas motioned with his eyes.

Reverend Crook's comeback was icy. "That's fine with Mr. and Mrs. Eagles, as long as the wedding is here in Apperley, at the Methodist chapel. Performed by me." *Pompous young Anglican. Never met one that's worthy of a Methodist girl.*

Bobby let his shoulders droop. He fidgeted in his chair. "But my sister and my mother are set on a wedding in Deerhurst. Daniel's mother has approved it, and she's Quaker."

"Then we do have a problem, don't we?" the reverend said. His tone made Bobby feel small and unimportant. "I know your family is Anglican. But you are marrying a Methodist, and she needs to have a proper Methodist wedding. It is customary for a bride to be married by her own minister. You know that."

A nagging thought came to Bobby. Life would be magical with Hannah, but it would be a nightmare with her parents and her minister. And Henry. "Why don't we ask Hannah what she wants?" He cut his eyes to the right.

Hannah stroked the yellow cat, afraid to speak.

Thomas folded his big arms across his stomach. "We are not going to permit our daughter to be married in an Anglican building by an Anglican preacher. Period."

Reverend Crooks coldly smiled, and his expression tightened. "Mr. and Mrs. Eagles have the perfect solution that will ensure a lifetime of happiness for you and their daughter."

Bobby rolled his eyes. He knew what was coming. "And the solution?"

"Become a Methodist. According to what we know, you haven't been much of an Anglican, anyway."

I knew I'd be ambushed, Bobby thought. "If I did, that would solve everything?"

Ann's face erupted into a contortion of delight. "Oh, it would Mr. Harris. It would." She nodded as if she couldn't wait to introduce all her good Methodist friends.

The voice of Thomas Eagles turned an octave or two lower to express his seriousness. "We'll make room for you at the dairy. We will buy some extra cows. You can live in one of Mr. Nightingale's cottages near us."

Bobby was not comforted to know that Thomas Eagles had suddenly taken an interest in planning the rest of his life.

"How can you say no?" Ann asked. "Just tell your sister have a separate wedding. Forget the double wedding nonsense."

"We talked about it with Hannah, just before you arrived," Thomas said, his voice calm now, even chatty. "You're a bright young man, hard worker, handsome. I know you're worried about Henry, but leave that up to me. I can handle him."

Hannah refused to meet Bobby's eyes when he looked to the kitchen.

Bobby was about to reject the offer outright, but Thomas and Reverend Crooks began a tag-team show that would have impressed John Wesley. They rehearsed every litany invented as to why Methodism was a better religion that the Anglicans. They berated everything from King Henry VIII and his wives to the mandatory tithes that even Methodists had to pay to the Church of England. Fifteen minutes passed before either one took a breath. Bobby suspected it might have been partly the wine's fault; Ann kept their glasses filled. Hannah stroked the cat.

The reverend was mid-sentence when Bobby stood up. "You'll have to excuse me. We have a family gathering at my father's place. They're waiting for me. Sorry, but I have to go."

"But you haven't given us an answer," Thomas said with an incredulous tone.

"How would you feel if one of your sons bolted the family religion and became Anglican?" Bobby asked, snorting.

"You're making a big mistake, young man," Thomas said.

Ann's eyes watered in disappointment.

Hannah pulled a face. Bobby couldn't tell which kind.

"My purpose in coming here tonight was to ask your permission for a double wedding in the Deerhurst church. That's what Hannah wants. Why don't you give it some more thought?"

"We have," Thomas said. "Our answer is no. She'll be married here in Apperley."

Without realizing it, Bobby's fists rolled into a ball. He retrieved his cap and coat and opened the door. "Good night. Thanks for the conversation." Before he left, he gave a forced polite bow.

Hannah remained in the kitchen, her head hanging low.

Under a black-vaulted sky, Bobby swung into the saddle resigned to the fact that the double wedding idea was in jeopardy. Perhaps it would be easier to elope. He knew of a place across the border in Scotland. Or jump over the broomstick. Or use the traditional handfasting ceremony. But that would be regarded as living together without a proper wedding.

He glanced back at the Eagles cottage. Reverend Crooks was making a triumphal gesture. Hannah had disappeared.

"Come on, Duke. Let's go home," he said in a disconsolate voice. Bobby kicked Old Earl's flank in anger. The gelding trotted toward Deerhurst in the dark.

"What do you make of all that rubbish, Duke?" Bobby asked, standing in the stirrups to soften Old Earl's hard trot. "Aren't you glad you don't have to deal with parents every time you sneak out courting, you sly thing you?"

Duke whined.

"How would you like to become a Methodist? I hear Anglican rabbits taste good to Methodist dogs."

The dog barked and looked up at his master, then bounced ahead of the horse as a very dim sliver of a moon disappeared behind a bank of heavy clouds.

Minutes later, Duke barked at a grove of trees. Bobby could see nothing. If Duke were chasing another hare, he would have to do it on scent alone. The barking turned ferocious.

Whommmp!

No more barking. The rustle of trees. The cracking of branches. Footsteps, running. Startled, Old Earl reared. A powerful arm, barely seen, jerked at Old Earl's bit.

"Let go of my ruddy horse! Who's there? Duke! Here, Duke!"

"Grab the rot! Pull him down!"

Drenched with concern over his dog, Bobby kicked at three sets of arms. He recognized the voices.

The three sets of arms had six powerful grips. The black gelding ran away in wild, surging gallops, without its rider.

There were kicks to his ribs, stomach, legs, and head. Three men, wailing away. As Bobby slipped into unconsciousness, he remembered voices.

"I think he's out. Let's not kill him."

"If he dies he won't be marrying my sister, will he? Make sure the dog is dead."

Whommmp! Whommmp!

Full of raisin pudding, bored and tiring of the incessant chatter of his grandchildren, his lower back muscles still aching from Saturday's work of dressing two beef carcasses, Robert Harris was not in a patient mood. Minute-by-minute he was growing more irritated that Bobby had not returned from Apperley. He peered out the parlor window into the darkness and listened for Old Earl to come clomping into the yard. The parlor was jammed with his family, all waiting to hear if Bobby had received permission from Thomas and Ann Eagles to marry Hannah in Deerhurst at the Anglican Church. Robert's daughter, Dianah, was there with her husband, Thomas Bloxham; so was his son John, and his wife, Lizzy; William and his wife, Victoria; his unmarried daughter, Elizabeth, along with Daniel Browett; and a house full of playful, screaming grandchildren.

"No, you can't have more pudding," Dianah scolded three-year-old Charles Bloxham, her oldest child. "We need to save some for Uncle Bobby."

"I think it was your husband who had seconds and thirds," Sarah said of Dianah's husband, Thomas. "I think he even ate little Lucy's and little

Tommy's portions," she charged, talking of her other two grandchildren.

Throwing his hands in the air, Thomas replied, "See here, not me. Not guilty. It was John who ate it all."

Sarah was the first to hear Old Earl outside. "I think that's Bobby," she said, glancing out the window.

Robert opened the door and peered into the darkness. From the faint light given out by the lanterns inside the house he could see the gelding. But there was no sign of Bobby. "I don't see him," Robert reported. He walked toward the horse, followed by John, William, Daniel, and Elizabeth. The heavily lathered horse let them approach. One rein was missing.

Elizabeth asked the obvious question. "Where's Bobby?"

In a shaky voice, Robert said, "John, saddle Queenie for me. One of you repair that rein and come with me. Something's happened, and it's not good."

Bobby didn't know how long he had lain in the road. When he awakened it was darker than before. Clouds still covered the sliver moon. A light rain was falling. His breathing was labored, downright painful. He knew he had broken ribs, and there was blood in his mouth, not to mention a splitting headache. He spit it out and wiped his face with his sleeve. The blood was caked and little came off. He touched his ear and the rest of his head where he found matted hair, damp with blood. Staggering to his feet with a loud groan, he instinctively but slowly began walking toward Deerhurst. Every step nearly took his breath away. He could hear the sound of something coming toward him.

Robert Harris, Sr. waited until daylight Monday morning to go see Thomas Eagles. He took his two sons with him, just in case there was trouble, leaving Bobby under the care of his wife and Elizabeth. The initial exam revealed multiple head wounds, a cut on his left cheekbone, cuts around both ears, three loose teeth, and three, perhaps four broken ribs. His next professional fight would have to be canceled. Duke's dead, mangled body was found in the trees.

Thomas was shocked to hear what had happened but told Robert and his sons that it wouldn't surprise him that the foul deed had been done by Henry and his two friends. He sincerely apologized. Accepting the apology, Robert felt it best to let Thomas deal with his own son. Thomas promised there would be a strict punishment in return for Robert's promise not to press legal charges against Henry. It was a deal. Robert asked Thomas if he thought the controversy over the wedding had anything to do with Henry's actions. Thomas said no. Robert asked Hannah's father if he was going to allow the double wedding to be held in Deerhurst. Thomas said no again. Not wishing to press the issue, Robert took his two sons and left.

Riding back to Deerhurst in his butcher wagon, Robert wondered why Bobby had to fall in love with a girl who came from such a stubborn, violence-ridden family. He was glad he was not narrow-minded like Thomas Eagles. Thomas ought to be more like him, loved and respected by everyone. Methodism had ruined the man and had ruined his family. Henry was obviously the worst of the lot, but the others no doubt had hidden personality traits that were going to come out as time went on. Personality traits that would be as disgusting as Henry's and his father's. What was Hannah really like? She may appear to be sweet and innocent now, but she may poison not only her son but also the entire Harris family in time.

After beating Henry with a stick two-inches around and four feet long, drawing ugly welts on his back, Thomas banished him to the fields to help the dairy servants do some fall plowing.

Then Thomas told Hannah what had happened. She was hysterical and told her father that if she could not go see Bobby at that very moment she would run away. He told her she could go, but she would have to walk. She ran all the way to Deerhurst.

17

BOBBY FELT EVERY bump in the road as Daniel's span of two bay mares, purchased with a small down payment he had made with profits from his barrel earnings, pulled a carriage toward Castle Frome parish. It had been three weeks since his beating. Most of his injuries had almost healed, but not his ribs. They were tender. Hannah, wearing a pink satin carriage dress her mother had sewn for her, held his arm tightly, careful not to bump his side. Two doves flew away, causing the horses to shy to the right. Bobby held his breath as the carriage jolted slightly. A large hare ran across the road but this time the horses did not flinch.

"How much farther to the Benbow farm?" Bobby asked, careful to breathe in shallow spurts. To his right, farm workers were spreading manure on a field. Near a barn, children were feeding chickens.

"Another twenty minutes, I suspect," Daniel said.

"Do your ribs *still* hurt?" Elizabeth asked again, jealous of Hannah's satin, wondering how a dairyman could afford to dress her that way. She wore a simple green printed chaley carriage dress with satin trimmings and a matching mantle and bonnet.

"Heaps. What do you think?" Bobby said. "Just don't let the horses go any faster."

Every bump festered an inner anger toward Henry and his two friends, reminding him of the pain he would someday inflict on the three of them. He knew it would have to wait until he married Hannah, however. The kind of revenge he had in mind would cause Thomas Eagles to resent him forever, maybe to the point of rejecting him as a son-in-law altogether.

Earlier in the day, he had attended church with Hannah in Apperley. The conversation with her father had not gone well.

"It's time you gave in, son," Thomas said.

"No thanks. I don't want to be a Methodist."

"You're a loser. Perhaps my daughter should marry someone else."

"That's strange. Three weeks ago I was bright, hard working, and handsome."

Hannah had taken a firm line with her father since the beating. It was like she developed a whole new personality. Today, for example, he had opposed her going with Bobby on a carriage ride with Daniel and Elizabeth.

"I'm going whether you like it or not, Father," she had said. "And keep Henry away from us."

Daniel's double marriage idea had brought a lot of feelings to the surface, including religion. In their private conversations, the four of them agreed that perhaps they ought to seek their own religion, not Anglican, not Methodist, not Quaker. Every time Daniel had delivered barrels to the Hill Farm, there was Thomas Kington repeating his invitation to learn about the United Brethren. Today was the day.

Bobby was impressed with the sun-drenched landscape of the Malvern Hills, surprised at its beauty. He had never been more than twenty miles away from Deerhurst.

"They say there's no prettier place in all England," Daniel said, pointing out flowers that were blooming along the roadside: buttercups, sweet violets, mignonettes, bilberry, white campion. Leaves were beginning to appear on the trees: willows, poplars, walnuts, birches, alders, oaks, elms, cypress. He pointed out Beacon Hill, site of ancient Roman bulwarks, where brown winter grass had turned a bright green.

"Farmer Benbow has this large mansion with a great hall attached that will seat nearly two hundred people," Daniel explained. " He's lived at the Hill Farm about three years, and been married ten years. They had two children of their own, but both died. Two adopted children live with them."

Hannah looked confused. "I thought Mr. Kington was going to talk."

"Superintendent Kington," Daniel corrected, chuckling. "Farmer Benbow is the money behind the organization. Superintendent Kington will explain all about the United Brethren. He also lives at the mansion, but he's not married."

"Not married? Does he believe in celibacy?" Hannah asked.

"I don't think so."

Hunched over, Bobby grimaced, his sense of humor intact. "Will there be refreshments?"

"Bobby, be nice," said Hannah, threatening to elbow him.

"Matter of fact there will be," Daniel said. "I was going to save the news as a surprise. But because we are potential new members, John Benbow is giving us full treatment, dinner and refreshments."

Bobby's eyes widened. "This is sounding better all the time."

Elizabeth held up a hand of caution. "You mind your manners and act like a *gentleman* today."

"I always do."

"There's a big difference in what you think a gentleman acts like and the real thing," she countered. "The meal will *betray* you."

As Bobby rolled his eyes and stared into the trees, Elizabeth commenced to lecture her brother on dining room etiquette: A gentleman should seat his escort to his left and remain standing until all the ladies are seated. The senior lady, either by age or social standing, would be led to the table first by the host, Mr. Benbow. The hostess, Mrs. Benbow, would arrive last on the arm of the senior male.

"And another thing, Bobby, *never* say 'meat' instead of 'beef' at a formal function such as this."

Bobby's face sobered. "Just as well take me home now. I'll never make it through the meal without making a mistake."

Elizabeth gave her brother a hard look. "Yes you will. And *another* thing – never take bread, even when it's within your reach. Instead, ask the servant to *pass* it to you. And never cut bread with a knife. Break it by hand."

Bobby groaned. "How did I get myself into this mess?"

The Benbow parlor was beautifully wallpapered, accentuated with a high ceiling. A fire that crackled from a massive hearth warmed the room. Aromas of roasting meats filled every nostril.

After introductions, Jane Benbow, wearing a jacconet-muslin seaside dress with a pink mantle, seated her guests at a large table in a heavily paneled dining room. Dark paint and heavy drapes gave an illusion of closeness although the room was large, furnished with elaborately carved walnut chairs. Each place was set with a dinner and side plate, heavy silverware, and two glasses. The table was decorated with an epergne, candelabra, decanters, and serving dishes.

Bobby, Hannah, Daniel, and Elizabeth knew some of the guests: John Hyrum Green and his wife, Susannah; Edward Phillips, and Levi Roberts. Two were Daniel's employees: James Pulham and John Davis. One was Bobby and Elizabeth's cousin, John Gailey. The others: William Jenkins, Mary Rowberry, Thomas and Ann Jones, and Joseph and Eliza Halford.

Bobby dove right into the food, trying to remember the lecture Elizabeth had given him. There was not only roast quarter of lamb and roast beef ribs, but braised pigeons fricasseed with bacon, cooked cabbage and squash, preceded by clear gravy soup. Dessert was baked plum pudding covered with sifted sugar. Their drink was the best blackberry cordial any of the young guests had ever tasted.

Between bites, and gazing at the walls decorated with guns, whips, and fox's brushes, Bobby wondered how a man like Benbow reached Yeoman status, a tenant farmer.

As Kington began speaking, a hush came over the guests.

"The best way I can describe our unique congregation," Kington began, his hands at his side, looking comfortable, experienced, and in charge, "is very simple. We seek light and truth. I hope you noticed in the prayer that I said as we began that we, all of us, need to pray continually that the Lord will open up a way to send us further light and knowledge, that we can know the true way of salvation. We seek the omnipotent influence of the Holy Ghost. We don't think it is necessary to belong to any of the sects that are organized on the earth today; none have any resemblance to the original church set up by the Savior with apostles, teachers, priests, elders, pastors, and evangelists. Why don't I take it upon myself to organize the United Brethren that way?"

Kington paused, choosing his words carefully, bringing his arms in front of his body and pointing the forefinger of his left hand to his chest.

"Simple. I have no authority from God. There's not a man I know of here in England, representing any church, that has that authority."

Daniel began assessing Kington's words. He particularly liked the phrase, *light and truth.*

"I, or we," Kington continued, partially closing his eyes in deep thought, "don't pretend to have all the answers. We are just trying to improve on the reformation that has taken place in England, and all over Europe during the past many years. We are a break-off group from the Methodists, so we are closely tied to the Methodist beliefs; indeed we believe that the outstanding religious figure of the eighteenth century has been John Wesley."

Bobby grimaced. *Methodist.*

"Wesley felt it very important to preach the gospel of Jesus Christ to all people, and there was a duty laid on those able to preach to do so. He felt, and we sustain that feeling, that the gospel also includes the necessity to improve the physical and social conditions of the less fortunate. During the past fifty or more years there has been an increased enlightenment in England, a time when people have questioned formerly accepted ideas. Political developments ensued from these social concepts, and the culmination was the French Revolution which had an impact far beyond the borders of France, even to England, I dare say."

Kington began pacing back and forth, still talking in sober, reasonable, pedestrian tones.

"These new ideas have taken time to permeate into the religious societies in England but they have inspired certain individuals and that is where I, and the preachers I supervise, get our inspiration. We seek to improve the lot of the English people – to improve education, to help establish schools, as well as emphasize evangelism and the preaching of Christian doctrine. Some Christian leaders, some preachers, some reverends – without naming names- are slow, too slow, in moving society forward. That's one area where we part. We wish to move forward at a more rapid pace."

Daniel stole a glance at Bobby. There was no expression he could read.

A serious look swept over the face of Kington as he snapped his hands to his hips. "Within our embrace of noble causes we acknowledge, openly acknowledge, a weakness. We love the Bible and its teachings. We advocate daily reading of the Bible, and the living of Christian principles. But we do not have all the answers. I believe no church on the face of the earth has all the answers. None of us as preachers, within our movement or without, can answer all the many questions common people have of Christian theology. We cannot tell you, with exactness, the purpose of life. We cannot tell you what happens after death with any detail. Something in Christianity is lacking, and it has been lacking for centuries. I think we ought to be together as families in the hereafter, but nothing in Christian theology that I know of teaches that kind of doctrine. I pray for further light and truth."

Daniel blinked. There were those words again, *light and truth.*

"How are we truly saved? One church teaches one concept about baptism, another church teaches another. Are we to be baptized by sprinkling, immersion, or pouring? Does the Trinity consist of three Gods or is there just one God? Are we to believe in the rigid Puritan doctrine of predestination or a more open view of it? Are we saved by our works or by Christ's good grace, or both?"

Kington said that the United Brethren differed with Wesley in that they favored a kinder approach to raising children whereas Wesley had advocated a strict – sometimes even brutal – approach and even supported child labor. Kington was in favor of lessening the amount of hours children could work in factories. Wesley was opposed to teaching writing in Sunday Schools, Kington was in favor of it.

The church superintendent then brought his audience up to date on current events in England as well, telling them that the Industrial Revolution that began around 1780 was well entrenched, and that the country was still moving from an agricultural economy to one based on manufacturing. However, the revolution was putting increased pressure on women and children to tend steam-powered machinery. Kington said that leaders of all churches needed to become the country's watchdogs so that abuses of women and children did not continue.

He said the upper classes, the aristocrats, and the Anglican Church still owned virtually all of the land in England. Many people supported a continuation of the Corn Laws, which kept prices up for grains, but that workers hated it because it made food too expensive. Activists under the name of the Chartist movement were pressing for annual parliaments, voting rights for all adult men, the end of property qualifications for members of the House of Commons, voting by secret ballot, equal electoral districts, and salaries for members of Parliament so that men without private wealth could afford to run and be elected.

Land ownership sparked Bobby's interest, but the discussion about the Chartists bored him.

Kington glanced around the room, his forehead wrinkled in thought. "All this is continuing to bring change in England," he said. "There is still an atmosphere of national pride sweeping the country ever since the Duke of Wellington defeated Napoleon twenty-two years ago. There are more and more miles of railroad. New surfaces have improved major roads. Stagecoach lines, many of which will be replaced by railroads, connect every corner of England. Our country has strengthened its role as a major military power. We control much of the world, and our products are exported to faraway places."

Kington added that religion was changing, too.

"We need to implement many other changes, however. We think it is wrong that the aristocrats have the power to appoint clergy simply because they own the land surrounding the village. The people ought to have the power to appoint their own clergy. Better yet, those positions ought to be appointed by people within the church, people who in all righteousness represent the God in Heaven. And we think it is evil that a tenth of all agricultural wealth has to be paid to the Church of England. It gives the Anglicans an unfair advantage. The tithing tax ought to be paid voluntarily and paid to the church people attend, not the church that still thinks it is the official church of our country."

Despite the tithing disadvantage, Kington said, nonconformist Protestant sect members could now hold office in a borough, a change that had been in effect only a short while. "If you could afford it, you can now attend Oxford or Cambridge. Now that's progress," he laughed.

Kington told his audience that last year the United Brethren congregation had gained enough size and strength to purchase land, at a cost of twenty-five pounds, so that a chapel could be built in Gadfield Elm with a seating capacity of a hundred persons. Daniel was pleased to learn that the chapel location was only six or seven miles west of Apperley, tucked in the quiet countryside where the borders of three counties come together: Gloucestershire, Herefordshire, and Worcestershire. However, most meetings were held out-of-doors (in good weather) or in the homes of members so that people could walk to church services.

The meeting lasted more than two hours with all the guests asking many questions and Superintendent Kington and Farmer Benbow answering the best they could. The invitation was clear: attend church at one of the United Brethren locations. They detailed an elaborate meeting schedule for several congregations throughout the three shires. Lay preachers were used, trained and supervised by Kington.

Kington paused, standing in thought for a moment, then continued his invitation. "Take your time to think and pray about it. If you come into the United Brethren, you will find that we believe in vocal, private prayer. In the coming weeks and months I will have time to visit you in your homes if you wish and we can talk more. And please attend church with us on any Sunday in the future."

After a chorus of "Amens," Kington and Benbow began handing out copies of the United Brethren schedule, complete with times, locations, and the preacher assigned to minister each location. Each location, mostly homes of members, had been properly licensed, Kington said. It was too early to ask, but Daniel wondered if some day he could be one of the lay preachers in the organization. Even women could participate. He wondered if Elizabeth would be interested.

Dessert was baked plum pudding covered with sifted sugar. Bobby helped himself to three servings as the gathering began to break up. Licking his lips, he approached Farmer Benbow. Within earshot of Daniel, Bobby asked, "How does one get to be a Yeoman?" It stuck in his craw that the nobility and gentry, along with the Church of England, owned all the land. It was Lords and serfs. The working class could never own land. Benbow was a yeoman, sort of in between the nobility and the working class.

Not anticipating the question, Benbow appeared startled. "Why do you ask?"

Noting the rich atmosphere of the room and the way the Benbows were dressed, Bobby said, "It beats the life of a butcher."

Benbow laughed. "It is quite difficult, really. In my case I had a connection to Squire Francis Freeman, who is now deceased, through my wife's family. I would guess most farmers who have leases with the gentry have some kind of connection. You just can't get in a line and sign up."

"What if I were British heavyweight champion someday? Is that the kind of connection we're talking about?"

Hannah was clinging to Bobby. Benbow turned his eyes to her. "Is he serious?"

"I'm afraid so, Mr. Benbow," she said.

"If you were the champion, why would you want to be a farmer like me?"

"Pugilists have a short career. I'm talking afterward."

"What about your family livestock and butchering business?"

"I have two brothers. They can work in a blood-soaked apron all their lives if they want to. I'd rather be like you."

Benbow flinched. "Your father may not like that."

"I know. But I have my own life to live."

Bobby's bold and cynical tone made Benbow uneasy. He excused himself. "I think my wife needs me."

When it was apparent that all questions had been asked and answered, the young guests congregated at the hitching posts. John Hyrum Green and Susannah announced they were going to join the United Brethren regardless. So did Edward Phillips, Susannah's brother, and James Pulham. Levi Roberts was a maybe. John Davis expressed concerns about his staunch Anglican mother, fearing retribution.

"What about you, Daniel?" Green asked.

"I was very impressed with Thomas Kington and what he had to say," he answered. "I keep thinking about the words, light and truth. It's quite open minded."

"And you, Elizabeth?" Susannah queried.

Elizabeth knew her answer was not what Daniel wanted to hear. "Just like John, I'm concerned about my parents. I don't want to *jeopardize* my relationship with them."

"Hannah?"

"It's up to Bobby," she said.

"Bobby?"

"The dessert was really good."

CHAPTER NOTES

Thomas Kington's speech is pure fabrication on the part of the author. However, it is based on research of social and religious history in England at the time.

After his emigration to Nauvoo, Levi Roberts became a bodyguard to Joseph Smith (Arvilla Roberts Ford, *A Biography of Levi Roberts*, unpublished, April 16, 1964).

18

THE DEERHURST Saxon Priory Church of St. Mary, once a monastery of Benedictine rule, was regarded by Reverend Spencer Hobhouse as one of the finest Saxon churches in all England. It occupied a prominent spot in the parish, surrounded by rich farm ground, green pastures, and quaint cottages. The granite structure was rich in history. The apse dated to the seventh century, the nave the eighth. Like most Catholic-Anglican structures, it had been added onto decade-by-decade, century-by-century.

With the Sunday worship service completed, Elizabeth and Daniel and Bobby and Hannah rose from their pew, ambled along the main aisle in the nave, shook hands with Reverend Hobhouse near the Saxon font that graced the entry, and stood near the stain-glassed windows and gargoyle water spouts talking with Dianah. Robert Harris cast them a furtive glance, motioned for them to follow, and walked toward their cottage with Sarah.

"Wish us luck," Elizabeth said to her sister. "Today's the day."

Dianah fussed with her three children.

"Any suggestions?" Daniel asked her husband.

Thomas Bloxham shrugged. "Just give her father everything he asks for. That's why I get along with him so well. I concede that he's always right on every point, no matter what he says. I help him with the cattle, or at the shop, whenever he wants. I've promised to remain Anglican until I die. I contribute what I can to the plate when it comes around in church. It's simple really. Just give in. I do the same with my own father."

"In other words," Daniel said, chuckling at Thomas's cynicism, "give up being a Quaker, give up the double wedding idea, and give up our independence."

"That's about it."

Bobby's face took on a hard, sullen look.

"Seriously," Elizabeth said to her sister, "What do you *think* Papa will do if we tell him we want to agree to be married in the Methodist chapel just to solve the problem?"

"Tell you no, not speak to you for a week, then tell you no again."

"You two are no help," Elizabeth said mournfully. Deep in thought, she began walking home.

Sarah was checking her pork roast, and Robert was reading in the Old Testament when the two couples walked in. Robert pointed to a wooden bench opposite him. Abruptly, and without inviting discussion, he began his lecture before his wife sat down. For twenty minutes he berated all dissident religions in England, especially the Methodists and Quakers. Then just as abruptly, and with a tone of finality, he made a declaration.

"Your idea of a double wedding is genius, Mr. Browett. I've spoken to Reverend Hobhouse. He's given me some open dates. Let's settle on an exact date, and my wife and I will handle everything."

Bobby was grinding his teeth in frustration when it appeared his father was finally taking a breath. He jumped in. "Father, I would like nothing better. But there is no way Hannah's father will permit her to be married any-where but in her own Methodist chapel. The reason we wanted to meet with you today is to ask permission for the double wedding to be held in Apperley. One set of parents has to give. I was hoping it would be you."

Robert's comeback was smug and authoritative. "We've been over this before. In order for your marriage to be official, it must be conducted by a minister representing the Church of England. Not a Methodist minister. Not a Quaker minister. You know that you are required to have banns read here in the Deerhurst church on three consecutive Sundays. And I hope that I don't have to remind you in the future, that when you have your own children, you must have each child christened by an Anglican minister."

A face muscle twitched. Bobby frowned, thinking how behind the times his father was. That was true twenty or thirty years ago, but British citizens right and left were ignoring Church of England mandates. Countless mar-riages were being performed by other ministers of other faiths. Countless chil-dren were being christened by other ministers as well. His father was blind as a bat, clinging to yesterday's religious traditions. The trouble was, Bobby did-n't dare say it.

"Papa, I have an *idea*," Elizabeth said suddenly, her green eyes on fire, and her mouth curled in female anxiety.

"It better be good," her father responded with a defiant glare. He could not think of any of her spur-of-the-moment ideas that he had ever liked.

With imploring eyes, Elizabeth began. "I *promise* that all four of us will have an Anglican wedding."

Hannah furled her brow in doubt.

A winning smile came over Robert Harris.

"Let me *explain*," Elizabeth said, beginning to rush her words, and over-emphasize too many of them. "All *four* of us want a double wedding. Our hearts are *set* on it. Yet we can't blame Hannah's parents for wanting a

Methodist wedding. Every set of parents wants their daughter to be married by their *own* minister in their own church. Thomas and Ann Eagles are *not* going to change their minds. Hannah thinks that her parents are a little narrow minded in that regard."

Robert gave a nod. *All Methodists are narrow-minded.*

"Papa, Mama, I believe you to be fair-minded, not narrow-minded. So here is what I propose. Please don't say *anything* until I get the whole thing out. First, we'll have a double wedding ceremony in Apperley performed by Reverend Crooks in the Methodist chapel..."

Robert stomped his foot on the floor. "That will not happen!"

Sarah covered the distance to her husband's chair in two quick steps. She placed a hand over his mouth. "Shush! Listen to your daughter."

Elizabeth pondered her words carefully. "After the wedding, we will also have our wedding breakfast in Apperley. *Everyone* will be invited. Now here's the part that will make you happy, Papa. We will regard that wedding as 'unofficial.' A few weeks later, we'll have our 'official' wedding right here in Deerhurst."

For a moment there was dead silence as Robert rubbed his chin. He lowered his heavy eyebrows and cocked his head, reluctant to give in. "What about your honeymoons? You can't go on your honeymoons until after the official Anglican weddings. We will have to keep you separated until then."

Sarah threw a bony forearm across the chest of her husband. "Mr. Harris, don't be silly. They will honeymoon right after the Apperley wedding. Elizabeth, I like the idea. June will be here before we know it. We have a lot of planning to do."

Surprised at the depth of her victory, Elizabeth sat back in her chair. "You approve of having *two* weddings? You mean you *approve* of us being married twice?"

Elizabeth's mother bit her lip, deep in thought. A light came to her eyes.

"Instead of Deerhurst, why don't we have the second wedding in the St. Mary de Lode Church in Gloucester?"

Elizabeth regarded her mother as though she were having a vision. She broke out into a wide smile. "You mean the church where you and Papa were married? And where Dianah was married?"

Hannah was taking this all in with amused delight.

Bobby was cautious, expecting his father to erupt.

Daniel prayed that Mrs. Harris would get her way.

Robert glared at Sarah, still despising the idea.

"Yes, yes!" Suddenly fifty-six-year-old Sarah Harris was acting girlish. She could remember standing at the altar thirty-one years ago, clutching her handsome young groom as they recited their wedding vows in front of the minister. She began to ramble about her own marriage, often repeating herself, remembering how perfect everything was. The perfect late September weather, the flowers, the gifts, the large crowd, the stained-glass windows behind the vicar who married them. Having her own daughter and her own son married in the same church sent chills up and down her spine. There wouldn't have to be a second wedding breakfast, just a wedding in the historic building that stood near the Gloucester Cathedral. That would bring back so many memories.

Robert held up a hand. "I don't like this at all."

"Elizabeth's solution is the perfect compromise," Sarah told her husband in a concluding tone. She was still livid, reminiscing, smiling, and already visualizing details of both weddings. "We girls have a lot of plans to make. Don't you have a beef carcass you need to carve up?"

Lost time was soon made up. The three mothers began meeting almost daily with the two daughters. Tradition took over. Something old, something new, and a sixpence in her shoe.

Martha Browett surprised them with her knowledge: "Did you know June takes its name from Juno, the Roman goddess of marriage? Did you know it has always been the most popular month for weddings? That because traditionally if a bride took her wedding vows in June, she was most likely to give birth to her first child in the spring. That gave the mother enough time to recover to help with the fall harvest. Did you know that in the old days June also signaled the coming of warm weather, and a good time to partake in one's annual bath?"

Martha rehearsed nursery rhymes and recited tradition as Elizabeth and Hannah struggled over the color of their wedding dresses. "Pink, of you he'll aways think," she chimed, holding a bolt of pink material to Elizabeth's face.

Elizabeth favored it, but Hannah preferred a light pastel green because Martha said it was a traditional sign of fertility. Elizabeth thought it over and chose green also. Rebecca Browett was assigned to help sew the silk and cashmere dresses, both with a fitted bodice, small waist, full skirt over hoops, and petticoats.

The best idea Martha came up with was the final decision on the wedding date. "June eleventh, of course," she said. "Double ones for the double wedding."

Martha told Daniel and Bobby to pick out identical turquoise engagement rings and present them to the girls on May twenty-second-double twos. The boys thought it a little ridiculous, but the girls loved the idea.

"Just go along with it," Martha told her son. "Perhaps each bride will give birth to twins eleven months after the marriage."

They had a good laugh over that.

"And maybe both of you ought to have two best men each. Double up."

That's where Daniel and Bobby drew the line on Mrs. Browett. Bobby chose Levi Roberts. Daniel chose his cousin, James Pulham.

19

ON THE MORNING of June eleventh, two identical rented coaches brought Hannah and Elizabeth to the Methodist chapel in Apperley, arriving precisely at eleven o'clock. Nancy and Jane were among eleven village girls that spread eleven varieties of wildflowers in the path of the two brides as their fathers, under a canopy of elm and oak trees alive with the chirping of jays and robins, escorted them into the chapel. Bobby and Daniel, wearing flowers in their frock coat lapels that had been in the bridal bouquets, stood as erect as twin soldiers to receive them.

The old butcher, Robert Harris, felt low and betrayed. He regretted that the chapel was filled to capacity. He refused to shake hands with Reverend Crooks. He stood next to Sarah, mouth turned down, wondering why things appeared so well organized.

Rather that concentrate on the ceremony, he began to compare the chapel to the splendor that characterized Anglican structures such as the St. Mary de Lode in Gloucester where he was married, the St. James Church in

Charfield where his grandfather was buried, and the Saxon Priory Church of St. Mary in Deerhurst, where his remains would be laid to rest someday.

In his view, this puny simple plain building had no character: Where was the traditional nave, the main body of any church building, the ship that led to life eternal? His Deerhurst parish church had a nave that was built in the eighth century. Where was the bell tower? His Deerhurst church had a Saxon tower with a fourteenth century belfry. Where were the cloister doors, the corbels, the carvings of the Virgin with Child, the gargoyle water spouts, and Madonna panels? His church had the finest Saxon tub font in all England, where Bobby and Elizabeth had been christened as babies. His church also had some of the finest medieval stained glass in England. The stained glass in this meager brick building was scandalously under detailed. How Methodists could worship like this was beyond his belief. Not even a nuptial mass at high alter before the ceremony. What was the world coming to?

He was equally critical of Reverend Crooks: He was too tall, too skinny, too bent over, too hook-nosed, voice too high-pitched. Too arrogant, too proud, and too under-qualified. He had to read the ceremony from thick, wire-rimmed glasses. His Adam's apple bounced as he spoke. If he blew his nose, his head would cave in. The reverend was death warmed over, ready for purgatory.

Robert Harris seldom felt worse.

Sarah was a picture of happiness: Methodist wedding today, Anglican in a few weeks. What a beautiful daughter she had. What a beautiful daughter-in-law she was gaining. She clasped her husband's hand and pressed it to her thigh. A perfect day.

Thomas Eagles stood erect, arms folded, jaw set, feeling authoritative. He shot an acid look at Robert and all his Anglican family and friends. He followed every word of the ceremony with unfettered respect and loyalty. He was a picture of contentment and pride.

Ann Eagles cried about everything: Memories of her daughter, Editha, married in the same redbrick building two years earlier, now dead. Losing Hannah to an Anglican family. Rumor that Bobby and Hannah were investigating another religion. The conflict between Henry and Bobby. Bobby's dubious pugilism career.

Henry stood slightly hunched over, his face somber and rigid. He wondered what his sister saw in this proud transparent excuse for a man.

After a ten-minute oration, Reverend Crooks raised his hands in a graceful resigned gesture. "Please join your hands."

The reverend removed his thick spectacles. He knew the rest of the text by heart. He addressed Bobby first. "Do you, Mr. Robert Harris, Jr., take Miss Hannah Maria Eagles, to be your lawfully wedded wife, to comfort her, honor and keep her, forsaking all others to cleave only to her, until death do you part?" The question was repeated to Hannah, Daniel, and Elizabeth.

Reverend Crooks finished the ceremony. "What God has joined together let no man put asunder."

Rings of gold were exchanged. So were kisses.

The old butcher fumed at the thought that Reverend Crooks professed to have any authority at all. He began drinking wedding wine. As the wedding line formed, he began to relax.

He was glad to see Bobby's Anglican friends: Levi Roberts and his fiancée, Harriet Ann Efford. Joseph Hill and his new wife, Ann. John Cox. William Pitt. John Davis. Edward Phillips. John Gailey.

It puzzled the old butcher when Thomas Kington came through the line.

It puzzled him more when several members of the United Brethren congregation walked through: David Wilding, John Cheese, William Jenkins, John Parry, William Barnes, John Hyrum Green, Mary Rowberry, Joseph Pullen, William Parsons, Thomas and Ann Jones, James Robins, Elizabeth Lambert, Joseph and Eliza Halford, John and Ann Deveraux.

Despite the joking, eating, drinking, and general merriment of the wedding breakfast, the only time Robert really enjoyed himself was when the chimney sweep from Cheltenham showed up. Robert had hired him as his private surprise. As the two couples boarded their carriages to leave for their honeymoons, the chimneysweep, dressed in a weather-torn hat and tails complete with his brush and bundle of rods and a sooty face, gave Hannah and Elizabeth a keepsake gift. They had no idea where the gifts came from. Robert would keep it that way. Inside each small, brightly wrapped package was twenty pounds. Then the two carriages prepared to depart, each to its separate destination.

There would be no double honeymoon.

As Daniel and Elizabeth's carriage disappeared toward Gloucester, Bobby was startled to see Henry Eagles striding toward him and Hannah. Hair combed, clean-shaven, a big smile showing his two missing teeth, Henry was the picture of Mister Friendly. Holding out his right hand and grabbing Bobby's, Henry said, "Welcome to the family, brother. Is it all right with you that I call you brother now? You married the sweetest girl in the hamlet, you know. Congratulations."

Bobby blinked hard as his mouth fell open. After a moment of silence he managed to say a weak, "Thank you."

"Hope you have a nice honeymoon. You'd make a good dairyman. Maybe you ought to think about it when you get back. You could work at the dairy instead of your father's butcher shop. You'd be welcome." With that, Henry shook Bobby's hand again, kissed Hannah, and walked happily toward the chapel.

Bobby stared at his brother-in-law's back. "What was that all about?" he asked Hannah.

"Oh, that's the other Henry," she answered. "There's two of him, you know. This one can be quite pleasant when he wants to be."

20

BOBBY AND HANNAH honeymooned at a quaint hotel hidden deep in the Royal Forest of Dean, on the banks of the River Wye. Late the next morning found them strolling through daffodil woodlands, with plans later in the day to see the Clearwell Caves, and take a boat tour down the river. They had already watched the harvest of trees, learning that the logs would be used to build ships for the British Navy, and for ships shuttling British passengers across the Atlantic for a new life in America. A brief morning shower had given way to high clouds, resplendent in their colors.

"Remember that first Sunday when we talked about our dreams and goals?" Hannah asked, her fingers intertwined with those of her new husband.

Still stunned by Henry's act of friendship yesterday, Bobby picked a bouquet of yellow, blue, purple, and red wildflowers, and handed them to Hannah. "We were talking about predestination, weren't we?"

Hannah pushed the sweet smelling bouquet into her nose. "That was six months ago," she said, pleased that he remembered. "We talked about our goals. I want to know what your real life goals are now that we're married."

"What kind of goals?"

"The obvious, sweetheart. Family. Children. Which church are we going to go to? What's on your mind right now?"

Taking off his jacket and draping it over his forearm, Bobby's answer was instant. "Heavyweight champion of Great Britain."

Hannah's eyes dropped in disappointment. "Bobby, I know you well enough now to think there is more to you than just a fighter. But I want you to know that I would be proud if you really became champion of all England. Really, I would. But after that. I mean long range, what do you want out of life? What do you see for you and me together?"

Bobby reached to pinch his lower lip for a moment. "When we were at the Benbow farm, I asked about how to become a yeoman. After I'm champion for a few years, I'll be able to lease a large farm from somebody like Squire Hastings. That would set us up for life."

"What if your fighting career doesn't work out? What's wrong with being a butcher, like your father? You could take over his business."

Bobby pulled a face. "I couldn't think of anything worse, unless it would be to work with Henry at the dairy."

"What about a family?"

A look of bewilderment. "You mean how many children? Never thought much about it."

"I have. The more kids the better. I love children." Hannah pushed the wildflowers to her nose again.

"Maybe we will have our first in about nine months," he chuckled.

They sat at a park bench, near the river.

"What about religion, Bobby?"

Feeling trapped, Bobby stared at the billowing white clouds, moving west to east. "I don't want to be an Anglican. I don't like the Reverend

Hobhouse. I've never met a vicar or a rector that I really liked. I don't like your Reverend Crooks, either."

Hannah was surprised that Bobby would base his religious choice on the personality, or lack of it, of a minister. "So you don't want to be a Methodist?"

"After what your father put me through?"

"Then join the United Brethren. You like Thomas Kington, don't you?"

"This religion business is really important to you?"

"I say my prayers every day. And our family reads the Bible every day. I want those things to be important in our family. I think we should go to church every Sunday."

Bobby remained silent.

"Will you go to church with me every week?"

"Maybe."

"United Brethren?"

"Maybe."

"I love you anyway."

"You, too."

Bath, England. Site of Britain's only hot springs, only twenty miles from Gloucester. Once the greatest Roman spa in Northern Europe. Daniel and Elizabeth Browett's honeymoon spot. For two days they walked on ancient stone pavements around a steaming pool, visited the thermal spring, marveled at the life-size head of the cult goddess Sulia Minerva, and dined in unique restaurants.

"I have an idea," Elizabeth said over veal cutlets the second evening.

"Your ideas usually impress me," Daniel muttered, his mouth full. Her idea made his idea work: they had pulled off the double wedding.

"Have you *ever* been through the St. Mary de Lode Church where we'll have our vows repeated?"

"No."

"How about the Gloucester Cathedral? It's right next to the church."

"No. Why?" He had seen it from a distance, during the fair.

"Let's spend our last day in Gloucester. We could tour the cathedral and the church."

"Sounds fun. Are you trying to make an Anglican out of me?"

"I'm thinking about my father. It would make things so much *better* for us. Your shop is right next to the butcher shop."

"My heart tells me to affiliate with the United Brethren."

"Let's take it *slow*. Papa will mellow out."

"Agreed."

"After tomorrow, you might like Anglicanism."

"We'll see."

The Gloucester Cathedral impressed Daniel from the moment the stagecoach dropped them off at the Golden Cross Inn. He let his eyes trace its two hundred and twenty-foot high spires, which seemed to reach all the way to heaven. A gigantic medieval Bourdon Bell, named the Great Peter, struck two o'clock as their baggage was unloaded.

"Wow," said Daniel, anxious to tour inside the abbey church. The medieval glass of the great east window dazzled him. The coachman had already told them the church had been founded 1,300 years ago. An impressive survivor of Norman architecture.

Within minutes they joined a group led by a mustached tour guide named Nicholas, dressed in a green frock coat. His dark, unruly hair was heavily greased. The guide's first remarks bored Daniel: History traced back to 678 AD. Benedictine monks were in residence here in 1017. St. Peter's Abbey was consecrated in 1100. The coronation of King Henry III took place here.

They came to the tomb of King Edward II, in the north ambulatory. A woeful king who was murdered while imprisoned at Berkeley Castle in 1327.

"Why do they bury Kings right inside the church?" Daniel asked Elizabeth in a low whisper.

"It's the most prestigious place they could think of, I guess. And for protection of the tomb, too."

The king's effigy was made of alabaster, sitting upon a tomb chest of oolitic limestone, clad in Purbeck marble.

"I just think it's strange. It detracts from the purpose of worship, don't you think?"

"Never has bothered me," Elizabeth said. "You're the *first* to complain."

The entire south ambulatory was a virtual "who's who" in English history, the guide explained. It included Robert, Duke of Normandy, eldest son of William the Conqueror, who died while in captivity in 1134 because he was embroiled in a struggle for succession to the throne with his brother, the eventual King Henry I.

Daniel was amazed that the church was filled with statues, monuments, wall plaques, chalices, and effigies. Even a statue of King Henry VIII, his father-in-law's hero.

Daniel whispered again. "You know what? I think I liked the little red-brick chapel better. Not so gaudy."

The guide was doing his job: "Here we see the east-west nave with its massive Norman columns, extending upward some thirty-two feet. It, along with the roof vault, date back to 1242. And here is the magnificent quire, constructed as a lierne vault eighty-eight feet above the floor. You probably noted the window before you came in. You are looking at the largest stained-glass window in all England, assembled during the 1350s. Its centerpiece is a representation of the coronation of the Blessed Virgin Mary."

To Daniel, everything seemed to be more of a monument to man than a tribute to God.

"Here we are at the eastern prospect of the cathedral organ," Nicholas said. "See the Front Great organ case designed by Thomas Harris in 1665?"

"Was he a relative?" Daniel whispered again to Elizabeth.

"I'm *sure* he was," Elizabeth winked. "Only a Harris could build something that impressive and that ornate."

Daniel shook his head. "The guide said Thomas Harris designed the organ case, not built it. Your family is a bunch of butchers. I'm the talented carpenter of the family."

Elizabeth chuckled quietly. "Could *you* build something like that?"

"Give me time."

As Daniel and Elizabeth exited the building and walked a few steps south they looked up at the tower of the cathedral again. Its lofty parapets and tall corner turrets uniquely matched, albeit on a smaller scale, the design of the tower itself.

As they strode toward the nearby St. Mary de Lode Church, a thought came to Elizabeth. "Tell me the truth, Daniel, was it *really* Bobby's idea to have a double wedding?"

Daniel was evasive. "One has to agree, Bobby always has good ideas, don't you think? Just like you. Runs in the family, I guess."

Elizabeth gave Daniel an elbow in the ribs. "I think it was you. Hannah thinks it was you. Come on, fess up."

"Okay, it was me."

"Well, good show and *thank* you. It couldn't have been more perfect."

The St. Mary de Lode Church reminded Daniel of the Priory Saxon Church in Deerhurst: Granite construction. Added onto. Damaged by fire. Repaired. Added onto again. The Norman nave dated to the eleventh century. Aisles added the next century. Tower fell in and destroyed the chancel at the end of the twelfth century. Tower and chancel rebuilt in a different style. Its name was old English, referring to the ford or lode that crossed the River

Severn, which ran near the west door.

The building was a beehive of activity. Members were preparing for a late afternoon funeral. Daniel and Elizabeth approached the altar.

"In a few days we will be standing at this altar getting married," Elizabeth told one of the church members.

"Oh, that's lovely," said the round-faced lady. "You do look like a happily engaged couple."

"We're already married," Daniel stated, waiting for a reaction.

"But I thought you just said... ."

Elizabeth laughed and then explained the double wedding in Apperley, the tug-of-war between their parents, and the fact that her own parents were married in this very chapel.

"Oh, then you should meet the vicar, the Reverend John Bishop. Come back in two hours and he will be here conducting the funeral."

"I've already met him," Elizabeth said. "He married my sister, Dianah, just a few years ago."

In their room in the Golden Cross Inn, Elizabeth chuckled to herself. "Our situation is a little *confusing* to people isn't it, dear?"

Daniel smiled. "About our marriage, you mean?"

"Yes. We were married in a Methodist chapel. We're going to have our vows repeated in an Anglican Church. I want to remain an Anglican. You, a Quaker, are more favorable to the United Brethren."

Daniel collapsed into a wicker chair. "Just do me a favor."

Changing into another dress for dinner, Elizabeth turned her head. "Sure. What?"

"Reverend Kington told me that he would be glad to meet with prospective members, one on one. I propose we go back to the Benbow farm after our marriage ceremony here, and listen to him again. He's really well backgrounded on all the religions, the doctrines, history, everything."

"No harm in that. What will your mother think if you join another church? She's *deeply* devoted to the Quakers."

"Probably not much compared to what your father will think."

Elizabeth shuddered at the thought.

21

Summer 1835

PRIDE BOILED OUT of the ears of Thomas Eagles. Holding his bowler hat in his hand, he compared the number of people attending the repeat wedding ceremony of his daughter to the number that attended in Apperley. Less than a fourth. Only family members. Had the first wedding been held in an Anglican Church, the whole thing would have been an embarrassment. Most of the wedding cake would have been thrown away.

To him, the cold granite of the St. Mary de Lode Church felt like a prison. In fact, Royalist soldiers during the British civil war had used it for that purpose in 1643. Its history was downright shameful. That bloody queen, Mary the Catholic, burned John Hooper at the stake in this very spot. He had been the Anglican Bishop of Gloucester and Worcester. In retrospect, Mary should have caught all the Anglicans and torched them, too. How dare today's Anglicans call him a dissident, just because he was a Methodist.

When the ceremony was complete and Hannah and Bobby and Daniel and Elizabeth were pronounced man and wife for the second time within a few weeks, a peal of the six bells rang from the St. Mary de Lode tower. Thomas Eagles put his hands over his ears in disgust.

"Such a lovely ceremony," Thomas told the Reverend John Bishop minutes later. "And such a lovely old church. Thank you so much for marrying my daughter." He hoped the reverend would forgive him for squeezing so hard during the handshake. After all, he was a dairyman, the beefy man with a crushing handgrip. He wanted Reverend Bishop to remember that.

A canvas bag filled with sand and dirt dangled on a short tether, looped over the branch of an elm tree near the cattle corral at the back of the butcher shop, was now Bobby's training spot. Drenched with sweat, shirt off, his bulging muscles glimmering in the late afternoon April sun, Bobby shifted his weight from foot to foot to drive his canvas-wrapped fists into the bag, sending it spinning backward.

Whommp! Whommp! Whommp!

Bobby stepped back, waiting for John and William to steady the bag. He stared at the bag, picturing Henry, Alex, and Richie.

Whommp! Whommp!

It was time for revenge. Bobby had been working on his plan for weeks. At first he thought of just walking into the pub and breaking their jaws in front of everyone. No. He would hide in the trees, just like they did. Surprise them. Make their hearts jump out of their chests. Whatever he did, it would embarrass Hannah. Upset his mother. Make things worse with his father-in-law. He didn't care.

He chose a sultry night in August, with a full moon. From deep within a dense grove, with raindrops splattering on the leaves overhead, he waited for his brother-in-law to walk by, on his way home from another night of drinking at the pub.

Bobby appeared as a shadow from the fog, startling Henry.

"How's my brother-in-law this evening?"

Moonlight revealed Bobby's taunt face, his fists balled.

"Bobby?"

The smells: rum, dairy barn, and an unbathed body.

"Would you like ruddy dueling pistols, swords, or fists?" Bobby took a menacing step toward Henry.

Henry broke off his dumbfounded stare. Reaching to the ground, fumbling at first, he picked up a rock, six inches in diameter. He swallowed hard, fear gripping him. "How about rocks?"

"You just about killed me that night, you and your thug friends," Bobby said, his eyes burning with intense hatred. He touched himself on the ribs.

"I'll bash your head in if you come at me," Henry said. He held the rock up high. His eyes shot to his left and right. He was alone, no Richie, and no Alex. The moment he feared had arrived.

Bobby stared at the rock, momentarily hypnotized by its ugly appearance. He issued an ultimatum. "If you want to fight with that rock in your hand I'll break your jaw and your ribs. If you put the rock down and fight fair, I'll just break your ribs like you broke mine. Your choice. Then there's the matter of my dog. I haven't decided what to do with you to revenge my dog."

With widening eyes and a pained look, Henry threw the rock at Bobby. It hit him on the arm, causing a stinging sensation and a temporary numbness.

"That was the wrong thing to do, Henry," Bobby said, hands up, fists cocked. He knew that Henry would be no match for him, his equilibrium fouled by a night of drinking.

Henry lunged, swinging a right hand at Bobby's jaw. It missed my several inches. Bobby delivered a powerful uppercut to Henry's chest, and another, and another.

Henry hissed as his air escaped him.

Another punch to Henry's jaw. A cracking sound. Two more blows to the stomach. Another blow to the ribs. Henry crumpled to the ground, vomiting.

Bobby stood over his foe, rubbing his knuckles. "Enjoy your drinks, Henry." In an eerie way, the scene reminded Bobby of their fight at the fair. Déjà vu.

An hour later Alex and Richie lay crumpled at another roadside. Bobby walked away nursing swollen knuckles but he had a satisfied smile on his face.

CHAPTER NOTES

In real life, Bobby and Hannah were married first in a Methodist chapel, then three months later had their vows repeated in the St. Mary de Lode Church, so the novel is accurate in that respect. However, Daniel and Elizabeth were married earlier in a separate ceremony. The descriptions of the churches are accurate, based on research and a visit to each chapel by the author.

PART TWO

The
United
Brethren

22

THOMAS KINGTON, his shoulders square and erect, led Daniel and Elizabeth to a shady spot under a sprawling oak tree two hundred yards south of the Benbow house. A warm August sun beat down upon them.

"I hope we're not imposing on you too much," Daniel said apologetically. "I know you are awfully busy."

"Not at all," Kington responded, his soft eyes and open collar giving him a relaxed look. "I do this all the time. Before people give up their old religion and align themselves with the United Brethren, they want to hear my detailed reasons for our organization, and why I am not a member of any other church."

Daniel's eyes slid across the horizon. From his vantage point at the Hill Farm he could see the imposing Malvern Hills, with Beacon Hill looming to the east and the parishes of Catley-Southfield and Bosbury lying peaceful in a southern vale.

As they settled under the tree, Elizabeth took off her small-brimmed yel-

low bonnet and shook the road dust off of it. Her long blonde hair was parted in the middle without curls, flowing gently in the breeze. A pair of yellow
and black birds darted past them, swooped to a branch in the mighty oak tree,
and began a melodious chorus. From a pond near the oak, frogs jumped into
the clear, inviting water.

A farm servant opened a picnic basket full of cheeses, bread, fruit, and
both pear juice and apple cider. As the servant left, Kington shooed away six
or seven curious yearling Jersey heifers that were grazing in the pasture. In an
adjoining field several calves, separated from their mothers, bawled for attention.

Kington's statement piqued Daniel's curiosity. He wanted to hear what
the United Brethren superintendent had to say about every other major religion in England. He knew that the man had made a thorough study of those
religions. Kington was older, wiser, more knowledgeable, and had access to
books and information that Daniel had never investigated. All Daniel knew
about Kington's previous church membership is that at one time Kington, just
like nearly everyone else in England, had been christened into the Anglican
Church. Later in life, he had felt impressed to join the Primitive Methodist
faith.

Taking a drink of pear juice, Kington wiped his lips, changed from a
kneeling position to sitting on his haunches, and said, "I understand you were
put through quite an ordeal when you got married."

"Yes," Elizabeth responded, nodding her head, still kneeling, struck with
Kington's remembrance of their struggles. She was impressed with his kindly
eyes, his concerned personality, his judgement, and his intelligence. "You
probably know about Hannah's parents – the *devout* Methodists, and my parents – the *devout* Anglicans." She did not put her bonnet back on. It felt better off. It was a muggy day.

Letting a brief smile come over him, Kington cut to the heart of the matter. "Certainly, but when we get done today I think you will understand why there is so much seething hatred between Anglicans and Methodists, and between Anglicans and Catholics."

"I hope so," Elizabeth said, reaching for the cheese and bread.

Kington brought his hands in front of his knees and clasped them together. "Let's begin with the Methodists, since that was my religion before I organized the United Brethren."

Elizabeth nodded her approval.

"First, I'd like to say that I really admire John Wesley, who is credited for founding the Methodist religion. Actually, it was his followers who broke away. You probably know that Wesley remained an Anglican all his life. But historical circumstances and his organizational genius conspired against his desire to remain in the Church of England. At first Wesley had his followers meet in private homes, then he organized societies, each with eleven members plus a leader. They met weekly to pray, read the Bible, discuss their spiritual lives, and to collect money for charity. He attracted quite a following and coined a lot of aphorisms. My favorite is, 'Do all the good you can, by all the means you can, in all the ways you can, in all the places you can, to all the people you can, as long as ever you can.' He was a good man."

A puzzled look crossed Elizabeth's face. "Then why do Anglicans like my Papa look down on Wesley and his followers so much? And why does Thomas Eagles seem to hate the Anglicans?"

Ignoring the cheese and biscuits, Kington continued. "The Church of England was losing membership to the Wesleyans. Critics called Wesley's followers 'Methodists,' a label they wore proudly. As the movement grew, critics grew more critical, calling them bad names and resorting to violence. Paid ruffians broke up Methodist meetings and threatened Wesley's life. Wesley tried to schedule his itinerant preaching so it wouldn't disrupt local Anglican services but the bishop of Bristol still objected. Wesley became even more aggressive, declaring that the world was his parish. Soon he was traveling more than four thousand miles a year. At first he employed lay preachers, but the Church of England would not allow them to serve Communion. You can see how the friction was building. Wesley then organized his followers into 'connections,' and a number of societies into 'circuits' under the leadership of a superintendent. That's basically how I organized the United Brethren. I took a page out of Wesley's book."

As Kington paused to take another drink of cider, Elizabeth thought about Bobby, and Hannah. She wished they were here.

Kington threw a rock in the direction of the curious heifers that were returning. "Hyaa! Get back!" Then he continued. "As you can guess, I felt better about being a Methodist in my earlier years than I did an Anglican. I never did like the formal written prayers. I think praying has to come from the heart, so people should say their own prayers."

"Then why did you start the United Brethren?" Daniel asked, trying to remember what Kington had said on his visit to the Benbow farm five months earlier.

Kington fixed his eyes on Daniel. "Very simple. I was expelled from the Primitive Methodists."

One eyebrow went up on Daniel's gaunt, handsome face. He fixed his cobalt-blue eyes on the superintendent, probing him to the very core, wondering what Kington meant by the word "expelled."

Elizabeth's mouth dropped and she looked at the ground while she accepted the shock. Negative thoughts flashed through both of their minds. Did "expel" mean the same as "excommunicate?" What did Kington do to deserve to be expelled? Was it a morality problem? Insubordination?

They heard soft chuckles.

Taking in Daniel and Elizabeth's surprise, Kington made a chuckling sound again. "I suppose I better explain. I always like to see people's reaction when I tell them I was expelled from the Primitive Methodists."

Daniel and Elizabeth exchanged awkward glances.

"I was expelled for very simple reasons, really. I felt the dead influence of formal religion was not sufficient to save a soul. It seemed to me that too many of the other preachers were merely tickling the ears of their congregations, telling them what they wanted to hear. I wanted to preach the gospel as it really is, that the Lord requires accountability. The Methodists had settled into a rut of self-satisfied formality. I suppose I rather annoyed my superiors with my zeal over those things. Neither the preachers nor a lot of the members liked to have the gospel of repentance taught to them."

"I guess none of us do, if one has sin in his life," Daniel said.

"Precisely," Kington added. "But all we have to do is try harder, and try to eliminate sin. I believe repentance means to just change. If we are leading sinful lives, stop. I don't believe in being a Sunday Christian. We have to act like Christians every day of the week. We can't sin on Wednesday and act like nothing happened on Sunday. Now that doesn't mean that during those years I was a traditional Methodist preacher, that I personally held to a grim emphasis on hellfire and damnation. Sometimes people use the word 'Methodist' as a by-word for dour, uncharitable, churchgoing fanaticism. Methodism has a reputation of taking the form of a very radical evangelical movement."

Elizabeth thought of Bobby again.

"So repentance became your battle cry?" Daniel asked.

"I guess you could say that. I really believe that the gospel should be reduced to its most simple, understandable forms, or the basics. The basics are faith and repentance."

"When did this happen – your *expulsion* from the Primitive Methodists?" Elizabeth asked.

"Just last year."

"Did you receive a salary as a preacher?" Daniel inquired.

"No salary at all. That's why I work for John Benbow. He gives me room and board for part of my income. That's why I live there."

"Some preachers get a little money by passing the collection plate," Elizabeth stated with a cryptic smile.

Kington was quick to reply. "Our members are from the working class, so they don't have a lot of money."

"Do most of your members live near Mr. Benbow's farm?" Elizabeth asked.

"Yes. We extend into three counties: Herefordshire, Worcestershire, and Gloucestershire, where you live. We meet out of doors, just like the Primitive Methodists. In bad weather we meet in the homes of some of our members, and we use the great hall attached to Mr. Benbow's house. What else would you like to know?"

"I've heard that Pilgrim's Progress shaped your thinking as well," Elizabeth added.

"Certainly, yes," Kington acknowledged. "That book struck hard into the consciences and inner lives of all common people. I think it has produced more genuine religious thought than all the formal religious preaching done by the various orthodox ministers of our day. After I read it, it somehow gave me a deeply devout feeling. It tends to strip one of pride, profanity, and all forms of immorality."

"What about other religions, then?" she asked.

"The more I studied about Methodism and Anglicanism, the more I wanted to know about the origins of Christianity, the Church of Rome, the Reformation, King Henry VIII, and all the other churches that sprang from the Reformation. The more I learned the more I felt disenchanted with all religions, but at the time I still liked being a Methodist over the other choices. Then after I was expelled, and after I organized the United Brethren with the five hundred people that followed me, I had a feeling – as a result of my study and personal prayers – that the best thing for me to do was to wait for additional light and truth. I really feel, deep down inside, that somewhere out there, there is something better, something true, and something that will answer all my questions. I don't know when or where, but that additional light and truth is somewhere out there. But be assured that I do not believe the United Brethren to be that light. It is just a place to set myself, and others who want to join, to keep studying the Bible, to encourage one another to keep the commandments, and to teach one another. Again, it is patterned somewhat like the Primitive Methodists. But even though we have licensed lay ministers and licensed places to meet – to keep ourselves within the law – the organization really isn't a church and we don't profess to be the 'true church.' We are merely seeking more light and truth. Seems to me we preach the same things over and over. There has to be more."

Daniel bit his lower lip, thought deeply, then commented, "I'd be interested to hear your comments about King Henry VIII, and the origin of the Church of England."

Nodding, Elizabeth said, "I would too," wondering why her parents had never discussed those things with her.

Kington smiled, leaning, resting with his right arm and hand supporting him while he sat on the pasture grass. "I'm sure you have heard a lot of wild stories, but in a nutshell here is what happened. Many consider Henry to have been a dilettante king, letting his ministers run the country while he hunted stag. In truth, he was actively involved in the details of anything that he judged important. He demanded the facts be boiled down to their essence. Then he would listen to the issues and make a quick decision, often in the time it took him to dismount from his horse. The most important decision of his reign, however, he struggled with for years. But once Henry determined his course, he followed it with a flurry of decisions that forever changed our country."

"He must have been a good leader," Daniel said.

Kington continued, ignoring the food. "You probably know that Henry was born the second son of Henry VII. He was intelligent, handsome, physically powerful, talented in music, and an avid hunter and sportsman. He was sole ruler of England and the richest man in the world at age eighteen."

"Only eighteen?" Elizabeth gasped at the revelation, raising both eyebrows.

Kington nodded several times. "True. Even at that young age Henry knew he had to cement England's alliance with Spain, so he married the Spanish king's aunt, Catherine of Aragon – who was also the widow of his brother. When Henry defeated France and Scotland in successive battles, his popularity soared. He could do no wrong. Over the next decade, Henry made and broke peace treaties, stood for election as Holy Roman Emperor, engaged in the power politics of Europe, and turned his attention to religion.

"Was he really and honestly a religious man?" Elizabeth asked, seeing an earnestness in Kington that she had not seen before. She had heard so many stories about Henry, most not fitting the description of a religious man, and was taking Kington's remarks as gospel.

"Henry had always been a religious man, or at least pretended to be," Kington continued, his voice brimming now with an academic zeal. "He heard mass five times a day – unless he was hunting, then he could hear only three – and he was deeply interested in theological disputes. In 1521, with Lutheranism infecting the English universities, Henry wrote Defense of the Seven Sacraments against Luther. A beleaguered and grateful pope rewarded him with the title of 'Defender of the Faith,' quite appropriately."

"That changed in a hurry, didn't it?" Daniel commented, deeply struck by Kington's steady manner, by his apparent moral conviction, and by his broad vision of history. He radiated a personal force that Daniel had seen in few other men.

Kington chuckled again. "Yes. By 1526 Henry began to seek ways to end his marriage with Catherine. The alliance with Spain was restricting his international aspirations. He had fallen in love with nineteen-year-old Anne Boleyn, and, most importantly, Catherine had failed to give him a male heir. She did give birth to a daughter they named Mary. England had recently survived a bloody and costly civil war so Henry felt he needed a male heir to insure a peaceful succession upon his death. So he blamed his wife, Catherine. Mary should have been a boy. Getting an annulment from the church was fairly easy in the sixteenth century – if both parties wanted one. Divorce no, annulment yes. But Catherine was unwilling, and sought the support of her nephew in Spain, Charles V, the emperor of the Holy Roman Empire. The Spanish ruler didn't want to see his aunt disgraced so he routed the pope's troops."

Elizabeth blinked in amazement. "The pope had troops?" Despite the total conviction in Kington's eyes, her gut reaction was one of stark disbelief.

Kington nodded again. "Yes, the pope had an army back in those days. The pope was more of a king than a religious leader in some ways. Pope Clement could see the handwriting on the wall and had no choice but to refuse Henry the annulment. When Anne found herself in a family way in 1552 – good ole religious Henry – the king moved ahead on his own. Henry had already forced the clergy to submit to his supremacy in all ecclesiastical matters. Next, he married Anne in secret, had his new archbishop of Canterbury, Thomas Cramner, declare his marriage to Catherine invalid, and crowned Anne queen in 1533. Henry and the church teetered on the brink of schism."

Elizabeth sensed in Kington's patient smile that he empathized with her confusion. Nevertheless, she shook her head in disbelief, wondering if her parents knew all these gory details. "We have an interesting history, don't we – we English?"

Kington smiled and sighed. "It gets better – or worse, depending on your viewpoint. When the pope threatened excommunication, Henry plunged ahead. He passed one act forcing everyone to recognize the children of his new marriage as heirs to the throne. Then he passed another making him the 'supreme head' of the church in England. He dissolved monasteries, redistributing their property to his nobles to reinforce their loyalty. Monks who resisted were executed – good ole religious Henry – and the money from their treasuries went into his coffers."

Elizabeth's mouth fell open. "He killed some of the monks?"

"Yes, he did. Nevertheless, Henry's church reforms were conservative. He appeared to want to retain the Catholic Church, as long as it would be loyal to him and to England. Even though he broke with Rome he continued to uphold the doctrine of transubstantiation – that the body and blood of Christ were literally present in the sacrament wafer and wine – and demanded clerical celibacy. Meanwhile, Henry tired of Anne because she had produced only a girl – Elizabeth. Is that where you get your name, Elizabeth?"

Elizabeth grimaced slightly. "Oh, yes. Papa really is a dyed-in-the-wool Anglican."

"To get rid of Anne," Kington continued, eyes twinkling, clearly enjoying his history lesson, "Henry trumped up charges of infidelity against her and had her beheaded. Then he married Jane Seymour. Good ole religious Henry. After Jane gave birth to a son, Edward, she died. Henry married three more times before he died. As we look back, we know that Henry's break with Rome was fundamentally over control of the English church. Though he instituted some Protestant measures during his reign, such as putting English Bibles in all the churches, and though he had always supported his Protestant-leaning archbishop, Henry sided with Rome on key issues of doctrine and practice. But England could not return to its past. During the reign of his son, the sickly Edward VI, our country turned staunchly Protestant. But Edward died as a young man and Mary, Henry's daughter, became queen. 'Bloody' Mary reigned five years and forced a return to Catholicism. After Mary died, Henry's next daughter, Elizabeth, became queen. Elizabeth set England on a permanent Protestant course and we've been there ever since. She and others made the Church of England the 'official' religion."

"I don't see how Papa can be proud of our Anglican roots," Elizabeth said, shaking her head as she drank some more cider.

Kington lifted a pointing finger. "I want both of you to remember that although historical facts condemn the Church of England and the Church of Rome, that doesn't mean there are no honorable people in those churches and in all churches. There are – lots of them. They, for the most part, are trying to do the right thing. They can't help their past."

"You brought up the Church of Rome," Daniel said, digging for more history.

"As you know, there are still quite a few Catholics in England and elsewhere in the British Isles. But I believe the Church of Rome was so corrupt, especially in the Dark Ages, that I could never feel comfortable considering becoming a Catholic myself. After the Reformation the Church of Rome was forced to reform, but I don't think they have done enough."

Elizabeth blinked hard. "What do you mean by corruption?"

A serious look came over Kington as he paused for a few seconds to collect his thoughts. "I think the popes, bishops, and priests back in those days simply forgot their duties and began pursuing money and worldly recognition rather than ministering to people. Celibacy brought corruption. Unmarried church officials fell into excesses. Historians claim that most of the early popes, cardinals, and priests had mistresses and fathered illegitimate children. The worst was when the pope took it upon himself to sell the forgiveness of sins for money. I certainly don't blame Martin Luther for rebelling against indulgences, a move that eventually broke the back of the mother church. And

I don't blame King Henry VIII and others for breaking away from the Church of Rome."

"So there is no way the Church of Rome is the same church that Christ organized on the earth during his personal ministry?" Daniel asked.

"No way, I believe," Kington responded. "Listen to these interesting contrasts. The Savior was born in a stable, and had no place to lay his head throughout his life. The pope lives in a palace with hundreds of rooms. The Savior told the rich man to sell all his possessions and follow him. The Vatican is full of treasures that ought to be sold and the money given to the poor. Jesus lived simply and died naked. The pope is clad in gold and the costliest silks and jewels. The Savior washed the feet of His disciples to teach them the importance of serving others. Visitors kiss the feet of the pope. I could go on and on."

Elizabeth shook her head in amazement again. "We understand your point. By default, your organization looks *very* attractive to us."

Kington didn't know whether to take her remarks as a compliment or not. "Thank you," he replied awkwardly.

Daniel changed from sitting on his haunches to his knees. Clearing his throat he said, "One would think you have done a wonderful thing in leading the United Brethren. Could both Elizabeth and I become lay preachers?"

Kington inclined his head, smiling, as though he appreciated the praise yet wanting to appear humble and modest. "Yes, we need good people like you, if you have the time. First you would have to be trained. After your training I would put you through a trial period. If, in the judgement of myself and the other trained preachers, you pass, then you would help us conduct meetings throughout the circuit."

Daniel's eyes brightened. "How big is the circuit?"

Kington pulled papers out of his satchel and showed them to Daniel and Elizabeth.

"We have homes licensed as meeting places throughout Herefordshire, Worcestershire, and Gloucestershire. As we grow, others are added. We would have to license both of you as preachers, if you were accepted after your training. The paper you are looking at is what we call the 'Preacher's Plan,' which shows where meetings are to be held for the next three months and who is assigned to conduct those meetings."

"One would conclude that you are very well organized," Daniel added.

"Thank you," Kington replied. "So can we count on you? Would you like to begin your training?"

"Yes," Daniel responded. "What about you, Elizabeth?"

"Oh, yes," she said. "This sounds *wonderful!*"

CHAPTER NOTES

Superintendent Kington's visit with Daniel and Elizabeth is fiction, of course, but in all likelihood it represents the process that Kington used to gather converts to the United Brethren.

23

Spring 1836

THE SNOWS AND WINDS of the Cotswold and Malvern Hills winter were past for another season and the hills and fields were awakening from their winter sleep. Farmers were beginning to spread manure and plow their fields, bringing the first scents of fresh-turned earth. Wisps of green grass were starting to show. Wrens, sparrows, robins and all manner of birds sang an appreciation of the coming of spring as Elizabeth Browett and Dianah Bloxham walked under a canopy of billowing white and slate-gray thunder-clouds, up a rutty lane that led to Bobby and Hannah's small stone cottage, located near Robert's butcher shop and cattle corrals. A lightning bolt danced a few miles away through the purple belly of storm clouds to the southwest that would soon turn Deerhurst into a rain-swept gloom typical of late March days in England. Elizabeth and Dianah, rain shawls over their shoulders and umbrellas on their arms, each carried a gift for a new baby at this mid-after-noon hour. Hannah had delivered a healthy, wiggling, robust boy three days earlier.

Elizabeth raised a finger to her lips. "Maybe we better knock *softly*. We don't want to disturb the baby if he's sleeping."

Dianah, upbeat, vigorous, pregnant for the fourth time, her delivery date only two months away, held her tummy and laughed. "Trust me, little sister. When newborn babies are asleep, simple sound like a knock at the door doesn't bother them much. When they're a little older, it's different." Brushing locks of dark-blonde curls out of her eyes, she reached out and gave the door a knock. The wind picked up as they waited for Hannah to respond, blowing a few of the previous year's dead leaves onto the stone step.

Hannah opened the door and grinned. Her baby was wrapped in her arms, but aside from looking a little worn out, she radiated happiness. "Oh, come in, come in please. Thanks for coming. It's so good to see you." As she stood in the doorframe Hannah gloried in her pride of motherhood. She opened the blanket that shrouded her son, letting her visitors have a peek at the scrawny infant, awake now with blinking big brown eyes in a triangular face; clearly a boy, evident in the rolls of baby flesh.

"Have you picked out a name yet?" Dianah asked.

Hannah nodded. "Joseph. We considered Robert, but that would be three Roberts in a row. We considered Thomas, but Bobby is still a little put out at my father. We thought about John and even William, but Bobby wanted a name that wasn't used yet by anyone in his family, so we settled on Joseph."

"I've already marked March twenty-sixth on the calendar so that I'll remember his birthday next year," Elizabeth said, beaming. "Dianah and I each brought you a new blanket as a gift." She held up a dark blue cotton blanket and Dianah unfurled a red one with yellow stripes.

Hannah smiled in appreciation and swaddled Joseph in the new blankets. "My baby would stay warm now, even if I took him outside. Come and see the layette my mother brought me, and all the other gifts. How are you, Dianah? Not too long until you have your baby, true?"

"End of May," Dianah stated, gently patting her stomach where the unborn baby was kicking.

Opening the blankets again to expose Joseph's face, Hannah asked, "And how are you, Elizabeth?"

Elizabeth pinched the baby's rosy cheeks, trying to hide her jealousy. "Oh, I'm fine. *Disgustingly* fine. Can I hold him?" *Why didn't I become pregnant at the same time? I should be nursing a child, too. It was a double marriage, why wasn't it a double birth?*

Joseph whimpered as he was transferred.

"He's *beautiful*," Elizabeth said.

Hannah regarded Elizabeth's compliment, smiling. "How is Daniel?"

"Busy as ever," she said, her eyes still glued to the baby. "Between filling orders for barrels and furniture and training to be a lay preacher for the United Brethren he hardly has time to breathe."

"Is your father still angry that you abandoned the family religion?"

"Some, but he seems to be getting used to it," Elizabeth said, stroking Joseph's cheek with her forefinger. "If we had switched to Methodist it would have been a *different* story. He doesn't know much about the United Brethren, and the less he knows the better, I suppose."

That brought a chuckle to Dianah. "Maybe he won't have a fit if Thomas and I do the same thing someday."

"You think Thomas would change?" Elizabeth asked.

"Not right now, but I would," her sister said with a note in intrigue.

Elizabeth shook her head, her smile faltering. "I'm just glad those awkward days seem to be *over* for Daniel and me, and for you and Bobby, too, Hannah. Remember how Papa blew up when I told him we were going to quit going to the Anglican Church, that we were grown up, married, and had our own religion?"

Hannah nodded and laughed. "I'm glad I wasn't there."

"Good old Papa," Elizabeth said, settling into a chair. "At least he does-n't hold a grudge forever. He's back to being the same old Papa, narrow-mind-ed, but otherwise pleasant to be around. He has his religion, we have ours."

Hannah shivered, suddenly chilled. The remarks caused her to think about Bobby, who more and more seemed to resemble his father. Even though he had told his father that he wouldn't be attending the Anglican Church any-more, he was a member of the United Brethren by name only. The whole process seemed to make Bobby a little more withdrawn from religion, and the more she and her friends pressed him about it, the more withdrawn he became.

Elizabeth was thinking how the baby resembled her brother, and what her first baby would look like. As if on cue, she asked, "What's Bobby doing today?"

The words brought Hannah out of her stupor of thought. "He is still with his father and brothers. They bought some Old Spots pigs from Cheltenham, and they are butchering them to sell in the butcher shop. Then he wants to train some more. He has another match next week. And Daniel?"

Elizabeth handed the baby to Dianah. "He's home, trying to improve our cottage. The shop employees are helping him. They built some new benches last week to go with our table. Soon we'll have a house full of furniture. Your home looks *nice*, Hannah."

Hannah glanced around her small parlor. "At least we were able to move out of your parents' home, but there is still a lot to do." It was a small stone cottage that had a single room downstairs, a small stairway, and a sleeping loft above.

The first raindrops came splattering against the small window. Elizabeth looked outside for a few seconds, and then returned her eyes to Hannah.

"Daniel can come and help some more."

Hannah gave Elizabeth a wistful look. "Maybe Bobby will have more time to finish fixing it up as soon as this next fight is over. But he might be so stiff and sore for a few days that nothing will get done."

"At least his fight is before our anniversaries. He won't be stiff and sore for our supper together."

"I know where his mind will be. Mostly on that fight," Hannah said, dejectedly.

Gently rocking the baby, Dianah asked an inquisitive question. "Do you think Bobby will buy you two presents, one for your anniversary and one for your birthday? Or just one for both?"

Hannah hunched her shoulders and stared at the floor. "He is so into preparing for the fight, perhaps none."

"What do you think Daniel will do?" Dianah asked Elizabeth.

Without thinking, Elizabeth blurted. "He already said he would buy me one for each." Then she noticed Hannah's dejected look and decided that she had better change the subject.

"We're going to be walking home in the rain, Dianah. Look outside. Ever see such large raindrops?"

Robert Harris was beginning to share his son's vision. As he watched Bobby attack the heavy bag tied to a tree with his other two sons, feelings began to well up in him. Perhaps Bobby did have the potential to become one of the top fighters in Great Britain. The more the old butcher thought about it, the better he liked it. What if he did become champion?

Congratulations, Mr. Harris. You have a wonderful son. He reminds me of you. I'll bet you were quite the fighter in your day, too, weren't you? You must have been quite brawny, quite dexterous. Your son puts in blows about the face with surprising timing and judgement. He hits most prodigiously. No one will ever beat him. The King and Queen want to meet you and your son. Do you think you would have time to go to London?

"Keep your balance, son," Robert said, playing the part of the expert. "Don't swing wildly with your arms. Keep your elbows in. Twist your fists with every punch. Think about cutting your opponent's skin. More leverage. Power comes from leverage. Fine. Rest now. Do you want to spar with your brothers again? John. What about it? Ready to spar?"

John pointed to a black eye and a missing tooth. "Father, no more. You've got to find someone else to spar with him. If I spar anymore with him today I won't be any good for work tomorrow. I have a habit of leading with my face, and it's not fun."

Bobby reached for a towel and wiped the sweat off his body, then reached for the mufflers that protected a fighter's hands during sparring sessions. He threw one pair in John's direction and donned another. "Just give me another ten minutes."

John shook his head. "No thanks. Try William."

Pointing to a cut lip, William declined. "I agree with John. It's time to find Bobby some other sparring partners. Why don't you hire Henry Eagles? He'd work cheap."

"Funny," Bobby said derisively. "You girls stay here. I'll do my running. Ten miles this time. Go in and have some bread and jam with your mother. See you later."

John watched Bobby disappear behind the line of shops along the road. He turned to his father and said, "I don't think he appreciates us anymore."

Robert smiled to himself. His two sons were probably right. Bobby had proved a worthy fighter, winning three straight pub matches in Ledbury. Perhaps he ought to talk to the promoter in Gloucester about arranging a fight between his son and another promising young fighter. The winner might have a chance to go to Manchester and fight a reputable leading challenger. At times, however, it seemed as though hundreds of young Brits were in the fight game, jockeying with their supporters and families for a chance to be invited to London. It was London where the promoters with real savvy and influence could see young fighters and perhaps get them billed into a match that would pay big money and obtain recognition. Robert Harris, Sr. knew that right now Bobby was just another fighter, lost among the hundreds that had the same aspirations. He was becoming somewhat respected in Gloucester, but no one beyond that had noticed him yet.

24

THE FADING OF the sun into the western sky, shrouded by a scattered array of pink and purple clouds, found Daniel ending his June eleventh work day a little early in order to celebrate his first wedding anniversary with Elizabeth, Bobby, and Hannah. Brushing the sawdust off his clothing, he walked from his shop to his small stone cottage where the aroma of four steaming loaves of bread, cooling on towels on the kitchen table, welcomed him. Elizabeth was bent over an open fire in the hearth, in her spotless, austere kitchen, checking her cast iron ovens. She was baking beefsteak pies and crumpets. He gave her a kiss, washed, discarded his dirty clothing, and then pulled on a clean pair of trousers and a clean shirt. He lit a lamp, withdrew his uncle's letter from his desk, sat in his rocking chair, and began reading – thinking about what he was going to say to Bobby and Hannah.

Ever since Daniel and Elizabeth had begun training to be lay ministers, Daniel was heartsick that Bobby was seldom seen at any church service, United Brethren or otherwise. The only time Hannah attended was when services were held in either Daniel's home in Deerhurst or at the home of another nearby member in Tirley, Tredington, Corse Lawn, or The Leigh. Bobby remained his best friend but he was arms length when it came to religion. That didn't keep Daniel from trying, however.

The minute they were done eating, Daniel said, "I received the most curious letter a few days ago. I want to read it to you."

"Your French-Huguenot relatives?" Bobby asked, leaning back in his chair. He wondered why a letter from France would be of any interest to him.

Nodding, Daniel continued. "That's where the Browetts are from – you're right. First, let me tell you why the letter came. As you know, Elizabeth and I spent an afternoon with Thomas Kington recently and he was kind enough to tell us not only about the United Brethren but also about the differences between Methodists, Anglicans, and Catholics. My mother and I frequently exchange letters with the Browetts in France and they in turn exchange letters with relatives they have in Switzerland. My uncle has a cousin in Basel, Switzerland."

Bobby coughed, pulling a face. *So what?*

Daniel gathered his thoughts. "My uncle could tell that I was very much interested in studying different religions, so he forwarded me a copy of a statement written by a Catholic priest there in Basel in 1739, almost a hundred years ago."

Daniel held up the letter, and then lowered it. He placed a finger on the written lines of the letter. "The priest published a formal statement called 'Hope of Zion.' I'm going to read to you directly from my uncle's letter, and remember, he is quoting this Catholic priest named Lutis Gratius."

A puzzled look came over Bobby's face. Hannah leaned forward in her chair, eyes wide open, waiting.

Quoting, Daniel read:

The old true Gospel and the gift thereof is lost, false doctrines prevail in all the church on the face of the earth. All we can do is exhort the people to be just, fear God, shun evil and pray.

Prayer and purity may cause an angel to visit a deeply distressed soul, but I tell you, God will have spoken within a hundred years. He will restore the old church again. I see a little band of people led by a prophet and faithful leader. They are persecuted, burned out and murdered. But in the valley that lies on the shore of a great lake, they will build a great city and make a beautiful land. They will have a temple of magnificent splendor and also possess the old priesthood with apostles, prophets, teachers, deacons, etc...

From every nation shall the true believers be gathered by speedy messengers and then shall Almighty God speak to the disobedient nations with thunder, lightning, destruction such as we have never known before.

Daniel finished his reading and then, one by one, glanced into the eyes of both Bobby and Hannah. Taking a deep breath, he sat forward. "What do you think?"

Bobby brought his hands together, and then spread them apart, palms open. "What am I supposed to think?" He sighed, too tired to play games.

Elizabeth spoke, reeling in disbelief at Bobby's sarcastic reaction. "Bobby, I think this letter is significant. It was written just about a hundred years ago. Maybe the little band of people being led by a prophet is somewhere on the earth today, right now, as we speak. If that's true, I want to know about it."

"Obviously something like that is not happening here in England," Bobby said, crossing his feet, and turning a deaf ear to his sister's logic. "That description doesn't fit the Methodists or the Anglicans – or even the United Brethren. I don't think Thomas Kington is any kind of a prophet. Do you?"

"No, of course not," Elizabeth said, shaking her head in agreement.

Daniel held up the letter again. "But Bobby, one could perhaps conclude that the additional light and truth that Reverend Kington has always talked about is with this little band of people. Reverend Kington may, without knowing it, be waiting for some kind of a message that will be delivered in the not-too-distant future. If the Catholic priest is correct, something is about to happen, or it has happened already and we don't know about it."

Bobby let his chair drop back to all four legs, and he rose to pour himself a cup of tea. "Your letter says that the Catholic priest also talks of persecution, burning people out, and murders. Maybe that's happened already. Maybe the so-called light and truth has already been snuffed out. That's very likely, you know, given the history of the world's religions. Just take the Anglicans and the Catholics for example. Lots of gory history."

Elizabeth sighed. In her opinion, although he was making a very good point, Bobby clearly was trying to promote more turmoil about religion in general in order to avoid making any kind of commitment. He was United Brethren by name and convenience only, not by devotion. The more she and Daniel talked to him about religion, the more arrogant he became. He was completely inconsiderate of Hannah and her desire to attend any church. If Reverend Kington, or anyone else for that matter, could give him plain answers to the key questions he always had, Elizabeth knew it might be different for her brother. The thought that their mother's babies, who died before they were baptized, might be in Hell tormented him. She knew that her brother couldn't stand the thought that some religions believed in a literal resurrection of the body and some did not. Bobby had told her that he wanted to know if resurrected beings had any purpose or if they were just going to "float around on a cloud" forever. The questions proved to her that deep down inside her brother was indeed religious. But right now, unless something could ignite that buried passion, he would continue to drift further and further away from a desire to attend religious services of any kind. Well, even if he wouldn't participate in the conversation in a rational way, perhaps just by listening to what the other three of them had to say would soak in a little bit. If he said anything at all it would probably be negative.

Reaching for a fresh-baked crumpet, Elizabeth turned to Hannah. "What do you think, Hannah? How do you feel about the letter?"

Hannah leaned over her baby at the sofa, opened the blanket and peeked at Joseph, who was still asleep. She stepped back toward the table again. "I don't know. He predicts that God will have spoken within a hundred years and we know nothing about it if he actually did, do we? In England, we have heard nothing like that. If God spoke to the pope in Rome, nothing has been announced. If God spoke to head of the Anglican Church in England, we haven't been told. If God said something to the Methodists we haven't been enlightened by them, either."

Bobby folded his arms, and then hissed, "It's just an old Catholic priest gone partly off his rocker. I don't know anything about a church being restored, or about a real prophet. I haven't heard about a valley by the shores of a great lake, none of us have. Reverend Kington doesn't even preach anything like that."

Daniel folded the letter, placed it on the table, and then pointed an index finger toward his friend. "The old Catholic priest may prove to be somewhat of a prophet himself."

"What do you mean?" Hannah asked.

Daniel shrugged his shoulders. "It's just a feeling I have. The old priest's words just have a ring to them, a fabric of truth, a familiarity." He had read, re-read, and contemplated the letter over and over again since he had received it. "One doesn't quite know how to describe it properly, I guess. I just thought it the most unusual thing I've ever read."

"It rings true to me, too, in some strange way," Elizabeth said.

Hannah bobbed her head. "The more I think of it, I guess it does to me, too."

Slowly, Hannah, Elizabeth and Daniel turned to Bobby, expecting him to say something in agreement.

"Any more crumpets, Elizabeth, or are they all gone?"

Bobby won his next fight in eighteen rounds, knocking down his opponent fifteen times. When his opponent faltered, after being knocked down the fifteenth time and given a thirty-second rest, he could not "come to scratch" within the thirty-second time limit, so Bobby was declared the victor.

Afterward it seemed to Bobby that his father regarded pugilism as his new god, almost replacing his devotion to Anglicanism. Robert felt that it was time Bobby began challenging top fighters in other cities. He began working on Bobby's psychic, convincing him that if he trained harder than anyone else, instilled a can't-be-beat attitude in his brain, he could indeed challenge for the championship one day.

Robert studied newspaper accounts and listened to conversations at the pubs, learning everything he could about the current champion, James "The Deaf'un" Burke. He won the championship in 1832, beating Jem Ward senseless. Since then, he was undefeated. But Burke was getting older, more vulnerable.

"Your time will come, son. Your time will come."

Daniel Browett retreated fifty paces into the trees with Thomas Kington, where they stood admiring the only United Brethren chapel in the England. Daniel gloated in its simplicity. It took no inspiration from the Anglican churches that dotted the landscape: no chancel, no nave, no aisles, no towers, no porches, no bells, no stained glass, no statues, no idols, and no tombs. It was about the size of the Methodist chapel in Apperley where he had been married. Using local stone, masons had worked seven months to erect the outside walls and the hearth. Daniel had helped construct the roof, install the doors, and frame an upstairs office. The project had been made possible by a twenty-five-pound donation from United Brethren members, most of it coming from John Benbow.

Kington gave Daniel a pat on the back. "All we need now are benches."

"Just give us a few more days," Daniel said, watching James Pulham, John Davis, and other carpenters at work with their tools, sawing, planing, and pounding away.

Daniel loved his involvement with the United Brethren. With Elizabeth, he spent all his extra time in training to become a lay preacher. He was learning how to conduct meetings and preach sermons. And he did it without pay: Matthew said, *freely ye have received, freely give.* Paul said, *I preach the gospel of Christ without charge.* Peter, *feed the flock not for filthy lucre.*

The only thing Daniel didn't like about the United Brethren was that sometimes their services reminded him of the Quakers. Noisy fits of religious ecstasy did not set well with him.

"Are you making any progress with your friend Bobby?" Kington asked Daniel.

Daniel slumped and his mobile face went weary and grave. "I keep trying. He seems more interested in his fighting career than religion. Between that and making a living as a butcher, he claims he's too busy."

"What about his wife?"

"She wants to join with us, but she's afraid Bobby will be upset if she does."

"Keep working on both of them."

Daniel rubbed his eyes hard with his thumb and forefinger. "I will. I certainly will."

25

December 1836

THOMAS EAGLES became sick when the weather turned cold and damp – it rained for ten days straight. His coughing and fever became acute right away. Hannah had hoped that he would have the strength to recover, even at sixty-one years of age. Her mother, who had inherited from her own mother a familiarity with medicinal herbs, had used some of her supply of foxglove, dandelion, coldsfoot and other herbs that helped – perhaps too much. Thomas got out of bed and worked at the dairy for part of a day. That made his illness worse and in three more days he was near unconsciousness.

The day he died Nancy had arisen early and taken the dairy's horse and carriage to Deerhurst to notify Hannah that their father was near death. Hannah and her little son, Joseph, arrived as her father was drawing his last breath. Within a short time he passed away. Hannah cried especially hard.

Though all her family was there, she felt lonely without Bobby. Despite the bad time her father had given them over their marriage she loved him very much. Hannah was thankful that George, not Henry, was the oldest and heir of her father's holdings. George had already received assurance from Farmer Nightingale that George could take over management of the dairy farm.

Hannah helped her mother through the requisite mourning rituals. They closed the curtains and stopped the clocks at the time of her father's death. They covered the mirrors so that her father's spirit would not be trapped in the reflective glass. Assignments to watch the body every moment were made so that grave robbers could not abscond with the corpse before burial. Weeping willows and extinguished torches were ordered. The official mourning period had begun. It would last nine months.

Bobby was in Bodington buying hogs with his brother William when his father-in-law passed away. He didn't hear the Methodist chapel bell when it rang the traditional "nine tailors" to signify the passing of a man, followed by a peal for each year of his life. He didn't know Thomas had died until he saw a note from Hannah telling him that she was at the Eagles home. He quickly went there. He felt sorrow for Hannah, who sobbed in his arms, but he didn't feel much personal remorse. He just hoped the old dairyman would be more open-minded when he faced his Maker on the other side, wherever that was.

Bobby paid his respects to the family, then brought Hannah and Joseph home for the evening. He didn't object when she began putting together a wardrobe of all-black clothing, made entirely of crepe, a dull fabric without any sheen to reflect light. She told him he would have to wear a plain black suit with black armbands to the funeral.

The next day Hannah helped her mother and sisters write notes to family and friends, notifying them of the death. The notes were written on black-edged paper and sent in black-edged envelopes sealed with black wax. She knew she had to help in every way to give her father the best funeral possible with the limited financial resources available to her mother. They planned the funeral for Sunday, five days after the death. A hearse was negotiated. A single black horse would draw it. They made certain his will would be read at the church gravesite just before burial. It was a foregone conclusion that everything would be left to Hannah's mother.

It snowed on the day of the funeral. Huge, wet snowflakes fell heavily upon their umbrella as Bobby escorted Hannah into the chapel to sit with her family. It was one of the few times he had seen Henry since he had exacted his revenge. Remarkable, he thought, how Henry had managed to stay out of sight after that. When he and Hannah had been invited to the Eagles home for Sunday afternoon dinners, Henry was nowhere to be found. There were no words exchanged today even though Henry walked close to Bobby and Hannah. Bobby suspected that he had the capacity to act like a real human being. He hoped today would be one of those times.

It was also the first time Bobby had seen the Reverend Stephen Crooks since the old stuffbox had married him. His father shared with him how he'd watched Crooks' Adam's apple jump up and down during the wedding. He wished his father hadn't pointed that out. Bobby would probably watch that more than he would listen to the funeral sermon. As Bobby suspected, the sermon did nothing to make him or Hannah feel better.

After the funeral, Hannah walked through the next few weeks in a fog of shocked grief. Until her marriage and the problems over the double wedding, Hannah had always taken her father seriously. Since then, although she loved him deeply, she had become more and more aware of his insensitivity, his peculiarities, and his biased opinions, especially about religion. Yet she was prostrated when he died. She could not eat and she could not sleep. Bobby could do nothing to comfort her. Even her own mother, Ann, pulled out of her own grief and tried in vain to help Hannah. Some days she would lay on her bed and wail and bawl, almost constantly at first, then in spells every day for weeks afterward. She suffered agonies of guilt for the chasm that had separated her from her father after her marriage, mostly because her father did not get along very well with Bobby. She regretted that their relationship had eroded at the cost of her marriage to Bobby.

But Thomas Eagles was gone, and there was nothing she could do now but repair whatever damage might also have been done to her relationship with her mother. Her father was unreachable by love or regret, but her mother was still very much alive. Hannah vowed to renew her relationship with her mother, making it stronger, more loving than ever. To her credit, Hannah did just that; after a few weeks of self analysis, and she began to spend more time with her mother and her sisters. Still, she avoided Henry whenever possible.

Bobby's next fight came a week after the funeral, at the Gloucester horse fair. He was matched against another top local fighter, who was expected to give Bobby his toughest match yet. Bobby still won handily in eighteen rounds, and was only knocked down twice. He thought about his deceased father-in-law. He wondered if old Thomas Eagles knew he'd won his fight. He wondered if in heaven – or hell – people cared about such things.

26

WILFORD WOODRUFF stood on the porch of the Newel K. Whitney store, scanning the Ohio horizon with Brigham Young. "It's amazing how Kirtland has grown."

"It's too bad you missed the temple dedication," Brigham said. The Kirtland Temple stood on a low bluff, just above the store, majestic in its white color. For a few minutes Brigham described it: Joseph Smith's dedicatory prayer. Angels descending from heaven. Visions. People in the neighborhood hearing unusual noises. Sound of a mighty rushing of winds. Reports of a bright light above the temple. His own experience speaking in tongues.

"When I left for Zion's Camp in Missouri in 1834, Kirtland was nothing like it is today," Wilford said, sweeping his arm across the horizon. The city, three hundred miles west of Washington D. C., had a brief history: First permanent clearing in 1811. Influx of settlers following the War of 1812 and especially in 1815. And arrival of Mormon settlers in the early 1830s. At one time, Joseph and Emma Smith had lived in the Whitney store. He had received around twenty of his revelations here, recorded in the Doctrine and Covenants.

"We're glad to have you back," Brigham said. "Someone told me about an old man that was a big influence in your life. A Mr. Mason?"

Wilford chuckled with a fond remembrance. "Old prophet Mason, we used to call him. I regret that he died before the church was organized. It's amazing what he knew."

"Such as?"

"He knew nothing about Joseph Smith and the restoration. But I remember Mr. Mason telling me a few years back, before I was baptized, that the Lord would raise up a people and a church in the last days. That the church would be complete with prophets, apostles, and all the gifts, powers, and blessings, necessary to bring true salvation to the people of the earth."

"That truly is amazing."

Wilford danced his fingertips together. "When I was a child, Mr. Mason told me about one of his dreams."

Brigham's eyes opened wide in anticipation.

"In this dream, he had seen himself in a vast fruit orchard with numerous trees that were barren of fruit. Suddenly, all the trees fell to the ground. Afterward, he saw young sprouts springing up from the roots of the fallen trees. These suddenly grew into full-grown trees, heavily laden with fruit."

"Did he ever know the meaning of the dream?"

"He told me he prayed night and day about it. Soon, he knew. I think it came as some sort of personal revelation. The barren orchard represented his generation, his past life. Sadly, he knew that the true church of Christ was not upon the earth. However, the dream meant that in the days of his children the church and kingdom of God would appear with all of its gifts and blessings. He knew he would not live to enjoy its blessings, but would do so after death because he had followed the dictates of the spirit during his life."

"When did all this happen?"

"I can't remember the exact year. As I look back on it, I think it probably happened near the time when Joseph Smith had his first vision. I would have been twelve or thirteen at the time."

Brigham uttered the word "amazing" again.

"There's one other thing I remember Mr. Mason telling me. He looked at me with his searching eyes and testified that although he would never enjoy the blessing of the gospel, I would. His exact words were, 'I shall never partake of the fruit in the flesh; but you will, and you will become a conspicuous actor in that kingdom'."

"Brother Woodruff," Brigham said, a warm feeling coming over him, "There's no doubt in my mind that is true. Think of it. Think of all the great experiences you had on your mission to the Southern States. All the things you told us in your report. Think of your ordination to the Second Quorum of the Seventy. Your are a conspicuous actor in the Kingdom of God. I suspect the Lord has much more in store for you. I don't think the surface has been scratched."

A chill went up and down the spine of Wilford. He thought of the time he had spent in the temple since his return to Kirtland, the church services, washing and anointings, the sessions of gospel instruction at the hands of Joseph Smith, the prophet. He thought of the special blessing just given to him when he was ordained to the office of a Seventy: *You will preach to the nations of the earth and to the inhabitants upon the Islands of the Sea.*

These things flashed through Wilford's mind for several seconds. His eyes shot up the hill, at the temple.

"Something else is truly amazing," he said, his eyes glowing ominously. "And that is what has happened in that temple while I was gone."

"You're right," Brigham said. "And our job is to tell the world about it. The world needs to know that the Kirtland temple was built for a place for prophets of past dispensations to restore the keys, powers, and authorities to their dispensations and ministries. Moses has appeared in that temple. He restored the keys relative to the literal gathering of Israel and the restoration of the Twelve Tribes. Elias restored keys that we may enjoy the blessing given to Abraham, eternal posterity and family relationships through the patriarchal order of the priesthood. Elijah restored the keys to the priesthood."

"I like your word, amazing, Brother Brigham," Wilford said.

"Not a better word. It can be used to describe the Savior's appearance in the temple. Perhaps in a coming teaching session, the prophet will tell you details about that. He even describes what the Savior looks like: bright silver gray hair, penetrating blue eyes. The Savior has accepted his temple."

A tear of appreciation came to Wilford's eyes.

27

March 1837

THE DEATH of Hannah's father was one thing, but the death of his own mother, Sarah, was another.

Bobby was devastated by her death. He loved her very much, and he had expected her to live much longer. But a wetter, colder winter than normal had given her such a bad case of influenza that, along with longstanding heart disease and dropsy, her body did not have the strength to recover. She passed away suddenly on the second of March. It was the first time someone so close to him had died. He regretted all the times he had disobeyed her, refusing to admit she was right and he was wrong, even over trivial things. He had to admit that the older he got the worse he was in that regard. Although his mother was not as vocal as his father, she had, in her own quiet way, let him know she was not happy when he quit attending the Anglican Church. And she had been disappointed even more when she found out he wasn't even attending the church that he claimed he was attached to. If he had it to do all over again, he would attend once in awhile just to make her happy. He felt bad that his sister, Dianah, and her husband, Thomas Bloxham, had just followed suit and joined the United Brethren. They had the right to do it, though their timing could have been better.

Elizabeth was filled with guilt at her mother's passing. She knew she had disappointed her mother by abandoning the family faith. At the time, she didn't think it bothered her mother but now, as she reflected back, Elizabeth could recall several things her mother had said that made it clear her mother supported her father's feelings all the way. Now she was gone. In her private prayers, Elizabeth asked God to forgive her. She wept several times.

Hannah was extremely helpful. She related what she went through when her father died and how she had resolved to keep making the relationship with her mother better. Elizabeth thought that was a great idea and decided to put the philosophy to practice in the future relationship with her frosty old butcher of a father.

As expected, Robert took his wife's death badly but he made certain the mourning rituals were followed and that a proper funeral was conducted. She had died firm in the faith and she would have a proper Anglican funeral, conducted by the vicar, the Reverend Spencer Hobhouse. This would be a funeral that would make his father, his grandfather, and his great-grandfather proud. They had all died firm in the Anglican faith. Not one of them, or any of their children or their children's children, as far as he knew, with the exception of Bobby and Elizabeth, departed from the faith. He had to live with the embarrassment that his own son and both daughters were probably the first to depart from the faith. But it wasn't over. Bobby wasn't even attending the United Brethren. When he was champion he would be back. His return to the faith – and surely Robert's two daughters would follow Bobby's example and

return also – and the championship would bring honor to his dearly departed Sarah. They had been married more than thirty-four years. She had been a
faithful wife, mother of three sons and two daughters, not counting the
infants who died. He had been a faithful husband and a good provider. God
would be pleased with him, too. *Thou shalt not commit adultery. Thou shalt
not covet thy neighbor's wife.* Of all the men who had ever lived upon planet
earth, he was in the minority. He knew a lot of men who violated those two
commandments. But not him.

After the funeral – a walking funeral, which was customary among working-class people of the Anglican faith who lived in the country – and at
Bobby's suggestion, Bobby's oldest brother, William, moved into his father's
home to care for him and to continue managing the purchase of livestock for
their butcher shop. Bobby knew his father was four years older than their
mother and he privately worried how many more years he would live.
Occasionally Robert complained about his lungs. Bobby had to treat him better, spend more time with him, eat more Sunday dinners with him, take him
on walks, and not complain anymore about the blood and the offal. There
were worse jobs than being a butcher. He hoped he would win the championship before his father passed away. Then they could all quit the butchering
business. There would be money enough to spare.

28

BOBBY NEVER SAW the left hand cross coming from his opponent. It staggered him. Jem Taylor moved in for the kill. Another left to the forehead. Dizzy now, Bobby collapsed to his knees. Bobby's brothers rushed to him. Noting the glazed look in his eyes, they knew Bobby was in trouble for the first time in his career. Hannah was crying. Elizabeth was screaming.

The crowd at the Gloucester Pugilistic Club roared its approval. Taylor, because of his experience, was the favorite.

John and William brought Bobby to scratch for round two. Taylor moved in, sensing an early victory. He threw another left. Bobby instinctively ducked. The punch missed. Dancing away, his head still spinning, Bobby knew he had to buy more time. He backpedaled. Taylor rushed him. Bobby wrapped his arms around Taylor in a bear hug.

Bobby had never fought an opponent who was left-handed. Taylor's style was confusing to him. Taylor rushed in again, throwing combination rights and lefts. Bobby went down again.

Round three.

Physically stunned, but his head clearing in thought, Bobby knew that unless he changed his strategy, he was doomed to lose.

Though it felt awkward, he changed his stance. He led with his right, instead of his left, just like his opponent. Jab, jab, jab. Circle left instead of right. The sudden change in style brought a sneer from his opponent. He attacked as though he were insulted. *A right-hander cannot fight left-handed.*

The strategy seemed to work for Bobby. He was still absorbing most of the punishment, but Taylor was unable to land the type of devastating blows that had knocked him down earlier. Bobby was buying time.

Minute-by-minute, Bobby learned how to block Taylor's blows. Occasionally he was successful with a quick counter punch, which maddened Taylor. Gaining confidence, Bobby lashed out with jabs, crosses, and hooks. Taylor lashed out with a savage counter-attack. A left uppercut landed to Bobby's chest. The powerful blow put Bobby down again. Bobby took a long count and came to scratch.

Round four.

Taylor rushed in. Bobby crouched low, and grabbed a thigh. Defenseless, Taylor pounded the back of Bobby's head. The referee parted them.

Bobby struck Taylor with right hand jabs, followed by a stinging left.

"Hit 'im, Bobby, hit 'im," Elizabeth screamed. "Watch out for his left hand, Bobby! Atta boy, *step away*, now at 'im again!"

The two fighters wailed at each other for a four-minute period with no knockdowns. Bobby perceived that Taylor was tiring.

Taylor made a move that shocked Bobby. Taylor, sensing that Bobby had neutralized him, switched leads. He began fighting right-handed.

Quickly, Bobby switched, too. Jab, jab, jab. Left crosses. Right crosses. Right uppercuts. Taylor fought gallantly with his own punches. He swung a powerful right cross. It was just the punch Bobby was waiting for. He ducked under the right with a right of his own, square into Taylor's ribs. He went down.

Round five.

Bobby knew the fight was gone out of Taylor as his handlers brought him back to scratch. Taking no chances, he attacked with vicious combinations. Taylor collapsed in a heap. He was done.

"The squire wants to talk to you."

Bobby was wiping beads of sweat from his face with a towel, amid a chorus of praise from his family and friends. He turned to face his father. "You mean Squire Hastings?"

"None other," Robert answered, wearing a saucy, proud grin.

Bobby followed his father a few steps from the ring apron.

"Squire, this is my son, Bobby."

The squire offered his hand, and Bobby shook it. The squire's hands were soft like a woman's. They exchanged awkward glances for a few seconds, sizing up one another.

Squire Hastings looked like the aristocrat that he was. He was dressed in a black frock coat, and held a tightly furled umbrella that the upper class called a "doppelganger." Rumor had it that the squire spent more than a thousand pounds a year on his wardrobe. Between him and Squire Nightingale, they owned most of the land around Deerhurst and Apperley.

"That was an impressive display of courage and talent, young man," the squire said, scanning Bobby's physique top to bottom.

Bobby mentally shook himself, his chest still heaving. He had never received a compliment from an aristocrat. "Thank you, sir," he said, returning a cheeky grin. In his youth, he had poached more than his share of rabbits off the squire's lands. He hoped the squire knew nothing about it.

Up close, Squire Hastings looked much older than his fifty-five years. He had a hard face with deep-set, blue-gray eyes, long, bushy gray eyebrows and mutton-chop sideburns. His nose hairs needed clipping and long hairs protruded from his ears. At only five-foot-five, he looked up at Bobby. He was well fed; his stomach spoke of it. And he was an ugly man; his clothes, although immaculate, did little to mitigate the ugliness – the crooked bulbous nose, protruding chin, and bony cheeks.

A woman that Bobby took to be the squire's wife waited in the background, ignored by the squire. She was slightly younger, ashen-haired, with eyes that glittered clear blue like the diamonds on her neck, her arms, her fingers and her ears. She was patiently waiting, humming an old English tune, *Lavender Blue*.

"I have a proposal for you," the squire said as a twisted grin appeared on his face.

Bobby grew pensive. *For me?*

The squire's head tilted to one side and his eyes riveted on Bobby. "I have seen you fight three times now, and I think you have the potential to be groomed as a contender for the championship. I am inviting you to become a member of the Gloucester Pugilistic Club, which I own. That means that you'll receive some professional training at my sparring house, and we'll match you with some opponents that will attract a crowd. You'll soon be earning a purse of a few pounds for each fight. Out of those earnings you can repay me for your training. If you're good, you'll eventually fight for some big purses, and earn some real money."

Bobby's eyebrows raised and his eyes flashed wide open. Trying to crush down his elation, he glanced at Hannah, then back at the squire. "How much money?"

Pulling a cigar out of his vest, the squire showed no visible signs of nervousness over his business proposal. "Not much at first – three, four, five pounds. If you're as good as I think you can become, in a few years you could be fighting for a twenty or thirty pound purse. If you contend for the championship, maybe a hundred pounds or more." The squire put the cigar into his mouth. "Interested?"

Bobby dabbed at his forehead with the towel. "I'd be a fool not to. But why me?"

The squire momentarily forgot about lighting his cigar and stared at Bobby. "I've already told you that I am impressed with your talent. Now see here, lad, I'll confide in you. Pugilism in England has lost some of its glamour. We are infested with moralists who attack the sport, and think that we ought to be playing cricket instead. Part of the criticism of pugilism is warranted. Some of our fighting chaps are low-life sods, unscrupulous, heavy drinkers, loud, vicious. Lot's of bloody fools out there. We need a new breed of fighters, fighters that can help restore credibility. That's what I see in you. You strike me as a nice young chap who has a natural instinct for fighting. You put on a splendid good show today."

Bobby's father nodded with high-strung eagerness. "I think we're jolly well interested, aren't we son? But we need to go home and talk about it."

A big grin was lighting up Bobby's face. As far as he was concerned, they ought to make an agreement with the squire right on the spot.

Lighting his cigar, out of which curled a thick smoke that offended Bobby's sense of smell, the squire coughed four times. He spoke again with a self-satisfied tilt of his head, showing his relish for power and his satisfaction in bestowing largesse. "You and your father think it over, no rush for a decision. But if you accept, I will make another proposition as well."

Bobby's curiosity was aroused. "Another proposition?"

The smoke-wreathed puddle of an old squire came straight to the point again. "As your father knows, I own a lot of the land around Deerhurst and Apperley. I hear through the grapevine that you have been looking for land to lease. If you sign with me, I will make every effort to transfer a lease to your name so that after your fighting career you will make a good living as a tenant farmer."

Bobby's eyes sparkled. "Do you have enough land for my friend, too?" He motioned to Daniel. "Both of us would like to become yeoman farmers."

With a mere shrug of the shoulders the squire made a reply. "I have two hundred acres that will become available within a year. You can take it all in your name or split it with your friend. It makes no difference to me. I will trust your friend Browett with a lease if that is what you two chaps want. A hundred acres isn't much but perhaps in another year or two more land will become available for you."

Squire Hastings gave Daniel a quick perfunctory handshake that made Daniel feel small and unimportant, and then quickly turned his attention back to Bobby.

"Thank you, sir," Daniel said, almost unnoticed.

The squire withdrew the cigar from his mouth with his right hand, and shook off the built-up ash. "Mind you, I'm not doing this out of benevolence. I am a businessman. Mr. Harris, I believe your son has the potential to eventually fight for the heavyweight championship of England. It will take another three or four years of very hard training. He will have to win all his matches. Then we can challenge the other top fighters. If he makes it to the top, and once he is the champion, both of us stand to make a lot of money. But first I have to get him in the right circles with the right connections, and eventually have him fight in London where he will get noticed. If my hunch is correct, I will make my money in wagers, all of which will make my investment pay off. This is all fairly clear, isn't it?"

The squire turned to face Bobby again. His mouth wrinkled in gratification. "I can't lose in leasing my farm ground as long as the tenant farmers are responsible. I believe you will be. Both you and your friend. You will eventually make more than a reasonable amount of money, and you will have a farm to fall back on when you retire from fighting. I'm gambling on your ability as a fighter, but after watching you today, I think you are not only a gifted fighter but also a smart fighter. You turned a potential loss into an impressive win."

Hannah listened to the conversation with a blank look on her face. She didn't know if the arrangement would prove to be a blessing or a curse.

Bobby walked away from the conversation with a smug smile. *Who needed the United Brethren? Who needed any kind of religion?*

The home of the Prophet Joseph Smith was the setting of the marriage between Wilford Woodruff and Phoebe Carter, whom Wilford had known since January. Their April thirteenth marriage culminated a three-month courtship. Two days after spending his wedding night in the prophet's home in Kirtland, he went to the temple to receive his patriarchal blessing at the hands of Joseph Smith, Sr.

He was told he had a "great work to do in the earth." If ever he believed in anything, he believed in his blessing. It was given by the father of the prophet, the first prophet on the earth since the apostles at the time of Christ. The prophet's father had the priesthood, conferred upon him by his prophet son, who had received it directly from Peter, James and John. It was a blessing to be believed, to be revered and to be treasured. Wilford didn't know exactly how to interpret the phrase that stated he had a "great work to do in the earth," but that didn't matter. He had the faith that it would happen. All he had to do was continue to keep the commandments and accept every calling that the prophet would give him.

29

THE BRITISH FLAG fluttering from the rooftop of Squire Hastings' two-story mansion near Apperley struck Bobby with a pang of pride as he turned his head. Its colors seemed so rich, its slow waving in a steady breeze so full of majesty. For a moment he forgot about his normal cynical attitude toward England's stratified social structure, the distinctions blurring in his mind. He had a coveted pugilism contract. And he was about to become a yeoman.

As a new yeoman, he knew he would still be classified as a commoner. That's because England had only two classes of people, aristocrats and the working class. The aristocrats were people like Squire Hastings, who inherited titles and land. The commoners, or working class, included everyone else. As soon as he and Daniel took over the two hundred acres from the squire, his class status would suddenly become elevated from the poor working class to upper middle class. He would be on the same level as people such as John Benbow, even though it would take him several years to accumulate what

Benbow had. He would also be on nearly the same level as Mr. Nightingale, the man who owned the dairy where Hannah's father had worked. He would be above shopkeepers, clerical workers, lower-level government workers and the like. And just below the status of merchants, manufacturers, bankers, military officers, clergymen, and university professors.

Bobby closed his eyes and imagined what his social status would be when he became the heavyweight boxing champion of England. Combined with being a yeoman farmer, he would eventually become one of the wealthiest and most respected upper middle class people in all Gloustershire. He felt certain that as he rose in the ranks of pugilism, he would also rise in the number of acres that the squire leased to him.

It was his sister Elizabeth who broke Bobby's trance. In her usual giddy, bubbly way, she was going on about the squire's house as Elizabeth, Daniel, Hannah, and Bobby were leaving the squire's property.

"I've always wanted to go through this house, haven't you, Hannah? Ever since I was a little girl, when Papa would drive us by the squire's mansion, I couldn't imagine how anyone would need such a large home."

All the guests – about ten couples – had been brought first through the principal court of the estate. They entered the mansion through an elaborately decorated porch which led to a sub hall, then the grand hall which was connected to the dining room where they had a dinner consisting of filet de boeuf with Spanish sauce, larded sweetbreads, rissoles, boiled leg of lamb, roast fowls garnished with watercress, boiled ham, spinach garnished with croutons, and ice cream for dessert. Flanking the dining room were the library, drawing room, morning room and a smaller dining room. Another wing of the mansion housed the kitchen court, kitchen, servant's quarters, washhouse, laundry house, scullery room, and the pastry room. Bedrooms for the family and guests were on the second floor.

Hannah was looking keenly at Elizabeth. "How many servants do you think the squire has to have to run his manor?" She began counting them on her fingers – a housekeeper, lady's maid, upper housemaid, under housemaid, kitchen maid, scullery maid, and a cook. That included only the women they saw. In addition, Hannah began counting the men servants – house steward, valet, butler, gardener, footman, coachman, groom, page, and stableboy. She made a face and quit counting, then changed the subject. "The squire never did tell us, but I'm wondering. How many acres of land does he own? Must be more than a thousand."

Elizabeth shrugged her shoulders. "I don't know."

"More than three thousand," Bobby said, sounding confident with his dazzling smile. "I found out by talking with Mr. Nightingale."

Elizabeth's face fell. "Three thousand acres? Isn't that just *obscene*? And he rents it out at a pound an acre per year. That's three thousand pounds a year. How many squires are there in our country these days do you suspect?"

"I know that, too," Bobby said. "Around two thousand."

Elizabeth shook her head. "Just two thousand men own virtually all the land in England, then. Would that be *true*?"

The statistics knifed through Daniel's mind. "I guess that's true. All except the land the Church of England owns." He thought of the hundred acres that John Benbow rented from the Castle Frome glebe.

"And to think you're about to become a yeoman, Daniel," Elizabeth said, her face lit with happiness. "Even if it will be only a hundred acres to begin with."

During the afternoon, the squire had told Daniel and Bobby that their lease would begin at the end of the year so that the current men who leased the land could harvest their crops.

Elizabeth said, "I didn't realize what an *important* man the squire is to our community until now." She had learned that Squire Hastings served as justice of the peace, appointed the Anglican priest, spent nearly half of his time in London where he maintained another residence, had friends in Parliament, and promoted local charities. His wife, although a lady of ostentatious tastes, provided layettes for new babies born in the parish, soup for poor elderly people, and occasionally taught a class in Sunday School.

Hannah turned with Bobby to get a last close-up glimpse of the mansion and the British flag flying above it before they left in their carriage. "I wonder if the squire has met the new queen?"

One of the hot topics of conversation at the party had been the fact that a seventeen-year-old princess by the name of Victoria had just become Queen of England. It had happened June twentieth, upon the death of her uncle, King William IV, just two days after the national holiday celebrating Napoleon's defeat in 1815.

Hannah chuckled. "If not, he'll probably get to kiss her hand on his next trip to London."

Elizabeth regarded her brother with another concern. "Now that you're going to be a yeoman, Bobby, you'll need to learn how to *behave* like a gentleman. You didn't do all that well today."

"What's this?" he grimaced. "Another lecture?" He recalled the one she gave him on the way to the Benbow mansion prior to their double wedding.

"Yes, it is," she said.

Bobby covered his ears.

Elizabeth began to recite from memory the qualities of an English gentleman: Never arrogant but never weak. Bears himself with dignity but never haughtiness. Too wise to despise trifles but too noble to be mastered by them. Commands with mild authority but asks favors with grace and assurance. Respects the prejudices of men whom he believes are honest. Keeps his honor unstained. Retains the good opinion of others he neglects. And on it went.

"Why are you always picking on me?" Bobby snorted. "Is this the first time Daniel has heard all this rubbish?"

"Believe me, no," Daniel said. "It's all she's been talking about lately."

Bobby exchanged a serious glance with Elizabeth. "You've already violated the qualities of an English lady," he charged.

"In what way?" she asked, with an incredulous look on her face.

"An English lady should always be quiet in her manners, be natural and unassuming in her language, and careful to wound no one's feelings. I know that much about these things. You've wounded my feelings, so hush up."

Elizabeth drew her face into a smirk. "And now you've wounded *mine*."

"Be wounded, woman."

"Then in my wounded condition, I am going to make a demand right here and now. From now on, we will have to be concerned about the etiquette of dress for a proper English lady. Both of you men should know that as the wives of yeomen, our wardrobes will have to be increased."

Bobby and Daniel chafed at the thought, shaking their heads.

"Oh, yes, Hannah," Elizabeth said with a twinkle in her eye. "Think of all the new silk dresses, the lace collars and cuffs, the jewelry, the broaches, pendants, and earrings, and all the costly furs in your future."

30

Spring 1838

BOBBY STRODE out onto his one hundred acres of leased land between the Deerhurst Parish Church and the hamlet of Apperley until he reached the highest point on a hill. He stooped down, grabbed a handful of soil, brought it to his nose and smelled it. It was rich and black, with a hint of the manure that had been spread prior to the planting of the crops – wheat, rye, barley, and oats. He rose to his feet and studied his kingdom, letting the soil slowly sift through his fingers. To his left were fields of hay, to his right the fields of grain, their green shoots rising several inches in the air, reaching for the warmth of the sun on this bright morning in late May.

Below him, Bobby surveyed a painted barn, corrals, and a large stone thatch-roofed cottage where Hannah was caring for two-year-old Joseph and their newly born daughter, Elizabeth, only six weeks old. With a rise of satisfaction he thought of the small herd of sheep, the twenty-six steers, and the ten pigs that were his – at least in theory. Technically, since Squire Hastings had financed the crops and the livestock, everything belonged to the squire. No matter. Someday, they would be his.

Bobby stared a mile south in the direction of The Leigh, where Daniel Browett was settled on his own farm, also nearly a hundred acres, complete with outbuildings, livestock, and an equally opulent cottage. He thought about the previous tenants of the two farms. He wondered how they had fallen into disfavor with the squire. One day they were tenants, the next day they were not. Bobby didn't know the details and didn't want to think about it.

He looked farther south, in the direction of Gloucester, where he was expected to spend a good portion of his time at the squire's sparring house, training to become a serious contender for the British championship. In time, Bobby knew that if all went well, he would begin earning attractive purses from his fights, a small profit from his farm, and the opportunity to increase the number of acres in his lease. On the downside, he knew that he had sold a large portion of his soul. Squire Hastings owned him.

As a gentle breeze rippled across his face, he began to smile. Despite the squire's hold over him, he was on a career path that few others could match. Soon he would be the envy of thousands, known throughout England as a champion, and a wealthy yeoman employing dozens of farm servants.

Elizabeth saw less of Daniel during the summer than any other time now that he was both owner of his cooper and furniture shop, and a small tenant farmer. She was grateful that Squire Hastings had made good on his promise and his two hundred acres were made available early in the spring prior to planting season.

Daniel and Bobby were quick learners and Farmer Benbow of Castle Frome had given them advice on how to raise crops, manage livestock, and supervise farm servants. She marveled how quickly they had progressed from a household with only one servant to tenant farmer status with a small army of servants – even though Daniel and Bobby leased only a hundred acres each. In June Daniel had the "army" out in the grass fields with scythes harvesting hay; today they were harvesting corn. Between the two of them, they kept their friends Levi Roberts, Joseph Hill, and James Pulham busy full time. Daniel calculated that it took five farm workers to knock down two acres of grain per day. Daniel and Bobby were doubly grateful to Squire Hastings because he not only contracted to lease them the land but provided financing as well so they could hire laborers, buy livestock, and purchase corn seed. They understood now more than ever that farming was a tremendous gamble – what if their yields were down? What if corn prices suddenly fell? What if disease wiped out their livestock, even by a small percentage? What would the squire do to them if they could not repay their loans?

Together they now had a small herd of sheep. They were marked with raddle dye to distinguish them from other sheep that roamed through the Cotswolds. At night they placed them in pens in fields they wanted fertilized.

Both Hannah and Elizabeth were elated about having house servants. Hannah even had a nursemaid. They had met together to review rules for servants: Always move quietly about the house. Do not let your voice be heard by the family unless necessary. Do not enter into any family conversation. Do not offer information unless asked. Do not smile at droll stories. When meeting any lady or gentleman about the house, stand back and let them pass. When you walk with the lady or gentleman of the house, always keep a few paces behind.

After a few weeks of having house servants, Hannah and Elizabeth began to feel relieved of some of the hard work they previously had to do: Opening the shutters first thing in the morning. Lighting the kitchen fire. Shaking soot from the rugs and curtains. Emptying the stove soot outside. Sweeping and dusting the rooms. Laying the hearth. Cooking breakfast. Making the beds.

Emptying the slops. Cleaning the kitchen. Picking and gutting geese and chickens. Blackleading the scraper. Scrubbing the floors. Washing the dog. Making supper. And doing more dishes.

Daniel and Bobby estimated that Squire Hastings must have been banking on making a lot of money through Bobby's fight contract, and bets, along with the five percent loans and the pound-per-year per-acre rental contracts on his land. They marveled again at how many total acres the squire owned and what his annual income might be. The often talked together about what determined whether a man was born into the aristocracy or into a working class family. What did the squire do to deserve the wealth he had? Did he deserve it just because he was the oldest son and inherited everything from his father? How many centuries had the Hastings family owned all this land? Why was the squire born into such circumstances?

Their farm lease agreements not only included the land but also homes to live in, cottages for the servants, plus barns and other outbuildings. Elizabeth and Hannah were pleased with their country farm homes complete with large parlors, several bedchambers, and servant quarters.

Elizabeth was still disappointed that no children had come to her and Daniel. She stared at the empty bedchambers, and longed to one day fill them with children. Privately she was somewhat jealous of Hannah and her two children. She was honored deeply to have Bobby and Hannah name the baby after her – Elizabeth. She had been at Hannah's side during the birth, assisting the midwife and servants. If she couldn't have children of her own she wanted to help others in every way possible.

Squire Hastings had secured a big piece of Bobby's life, and demanded that Bobby spend a large amount of his time in training. Bobby no longer trained at home with a punching bag tied to a tree. He spent time in Gloucester at a facility where he met other professional fighters and began fine-tuning his skills. He was judged to have above average natural skills, a strong frame, and superior motivation. Trainers projected that with those attributes, combined with new skills they would be teaching him, Bobby could be ready within a year to fight other leading contenders. And, if he won those fights, he could stand to be invited to fight for the championship in London. James Burke, the reigning champion, had held the title for five years now, but was aging and starting to look vulnerable.

Maybe there was a diamond broach in Hannah's future, Bobby thought to himself.

31

REVEREND SPENCER Hobhouse, short, slightly overweight, brown-eyed, his unruly gray hair heavily greased and his leathery face wrinkled by time, slowly walked through the nave of his Priory Church of St. Mary the Virgin. He glanced at the Saxon sculpture of the Virgin with Child. He approached the Saxon font that graced the entry. He placed his right hand on it and slowly traced the circle, thinking of two unchristened infants that blemished the records of his Deerhurst parish: Joseph Harris and Elizabeth Harris, Bobby's children. This thought seared his conscience. It made him uncomfortable.

His eyes narrowed as he thought about the competition he constantly received for the saving of souls, whether from the Quakers in Tewkesbury, the Methodists in Apperley, or the Baptists in Ledbury. Now there was a new threat: the United Brethren, another dissident group. To Reverend Hobhouse, the United Brethren seemed to be unique to the Malvern Hills. He perceived them to be weak, meeting in very small groups, patterned after the "primitive" Methodists. They owned only one chapel, in Gadfield Elm, an unattractive stone building.

The reverend shook his head. How could a faithful member of his congregation like Robert Harris permit Bobby and Elizabeth to engage in such heretical behavior? Surely Robert knew that the United Brethren were just a bunch of heretics. Didn't Robert realize the burden he was placing on the Anglican congregation? It was a simple matter of numbers. The fewer members of the Deerhurst parish, those who attended the Deerhurst Priory Church, the more the reverend had to rely on those who remained to cover the costs, including his salary, of running the congregation. The larger the flock, the greater the potential for coins to fill the plate that was passed each Sunday. By habit he looked for coins that made him smile – half sovereigns, crowns, half crowns, double florins, and florins. A man of God could not supplement his salary very well with penny coins such as a farthing, halfpenny, twopence, threepence, groat, or sixpence. Times were so bad that the fees collected for pew rental for the best seats during morning communion and afternoon Sunday School were even down. He wished Anglican priests had their old powers back, the powers they had at the turn of the century when only Anglican clergymen could conduct marriages or bury the dead. What was the world coming to? Dissidents were ruining everything.

Reverend Hobhouse shook his head in dismay as he exited, walked a few paces, and turned to face the stone structure. Why couldn't young Bobby appreciate this old church as he did? The Tudor windows of the nave and south aisle. The tell-tale bands of herringbone masonry work that ensured its Saxon origins. The seventy-foot high tower, dating from before the Norman Conquest. He closed his eyes for a moment. He thought he could see herds of deer bouncing through the trees. *Deerhurst, woods frequented by deer.*

Full of regret, he began his walk toward the old butcher's cottage, determined to engage his parishioner in a meaningful conversation. He had to persuade butcher Harris that it was a joint responsibility to convince Bobby to remain a faithful Anglican and keep all new children christened and safely in the fold. He couldn't afford to lose them to Methodism, Quakerism, United Brethrenism, or any "ism" for that matter. Not only did the contributions go up and down depending on the numbers, so did his salary. He determined to regain the souls that had wandered to other flocks, one by one. Although he was deeply suspicious of Catholicism, which he and other Protestant ministers called "Popery," their doctrines were basically the same. After all, that's the way Henry VIII wanted it. Baptism was by pouring, however, not sprinkling.

All his life Reverend Hobhouse had been a parish priest who had been willing to confront issues head on. He thought about his courage and his boldness as he walked past several stone cottages – some with new tile roofs and others with traditional thatched roofs – down the street scattered with shops, then to the nearby cottage occupied by Robert Harris. He pounded on the door, sweating slightly from the quarter-mile walk on the warm, humid day. He found his faithful parish member, the elderly butcher, in a cluttered house, lonely, and anxious to talk to anyone. For twenty minutes over several cups of tea they talked about old times, Sarah's life, the burial plot in front of the Deerhurst Church, and one-by-one all of the children that they had raised. They discussed how faithful William, John, and Dianah had been in marrying within the church, that their lives were blessed for it. They had obediently brought each of their children into the church where each was christened in the Saxon font, in a proper ceremony, befitting a loyal Anglican. That brought Reverend Hobhouse directly to the purpose of his visit.

Sipping a third cup of hot English tea, he looked over the brim of the cup. "I can't help but notice that two of your grandchildren have not been christened, Brother Harris. I'm sure you're quite aware of it."

The old butcher meditated, and a sad look came on his face. The glance of his sunken, pallid blue-gray eyes was straight ahead and far away. He spoke in a quiet tone, almost ashamed that the reverend had unveiled the unsettling truth. "I assure you I am aware of it. My heart is broken over it. It's wearing me down. I've talked to my son about it, and to his wife, but I'm getting nowhere."

"I say, what do you mean, at a later time?" posed the parish priest.

"Just what I said. You mustn't make me repeat."

The reverend sat his cup of tea on the table and stared deeply at his parishioner. The issue before them was far too important for it to be delayed to a "later time." After all, the Bible taught that the Kingdom of Heaven is unattainable for those not properly baptized. It was thus customary for little children to be christened as soon after birth as possible. Infant baptism had been practiced in the Christian church since the early days of the Church of Rome, and it was properly embraced by the Anglican faith. As far as Reverend Hobhouse was concerned, Bobby was still Anglican, married in the St. Mary de Lode Church, even though he and his wife had "toyed" around with a dissident group called the United Brethren. It was not too late to save them and their two children. Their spiritual lives depended on it, in his opinion.

Robert Harris again shook his head in sadness and futility.

"Believe me, reverend, I've spoken to him about it, many times. It would please me if he did. I've reminded him time and time again. He's a fine lad, but I'm having a bit of a problem; he won't listen on this subject. We get along fine on everything but religion. He'll be the champion some day. But like you, I wish he would have his children christened. I'm afraid he attended the United Brethren congregation recently. Do you wonder if Bobby had his children christened there? I don't think so, because surely they would have invited the grandparents. One hangs on and hopes."

The reverend's face reddened. "I say, such a christening would not be recognized. They would be placing their family in jeopardy. What if one of their children died without being christened? There is no salvation outside the church. The child would not be saved in Heaven."

"I have said all I can to my son," Robert said, throwing his arm in the air in an act of despair. "You talk to him if you wish. I hope he comes back to the Anglican Church but Bobby has a mind of his own and Hannah does, too. I feel rotten about the whole thing. They think they are old enough to make their own decisions about these things." For the first time in his life, Robert was a little exasperated with the Anglican ministry.

"Is there any truth to the rumor that your son has declared himself to be a member of the United Brethren?"

Robert shook his head slowly. "To tell you the truth Reverend, my son isn't fond of any religion. He was deeply troubled when his mother passed away. I think he still reads the Bible on occasion – I know his wife does, at least – but he doesn't feel particularly close to any religion, and that includes the United Brethren and our church as well."

"What do you recommend?"

"Like I said. Talk to him directly, face to face."

On a Sunday evening four days later, Reverend Hobhouse came bouncing along the road leading from his church to Bobby and Hannah's house, located between Deerhurst and Apperley. His little gig was pulled by a handsome white horse. He found Bobby and Hannah entertaining Daniel and Elizabeth for one of their customary Sabbath evening chats. His old eyes glistened at the prospect of confronting Bobby and Hannah about their children not being christened, and at chiding Daniel and Elizabeth for their affiliation with the United Brethren.

Hannah's mouth dropped when she saw the Anglican minister at the door, but politely let him in where Bobby scanned him warily, puzzled that his old parish priest had made a special trip just to come calling at his house.

Elizabeth rolled her eyes at Daniel, correctly guessing the purpose of the reverend's visit. This left her in a nervous slump, fearing that the man who had been the family priest all during her childhood, right up until the time she married, would question her about leaving the faith and becoming a member of the United Brethren. During a brief time of exchanging clumsy but cordial greetings and offering the reverend tea and crumpets, Elizabeth quickly concluded that compared to Thomas Kington, the reverend looked much older than she remembered. His face was wrinkled and heavy, his shoulders were slumped over, and his look withdrawn. He not only looked old, but suddenly Elizabeth remembered his past teachings, which now struck her as old-fashioned and terribly out of step with the way she now believed. They chitchatted about the weather, Bobby's boxing career, the farms they had leased from Squire Hastings, and the price of cattle and commodities. Reverend Hobhouse even complimented Hannah on her handsome, bright-eyed, healthy children. Then he began what seemed to all of them a lecture about religion in general, and the Anglican faith in particular. He related that he had been the parish priest in Deerhurst for seventeen years, that he knew what was right for their children, and that infant baptism was necessary for salvation. He stressed that even though Bobby and Hannah lived in the hamlet of Apperley they were still considered members of the Deerhurst parish, and that Elizabeth ought to continue being an Anglican instead of becoming attached to the heretical, nonconformist, dissenting group called the United Brethren.

The longer the Anglican priest talked, the bolder he became. The boldness startled Hannah, disconcerted Elizabeth and Daniel, and angered Bobby, whose face went tense. He seized a pause in the priest's remarks to bring the visit to a close.

"Reverend, we still respect you and honor both you and your church, but as you know, we made the decision some time ago to attend the United Brethren congregation from now on."

"But..."

Bobby held up a hand, cutting off his old parish priest. He knew he was telling a little white lie, because he had attended only once, though Hannah went with Daniel and Elizabeth more often.

"If our children are to be baptized, they will be baptized by Superintendent Thomas Kington." Truthfully, Bobby did not know what Thomas Kington preached about the baptism of little children and didn't care. He did not want to be drawn into another religious tug-of-war.

A scowl appeared on the reverend's face. "I shall not endure such a thing. We do not recognize such christenings."

"I can't believe that."

The reverend looked up, certain that he had been misunderstood. He repeated the worry that the children needed baptism to enter Heaven, this time telling them that if the children were not baptized, they were consigned to the Kingdom of the Devil. It was a doctrine retained from the Church of Rome – that all unbelievers, Jews and unbaptized children as well, would be excluded from Heaven.

Abruptly rising to his feet, Bobby glared at his childhood Anglican priest and instinctively clenched his fists. He felt like grabbing the man of God by his ministerial collar and manually tossing him out the door, wondering if he could throw him a full twenty feet and get another eight-foot bounce. Who did this abysmal, self-righteous, pious reverend think he was? God? No one could make a threat or insinuate that his own children were going to hell. He didn't believe it. Precious, innocent Joseph and Elizabeth? Impossible!

"Reverend, that's enough. Please leave my home before I ruddy well throw you out."

Hannah's mouth dropped to her lap. "Bobby! How can you say such a thing to your priest?"

Ignoring his wife, Bobby pointed to the door. "See here, sir, we are members of the United Brethren congregation, all four of us. Now leave us alone. Goodbye!" He grabbed Reverend Hobhouse by the arm, jerked him to his feet, and shoved him toward the door.

Equally shocked, his mouth agape, eyes wide open, Reverend Hobhouse walked out the door. He stumbled toward his white horse and gig, kicking the dirt. As he thought of his failure to sway any one of the four young adults in the cottage to his way of thinking and reasoning, he gritted his teeth and cursed at the silence of the warm summer evening. With a quick, deliberate motion he untied his horse, crawled into the gig, and left a cloud of dust as he disappeared into the dusky evening.

"Bobby," Hannah said, her eyes misting, "I think you offended the parish priest."

As he took in the shocked expressions of Hannah, Elizabeth, and Daniel, Bobby began to laugh. "Oh, I assure you I did, and I don't care. He has to get the message so he will leave us alone."

Hannah gave her husband a surprised look, not appreciating the humor. "I daresay he got it tonight."

"He'd better remember that we're members of the United Brethren."

Daniel chuckled and slapped his brother-in-law on the shoulder. "Aren't you the sly one! You mean you are waiting for additional light and truth, like Superintendent Kington talks about?"

At that remark, Bobby's face turned serious. "I don't know specifically what that means. All I know is that I am jolly well tired of all the controversy about religion, doctrines, infant baptism, life after death, funerals, the whole bit."

Hannah had to ask because the timing seemed right. "Then will you go to church at Gadfield Elm every Sunday with me from now on?"

"Hannah, I'm not promising anything," Bobby answered wearily, shaking his head. "But let's agree that we are settled about our religion. As far as our friends and the outside world are concerned, you and I are members of the United Brethren. I don't want to change again. This will be our religion for life. When I'm not so busy with boxing and farming, perhaps I will attend more. Until then, leave me alone on the matter."

Elizabeth posed another question to Bobby, pinching her brother's elbow with her fingers. "What if by some *miracle* we found the church mentioned by the Catholic priest in Switzerland – what was his name?"

"Father Lutis Gratius," Daniel quickly said.

"Probably just some wild dream he had," Bobby said sternly. "Doesn't mean a thing."

Elizabeth followed with another question. "What if the United Brethren leaders come up with what they call 'further light and truth' and they announce a lot of changes in how we practice religion?"

"Look, we can 'what if' this debate to death," Bobby responded. "All I am saying is that I want to settle on one religion and raise my family in that religion. I don't know if it is the ultimate true religion, but it is the best we have found and that's that. I am not going to change religions every year or two."

A month later Bobby won another major fight in Gloucester. Squire Hastings told him he was getting closer to being qualified to fight in London. Hannah didn't know if that was good news or bad. She had married Bobby because she was in love with someone who accepted her for the way she was – a religious girl who read the Bible every day and who had dreams of raising a large family. She had two children but she was alone in whatever religion the United Brethren was. She didn't know that much about it. She couldn't even discuss it with her husband. It was out of bounds. She couldn't go back to being a Methodist and attend church with her family in Apperley. That was out of bounds, too. If she went alone to the United Brethren she felt conspicuous and out of place. Bobby was all she had to hold onto. She needed his strength. She needed to cling to him. But he was becoming distant. She was competing with pugilism or religion. Maybe it was both.

Wilford Woodruff, now a father since Phoebe gave birth to a baby girl on July fourteenth, was on another mission for his church in the Fox Islands, off the coast of Maine. On August ninth, he received a letter from Thomas B. Marsh, president of the Quorum of the Twelve Apostles, dated on the day his daughter was born. The letter contained notice that the Lord, through the Prophet Joseph Smith, had called Woodruff to fill a vacancy in the Quorum of the Twelve. He was directed to report to church headquarters, now located in Missouri, the following spring.

He retired to his room to pray. He thanked God for the calling but acknowledged for the first time he felt inadequate. He had always felt he could handle leadership opportunities, but the apostleship? How could he place himself on the same level as Peter, James, John, and the other original apostles? Or even with the apostles who made up the Council of the Twelve in the modern-day church? He understood well that the word "apostle" meant "one sent forth." It was the same title Jesus gave the twelve whom he chose and ordained to be his closest disciples during his ministry on earth. He knew they had been "sent forth" to represent the Savior after his ascension into Heaven. He knew he must go forth and do the same thing – be a special witness of Jesus Christ in all the world, particularly of his divinity and of his bodily resurrection from the dead.

He was overwhelmed but knew there was no better way to serve the Lord. There was no better way to show appreciation for his blessings than to respond to the call, study the gospel harder than ever, be obedient to every commandment and work as hard as his physical body would let him.

He was anxious to meet with the prophet and begin the rest of his life.

"Mmph," said Bobby.

His end of the conversation with Hannah was nothing but a series of grunts. Perhaps, Hannah thought, he didn't mind being at the Gadfield Elm chapel at the end of January for Thomas Kington's wedding as much as he was putting on. She was just trying to keep the conversation going after Thomas was wed to Hannah Pitt by John Benbow, who had to get a special license to marry from the Justice of the Peace. The indifference to Daniel and Elizabeth's friends that Bobby showed hurt Hannah, much worse than the biting cold outside the chapel. Every time he was introduced to someone, it was "Mmph."

"Did you like the wedding?"

"Mmph."

"Do you like the chapel? "

"Mmph."

"Are you impressed with John Benbow and Thomas Kington?"

"Mmph."

Hannah knew from the outset that Bobby had agreed to attend the wedding only as a favor to his friend, William Pitt, because Hannah was William's sister. "Are you glad that your friend's sister married Superintendent Kington and that they'll live in Dymock?"

"Mmph."

"Do you think William's other sister, Mary, will ever get married, or will her handicap make her an unwanted Old Maid?"

"Mmph."

"Wouldn't it be nice if someday someone had enough faith to heal Mary so she could throw away her crutches?

"Mmph."

32

❧

Summer 1839

BOBBY THOUGHT he was strong enough to withstand any stumbling block in life. He was wrong. When his father died he broke down and cried for the first time since he was a child. He couldn't help it.

During the past two years he had actually become closer to his father than at any other time in his life. Despite their differences over religion, his father had become more and more involved in his dream to become champion. They talked and joked about it. When he was younger he always felt he knew more than his father did. The last two years he realized his father was much wiser than he had given him credit. Even after he was diagnosed with consumption, Bobby refused to believe his father could die. When the glitter disappeared from the old butcher's eyes, he wondered if he was wrong. When his father was confined to his bed, Bobby knew the end was near but still refused to accept it. He wanted to spend his share of time sitting with his sick father, but couldn't do it because he could not stand to see his father suffer. Advanced pulmonary tuberculosis was not pretty to watch. Elizabeth and Dianah did most of it. They would have made perfect nurses.

The day after Robert Harris died, Bobby didn't know anything better to do than go to the training camp and take his frustration out on his sparring partners and the punching bag. William was handling the funeral and burial details. But inside, Bobby was frustrated again. As he slammed his fists into the bag he wondered if he would ever see his father again, and if so, under what circumstances. Death confused him: Where did the spirit go after death? Was the resurrection spiritual or physical, or both? What do dead people do after they die? Was his father with his mother now? Were they reunited with the little children they had lost in infancy? Why couldn't anyone give him answers that made sense?

Bobby didn't expect any answers during the funeral. He didn't look forward to it. He didn't want to see Reverend Hobhouse, let alone listen to his funeral sermon. When the reverend said, "All people need structure and direction from the church," Bobby felt he was singled out.

Robert's will was read at the graveside. William, as expected, inherited the rights to his father's butcher shop and cattle trading business. That's the way it should be; that's the way Bobby wanted it. He was happy for his brother. Each of the surviving children – William, John, Bobby, Dianah, and Elizabeth – received sixty pounds. His father had it all worked out with a probate attorney months before he died. John quickly announced he would use his inheritance to get a start on a new life by managing a pub in Apperley parish. With Bobby now on his own as a tenant farmer, William would have the family business all to himself.

Walking into the butcher shop a few days after the funeral brought painful memories to Bobby. Seeing William behind the counter arranging the cuts of meat wasn't the same as having his father there. Nevertheless, he put his arm around his brother and wished him good luck.

Shaking his head in sadness, William said, "It would be nice if you were my partner here. I'm so busy I can't keep up. I need to be out buying livestock and butchering animals. My wife can't spend much time here with the children needing attention."

Bobby sighed. "If I weren't a pugilist and didn't have my own farm lease, I would sure do it." He lied. He had hated the life of a butcher. He didn't want to go back to it.

"How is Elizabeth taking Father's passing?" William asked.

Bobby related how Elizabeth was still totally devastated. "At first she was optimistic that Father would get well and his sickness never depressed her. But the night he passed away she refused to believe he was gone. I think she believed he would start breathing again any minute. When he didn't she began crying and wouldn't quit. Daniel had quite a time with her. Did you know that she gave her sixty pounds inheritance to Daniel so that it could be used to retire some of the farm debt owed to Squire Hastings? She was totally unselfish about it."

As William finished rearranging the cuts of meat, he began sharpening his knives. "Dianah is not doing too well, either. I guess women have a tougher time than we do." He told Bobby that Dianah accepted the fact that her father was going to die weeks before it happened. She offered to help William with details of the funeral and taking over the business, for which he was grateful. She seemed to be more appreciative of her inheritance than any of the others. She had a large family and her husband was a farm laborer. The sixty pounds was more than what he made in a whole year.

"How's Thomas doing?" Bobby asked.

"I've tried to talk Dianah's husband into working here at the butcher shop, but Thomas says he would feel out of place. He's a farmer at heart. He would make a good farm manager for you someday if you get to lease more land from Squire Hastings."

"I'll try to remember that," Bobby said. "Got to run, old top. Literally. I have to run ten miles a day now in my training. See you later."

William watched his brother go out the door and break into a trot.

Bobby wished his father were alive when Squire Hastings told him the big news a few days after the funeral. The squire had finally arranged a fight between him and a tough, up-and-coming young fighter named Sam "The Man" Gregory from London, where the fight would be held. It was the first big break of his fight career. The squire told him to train especially hard seven days a week. Fighters from the country usually lost the first time in London. He told the squire not to worry; he was going to dedicate the fight to his father.

At an evening dinner at the Browett house, Bobby was able to surprise Hannah, Daniel, and Elizabeth with the news that Squire Hastings was paying their expenses to go to London so they could watch him fight. Bobby said that the squire had told him it was a good investment. Fighters usually did better when they had family and friends ringside to watch them. It would be the first time any of them had ever been to London. It was a long distance away – a hundred and twenty miles.

Hearing the news, Elizabeth got all bubbly again for the first time since her father's death. "Imagine it – Bobby 'The Wild Bull Killer' fighting in London! I can see Bobby's name on the marquis. Can't you, Daniel? What's the name of your opponent? Sam the Man? Sam – now that's a *plain* name. Bobby is better. You'll whip him for sure, Bobby. And just think, we'll be right there to cheer for you. How exciting!"

Daniel was proud of his friend. Years of training and determination were beginning to pay off. He was still disappointed that Bobby did not attend church, but otherwise his life seemed to have purpose and direction. Maybe he really would be champion some day.

Daniel said, "Well, if we travel all the way to London, you better win."

"I'm going to be my best," Bobby promised, clenching his jaw.

Elizabeth was still dancing with excitement. "Father would be so *proud* of you, Bobby. And just think. This trip is going to be an opportunity of a lifetime for all of us. I've *always* wanted to see the London Tower, Westminster Abbey, and the Houses of Parliament. There's so *much* to see and do there. Just think of all the history!"

"What can I do to help?" asked Daniel.

"I might need another sparring partner," Bobby replied in jest.

"Anything but that," Daniel smiled. "I'm not *that* excited about going to London." However, he promised his brother-in-law that he would arrange for the farm workers to take care of everything while they were away, and make certain that work on both farms stayed on schedule.

Hannah stayed subdued. She recognized how important the fight was to Bobby even though she still had her frustrations over the way their private life was going, especially without religion and with him now training every day of the week including Sundays. Nevertheless, she wanted to demonstrate to her husband that she was supportive and would follow him anywhere, even if that meant London. She worried about what to do with the children but her mother and sisters would probably volunteer to take them.

"The squire wants me to shorten my nickname," Bobby said.

"Oh rot! *Why?*" Elizabeth asked in shock. "What to?"

"Just plain 'The Bull.' He says it's better for the fight promotion."

Elizabeth shrugged her shoulders. "Tell him no. I like it the way it is. Better than some of the *other* fighters. What're their names again?"

Bobby had them on the tip of his tongue. "Gentleman" John Jackson. Daniel "The Jew" Mendoza. Tom "The Light Tapper" Spring. And Bobby had more news from London. The man who had held the championship for several years, James "The Deaf 'Un" Burke, had just been defeated by William "Bendigo" Thompson.

"Do you realize what that means?" Bobby asked.

"Not really," Elizabeth said, shaking her head in a silly fashion and raising her eyebrows.

"Well, here's how the squire sees it," Bobby explained. "He thinks Thompson lucked out, catching Burke in the twilight of his career. The squire thinks any one of a number of leading contenders could probably defeat Thompson, including me, even though I'm still almost unknown in the London fight circles. So that's why this fight is so important. If I win, the squire says he can get me a match with one of those top contenders, and then another and another, and that could earn me a chance at the championship in maybe another ten or twelve months."

Patting her brother on the head, Elizabeth continued to be bubbly. "Jolly well. Train hard, brother. You're going to be *champion* yet!"

33

FIGHTING ALL TOO familiar anxieties, Hannah felt terribly out of place in the second-class train car on her way to London. Maybe it was because she was seven months pregnant, and the hard wooden bench was uncomfortable. Maybe it was because butchers and carpenters really should be standing in the open cars of third class instead of sitting here in second class. Or maybe she was afraid that their luggage, strapped to the roof of their coach, might fall off. Hannah knew she should be thankful for the new railroad linking Gloucester to London, and that the squire had paid the seven shillings per ticket price for them. A few years ago her father had paid one pound thirteen shillings just to ride a stagecoach to London. She was surprised at the amount of traffic on the busy turnpike near the railroad tracks, and how much faster the train moved than the collection of wagons, carriages, phaetons, cabriolets, barouches, and simple carts. Hannah wondered how long it would be until the cattle and sheep that she saw on the road, being herded to the market in London, would be carted on the railroad.

Hannah was glad that Squire Hastings was riding in first class with the other aristocrats, sitting on their soft, black leather cushions. It would have been just dreadful if he had bought them first class tickets, especially in her condition. She felt uneasy around him. He was too rich, too powerful. The squire would fit right in up there in first class with his big jowls and big girth.

Elizabeth chattered nonstop during the trip, over-emphasizing her words, ignoring the fact that the carriage car, only four feet wide, was packed. Two rows of benches sat opposite each other filled with a collection of men, women, and children. She was glad none of her group had been split up. She heard that sometimes they put men in one carriage and women and children in another.

"Do you think I brought *enough clothes*, Daniel? Did you know there are *two million* people in London? Can you believe we will get to see the financial district? I never *dreamed* I would stand by the River Thames and gaze at the Tower of London and St. Paul's Cathedral. Did you know the *Great Fire* destroyed thirteen thousand homes back in 1666, or that the fire started in a place named Pudding Lane? Do you think we will get to see Queen Victoria?"

Elizabeth wanted to ask the occupation of every other passenger in their carriage car. She guessed one man to be a bookmaker, another to be a packman or traveling peddler, and a third to be an upper servant wearing his master's cast-off clothing – judging from the quality of his waistcoat. She was amused every time the train made a stop at a station as servants riding in second and third class rushed up to the first class car to see if their employers wanted food to be fetched from a station restaurant.

Still talking incessantly as they arrived at Paddington Station in London, and as they took a large-wheeled hansom cab to their hotel, Elizabeth gazed in all directions, taking in everything she saw with amazement. "Look at the streets! They're paved with chips of granite. But where is all the *dust* coming from? It must be from all these horses. Every one of them have iron feet, they're grinding up the granite. And *look* at all the horse droppings! Oh, it *smells* just terrible here. You can hardly see the streets in some places. Why don't they clean this up? I know – it would take ten cartloads every mile every day. Who would pay for it?"

Elizabeth watched in amusement as men tipped boy and girl streetsweepers so that their lady companions could walk across the streets in relative comfort, but the women still had to raise their skirts. When she crossed the street with Hannah, Bobby and Daniel gave a tip to a pitiful little girl named Maggie. Elizabeth stopped to talk to her, curious to know why the girl, at only twelve years of age, was working instead of attending school. She learned that the girl's mother had been dead for two years, that her father was very poor. The girl pointed to a younger brother and sister, ages four and three, that she was tending while sweeping streets, working from nine in the morning until four in the afternoon. Elizabeth made Daniel tip the anemic-looking girl another sixpence.

Street musicians seemed to be everywhere: Fiddles, tin whistles, bag-pipes, accordions, triangles. Men from India with their tom-tom drums. A German band, with uninvited dogs in a grand chorus, noses in the air, wailing. A Savoyard hurdy-gurdy player, sitting as a model for artists. Blowhard bassoonists and trumpet players. Organ men and their monkeys. A petticoat quartet of young girls. Minstrels with blackened faces. A campanologist playing *Home Sweet Home* on a string of ten bells. The pleasing sound of *Ye Banks and Braes* coming from two rows of glass tumblers on a table. A ballad singer claiming to be the leading tenor for the London Opera Company.

Streetpatterers, some moving, some stationary, cried headlines for the newspapers they sold, or words of songs for the music they were selling: *The Pope He Leads A Happy life, Buffalo Gals, Jim Along Josey, Drink To Me Only, Kate Kearney, Chuckaroo-choo choo-choo-choot-la, Chockala-roony-ninkaping-nang, Pagadaway-dusty-kanty-key, The Standard Bearer, Widow Mackrel, Oh!*

That Kiss, The old English Gentleman.

Pickpockets, prostitutes, drunks, beggars, and vagabonds of every description were seen.

As evening approached, the city took on a fairground appearance with thousands of gaslights illuminating the city, even the bridges over the River Thames. Dram shops with great plate-glass windows were engraved with messages such as, "Gin at Threepence," or "Generous Wines." Hundreds of other shops lined the streets: pawnbrokers, haberdashers, hairdressers, glove makers, basket makers, bonnet makers, hatters, opticians, perfumeries, pipe makers, quill cutters, whip makers, yeast merchants, bakers. Endless shops.

The weather lapsed into rain. Soon umbrella humps crowded the sidewalk. The stormy weather brought seagulls from the sea, and they covered the lawns. Hundreds of white bodies all facing the same direction, waiting out the damp wind. The rain brought fresh welcome scents.

Just about everyone in London appeared to be somewhat anemic to Elizabeth. She attributed it to the foul air, the poverty of the people, and the lack of meat in their diets. When she found out how high the infant mortality rate was in London, she sank in depression for a bit. Her eyes locked on the crowded city streets, where homes of rich and poor were thrown together in close proximity. There were horribly overcrowded slums. Raw sewage flowed in gutters, emptying into the River Thames. The stench was terrible.

Told that thousands of milk cows were kept penned inside large barns throughout the city, Hannah was surprised. How could men similar to her father manage dairy farms in a congested city such as London? There were people everywhere! How could dairymen possibly provide enough milk, cream, and cheese for the thousands and thousands of people? To her, the entire city held a strange aura of foreboding.

The rain quit as suddenly as it came and in minutes Welch and Irish milkmaids bellowed in their native brogues, "Fresh milk for sale! Buy your cream, buy your cheeses!"

Others yelled, "New laid eggs ten for a groat, crack 'em and try 'em!"

Daniel tried counting the number of shops and booths. There was more variety than at the Gloucestershire fair – greengrocers, bakers, pastry cooks, cobblers, and butchers. Barrels were filled with everything imaginable, despite a depression that was beginning to grip England. He could sell millions of barrels here. Costermongers with barrows or carts pulled by donkeys were selling fish, fruits, and vegetables up and down every street.

"Here I am with my rabbits hanging on my pole," said one coster with gutted rabbits, their feet lashed together, draped on long poles. "Who will buy my rabbits?"

Still other vendors offered fresh tea, hot pies – beef, steak and kidney, pork, eel, or fruit and pudding – spicy gingerbread or Dutch biscuits, oysters, and roasted chestnuts. On the street corners knots of idle, unemployed men argued with loud voices and sweeping gestures. Children darted about playing their street games, boys in caps and long trousers and girls in simple but gaily colored frocks, their mothers gossiping as they watched them. Flower girls collected leftovers at restaurants, which were taken to poor houses to feed the people there. Other young girls sold matches and watercress. Boys earned small tips by holding horses, fetching cabs, and carrying parcels. On one corner a political rally was being held, with candidates trying to be heard over the shouting matches. At one point the unruly crowd threw eggs and rotten potatoes at the speaker.

Bobby watched in amazement as herds of sheep and cattle were pushed through the streets to urban slaughterhouses. Being a butcher here would be no fun at all. Just a man with a bloody leather apron and a sharp knife. No wonder people were escaping to America. On the other hand, he had never seen so many shops and customers. Butcher shops were selling meat faster than they could bring it in. Carriages and carts streamed both ways. People carried packages into and out of the stores, some stopping to look into the windows. The shops were stocked with heads, trotters, and innards of bullocks, calves, sheep, and pigs. One was called the "Piggy Wiggy Pork Shop."

The sights along a quarter-mile length of Whitechapel astonished Bobby. Six hundred slaughtered oxen, and seven hundred slaughtered sheep, hanging to cure. Children of butchers, ankle deep in blood and offal, mingled with troops of hogs, A herd of black cattle meandered up the street, tended by dirty-faced herders.

"If I lose my fight, I suppose Squire Hastings will banish me to here," he said, joking.

Pulling Elizabeth out of the way of an errant steer, Daniel said, "He has a lot of money bet on you, so don't even think about losing."

Elizabeth made an awful face. "Bobby, I just had this *terrible* thought. What if you did lose? Would Squire Hastings be so upset that he would *cancel* our farm leases?"

"I don't think so," Daniel said as he bought four muffins from a vendor. "Do you, Bobby? Lease contracts are pretty specific and landowners don't like to change tenants. They are all long term."

"But he took a *big* chance on us," Elizabeth reminded them. "All of us know that he gave us leases over others that would have been given the land if the squire had not wanted Bobby's fight contract. And they are *always* worded in favor of the owner."

"I get the message," Bobby said at length. "Either I win or we are all out on our ears." He harbored fantasies of the way the fight would end: five-round knockout, eight-round knockout, fourteen-round knockout.

"I was just joking," Elizabeth said.

But no one was laughing. They knew Squire Hastings was already making heavy bets in favor of his young fighter from Gloucestershire. He would be an angry man if Bobby lost. There may be another beheading in England.

34

A PAINED QUIETNESS came over Hannah the next day when she saw Bobby's opponent for the first time at the arena. She had never seen a man so ugly and grotesque. His body had been deformed by infantile encephalitis. Sam "The Man" Gregory's head was big and bulbous at the top, and his face pinched and narrow. His brown eyes were sunken deep within their sockets, and his cheeks were sallow. His physique, however, was impressive. Muscles bulged everywhere. He moved like a thoroughbred.

A newspaper account said that Gregory was born in the "house of a sinner," in a section of London "where thieves, rogues and ne'er-do-wells gathered to eke out their grimy, violent and precarious existences, even though the penalty for thieving out something as invaluable as a pocket handkerchief could cost a young man his life." The newspaper article said that Gregory, because of his penchant for violence, his hardened body and his cult celebrity status, was heavily favored to win his eighth fight in a row against an unknown fighter from Gloucestershire. The newspaper did not even mention Bobby's name.

From that moment on Hannah began to pray for Bobby as though she feared for his life. Her mouth compressed to a straight line every time she talked, whether it was in prayer or in response to Elizabeth or Daniel's questions. Everyone around her in London took on a ghoulish form, and her mood darkened with each passing hour. When Gregory came into the ring a crowd of more than two thousand screaming, chanting fans erupted when he took off his robe and displayed scarlet ribbons fluttering at his knees. The chanting further distressed Hannah. A thick haze of tobacco smoke gave the arena an eerie atmosphere. The entire arena smelled like a men's locker room. Pugilist aficionados revered the place, but not her. Breathing in short spurts, her bulging stomach stressing her, Hannah pushed through the crowd to Bobby's corner, trying to get his attention.

"Bobby! We've made a mistake. Let's go home – please!" Hannah had stepped into another world, one that she intensely hated.

Bobby shook his head in disgust. "Don't worry. I know what I'm doing."

He said the words without looking at his wife. His eyes were locked on Gregory, who was dancing in the corner with his two seconds, men who had an equally evil appearance.

When the bell rang Gregory attacked viciously, drawing first blood when he cut Bobby on the left side of the head with a series of right crosses. When Bobby went down, his ear was bleeding and, to Hannah, looked mutilated. She began to cry. Gregory leaped at Bobby again when he was brought to scratch, hitting him with an uppercut that split Bobby's lip, and left a cut as clean as a razor on the left side of his nose. He went down again.

"Get up, Bobby!" Elizabeth screamed. "He's not so *tough*! Show him who's the better man!"

Feeling pain around his ear, nose and lip, Bobby wiped at the blood and stared at the smears on his hands as he came to scratch again. He swallowed, trying to rid his mouth of a dry, sour taste, and he knew he had to clear his head. As Gregory lunged toward him, he ducked and grabbed Gregory by the waist in a bear hug, squeezing with all his might as Gregory beat him on the back of the head, but they eventually tumbled to the ground. Gregory cursed at him as they regained their feet, waited for the referee to signal the start of another round, and he lunged again. Bobby danced away this time, his head clearing.

He found that he was slightly quicker than Gregory, so he began to jab. Jab, jab, jab. Bobby's left hand flickered into his opponent's face. But Gregory pushed him into a corner and caught Bobby with another uppercut, this one to the midsection, causing Bobby to go down again, surging for breath. When he was brought to scratch he began to dance away again and as Gregory attacked, this time Bobby countered with all the strength he could muster, catching Gregory with a vicious right to the throat. The crowd settled into a stunned hush as Gregory went down, gasping and holding his throat. For a few seconds Bobby thought his opponent looked incapable of making it back to scratch, and when he did it was Gregory who began to retreat and finally administer a bear hug.

The fight then settled into a slower pace, each man trying to hit without getting hit, feigning, dodging, and assessing one another's strengths and weaknesses. A full ten minutes went by without either man going down but Bobby could tell Gregory was tiring. Bobby went on the offensive again, jabbing, throwing left and right crosses and uppercuts. One blow caught Gregory on the jaw and he went down, stunned, but rose quickly. Bobby then caught him with a left hook to the eye, drawing blood, which quickly flowed into Gregory's right eye, partially blinding him. From then on, Bobby took advantage, landing blows to Gregory's face and body. Gregory sank to the floor and lay in a pool of his own blood, unable to rise.

When Bobby was declared the winner, less than fifty persons cheered for him.

35

HE FELT TIRED, SORE, beat up, and exhausted. Black and blue bruises were showing on his head, arms, and torso. He had stitches in his nose. Bobby's first inclination was to skip the tour of London. It was his sister, the lioness of England, the woman who does as she pleases and you just get out of her way, who talked him into going. Her rationale was correct. It was their first time in their entire lives that they had been to London. It was an opportunity not to be missed. Limping slightly, Bobby joined them at ten the next morning, regretting that he had given in, but there nonetheless.

Elizabeth had studied about London so much she thought she could qualify as the tour guide. Nevertheless, she was grateful that Squire Hastings had provided not only a guide, but also a coach and driver to take them to see the main "financial" and historic district and the Tower of London. She'd heard that the squire won more than two hundred pounds in bets on her brother's fight. *Two hundred pounds!* It didn't break him to fork over a few pounds for a deluxe tour of the city before they returned home. She was glad he was not their guide, however. He was too boisterous, drank too much, and had bad breath.

"Doesn't it just give you *goose bumps* to be standing in the political heart of Great Britain?" Elizabeth asked the others as they exited their coach and began a circular walk around royal Westminster and aristocratic St. James, beginning on Bridge Street at Westminster station. She didn't care if Bobby, Daniel, and Hannah regarded her as overly passionate about the historical part of London or not. She had a great interest in it, regardless of the fact that she was a woman. She listened intently as the guide told them about Westminster Hall, that nowhere in the world was there a building that had so continuously been involved in the affairs of a great nation. And their nation certainly was the greatest on earth. Elizabeth learned that it was built more than seven hundred years earlier, that it measured two hundred and forty feet long and almost seventy feet wide, that it could hold six thousand persons standing or nearly two thousand five hundred seated. The guide said that the most magnificent event ever to take place in the hall was the coronation banquet of King George IV in 1821. Elizabeth was just a little girl then but she could remember hearing about it.

As they stood inside the hall, which was under renovation, the guide said the building shook to its foundation during the King George banquet when the raucous crowd toasted the king three times followed by nine rounds of cheers. Another celebration had been held here in 1501 to commemorate the arrival of Katherine of Aragon to marry Prince Arthur. The first king to have his coronation banquet in the hall had been Richard I in 1189. Anne Boleyn had hers here in 1533. The guide pointed to a cloister where King Henry VIII had watched the banquet from a closet. His daughter, Queen Elizabeth I, had her coronation banquet in the hall in 1559, Charles II in 1661, King James II in 1685, King George III in 1681. The list went on and on.

Elizabeth imagined what it would be like to be the queen and have a royal banquet in the hall: Richly decorated foods. Forty or more dishes of hot meats. Gold and jeweled salts. The sweet music of minstrels. Fine white napery. Lavish coronation robes with silken cloths of gold. A marble throne. Three thousand burning candles. Circus acts. What splendor!

Peeking inside the House of Lords at the invitation of their guide, Bobby formed a frown on his hurting face. All Bobby could think about when the guide explained the makeup of the House of Lords was the over-representation of the Anglican Church. First, there were the Lords Spiritual: the archbishops of Canterbury and York; the bishops of London, Durham, and Winchester; and all the senior diocesan bishops of the Church of England. No wonder the Anglicans had so much power in his country. No wonder his father-in-law went to his grave hating Anglicans. Who represented the Methodists? Who represented the United Brethren? It wasn't fair that only members of the Anglican Church were eligible for national or municipal office, or for admittance to most universities.

Second were the Lords Temporal. He heard the words "hereditary peers and life peers." He had a hard time understanding the complicated system.

Bobby's mood improved at the House of Commons. At least it sounded better. But the speaker, wearing his ceremonial robe and an ill-fitting wig, did not look like a commoner to Bobby. Let the speaker come out to Deerhurst and butcher a beef with him. He would show him what a workingman's life was really like. He wished his dog Duke were still alive and with him. He would set him on the speaker, letting him tear a bite out of the ceremonial robe.

Bobby was not comfortable in the gigantic Westminster Abbey either. In size, it reminded him of the Gloucester Cathedral back home.

"Is this a church or a graveyard?" Daniel whispered to him, learning that more than three thousand people were enshrined or entombed here.

"I don't know and I don't care," Bobby said, shuddering. The colossal interior burgeoned with the remains of musicians, poets, scientists, statesmen, and of course, kings and queens. Their tombs were packed into every last niche and alcove. Dozens of visitors were on their knees with charcoal grave-rubbing pencils. He read some of the names: Sir Isaac Newton, Oliver Cromwell, Mary Queen of Scots, William Shakespeare, Geoffrey Chaucer.

"Well I care," Elizabeth said as they approached the canopied sarcophagus of Queen Elizabeth I, inhabiting its own private, apsidal chapel.

Bobby scoffed at his sister's reverence. He felt like a tiny ant whether he stood in the quire, the nave, the cloisters, the north or south transepts, the Henry VII Chapel, or the Chapel of St. Edward the Confessor. So what if Queen Victoria was coronated here just last year? So what if "every sovereign of England has been crowned in that chair" except Edward V, Edward VIII and Mary I? In Bobby's pride-looking-upward opinion, all kings and queens made life comfortable for themselves and their "Lords," but worse for the working class. After he became champion and got to meet Queen Victoria, he would tell her just that.

Even though Hannah had been raised a Methodist she was in awe of the abbey. She listened to every story, and every explanation the guide gave. "This is the tomb of Elizabeth I who ruled England from 1558 to 1603. She was the daughter of Henry VIII and Anne Boleyn. Henry declared her illegitimate when he had her mother executed, but Henry later restored her to the line of succession in his will. Despite having many suitors she never married and hence left no heir. Her navy defeated Spain and the 'Virgin Queen' became very popular. Historians recognize her long reign as one of the most brilliant in English history. It was a time of great literary achievement, with writers such as Edmund Spenser and William Shakespeare producing enduringly famous works. Universal mourning marked her death."

Hannah listened just as intently to the story of Mary I, also entombed in the King Henry VIII Chapel. And to the stories of King Edward III in the South Ambulatory; Mary, Queen of Scots in the south aisle of the chapel; Henry V and Henry III, Richard II, and many others in the Chapel of St. Edward the Confessor. The abbey had so much history it made her head spin.

After the abbey they saw No. 10 Downing Street, home of every Prime Minister since 1732. Next came Buckingham Palace. Nearby was the home of Queen Victoria. Hannah was disappointed they did not get to see the popular queen.

"Why didn't the squire arrange for us to see the Queen?" Hannah asked Bobby, sidestepping a street ballad singer.

"Don't be silly," he answered. "He's just a squire, not a duke or a marquess or something like that. He has his limits, you know."

Elizabeth threw back her head and laughed. "Oh, I don't know, Bobby. *Ask and ye shall receive.* You didn't even ask. If you had *thought*, maybe the squire could have gotten us seats to the wedding last February."

"Dream on, silly sister."

"Well, I happen to *know* all about it, nevertheless," Elizabeth said, tossing her head again. With tinges of wonder she described the Queen's wedding dress in detail, the rich white satin, trimmed with orange blossoms with a matching wreath of the flowers on her head. The Queen had been sparingly decorated with diamonds, and Prince Albert had been dressed in the uniform of a British field marshal, decorated with the collar and star of the Order of the Garter.

"They were married at the royal chapel of St. James and the wedding breakfast was at Buckingham Palace," Elizabeth added. "We *should* have been there, Hannah. My brother, your husband, let us down."

"It's your fault, Bobby," Hannah said, pointing a finger.

"I have one tidbit of gossip, too," Elizabeth added with a trace of her high-strung eagerness.

"What?" Hannah asked, peering at roasted chestnut and ice cream vendors.

"The queen is *expecting* already. I hear the baby is due in late November."

"Oh, my," said Hannah with a saucy grin. "What will the baby be like? The king and queen are first cousins."

She giggled and so did Elizabeth.

Daniel's favorite part of the tour came after a lengthy and rattling Dover coach ride to the eastern part of London – with the girls still talking about Queen Victoria – to the Tower of London, the Norman castle of conquest and home of kings dating back to William the Conqueror in 1066.

"We have evidence to believe the tower was built by order of Julius Caesar," the guide said, pointing across a staggeringly expansive plaza. The tower rose like a citadel against the eastern London sky.

The guide spoke in rapid-fire English. Successive kings through the years had enlarged it until it had become the showplace of the nation in the eighteenth and nineteenth centuries. James I had been the last king to live here in 1604, as the tower structures became dilapidated. In 1639 much of it had been converted into a military store and gradually into ordnance storage.

The price of one shilling per head was well worth it, Daniel thought, except for the fact that the moat's filthy water needed to be drained. But he could tell what medieval life had been like in England in periods like the thirteenth century.

When Daniel saw the crown jewels he appreciated the historical detail and beauty but he thought how smug, self-righteous, and proud the English monarchs must have been through the ages. Each crown was worth thousands of pounds. The Savior had taught not to lay up treasures of the world.

Daniel was depressed when he saw gruesome reminders of England's terrible past: Axes and blocks used to behead the guilty and not guilty. Weapons ranging from swords to guns, and armor for both horses and men. King

234 Light and Truth

Henry VIII must have been a large man. His armor would fit a three-hundred-pound frame. The guide said Henry had it made for a May Day jousting tournament in 1540.

Daniel imagined what it would be like to be suited up in any of the battle armor he saw, whether it was the armor for King Charles I, Prince James II or the Earl of Worcester. It looked bulky but safe. He thought it would be great if he had an invisible armor that would protect him from the temptations of Satan. In fact, it would be great if everyone had that protection. He hated Satan. He thought of a scripture in Ephesians: *Put on the whole armor of God.*

As Daniel, Elizabeth, Bobby, and Hannah rode in the train back to Gloucester, Daniel wondered how long it would be until they returned to London. With luck, Squire Hastings would pay their fare when Bobby fought there again.

CHAPTER NOTES

Wilford Woodruff visited the Tower of London December 1840 and gave a lengthy account in his journal. He described the tower itself, the Horse Armoury, Queen Elizabeth's Armoury, the Train of Artillery, and contents of the Crown Jewel Room in detail. The author personally visited the Tower of London in 2001.

36

OVER A BREAKFAST of dark orange cheese, bread, cold pork, and fresh apples with the children, Bobby had asked Hannah how she enjoyed her trip to London. He sought to be complimented that he had not only won his fight, but through his connections with Squire Hastings, that she had been graced with a free tour of the city.

"I really didn't like London."

Hannah's words shook Bobby. "That so? I thought it was a perfect trip."

"Oh, I'm glad you won your fight," she said, biting into a shiny red apple. "And I liked the tour. It was very educational."

Still vexed over her first words, Bobby asked, "Then what do you mean?"

"I didn't like London, the city," she said with a gravelly growl. "In fact, I hated it."

Bobby contemplated her words carefully. Ever since their marriage he had slowly acknowledged their differences and knew that when he pushed her too far with unkind or domineering acts, she had a tendency to erupt.

However, he had his limits, too. Inside, he was frustrated that she seemed so detached and passive about his goal to become a great fighter. He was sensing that this was one of those moments. Or perhaps her prattling was due to the fact that she was close to delivering their third child and the trip had worn her out.

"Hannah, I can't believe you'd say something like that," Bobby said, cursing beneath his breath.

"I'm just speaking the truth. I was uncomfortable the whole time." She got up from the table and let Joseph and Lizzy outside to play.

"Why?"

Hannah sat opposite Bobby and avoided eye-to-eye contact with him. She took a deep breath, searching for a way to describe the trip. "There was a dark feeling. It was there at the fights. It was in the face of your opponent. I don't think I've ever been around a more evil man. Remember what we read in the newspaper about him? Remember the evil presence he brought to the ring? I kept looking for his cloven hooves, his horns, and his pitchfork. He was the devil incarnate. And you'll have to admit there were folks of a baser sort there, drinking, smoking, and betting. I didn't like those people, Bobby. And I didn't like some of the other things I saw there, either, like the cock fighting, the badger baiting, and the bull baiting. Letting dogs chew on animals that are tied up is not my idea of fairness. I hate the fact that society has always found a way to accommodate its brutishness."

"Some of those people you are talking about are my friends, Hannah," Bobby said, clearly aggravated at her starkness

Hannah glowered at her husband.

"It's not just them, Bobby. I had the same feelings just walking around, too. I think there is a lot of evil in London. I could feel it." Hannah sat back, knowing that it was hard for a man to understand fully the feelings women sometimes have.

"Hannah, don't ever talk this way around Squire Hastings."

"I don't like him either."

Boiling over now, Bobby's face turned red.

"You don't like him after he has given us land to lease, setting us up for life? And given me a fight contract? And the opportunity to make big money fighting leading contenders? And perhaps the opportunity to fight for the championship? Hannah – you're crazy! Didn't I hear the evil man you just described?"

He paused, waiting for a reaction.

Hannah stared at the floor. "Yes, you did."

Bobby turned up both hands in frustration. "How do you even dare compare him with me? Remember what the squire said when he offered to take me in, that he needs fighters like me to give pugilism a better image? Sure, Sam Gregory is one of those fighters that has given my sport a bad name, but I beat him. It's like I followed the script. Everything is going just like the squire said it would! Didn't you read the newspapers after the fight? They didn't come right out and say it, but they came close to saying it was a triumph of good over evil."

Bitten by her husband's words, Hannah finally looked at Bobby again.

"I don't think you had better get it into your head that you're going to be the sole savior of pugilism, Bobby. I don't think the Savior himself could save it. If He were to walk into that arena in London the Savior would probably be crucified all over again. That's the kind of people I saw there. I just don't like it, and I don't want to be around it."

Her defiant, self-righteous attitude made him laugh. "Ha! Do you just want me to drop it? Tell the squire thanks but no thanks? Go back to cutting the throats of steers and pigs? Give up our farm and our cottage?"

As Hannah looked away, Bobby flew into a frenzy, recounting the reasons why they were better off, how they were going to achieve a lifestyle that was better than the working class, better than the commoners, full of notoriety and plenty of money. They had to respect and like the squire. Bobby and his athletic ability were the tickets to the good life.

Knowing that she was not going to win the argument, having stated her opinion, Hannah withdrew into total silence, trying to stomach assertions that she was going to ruin everything. But no matter what he said, or how he said it, she knew her feelings would not change. Pugilism was evil, designed by the Devil to satisfy man's Neanderthal blood lust. The people around it were evil. Given time, it would make her husband evil, also. She would much rather be the wife of a lowly butcher than the wife of a famous, wealthy fighter. She would rather live in Deerhurst or Apperley than in the big, Evil City of London. She wanted to raise her children in the quiet peace of the country, bring them up as God-fearing people, embracing the teachings of the Bible. She wanted to be regarded as a Christian, as an active member of a church, and she really didn't care if it were Anglican, Methodist, Catholic, Quaker, or United Brethren. Any religion she knew of was better than no religion at all.

For another half-hour Bobby chided her for her feelings. Then he left. He said he had a busy day in front of him, running the farm and working in four hours of training. It hurt her when he threatened to stay at his brother William's house for the night. But their discussion hadn't changed her mind about London and about the squire.

37

THE SUMMER of 1839 was a time of struggle and sickness among members of the Church of Jesus Christ of Latter-day Saints in their new settlement along the Mississippi River in Commerce, Illinois. By the time Elder Woodruff had reported to Far West, Missouri, on April twenty-fifth, what once had been a thriving, growing community was now practically a ghost town. Persecution had driven the saints out of the Missouri settlements. He was directed to follow the trail of the Saints that led to the upper Mississippi River. On May eighteenth, Wilford culminated his journey to reunite with the main body of the church, arriving in Commerce, Illinois-soon to be renamed Nauvoo.

By now Elder Woodruff knew that his calling to the Quorum of the Twelve also included a call to serve a mission to England. Every available member of the Twelve was to serve and they were instructed to leave as soon as they could settle their families in Nauvoo. By July and August, however, nearly everyone in the settlement was suffering from malaria, including

Wilford. Despite the sickness, and a feeling that the Adversary was trying to keep him from serving a mission to England, Wilford departed with his companion, Elder John Taylor, and wrote in his journal a few days later:

Early in the morning on the 8th of August, I arose from by bed of sickness, laid my hands upon the head of my sick wife, Phoebe, and blessed her. I then departed from the embrace of my companion, and left her almost without food or the necessities of life. She suffered my departure with the fortitude that becomes a saint, realizing the responsibilities of her companion.

Malaria would not stay him. Nothing would prevent him from fulfilling his calling to serve a mission in England as a member of the Quorum of Twelve Apostles. The Lord needed him. When he got to England he would make certain he was successful. He was being sent there for a purpose and neither sickness, hundreds of miles separating Nauvoo from his port of departure in New York, nor the wide expanse of the Atlantic Ocean could stop him. With every ounce of strength he could muster he would somehow get to England and do what the Lord would bid him to do.

38

EXITING THE Gadfield Elm chapel on a cool and partly cloudy Sabbath day in October, Hannah had a question for her sister Nancy and James Pulham. "Did you have a chance to talk to Superintendent Kington about performing your marriage?"

It had rained hard during the sacrament service, and Kington had been forced to compete with the sound of the large raindrops as they pummeled the roof. Now, however, the dark clouds were moving east. As she walked over the moist withered leaves that were strewn around the churchyard, her unfolded umbrella in hand, Hannah was hopeful that the rain would not return on their carriage ride home.

Nancy Eagles shrugged her shoulders in guilt as they approached John Davis, who was unhitching their horse. "No, he was too busy talking with other people."

Hannah tugged on Nancy and James. "Then let's go back inside. You need to begin making arrangements now if you are to be married next month."

Nancy and James had been engaged for five months. Because Hannah's mother was alone now, there had been no opposition to the engagement, even though she had already said that she would like Reverend Joseph Crooks to perform the marriage. Both Nancy and Hannah had told their mother they had their own religion now and that the wedding ought to be conducted by their minister, not hers. Hannah desperately missed her father but knew if he were still alive he would not let Nancy have anything less than a Methodist wedding.

Watching his cooper shop partner walk back into the chapel with Nancy, John Davis experienced feelings of jealousy again. Everyone his age was getting married except him. He knew all about parental opposition when it came to religion. In his opinion, his own mother was far worse than Nancy and Hannah's parents. Mrs. Davis had thrown a literal fit when he began attending the United Brethren. She was the most radical Anglican he had ever known. Thinking about his mother depressed him. Disconsolate, he retied the horse to the hitching post. All during the meeting he had wondered who the pretty girl was who had been sitting with William Jenkins and Mary Rowberry. He had watched her come out of the chapel and now she was standing quietly while William and Mary were visiting other church members. He would like to meet the new girl but feelings of shyness prevented him from taking the first step. Instead, he took a few steps in the opposite direction to visit with Edward Phillips.

Suddenly, Mary Rowberry was pointing towards him. Next she was walking in his direction, dragging William and the new girl. John's heart jumped.

Still walking towards him, Mary spoke. "I want you to meet Mary Ann Weston."

John looked at Edward, and then looked to the ground. He didn't know if Mary Rowberry were talking to him or Edward.

Coming closer, making certain John heard her, Mary repeated her words. "Mr. Davis, this is Miss Mary Ann Weston. She is now living near us, taking up her apprenticeship as a dressmaker." Mary Ann had fair skin, a slender figure, flashing blue eyes, and brown hair set in curls.

Bowing politely and tipping his cap, John said, "Pleased to know you Miss Weston." He blushed and looked to the ground. He wondered how his light brown hair looked without his cap. He wondered if he had any mud on his trousers. He worried about everything. That was his nature. But Daniel had told him that was one of the traits he liked about him. He worried about the furniture and cooper shop so much he was very hard-working and reliable.

"Mr. Browett wanted me to introduce her to you," Mary added. "Mary Ann, this is the young man we have been telling you about, Mr. Browett's partner in the cooper shop. Mr. Davis, Mr. Browett suggests that you call on Miss Mary Ann at your pleasure."

John was speechless. He blinked while he groped for words.

William added, "I verify that, Mr. Davis. Also, Miss Weston's father told us explicitly that if their daughter were to court it would be fine with him and his wife. She has been raised in Gloucester and her father is a prosperous realtor there. We'll excuse ourselves so you can talk together."

As they strode away, William said to Edward, "I just saw Hannah and Nancy with James Pulham but I didn't see Bobby. Is he not here?"

Edward shook his head in disappointment. "I asked Bobby to come but he said no again."

"Please tell him hello for us and tell him that we miss him." William said.

"That goes for me, too," Mary added. "He has such a nice wife – I really like Hannah. It's too bad she has to come to church without him every Sunday." Mary stole a glance at John and Mary Ann, and smiled at their discomfort.

Not knowing what to say, John was relieved that Mary Ann broke the ice with a question. "Do you work with Mr. Browett?" she asked. She knew he did, but it was a good way to start a conversation.

John finally looked at her and nodded. "Yes, Miss Mary Ann, I do."

"Do you like working with him?"

"Yes, I sure do."

"How long have you been a United Brethren member?"

Hiding his emotions, John said, "Ever since Mr. Browett started attending – several months."

"Mr. Browett said it would be okay to ask me a question."

John's face changed. "He did?"

"Don't you remember what Miss Rowberry and Mr. Jenkins told you?"

"No..."

"About that it is okay to..."

"Court you?"

"Yes!"

PART THREE

The

Mormons

39

1840

OTHER THAN A SMALL handful of people, the fifteen million citizens of England had no idea that two apostles of the Lord and Savior Jesus Christ were aboard the packet ship *Oxford* as she docked in Liverpool on this cold eleventh day of January. Standing topside with dozens of other passengers was the American, Wilford Woodruff, accompanied by two men who were born in England: John Taylor, the other apostle, and Theodore Turley.

Apostle or not, Wilford was grateful to end the twenty-four-day gruesome trip on the Black Ball Line ship that had begun with seasickness, vomiting, and putrid smells, and ended with a severe gale that pitched trunks, boxes, and barrels around the steerage compartment. He recalled how excited he had been two days ago to finally catch a glimpse of the Irish coast, but that was followed by a heavy gale that had threatened to blow them into either Ireland or the Welsh coast.

As they had made their way up the River Mersey toward Liverpool, towed by a steamship, Wilford had been impressed that nearly everyone finally cleaned up, dressed up, shaved, and prepared to disembark. He was so anxious to get off the ship that the biting sea breezes from the southwest did not daunt him in the least. He had reached England.

A member of the ship's crew yelled at the top of his lungs: "When you disembark, watch yourself and your personal belongings at all times. Do not trust anyone. The people around the dock at Liverpool are not typical of the English — watch out for them. Poverty is so rampant that even children will steal from you. Gangs of slum children are highly organized."

Wilford shivered twice, once at the warning and once at the cold. He tightened his black beaver hat, and pulled his red scarf firmly around his neck. He talked in the direction of his traveling companions. "Whatever we are subjected to on the dock can't be much worse than what we've experienced on this dreadful vessel. I wouldn't board it again if they paid me the fifteen dollars steerage."

John and Theodore both laughed, knowing that Wilford wasn't serious. They knew Wilford would do it again — and do anything — if the Lord asked him to do it. However, the ship had taken in more passengers than it could comfortably accommodate, a mixture of American, English, Scottish, Irish, Welsh, and Dutch people. The three missionaries had shared the steerage compartment with sixty-one other passengers in quarters that were tight and nauseating. The weather topside had always been much too cold for comfort. Freezing salt-water spray had nearly always been in their faces. Staying below had been worse. Their quarters had been not far from the animal pens and the smell had reminded them of barnyards back home. Animals had been butchered for cabin or first-class passengers on a regular basis. With extraordinary clarity, each of them could recall on a moment's notice the details of the trip, the sickness, the terrible food, the creaking of the ship, the sounds of the sails flapping in the wind, the crudeness of the sailors, and the difference in accommodations between first-class and steerage passengers. Each of them hoped they would soon forget the experience.

The Liverpool port was startling in its bustle, its crowded quays, the Metropolitan Cathedral, and its clutter. Fat men and skinny men drank beer and gin, staggering dizzily. Everywhere Wilford looked along the Liverpool wharves he could see products imported from America: bales of cotton, and hogsheads and barrels full of sugar, molasses, flour, whiskey, lard, grain, lead, and cottonseed oil. And there were products from South America such as coffee, cocoa, and bananas. And tea from China. Lots of tea.

"Ah, this fresh orange. What a treasure!" said Elder Taylor cheerfully from his six-foot frame, contemplating the piles of fresh fruit and reaching in his pocket to pay the vendor. He peeled it and thrust pieces of the orange into his mouth, savoring its juicy sweetness.

"Lead on, Elder Taylor," Theodore Turley said. "Find us someplace to stay."

Taylor glanced up and down the familiar streets. Years earlier, he had worked in Liverpool as a cooper. He contemplated the city originally called "lifer pol" or muddy pool. The port of Liverpool was founded in 1207 by King John. England had just conquered Ireland and the king needed another port to send men and supplies across the Irish Sea. Soon a weekly market was started near the tidal pool, next to the River Mercey, giving life to the new fishing town. Medieval Liverpool had a population of about one thousand, but began to grow rapidly in the late seventeenth century. Brick and stone fishermen's houses quickly dotted the landscape. In 1699 Liverpool was finally made a parish town. The first docks were built in 1715 and the city soon grew to be the third largest port in the country, behind London and Bristol. By the turn of the century the population reached 77,000, grew to 115,000 within the next ten years, and stood at more than 400,000 in January 1840.

Smells along the streets of Liverpool were not much better than those on the ship, Wilford decided. The air reeked with the stench of decayed fish, rotting vegetables, and swarms of filthy, raggedly dressed children with pale, sallow complexions and stunted growth. The streets seemed far away and uninviting. Wilford's head swam with images of buildings full of dank offices, crowded restaurants, and hotels with busy, uncaring clerks.

John Taylor scanned the horizon of the visually stunning city, thinking of the best place they might stay. "I really have no idea," he said. "It's been so long. Everything has changed." He didn't know if the compact central area of Liverpool was a curse or a blessing.

Theodore Turley ventured to ask a local vendor for a recommendation. Right now Theodore would gladly sleep in a little log house, like the small home he had built in Commerce, now known as Nauvoo. In fact, he had raised the first house built by the saints in that place.

Pointing a bony finger, the man smoothed a palm over a greasy moustache and said docilely through crooked, discolored teeth, "Try the Birmingham Arms, right over there."

The next morning, Wilford wrote in his journal before they left: *May the Lord henceforth deliver me from such a place.*

Wilford Woodruff's Daily Journal
And
Travels in the Ministry
In 1840 in England and Wales

JANUARY 1, 1840. I find myself in company with Elders John Taylor and Theodore Turley on board the packet ship Oxford of the Black Ball Line on our way from New York to Liverpool to fulfill a commandment of God in preaching the gospel of Jesus Christ to the nations of Europe. We have had a very rough sea; high winds blustering and cloudy. Right now I am about 1,900 miles from both Liverpool and New York, in the center of the Atlantic Ocean.

JANUARY 3. Friday. Fair sailing and good breeze. We were in full view of two other sailing vessels, one fore and the other aft of us. We soon overtook the one and found her to be a British brig that had sailed from Halifax. She raised her British colors. Our ship raised the American colors.

JANUARY 10. Friday. Cloudy and cold. Smooth sea and fair breeze. It grows colder as we draw nearer to land. We are entering the channel of St. George. We went on the forecastle deck and after straining our eyes we could see the Irish coast, laying three points off our lee bow. This is the first land we have seen in 20 days. At 8 o'clock at night the lighthouse at Cape Clear came into view.

JANUARY 11. Saturday. We have a heavy gale commencing about one o'clock in the morning and we were in some danger of having the Welch coast on one side and the Irish coast on the other. There was a great bustle and noise on board from command of the captain and mates, whistling of the winds, and the roaring of the waters. We reached the pilot at daylight and raised colors for him to come on board. The pilot boat soon appeared and a pilot came on board and soon a steamship appeared from Liverpool. Despite high winds we gained fast toward Liverpool. There was much bustle among the passengers in shaving, washing and preparing themselves to go ashore. The city of Liverpool soon was in sight and the steamboat came alongside and towed us into port. We reached dock about the same time as two other ships, the Liverpool and the Independence. There were 109 souls of us all who reached shore in good health and spirits. Our company was composed of Americans, English, Scottish, Irish, Welsh, and Dutch. We went into Liverpool and visited several noted places - the customhouse, Lord

Nelson's monument, etc. We took supper and lodging at the Birmingham Arms (and may the Lord henceforth deliver me from such a place).

An embarrassed smile played on John Taylor's thin lips. "I hope you're not judging my country by our accommodation at the Birmingham Arms," he said to Wilford as the train pulled out of Liverpool's underground terminal, chugging toward Preston.

Wilford jerked his head back and laughed. "We're certainly not the first missionaries in this country, and we're not the first to be disappointed in the Birmingham Arms." He had gained a renewed appreciation for Liverpool when John had reminded him that Liverpool emigrant Robert Morris had been the financial genius behind the American War of Independence.

The three men were seated in a narrow, unheated car, riding second-class. The coach bench was hard and black smoke that belched from the engine seeped through the cracks in the door. The strong train smell was the same as in America. So was the hypnotic click-clack rhythm of the train wheels, on the narrow gauge rails.

"I've seen worse," said John Taylor. "You have a lot yet to see."

Wilford nodded in agreement as he contemplated his fellow apostle who, in his opinion, always maintained a heavenly countenance and a noble, dignified manner about him. All throughout the trip John – with his deep-set gray eyes, olive complexion, long English nose, and thick sandy hair – had been gracious, polite, and friendly to everyone. They were about the same age. Wilford would turn thirty-three on March first. John would be thirty-three in November.

Wilford took little solace in the fact that his arrival in England was hardly a novel event. Many early nineteenth-century revival movements had made their way across the Atlantic. Within his own church, several had preceded him, including Heber C. Kimball, the first president of the British Mission, along with Orson Hyde and Willard Richards, who was now living in Preston. Wilford hoped that Elder Richards had received word that they were on their way, and would be there to meet them.

As the train emerged from the underground tunnel and the English countryside came into view, Wilford stared out the window at the hazy gray sky, the leafless trees, the collection of people walking, and carts, gigs, and wagons that were pulled by horses and mules along the road that paralleled the track. A thought struck him as he contemplated his assignment in the British Isles. It was a thought that had struck him before, but the answers to it seemed more urgent now. Where did the British people come from? What was their history? Were most of the people still members of the Church of England? How many were Methodists, Quakers, Baptists, and Catholics? He bowed his head and put a hand to his face. After a moment he looked up with a curious smile.

"I'm certainly at a disadvantage, compared to you two brethren," Wilford said, sizing up his two native English companions. He told of his voracious appetite for knowledge, and his interest in history dating back to the time he was baptized. He expressed his concerns, his questions, with a wistful tone, while the engine hissed in front of them, picking up steam. As John and Theodore began explaining the history of their people, Theodore pulled some writing paper out of his valise, blew on his hands to warm them, and began scribbling with a pencil.

"Tell you what I'll do," Theodore said, continuing to make notes. "I've thought about doing this for a long time, even as we talked on the ship. I've always wanted to write a brief history of our country from a religious perspective. I'll write one up in the next few days and give it to you later. It will be a good missionary tool, especially for native Americans such as you and those who follow."

Wilford regarded the man who had been a clockmaker and gunsmith with a curious eye. He didn't know that his fellow missionary had any writing ability, but told Theodore he would be grateful for anything he could get.

Wilford glanced out the window again. He saw stout, whiskered men, bundled up women in shawls, and children. Washing hung outside apartments and cottages. A collection of churches loomed across the horizon. He thought of the laborers, the clerks, the schoolteachers, the farmers, the carpenters, the butchers, and the cobblers, and their diet, clothing, and shelter. He wondered about their habits, frustrations, family and social concerns, the plight of the poor, inequalities of income, achievements, and culture, as well as their religion, and knowledge of Christian doctrine. Were these people humble or proud? Egotistical or modest? Romantic or hard-boiled?

The sun momentarily broke through the cloudy gray sky, and the light shafted on the outskirts of Liverpool, its buildings, homes and churches, making him think of English architecture, literature, music, gardening, and painting. Wilford couldn't help but wonder how successful he would be in England as a missionary.

"I'd like to know more about the break between the Church of England and the Catholics," he said to Theodore. "And since your country is home to the Methodists and Quakers, tell me about them, too. And the translation of the Bible into English. All those things."

His long fingers still feeling dry and cold, Theodore continued to scribble. He came out of an abstracted stare to say, "I'll do that, and more."

The slow, even motion of the train began to lull Wilford. He thanked Theodore again and began to scan the English countryside once again.

JANUARY 12. Sunday. I arose in the morning and took breakfast (shall I say?). I ate it is true, and used a piece of bread for a plate and my fingers for a knife and fork, and was charged a high price for it at that. I heard some of the passengers boast of the superior accommodations in England to those of America. I confess I could not eat without smiling, thinking if this is the superior English accommodations, I do not know what those of the next nation will be. I would not wish the reader to understand this to be a proper sample of English customs. But we were strangers and we had the misfortune to be directed to a place of the above description. We changed our accommodation to M. Seymour Rotunda Place No. 7 Waterloo Rd. We attended church meeting at two places, St. Paul's and St. Thomas's. It was singular to hear those rectors preach against the form of Godliness without the power of it, which at the same time there is no people more formal than themselves. We also attended a meeting at the Pitt Street Methodist Chapel. The speaker appeared quite easy and simple in his manners. All of the above named chapels were quite splendid. They bury their dead in the yard all around their church and lay the gravestones flat upon the ground and it forms a pavement to walk upon. I find the people both rich and poor, male and female, to be much more plain in their dress than those of America.

CHAPTER NOTES

Elder Woodruff's journal entries are taken from *Wilford Woodruff's Journal*, edited by Scott G. Kenney, Vol. 1, Signature Books, 1983. The author has taken the liberty to slightly edit the material, correcting such things as original spelling, punctuation, etc. In a few cases, such as the entry for March 1, Elder Woodruff's entries have been supplemented by later writings from the apostle, such as *Leaves from My Journal*. In other cases, the daily entries have been shortened or left out altogether in the interest of space. The names of converts baptized personally by Wilford Woodruff were kept in a separate record, a small notebook. Those names have been merged into the journal by the author, as they happened. Since Elder Woodruff did not personally baptize every single one of the United Brethren converts, all baptisms are not listed. Other missionaries, some local, baptized converts as well. These included Elder Brigham Young, Elder Willard Richards, Thomas Kington, Daniel Browett, and John Cheese.

40

HALF SCREENED by the massive body of Willard Richards, Wilford sat at a kitchen table with John Taylor and Theodore Turley. Before them on the table lay an evening snack consisting of tripe, scrambled eggs, cheese and bread, prepared by Willard's wife, Jannetta. Wilford's cheeks were ruddy, his eyes were gleaming, and his whole face was brilliantly animated, despite the ordeal of the trip from Liverpool to Preston. The reality of being in England was jolting him, and it was sweet despite the fact that he was five thousand miles away from his pregnant wife, Phoebe, experiencing new sights, new smells, and new tastes.

Wilford peered curiously at thirty-five-year-old Willard, whose protruding forehead gave way to thick, curly brown hair and long sideburns. He had soft inviting brown eyes and big jowls. "Do you realize how long it's been since we've seen each other?"

"It's got to be around three years ago," Willard answered, filling his plate for the third time. "I left Kirtland in March of 1837, so that's two months shy of three years."

"And how long have you been in England?"

The big man leaned forward and his chair creaked under the burden. "We arrived on the twentieth of July that year."

Wilford shook his head in amazement. The apostle's memory surprised and impressed him. "I can already tell we owe you a big debt of gratitude for getting the work started here in this country."

"As they say here in England, thanks awfully," Willard said, his face coloring at the compliment. "Have some more eggs before I eat them all." He had told his visitors earlier that Joseph Fielding, the mission president, would arrive in Preston in two or three days to give them their assignments.

Amid a constant banter about the British Isles, missionary work, weather, and social conditions, the three new visitors were curious and respectful. Wilford asked remarkably naïve questions about everything, with Theodore still making little notes. Willard Richards related the details of his calling, how Elders Heber C. Kimball, Orson Hyde, and Brother Joseph Fielding had been set apart in 1837 to go on a mission to England, how he had been listening to Joseph Smith give them counsel while still in Kirtland, and how he felt his own heart burn inside him. Willard received his calling the next day. He recalled how the four of them had departed New York on the ship Garrick on June twenty-third, 1837, in company with three other missionaries, John Goodson, Isaac Russell and John Snyder.

Willard's deep love for England was evident: Despite the country's long history, age had proved an asset, not a liability. England remained the center of society throughout the world. It had a potent heritage, evident in its parish churches, cathedrals, medieval castles, and stately homes.

He knew much about Preston. The city got its name back in the Dark Ages following the withdrawal of Romans early in the fifth century. Monks had owned the town, thus the name "Priest-Town." Current population, around fifty thousand. Large concentration of Catholics and a proud gentry class of people. Main industry, textiles, supported by several cotton mills. Streets lit with gas. City survived an outbreak of cholera eight years ago, attributed to a lack of sanitary public works.

His visitors seemed more interested in the history of missionary work.

"Give us a brief report," John Taylor asked, his deep-set eyes alive in anticipation.

Willard's mouth began to twitch on his excited pudgy face and he launched into an enthused discussion of his experiences: The first visits with Reverend James Fielding of the Anglican Church, the brother of Joseph Fielding. Preaching to packed houses in the Vauxhall Chapel in Preston. Converting many of the reverend's congregation. So many, in fact, that the reverend soon became an enemy to Elder Richards and the church.

More experiences unfolded: Conversion stories. Baptisms in the River Ribble near Avenham Park. A growing congregation. The search for a large meeting hall. Opposition from Satan. Angry mobs. Casting out evil spirits.

A full hour and a half later, the day caught up with Wilford Woodruff. He rubbed his eyes, stretched his arms, and broke up the late night vigil with this remark: "You brethren have endured the school of hard knocks. You've established the church here in England. For that we are grateful. Now, where's my bed? I would like to write in my journal and get a good night's rest."

JANUARY 13. I took breakfast and went on board the Oxford and found the passengers taking their trunks and goods on shore to go to the customhouse to be examined. I found it to be a scene of the greatest confusion I ever passed through. But after much crowding and rocking about we were permitted to part with our things after paying six cents per pound to customs for all the books we had as duty upon them. The trunkman then took our trunks and boxes to Mr. George Cannon's house at No. 43 Norfork St. He was a brother-in-law of Elder Taylor's. We deposited our provision chest and a box containing our bed and bedding with him. We took our trunks and went to the railroad depot and took the train for Preston. For the first mile the cars run underground on a track that was cut out of solid rock, while there were buildings and inhabitants over our heads. We started from Liverpool about 6 o'clock and arrived in Preston about 8, where we called upon Brother Greenwood. He immediately sent for Elder Willard Richards and in a few moments I had Elder Richards by the hand. I truly rejoiced to once more behold his face. We immediately went to his house.

JANUARY 14. I spent the day in Preston writing and visiting with the saints. I dined at the home of John Parkinson and Elder Francis Mood. I took supper with Brother Robert Smith and spent the night again with Elder Richards. I found the saints in Preston (population about 60,000) poor but having warm hearts. The streets were crowded with the poor both male and female going to and from the factories with their wooden or clog shoes, on which makes a great rattling over the pavement. The poor are in as great bondage as the children of Israel in Egypt. I find that Elder Richards has had a hard school to pass through ever since he has been in England. I see that we have a great work to perform and we have need of much faith and humility before God.

Wilford stood in silence as he stared in grief at the woman described as "insane" and "possessed of a devil." Goose pimples quickly arose all over his body. He stuck his sweaty palms inside his pockets and rolled the English coins he thought were so strange looking. Three members of the church that he'd just met in Manchester – a day after leaving Preston – were holding the wild-eyed woman down, trying to control her violent shaking and keep her from tearing at her clothes.

"She's been like this for two or three days," said William Clayton, a counselor to Joseph Fielding, the mission president.

Wilford stifled a gasp.

The house he was standing in was filled with too many other people, members and curious nonmembers, who had heard an apostle of the Lord had been summoned to "cast the devil out of the poor woman." The woman was a member of the church.

Wilford had barely arrived in Manchester with Hiram Clark and Theodore Turley. When he first saw the city, he had been in a jocular mood. At first, he had seen a beautiful borough of more than three hundred thousand people. He had already met several members, including William and Ann Benbow and Alfred and Emma Cordon. Underneath the external beauty of the people and the homes, however, a depressing reality had set in. Unemployed factory workers stood on every corner. Wilford's mood had darkened as he witnessed penury, strife, physical and mental illness. And now this – a woman, who but for the three men who restrained her, would continue to tear at her clothing and her body. Her eyes were rolled in the back of her head and her hair was a twisted mat. She frothed at the mouth.

With an irrepressible spine tingle, Wilford calmly asked Elder Clayton, the Manchester Branch President, to clear the room. "Get everyone out of here except for you and me and the three brothers who are holding the sister down." Ordinances of the priesthood – including the casting out of devils – were not for public spectacle. They were sacred.

At first he wondered if he had made a mistake. The woman lunged at him, raging worse than ever. Her skin was cold and ghostly white. Her chin muscles seemed to spasm in an eerie, uncontrollable way. Her hands were taut, her fingers working outward at times, then balled into a fist at other times. Wilford thought of the story in the Bible of Jesus encountering a "man with an unclean spirit" in the country of the Gadarenes. My name is Legion: for we are many, the man had told the Savior. When the Savior had cast out the devils that possessed the man's body, they had entered the bodies of a herd of two thousand swine and the herd had run violently down a steep place in the sea, and were choked in the sea.

Wilford wondered how many evil spirits possessed the body of the poor woman who lay thrashing before him. He knew the spirit or spirits that were in the woman recognized him – as one having the Melchizedek Priesthood and being an apostle of the Lord – by the way she had reacted when he first entered the room. He thought of the billions of Heavenly Father's children who had been cast out of the presence of the Father for disobedience. He thought of how desperate those spirits were to possess the bodies of their own spiritual brothers and sisters who lived on the earth, those who, because of their obedience in the pre-existence, were blessed with bodies. Whether people gave them power to possess their bodies by sinful living or by whatever means, it didn't matter. Wilford just regretted that it was a reality. The reality lay writhing before him, a woman racked with torment.

"In the name of Jesus Christ, and by the power and authority of the Holy Melchizedek Priesthood which we bear," Wilford began, his hands laid on the woman's head along with those of Elder Turley and Elder Richards, "I command all evil spirits to leave the body of this sister." The woman immediately relaxed while Elder Woodruff continued, giving her a blessing.

Within minutes she was sleeping soundly. Her body needed rest.

JANUARY 17. Friday. At a meeting of council held at Elder Richard's house in Preston, Lancashire, England. Elder Joseph Fielding being called to the chair, and Elder Theodore Turley appointed clerk. Moved and seconded that Elders John Taylor and Joseph Taylor go to Liverpool, and that Hiram Clark go to Manchester, and Elders W. Woodruff and Theodore Turley go to the Potteries and there inquire the mind of the Lord upon the importance of going to Birmingham, and that Elder W. Richards have the privilege of going where the spirit directs him. Moved and seconded that Elder Wm. Clayton as one of the presidents, remain in Manchester to preside over the affairs of the church in that place and vicinity for the time being. It was moved and seconded that every elder communicate to the mission presidency the state and condition of affairs in the region in which they are laboring once every month for the time being.

JANUARY 18. Saturday. We met at Elder Richards' in the morning for a season of prayer and fasting before we parted. We gave each other our parting blessings. We have had many calls every day to lay our hands on the sick and pray with them, and in most cases they have had relief. I took the parting hand with Elder Taylor and Elder Fielding who were bound for Liverpool. Elder Richards will tarry in Preston. Elder Clark, Elder Turley and myself took the train to Manchester, where I had the happy privilege of meeting Elder William Clayton, one of the council of presidents in England, a wise and worthy brother. Manchester is the metropolis of the manufacturing districts in England. It is a beautiful borough of 320,000 inhabitants, larger land wise than New York City. There are 164 souls in the city who are members of the church. I had not been with Elder Clayton but a few minutes before I was called on to visit three sick persons and administer to them according to the order of the gospel, ie, by prayer and the laying on of hands. One case was very distressing. We found the sister possessed of the devil and a burning fever on the brain. She was raging and trying to tear herself, although in the hands of three or four men. We laid our hands upon her and commanded the devil to depart, and the fever to stand rebuked, in the name of Jesus Christ, and it was done; though not without a great struggle. We left her calm in her mind and principally delivered of her pain. I administered to 6 more people today.

JANUARY 20. Monday. There is distressing trouble in Manchester. About 3,000 souls are out of work at the factories, because of the pressure of the times and the lowering of wages. They are standing on every corner in the streets, counciling on what to do. Thousands are almost in a state of starvation. I was called upon with my brethren to visit a child possessed of the devil, that was endeavoring to destroy the child. It was the child of the woman that was possessed with the devil, upon whom we laid our hands Saturday evening. We laid hands upon the child that was writhing under the power of the devil, and commanded the devil to depart, in the name of Jesus Christ. It was instantly done and the child fell asleep. We gave blessings to 8 other persons, as well.

41

FRIGID AIR GUSHED over Wilford Woodruff as he sat on a hard wooden seat on top of a stagecoach that was taking him to Burslem, one of the main cities of the Staffordshire Potteries area. Four men paying full fare, sitting on comfortable leather upholstery, rode inside the coach below. He gazed to his right and to his left, watching the English countryside go by, listening to the muffled sounds of the horses' hooves and the wagon wheels plowing through four inches of mud and snow. A heavy and chilly rain, blown in by strong winds, was slowly melting the snow. The stage driver wore several layers of mud-encrusted clothing, but was skilled at the whip. Steam rose from the hides of the horses and trailed from their nostrils as they picked their way through the snow-covered ruts, past gloomy, run down gray cottages, and fields where horses and cattle waited to be fed meager portions of hay from a horse-drawn sled. A granite Anglican church came into view. They seemed to be everywhere.

Wilford thought of the woman in Manchester and the thankful testimony that she bore the next day at sacrament meeting in front of a large audience, and how the faith of the members there had increased. He recalled how shocked and frustrated he was on Monday to learn that the evil spirits had returned to her home, this time possessing the body of her small child, but a few months old. As he and his companions went to the home and cast the evil spirits out of the child, he had come to the conclusion that Satan did not want the gospel to be preached in England, or anywhere else for that matter. It was going to be a war. He recalled a scripture from Revelations: *And there was war in heaven: Michael and his angels fought against the dragon; and the dragon fought and his angels, and prevailed not; neither was their place found any more in heaven. And the great dragon was cast out, that old serpent, called the Devil, and Satan, which deceiveth the whole world; he was cast out into the earth, and his angels were cast out with him.*

As the stage bounced along, Wilford hung his head and said a silent prayer. He told the Lord how thankful he was that the gospel had been restored to the earth. That he understood the conflict that had taken place in the premortal existence among the spirit children of God. That the war referred to in Revelations was primarily over, and how and in what manner the plan of salvation would be administered to the forthcoming human family upon the earth. He thanked God for the principle of agency, which gave man the freedom to choose to accept the gospel or reject it. The gospel would not be forced upon people as Satan had proposed. Wilford knew that war in Heaven had broken out because a third part of the spirits had refused to accept the appointment of Jehovah – who would be known as Jesus Christ – as the Savior. Wilford felt sorry for those who rebelled, those who had refused the Father's plan of redemption. He had just cast some of them out of the woman in Manchester, and out of her baby. They were spirits who, while they were in the pre-existence, wanted salvation to come automatically to all who passed through mortality, without regard to individual preference or voluntary dedication.

A bump in the rutted road shook Wilford. He opened his eyes to see his traveling companions, Theodore Turley and Hiram Clark, eyes closed, chilled by the freezing rain, collars up, hats pulled on tight, trying to doze for a few minutes without falling off the coach. Perhaps they were uttering silent prayers, too. Wilford closed his eyes and continued to think about his experiences in Manchester, healing the woman and her baby, and administering to at least twenty other sick people. It was true-the war that began in Heaven continues on earth, especially here in England. Wilford thought of the conflict between right and wrong, and between the gospel and false principles. That the conflict remains between the same contestants and over the same issues, with the same salvation at stake. A third part of the spirits were cast out. The woman and her child were of the two parts of Heavenly Father's children who had been valiant in the pre-existence and were permitted to come to earth to obtain bodies. Wilford marveled at the fact that those spirits were not all equally valiant, both in the pre-existence and in real earth life. There was almost every degree of devotion to Christ and to the Father among them.

No doubt, Wilford thought, the war is still raging. The thought gave him goose bumps again. He concluded his meditation by promising God that he would be among the most diligent soldiers ever called to battle. The stakes were too important for him to be otherwise.

JANUARY 21. Tuesday. Anointed and blessed Priest Benjamin Davis, for the healing of his lame leg, and blessed four others. We said goodbye to Elder William Clayton and the saints in Manchester and took a coach to Staffordshire, passing through Mackelsfield, Stockport, Congleton, Tunstell and ending up in Burslem, where we stayed with Brother Alfred Cordon on Navigation Rd. According to the custom of the country we rode on the outside of the coach. We had a exceedingly strong wind and rain. Elder Turley took a cold and sore throat. I found the saints in Burslem numbering

66, in good health and spirits. We found Elder Cordon to be very faithful.

JANUARY 22. Wednesday. Elder Turley quite ill. I am now in the midst of the Potteries, which are so noted in England. The Potteries include the following market towns: Tunstell, Burslem, Hanley, Stoke, Lane End, and several other villages. The whole population of the Potteries in 1838 was 65,000. The potters are for the manufacturing of English china, crockery, and stoneware. We visited Hanley and sup'd at Brother William Benbow's place. He is keeper of a provision store, the Hanley Market Place. Brother Benbow was not at home but we were much pleased with his lady, Sister Ann Benbow. She was strong in the faith and manifested much interest at our arrival to England from America. We preached at Brother Wood's home in New Castle and spent the night at Elder Cordon's home.

JANUARY 28. Tuesday. I applied for a license to preach but the justice had not power to grant me one, that he knew of. I preached in Burslem at night to a large crowd. A Methodist preacher by the name of John Jones arose when I closed, and read a pamphlet called Mormonism Unveiled, written by Warren Parrish, Luke Johnson and John F. Boyington. I answered him when he got through, and he rejected our testimony as he had done a number of times before.

JANUARY 30. Thursday. I visited apartments near the silk factory in New Castle, and saw them manufacture silk from the raw article to the weaver's loom. The sun shone today and it was pleasant; the fields all looked green as summer. I preached in Hanley, and one man that the truth had hurt his feelings came to me full of all subtlety and mischief, and tried to catch me in my words by asking many questions. But he went away not accomplishing his designs. Spent the night with Brother William Benbow in Hanley.

JANUARY 31. Friday. Walked from Hanley to Burslem to post two letters, one to my wife, Phoebe, and the other to my father in Connecticut. Walked to Stoke and preached to a large congregation at Brother William Hume's place. There were several preachers present, but they went away silent. Spent the night at Benbow's.

FEBRUARY 5. Wednesday. Walked to Hanley, then to Newcastle. Read two papers. Found much talk about Queen Victoria's wedding. It had taken more than 200 persons nine months to make her bridal dress, and the weavers six weeks to make her veil. Preached at night at Brother Wood's.

FEBRUARY 6. Thursday. Received a letter from Elder Turley, so I answered the letter. Preached in Hanley upon the Book of Mormon to four or five hundred persons, some of whom were full of wrath. When I closed, those who were angry with me because of the word of God arose upon a bench and began to reject my testimony and rave like madmen. But I stood and gave answers to their questions until they were confounded. I then left the house while it was in an uproar.

FEBRUARY 7. Friday. Brother Grocott took me through the Copeland Pottery Works, and it was a great curiosity to see all kinds of earthenware, crockery, and the best of china being made, commencing with clay and bones in their first state, then go through every process until it is finished-grinding, mixing, sifting, drying, molding, firing, printing, stamping, gilding with gold, glazing, polishing. Cost of one set of china for dining and tea for 20 or 30 persons is 1,100 pounds or $5,500. The china is much superior to that made in China. Brother John Rowley made me a present of a china box as a token of friendship, plus three small china pitchers, and three small bottles. Preached in the evening at the home of Brother Humes.

FEBRUARY 10. Monday. Queen Victoria was married today to Prince Albert. They say that the queen's salary is $1,925,000 annually. As this is a day that many are celebrating the marriage of the queen, I thought it no more than just that I should honor the King of Heaven by advocating his cause and preaching the gospel of his Son, Jesus

Christ. So I walked out into the market place, accompanied by Alfred Cordon, William Bradbury and George Simpson, and we began to sing praises unto God, and call upon his name. A congregation soon flocked around us, and we preached the gospel to them, and I bore testimony unto them of the great work that God had set his hand to accomplish. When we finished many followed us, and we answered their questions. We also preached in the evening at Brother Thomas Amison's; baptized one. I received a letter from Elder John Taylor. They have baptized ten persons in Liverpool.

FEBRUARY 19. Wednesday. I spent the day at Alfred Cordon's and in the evening I walked to Newcastle and preached. There were two Methodist preachers present and they were filled with anger because of the truth of God. One, by the name of Robert Brown, rejected my testimony and said I should go to the bottomless pit, and all that followed me. It was manifest what spirit was in the man. After the meeting I baptized one person and walked to Hanley and to Burslem and spent the night at Cordon's.

42

WILFORD WOODRUFF had been awake since long before dawn on this second day of March, a Monday, his sixth week in England. The previous day he had spent a long Sabbath day on the Lord's errand in Hanley. He had preached twice during the day to a large assembly in the Hanley city hall. In the evening he had met once again with another assembly of church members and guests, speaking and administering the sacrament.

While singing the first hymn during the evening meeting, he had heard a voice.

It was a familiar voice, a voice that came to him while the Spirit of the Lord rested upon him. The voice had said to Wilford, *This is the last meeting that you will hold with this people for many days.*

The statement had astonished Wilford. He had so many appointments to teach the gospel to people in the area he didn't know how he was going to keep them all. Sunday, March first, had been his thirty-third birthday. What a strange way to celebrate. *What did the Lord want?*

Falling asleep seldom had been a problem for Wilford Woodruff, but the previous evening his thoughts had kept drifting to the voice he had heard during the meeting. He had gone so far as to tell the Hanley saints that he would not be with them for the next several days. They had been as astonished as he was, wondering why. The strange thing was he could not tell them why. He just knew he was needed somewhere else. Even after baptizing four persons after the evening meeting, his feelings had not changed. He had to move on. The question was – where?

Lying awake in the dark in Brother William Benbow's home in Hanley, as he snuggled in his bed, Wilford thought about a dream he had had while he was in New York. He had seen his wife in the dream, weeping and in great affliction because of their little daughter, Sarah Emma. In his dream, Phoebe had answered, "She is dead." He had wondered if the Lord was directing him to go home. Kneeling at his bed in Willard Richard's home, he prayed again. Where was he supposed to go? What was he supposed to do? Crawling back in bed, rewarming the covers with his body heat, he thought of his wife again. He could recall her features in every detail, the way she talked, her littlest gestures, the look in her eyes when he left for his mission. He tried to picture what his daughter looked like. Like a jewel in his possession, he could see her, too. He loved her very much. He prayed that she was fine, that the dream he had in New York would not come true.

A faint light was ebbing through his window as Wilford returned to his knees to plead with the Lord again. The sun would be up soon. Again, he poured his heart out to the Lord. Suddenly, the voice came to him again. In his mind, the message was clear. *Go south. The Lord has a great work for you to do. Go south. Many souls are waiting for you, waiting for the gospel.*

Wilford did not return to bed. He washed himself and dressed, reflecting on the months he had spent in Nauvoo with the Prophet Joseph Smith – the training, the instruction, and the messages of inspiration. Be humble and be not exalted, the prophet had told him. Beware of pride and do not seek to excel one above another, but act for each other's good. Honorably we must make mention of each other's names in our prayers before the Lord and before our fellow men. You are not sent out to be taught but to teach. Myriads of the prophet's words reverberated through his mind. Someday, Wilford would return to Nauvoo, perhaps in about a year. But for now – *go south!*

Still meditating, wondering, contemplating, Wilford left the William Benbow house and provision store for an early morning walk. When he returned, he found Ann Benbow in the store, getting ready for another busy day.

The Hanley provision store managed by William Benbow never changed. Day in and day out it was the same – boxes, bins, staterooms and drawers full of goods, account books laying on a desk, an apprentice coming in and out with new supplies. As Wilford opened the door the now familiar smell of blended teas, coffee, spices, sugar, molasses, currants, and raisins permeated his nostrils. An iron range with ornate grillwork, complete with an oven for roasting meats and baking, sat in the corner with the same "for sale" sign on it as two weeks ago.

"Good morning, Sister Benbow," Wilford said as he strode into the store. "I see you still haven't sold that fancy new stove. Where's Brother Benbow?"

Ann Benbow clapped a hand to her lips. "Oh, Lordy, you startled me. Where have you been? I thought you were still upstairs. Can I get you some tea?"

"Maybe later, thank you," Wilford wearily said. A night without sleep was taking its toll.

"No, we haven't sold the stove yet," Sister Benbow said as she piled new wooden buckets in a corner. "The depression is so bad here I guess no one can afford it. These days we sell ten times as many tallow candles as we do wax candles. That tells you how bad off people are. Elder Turley is with my husband in the back office."

Wilford found Elder Turley and Brother Benbow engaged in conversation, with serious looks on their faces. After exchanging greetings, Elder Turley turned to Elder Woodruff and said, "I have something to propose to you. I would like you to return with me to Birmingham." Knowing that their mission president, Elder Joseph Fielding, had assigned Wilford to the Potteries, Theodore sat back and waited for a reaction.

The proposal jolted Wilford. Three choices: go with Theodore, stay in the Potteries, or go south. However, the voice was still with him, profound and unsettling. *Go south. Go south.*

Wilford was silent for a few seconds, thinking of a way to break the news. "Why do you say that, Elder Turley?"

Theodore Turley was quick to answer. "When I reached the city limits of Birmingham, I didn't have the courage to begin preaching. Perhaps the old phrase 'a prophet is without honor in his own country' applies here because Birmingham is my native place. However, I would just feel more comfortable if you went there with me."

Wilford clasped his hands between his knees. Under normal circumstances he would happily comply. His face went rigid and serious. "I would do it except the Lord has directed me otherwise."

A startled Elder Turley widened his eyes and dropped his jaw. After being with Wilford nearly every day since they had departed New York, he thought he knew his fellow missionary inside and out. He gave his arms an exasperated wave. "What do you mean?"

Wilford gave Theodore a calm look of apology.

"I don't understand," Theodore said, his facial features screwed into a mask of disappointment. It was a crushing prospect to consider that Wilford was turning his proposal down stone cold. Although he had planned to preach in Birmingham, but had not actually set food inside his old native city. He lacked the courage to tackle it alone. He needed Wilford. It was a relief when

Wilford favored him with a smile.

A wave of warm delight swept over Wilford. Then he began to relate the experiences of the past evening, the voice he had heard while singing the hymn, the restless night, his long prayers, then the answer he received at daybreak to go south. He bore testimony to his two listeners that he actually did hear a voice, and that he had no choice but to do what he had been commanded.

There was a marked silence, broken only by Ann Benbow's busywork in the store and the chirping of birds outside. Theodore asked, "Where do you intend to go?"

Wilford turned to William Benbow, who also appeared startled and perplexed, his dark eyebrows turned down in concern. Alfred Cordon had baptized William and his wife back on January fourth. "I distinctly remember you telling me many times earlier that you have a brother who lives south of here," Wilford said somberly.

"Which brother?" Theodore asked with a certain aloofness, staring at William.

Benbow nodded. "John. He has a farm in Herefordshire, near Castle Frome." He went on to explain that he was the youngest of ten children, and that John Benbow was nearly two years older than he was. All were born in Herefordshire.

Wilford locked onto Benbow's eyes. "Would you take me there?" Creases of decision folded into his face, and his eyes were vivid as he waited for an answer. Theodore sat silent, his mouth still open.

William Benbow gushed at the thought. He had made the suggestion to Wilford a few times before, but the American missionary had previously manifest little interest. He could recall telling Elder Woodruff about his brother's affiliation with a religious order called the United Brethren, a group of more than five hundred persons who had broken off from the Primitive Methodists.

"When would you like to leave?"

"First thing in the morning," Wilford declared, his eyes sparkling despite his lack of sleep. "Can we make it in one day?"

"No. But we could do it in two days," William said, his mind racing. His wife could tend the store. He could take his son, Johnny, who hadn't seen his two cousins for several months. "We'd have to take a coach from here to Wolverhampton, which is twenty-six miles. We'd stay overnight there. Then we'd catch another coach that goes through Dudley, Stourbridge, Stourport, and Worcester. From there we might have to walk the last fourteen miles."

"I would appreciate it if you would lead me on that trip just as you have outlined it," Wilford said. "And the Lord would appreciate it, too. That's where He has directed me."

Theodore Turley sat heavily in his chair. "What about Birmingham?" His face sobered into the tired gravity of a portrait of the now-deceased King Edward that hung on the wall.

"It's all yours," Wilford answered with no apology. "William and I are leaving in the morning for Castle Frome."

Theodore heaved a big sigh, still puzzled, but resigned to Wilford's insistence. He reached for his satchel and pulled out a neatly bound document. He handed it to Wilford. "I brought you a gift. I was going to wait until we were on our way to Birmingham to give it to you."

Wilford thumbed through the pages, a thesis of some sort in Theodore's personal handwriting.

"I've been working on it for several weeks. Remember our conversation on the train from Liverpool to Preston? It's a paper I've written to help you understand our religious history. A few others helped me with their opinions. John Taylor, Alfred Cordon, and Joseph Fielding. I hope you'll read it."

"I promise you, I will," Wilford said in a grateful voice. "I'll read it on the way to John Benbow's farm."

43

The History of Christianity in England
Part One

The history of England is closely tied to the history of Rome. Not much is known about the British Isles until they were conquered by Rome, about forty-three years after the death of Christ. The people who lived here were part of the scattered members of the remaining tribes of Israel. As the Romans conquered England, armies brought with them a mixture of pagan religions and Christianity.

When the Roman Empire weakened in the fifth century, Germanic tribes called Angles, Saxons, and Jutes invaded Britain. These are the people who became the English. Britain came to the attention of Pope Gregory when he saw slaves from England on sale in the market in Rome. The Pope sent St. Augustine to convert the English to Catholicism. At the time, the English people were practicing their own Celtic form of Christianity. One can find old churches in England that can be dated back as early as 652 AD.

An interesting but tragic period of British history saw the Vikings of

Scandinavia, the last pagans of old Europe, conquer these islands. They founded the monasteries and the English people became easy prey for pillage. However, in the eleventh century the Viking King converted to Christianity and the fledgling nation began to revive.

In 1060, Normans under the leadership of Duke William, known as "William the Conqueror," gained control of England. He was of the same stock as the Vikings but he was already Christian. He brought in continental abbots and bishops to transform the English Church. Although the Norman leadership gave new life and impetus to the church, they removed all Anglo-Saxon "saints" from church records and actually pulled their bones from the ground. It was an ugly time.

Wherever the Normans settled England a system of land distribution called feudalism, learned from the Franks, was implemented. Feudalism divided English society into lords and vassals and introduced the notions of "free" and "unfree." The Catholic Church became organized on the same principles; bishoprics and abbacies became known as the "gift" of the lords. Some European men of authority retained a measure of integrity, such as Thomas Booket here in England. Others were corrupted by their temporal powers.

Now we come to the Crusades, which proved to be a dark period of European-Christian history. Jerusalem had been the ultimate destination of Christian pilgrims for many years but Islam or the Muslims now occupied it. In 1095, Pope Urban II issued a call to arms that affected England and all Europe. To get enough soldiers, the pope promised a "forgiveness of sins" to those who would go on the crusade. The first crusade to capture Jerusalem for Christianity was successful, but the city proved difficult to defend. A second crusade made the situation worse. The loss of Jerusalem in 1187 inspired a third crusade. Despite the efforts of King Richard I of England, it was not regained. In all, there were eight arrogant, bloody

Christian crusades to the Holy Land between 1095 and 1291. Shamefully, the knights from Europe turned into brutal beasts, surpassing in their cruelty all other conquerors of the past. They slaughtered men, women, and children, young and old, in houses and in streets, and with weapons or without. Thereafter Muslims looked at the Europeans as lustful murdering bandits without conscience.

The failure of the crusades caused some Christian leaders to preach the art of persuasion rather than conversion by the sword and thus the term "mission" was born. The Franciscans and Dominicans were organized to travel abroad, carrying the gospel of the Church of Rome.

During the fourteenth century, Christians in England had to deal with a variety of challenges. The English, along with the rest of Europe, were trying to cope with a rapid succession of popes and antipopes, abuses in the high office of the church, and outright corruption. With the Black Death, the Hundred Years' War and frequent famines, death was ever present. Pilgrimages to holy sites, with many people seeking some hope of spiritual gain, became a major element of medieval economics. Churches with important relics grew fabulously rich and corruption continued.

Finally, Europe emerged out of the Dark Ages, beginning when the Bible was made available in the English language. Previously it was in Latin only. From then on common people had access to the Bible for the first time. The Roman Church opposed the English translation of the Bible, and its printing, because the church had more control when its priests, along with the pope, were the sole interpreters of the Bible. The Renaissance followed, teaching people to no longer unquestioningly accept the dogma or doctrines of the Roman Church. The superstitious medieval world came to an end. There are additional details regarding the English translation of the Bible in part two of this document.

The movement against the dogmas of the Roman Church, which began to swell all over Europe, finally broke wide open in the figure of Martin Luther when he protested the sale of indulgences. That began what we know as the Protestant Reformation. With the invention of printing, the Bible was fully disseminated to all Christians. Despite the controversial history of King Henry VIII and his many wives, he was instrumental in the compilation of the modern Bible. During his reign, he commanded the clergy to install in a convenient place "one book of the whole Bible of the largest volume in English."

In 1534, Henry repudiated papal authority and established himself as the head of the Anglican Church, or Church of England. The cause was the Pope's refusal to annul Henry's marriage to Catherine of Aragon, who had not borne Henry a male heir. Henry's second wife, Anne Boleyn, bore him a daughter, Elizabeth, and brought to England the French reformist movement called evangelism.

Henry himself showed no desire to join the Protestant Reformation. It was Thomas Cranmer, the Archbishop of Canterbury and Henry's spiritual advisor, who became the theological architect of the reformed Church of England. At first the English church continued with traditional forms of worship, and differed with Rome chiefly in the seat of authority and in its liturgy (sacraments and ceremonies). But as the Reformation and the Puritan movement gained ground, most of the old forms of English religion – which were symbolic and colorful but full of idols and statues – began to disappear, its pictures and statues lost to whitewash or destroyed by Cromwell's directives.

The reformed church (Anglican) flourished under the brief reign of Henry's heir, Edward VI, but when his daughter, Mary I, came to the throne she restored the Church of Rome and sent reformers to the stake. Under the rule of Mary's sister, Elizabeth I, the Anglican Church was revived and it was the Catholics who suffered. Queen Elizabeth, by the Elizabethan Act of Supremacy and Act of Uniformity, made certain the Church of England was firmly established. Some Englishmen, despite the loss of social rights, remained with the Church of Rome and were called "recusants."

The act failed to satisfy extreme Protestants. They were not one group but many, united by a rejection of bishops and hierarchy. They became known as Puritans, professing loyalty to the queen but not to the Church of England. It was from Puritan thought that most, if not all, various denominations and groups of English Christianity arose. The Anglican Church was and is the established church of England, governed by bishops with the monarch as its head. The conflicts of the Civil Wars of 1542-1651 were as much religious as political. Later, under the protection of Cromwell, more radical groups emerged, such as the Diggers, the Levellers, the Shakers, and the Quakers. A rebellious spirit crept in among those who were called "nonconformists" or "dissenters" by the Anglicans. They include the Presbyterians, Congregationalists, Unitarians, and Baptists.

The elders of the Church of Jesus Christ of Latter-day Saints most likely will find the people of England to be Anglican, Methodist, Baptist, Quaker, and Catholics, but will find a mixture of the other religions as well.

The Quakers were founded by George Fox, who said that a justice first called his group "Quakers" because they "trembled" at the word of God. Their formal name is The Society of Friends.

Methodism, however, did not grow out of the Puritan movement but began as a Church of England club at the University of Oxford in the eighteenth century. The word Methodist was coined from the methodical studies of the group, led by John Wesley. They held frequent communion, fasted, and were more eager in their religion than the average churchgoer. For this they were eventually cut off from the Church of England, but not until four years after Wesley's death. Methodists appealed particularly to the working people during the upheavals of the industrial revolution, and they placed a lot of emphasis on social work. There seems to be a lot of bad feeling between Methodists and Anglicans, even today.

Between 1828 and 1832, a series of laws was passed in the British parliament of great importance to the Church of England and is relationship to the state. Previously civil servants had been required to be Anglicans and there were many restrictions on Roman Catholics and others. That is no longer true, legally, but hard feelings remain.

Many people here in England relate the legend of Joseph of Arimathea. It is said that he visited these shores. The legend says that he used a cup called the "Holy Grail" to catch drops of blood from Christ as he suffered on the cross, and that he buried that cup at the church he founded, known as St. Mary's Glastonbury, in Somerset. The church is reported to be the burial place of King Arthur as well. The king apparently sought to recover the Holy Grail when it was missing for some reason. Latter-day Saint readers of this document should understand that it is legend only, and it is highly unlikely that the legend of the cup is true.

Part Two: English translation of the Bible

Most people in England use the King James Version of the Bible. But the effort to get the Bible translated into English from Latin and other languages is equally as interesting as the history of Christianity in this country.

Although earlier attempts were made, the first English version of the whole Bible is associated with the name of John Wycliffe, beginning in 1382. But the honor of making the first translation into English belongs to William Tindale, born in 1490. We must understand that the Church of Rome opposed people having access to the Bible. As Tindale began printing his work in about 1525, he was forced to flee from Cologne to Worms and there he was able to print 3,000 copies. Most of the copies were burned when they were discovered. Tindale was put to death for heresy in 1536.

280 Light and Truth

In 1535, another man by the name of Miles Coverdale issued, with King Henry's permission, the first complete English Bible, translated out of German and Latin. And in 1537 Thomas Matthew issued, along with the king's permission, another edition that used Tindale's translation of the New Testament and half the Old Testament, and used Coverdale's translation for the remainder. This is the translation that King Henry ordered to be made available in all the English churches.

Mary's (Henry's daughter) ascension to the throne threatened everyone who had anything to do with the translations. Coverdale narrowly escaped with his life. Cranmer and Matthew (who also went by the name of John Rogers) were burned at the stake. After Mary died another version, known as the Genevan Bible, became popular. Some 150 editions were published between 1560 and 1616. It was improved with divisions of text and copious notes and eventually became known as the Breeches Bible. However, its strong Puritan flavor made it distasteful to many English churchmen and an effort was made to improve it. The improved version, regarded as the "official" English Church Bible, was presented to Queen Elizabeth I in 1568. It was used in public worship but otherwise had no great circulation.

Soon after King James I came to power, the Puritan party asked for a new translation, to which the king agreed. The king gave an outline of a plan for a new version, known today as the Authorized Version. In 1607 the work began at leading universities, utilizing the talents of 54 men, and then reviewed by bishops and other chief learned men of the Anglican Church. After review, it was presented to what is called the Privy Council, then ratified by the king. The new translation, the King James Version, was published in 1611.

Part Three: How original doctrines changed

Doctrinally, members of the Church of Rome, the Church of England, and all the other reformed churches, whether they are dissenters or non-conformists, trace their beliefs or dogma back to Rome. Their beliefs, accordingly, are quite similar but they have their differences. And they believe quite differently than members of the Church of Jesus Christ of Latter-day Saints.

The doctrines of the original church, as organized by the Savior during his personal ministry on the earth, and the doctrines of the Church of Jesus Christ of Latter-day Saints, are the same. But those doctrines differ drastically from those of the Church of Rome and thus of the Church of England and all the other reformist churches. What happened?

Unfortunately, Christianity did not destroy paganism when Rome adopted the church. Instead, the Christian Church, rapidly falling into apostasy, adopted paganism. The message of Christ and His gospel became subject soon after his resurrection to extremely controversial interpretations. Here is a more detailed history.

Passing of the apostolic age. With the passing of the so-called apostolic age the original church drifted into a condition of apostasy. Succession in the priesthood was broken and the true church of Christ, which original-ly operated under divine direction and had authority to officiate in spiritual ordinances, ceased to exist within two hundred years after the death of the Savior. Afterward, the Christian movement floundered.

Any student of the Bible will find that there have been times when the true gospel thrived upon the earth, but there have been other times when there was a temporary triumph of evil. This was true in the times of Adam, Noah, Moses, and all the prophets we study in the Bible. Because man has been endowed with personal freedoms to choose right and wrong, which we call agency, Satan and those who choose to follow him obviously try to frustrate the great plan of God the Father and Jesus Christ. Salvation is available to all those who choose to follow the Savior. God will force no man to heaven.

Even though the Savior organized his church on the earth, there are many scriptures that indicate that Christ, the apostles, and writers of the New Testament knew that church leaders and members would eventually lose their faith. The Apostle Paul referred to the problem many times. Even before he and other apostles had finished their earthly ministries, apostasy was spreading. Most of the early corruption came from within. Jewish converts and Gentile converts regarded each other with bitter aversion. Seeds of discord and controversy were easily sown. Soon the seeds broke out and divided the church.

Persistent persecution caused many early members of the church to renounce their faith. Many of the strongest leaders were the first to fall because opponents – Judaism and heathen sects – specifically targeted them. From the time of the crucifixion, people who professed a belief in the divinity of Jesus Christ were subject to persecution, especially if they tried to live the commandments. Even today, people who try to live the commandments are ridiculed by the people who do not. The apostles lived in the very shadow of death. Persecution was their heritage.

Not only did the Jews wage relentless persecution against the early saints, but they stirred up opposition on the part of the Romans, too. They charged that the Christians were plotting treason against Rome. To escape much of this persecution, the body of the church moved from Jerusalem into the provinces beyond Jordan. Pagans, or heathens, people who did not believe in the existence of Jehovah or Jesus Christ, caused problems. They worshipped idols. There were many deities and cults and most were forms of Satan worship. Pagans, though at times at war with each other, united in persecution of the Christians with incredible ferocity and indescribable cruelty.

Of all pagan persecutors of the church, the Roman Empire was the principle aggressor. The simplicity of Christian worship irritated the Romans. They could not imagine a religion without images to worship, without oracles, sacerdotal orders, sacrifices, etc.

Death of the apostles. Historians believe that the Apostles Paul and Peter suffered martyrdom in Rome, AD 68. All the other apostles were killed about this time, with the exception of John. During the reign of Domitan, AD 94, both Christians and Jews were persecuted because they refused to worship statues he had erected as objects of adoration. Because of Domitan's edict, the Apostle John suffered banishment to the isle of Patmos. During the reign of Trajan, AD 94 to 117, violent persecution against Christians was sanctioned.

Christians caught were put to death unless they renounced their faith. Romans demanded that men of every faith recognize Roman gods and burn incense before their statues. This the Christians steadily refused to do. The Romans believed this angered their gods, so when natural disasters such as drought occurred, they blamed the Christians.

During the reign of Diocletian, 284 to 305 AD, there was some tolerance toward Christians. However, the emperor turned totally against the church and undertook a movement to bring about the total suppression of the Christian religion. He ordered a general destruction of Christian books and decreed the penalty of death for those who had such books. Their places of worship were burned to the ground. Thousands were put to death in terrible ways-burned, thrown into the sea, tortured, and so on. Descriptions of the horrible extremes to which brutality was carried are sickening to the soul. A monument was erected to the mighty Diocletian which read: For having extinguished the name of Christians who brought the Republic to ruin.

Rome takes control. Eventually, the government of Rome took over the church, including the church here in England. It happened during the reign of Constantine, beginning in AD 306, when a great change occurred. During this time Rome's official religion was sun worship, the cult of the Invincible Sun. Constantine was its head priest. However, Christianity was on the rise. In a bold and cunning move, he combined the two religions, trying to make a hybrid religion acceptable to both. He fused pagan symbols, dates, and rituals into the growing Christian tradition. Because the Christian Church was now beset by internal apostasy, as well as persecution, it fell for the ploy. Even artists began fusing the two systems together. Egyptian sun disks became the halos of Roman Church saints. Pictograms of Isis nursing her miraculously conceived son Horus became the inspiration for modern images of the Virgin Mary nursing baby Jesus.

To strengthen the new "Christian" religion, in AD 325 Constantine called the now-famous ecumenical gathering known as the Council of Nicaea. Of 4,000 bishops invited to the council, only 250 came. From all of Western Europe only four bishops were present. The bishop from Rome was not even present. Many aspects of Christianity were debated and voted upon, such as the divinity of Jesus, the administration of sacraments, the date of Easter, and the role of bishops. However, Constantine did not subject himself to be questioned; he was the master of the conference. His ideas and concepts were accepted. There were no apostles to lead them, so the council floundered.

The council may have floundered by Constantine and Rome did not. Roman legions now marched under the emblem of Christianity. Conversions were made by the sword. (Constantine did not officially become "Christian" until shortly before his death. His baptism was by sprinkling, not immersion.)

Under the new system there was great competition for church prefer-ment that extended even to these English shores. The office of a bishop came to be more highly esteemed than the rank of a general in the army. The emperor himself was the real head of the church. The church under the patronage of Constantine was vastly different from the church as estab-lished by Christ and built up by his apostles. It had now become apostate as judged by the standards of its original constitution.

Because of external persecution from Rome and pagan groups, vast numbers of Christian converts lapsed into idolatry immediately. Many ran to the forum and sacrificed to the pagan gods as they were ordered. Under pressure, many Christians bought a document from their provincial gover-nor that attested they had complied with Roman law and sacrificed to Roman gods. This document usually guaranteed their immunity from perse-cution, but affected their standing in the church.

Bishops of the church complained that even their best members were beset with problems. Many put amassing wealth above being faithful. They forgot their duties in the church. Frauds and deceit were practiced. They married outside the church. They did not help new converts. Soon, bishops themselves neglected their duties and gave themselves up to secular pur-suits. They deserted their places of residence and their flocks. They gave no assistance to the needy but were insatiable in their thirst for money. The office of a bishop was sometimes sold to the highest bidder. Common peo-ple suffered.

By the end of the third century, there remained little proof of any close relationship between Christ and the church. Many historians say the evils of persecution were brought on not by Christianity itself, but the departure from it. It would seem that God allowed the persecution because of the wickedness of the apostate Christians.

Mixture of philosophy. Other major problems occurred in the church by the corrupting of simple principles of the gospel, achieved by mixing in philosophic systems of the times. These philosophies caused an eventual change in the core belief in God. Even in early times, evil men attempted to graft foreign doctrines into the Church; the sorcerer Simon, in Acts Chapter Eight, is an example. The apostles, however, preached strongly against the toleration of doctrines and practices alien to the gospel. Judaistic converts to Christianity sought to modify and adapt the tenets of their new faith so as to harmonize them with their inherited love of Judaism. The result was destructive to both. Also, the philosophy of the Gnostics damaged the church. They taught that Jesus did not have a body, and that eventually the earth will dissolve into nothingness. This philosophy became the forerunner to Agnostics, who deny the existence of God.

While no one can deny the good all churches do today, the Church of Rome had a deceitful and violent past. They employed brutal crusades to reeducate pagans, employing methods as inspired as they were horrific.

The trinity. From that point in history, and as an outcropping of the Council in Nicaea, a new doctrine was established called the "trinity in unity," as characterizing the Godhead. Leaders within the church began to argue who was the most important, God the Father, or the Son, or the Holy Ghost. This new doctrine regarding the Godhead became know as Arianism. Historians say it shook the church to its foundation. Thus the Nicene Creed became the law of the Roman Empire. Orthodox Christianity became an essential qualification for Roman citizenship. The Nicene Creed attempted to describe the Godhead. From that creed the church adopted the doctrine of the trinity – that God the Father, God the Son, and the Holy Ghost are all one person; that none have a physical body; that they are all spirit only.

This was a radical departure from the original concept of the trinity-that God the Father is a separate person from God the Son, and that both personages have bodies of flesh and bone. The Holy Ghost is a personage of spirit only.

The concept of the trinity was forced upon the world, as the Roman emperor wanted unity among his various provinces. He used Christianity as the tool to establish this unity. The Christians, who had been persecuted during the first centuries after the resurrection of the Savior, now became the oppressors, paired with the power of the Roman Empire. Later, the Roman emperor who was called Theodosius "The Great," helped make the Nicene Creed survive by having 30,000 Arian Christians killed during a single night in an amphitheater.

Orders of hermits and monks and the doctrine of celibacy. Another heresy that grew out of the alliance between Gnostics and the church was the doctrine of antagonism between body and spirit. As a result of this grafting in of heathen practices, men sought to weaken, torture and subdue their bodies, that their souls might gain greater freedom. It was this unnatural view of life that gave rise to the orders of hermits and monks.

An outgrowth of this false teaching was the growth of numerous orders of monks and the maintenance of monasteries. Celibacy was taught as a virtue and came to be made a requirement of clergy in the apostate church. An unmarried clergy, deprived of the elevating influences of family and home life, fell into much excess and the priests became corrupt. Historians claim that most of the early popes, cardinals, and priests had mistresses and fathered illegitimate children. Celibacy and chastity were two different things to those church "leaders." Celibacy, apparently, meant just to be unmarried, not chaste. But had they been true servants of God, they would have been chaste. They would have had no sexual relationships of any kind outside the bonds of legal marriage between a man and a woman. Christ never taught that clergy should not be married. He chose Peter as an apostle, and Peter was married.

Strange rituals adopted. The corrupt church moved forward, even adopting a doctrine that taught that lies are acceptable unto God if perpetrated in a cause that man calls good. Simple forms of worship were changed with elaborate ceremonies patterned after Judaistic and heathen rituals. Church members became hopelessly committed to formalism and superstition. Instead of decent respect for early martyrs of the church, members began to worship them in a superstitious reverence. The form of public worship in the church changed drastically during the second and third centuries. Worship bore little resemblance to the original church. Philosophic discourses took the place of testimony bearing. Applause was allowed as a measure of the preacher's popularity. Burning of incense was allowed. In the fourth century, adoration of images and pictures was allowed

Ordinance of baptism changed. In the early church, baptism was administered on profession of faith and evidence of repentance. It was performed by one who properly held the priesthood. There was no delay in performing baptism once the eligibility of the candidate was shown. In the second century, priests in the church restricted the times when baptism was offered to two church festivals, Easter and the time of the Pentecostal celebration. A long and tedious preparation time was mandated, amounting to three years training before baptism was allowed. The proper form of baptism was immersion, typifying the death, burial, and resurrection of Christ. In the apostate church, immersion was no longer deemed an essential feature of baptism. Sprinkling was allowed instead. It started when apostate bishops allowed deathbed baptisms by sprinkling and soon it became widespread because of convenience.

Infant baptism. Popes began to teach that unbaptized infants would not go to heaven. The Savior never baptized infants. He blessed them. Baptizing infants is a doctrine foreign to the original church because the philosophical basis upon which it rests is one that denies the efficacy of the atoning sacrifice of Christ. Infant baptism assumes that all men are born in sin and that to be cleansed they must be baptized. Little children are already alive in Christ and do not need to be born again spiritually until they reach the age of accountability, which is eight years old.

The Lord's Supper. Changes in the sacrament of the Lord's Supper were made. The sacrament, as instituted by the Savior, was simple, sacred, and solemn. However, the apostate church introduced long sacramental prayers, and much pomp and ceremony. Vessels of gold and silver were used with an ostentatious display. That leads to the next troublesome doctrine – transubstantiation. The Church of Rome taught that the bread and wine lose their character as mere bread and wine and become in fact the flesh and blood of the crucified Christ. Together, all this means that the plain purpose of the sacrament became hidden beneath a cloud of mystery and ceremonial display. Contrast that with what we believe is a correct view of the sacrament as instituted by Christ. He took bread and wine, blessed them, gave it to his disciples and said, This do in remembrance of me.

Officers in the church. Christ organized his church with apostles, prophets, high priests, seventies, elders, bishops, priests, teachers, and deacons. One can find no evidence that the organization of the Twelve Apostles continued beyond the earthly ministry of the apostles mentioned in the New Testament. While the apostles were alive, they established branches of the church and selected bishops. Names of bishops were submitted to the congregations for the vote of the members. After the apostles were gone, existing authorities nominated bishops and other leaders. The Christian churches became independent of each other. There was a recognized equality among them. During the second and third centuries, however, marked distinctions and recognition of rank arose among the bishops. Bishops of larger cities took different titles. There began to be a power struggle for authority.

Bishop of Rome. The city of Rome promoted itself to a position of pre-

290 Light and Truth

eminence in church matters. Because it was the center of Roman power, the bishop of Rome claimed supremacy over all other bishops. It is true that Peter and Paul organized the church at Rome. Tradition, founded on error, said that Peter was the first bishop of Rome. However, apostles did not serve as bishops. They appointed bishops.

After the apostles were killed the bishops contended mightily for office and the bishop of Rome thought he ought to be the head of the church. So today we have the claim that the present pope is the last lineal successor – not just to the bishopric but to the apostleship as well. The rightful supremacy of the bishops of Rome, or Roman pontiffs as they came to be known, was early questioned by many even inside the church. When Constantine made Byzantium, or Constantinople, the capital of the empire, the bishop of Constantinople claimed equality. This dispute divided the apostate church. The bishop of Constantinople disavowed all further allegiance to the bishop of Rome. Today, followers of the bishop of Rome are known as Roman Catholics and followers of the bishop of Constantinople are known as Greek Catholics.

The right to vote. Originally, church members had the right to vote on the bishop of Rome, or any other bishop, after the apostles had nominated him. As the church became apostate, the vote was taken from the members and given to the leaders alone. In the eleventh century the power was given to the College of Cardinals, where it remains today.

The office of a pope. Successive bishops of Rome, over the years, strove hard to acquire temporal or worldly authority as well as spiritual authority. By the eleventh century they claimed the right to direct princes, kings, and emperors in the affairs of several nations. Bishops (or pontiffs) of Rome took the title of Pope, which literally means papa or father, and applied it in the sense of a universal parent. The power of the popes reached its height during the thirteenth century. Popes claimed the right to authorize and direct the internal affairs of nations, and to make lawful the rebellion of subjects against their rulers if the latter failed to keep favor with the papal power. They exercised all the authority they could against kings and princes of the earth. Compare this arrogant and tyrannical church of the world with the church of Christ. Unto Pilate our Lord declared, *My kingdom is not of this world.*

Selling indulgences. In the fourth century the Church of Rome began to punish church members with civil penalties. It imposed fines, imprisonment, bodily torture, and even death when church regulations were ignored. To avoid those penalties, church members paid money to church leaders. This led to the shocking practice of selling indulgences, or pardons. It then became the custom to pay an indulgence before the committing of a specific offense. This became a license to sin, with a promise of immunity from both temporal and spiritual penalties.

This in turn led to the dreadful doctrine of supererogation. This granted authority for the popes to remit the penalties for sin in the hereafter on payment of a sum of money. This official doctrine put forth the belief that because other saints had lived such good lives, beyond what was necessary for their own salvation, that their good deeds could be transferred to others, to save them. The so-called guardian and dispenser of this precious treasure was the Roman pontiff – for a price. This is contrary to scripture; in Romans chapter twenty and verse thirteen we read: *And they were judged every man according to their works.*

Agents of the pope traveled all around Europe selling forgiveness of sins. By paying money to the church, they claimed that the souls of departed loved ones could be redeemed from hell. Copies of such indulgences, written by representatives of the pope, are preserved in history. This practice continued for four hundred years.

Today, many church historians believe it was an act of blasphemy for the popes of those times to take to themselves divine prerogatives and powers. Here we find the pope of Rome, the head of the only church recognized at the time, assuming to remit the punishments due in the hereafter for sins committed in mortality. A pope assuming to sit in judgment as God Himself!

We recall the Catholic Inquisition. Proponents published a book called *The Witches' Hammer,* instructing members of the clergy how to locate, torture, and destroy freethinking women. All those deemed witches, such as female scholars, mystics, herb gatherers, priestesses, gypsies, and midwives, were hunted down. It is estimated that the Church of Rome burned at the stake at least five million women during this time.

Scripture. Another obvious abuse of the Roman church was regarding the reading and interpretation of scripture. The church prescribed rigid regulations forbidding the reading of the scriptures by the people. Only the pope was allowed to determine the true meaning and significance of any scripture. Policy was adopted that stated the Holy Scriptures were not composed for the use of the multitude, but only for their spiritual leaders. But the Lord said in John five and thirty nine: *Search the scriptures, for in them ye think ye have eternal life; and they are they which testify of me.*

Corruption in the church was largely responsible for what we call the Dark Ages. There was stagnation in the useful arts and sciences. And there was a general condition of illiteracy and ignorance among the common people. Too often the apostate church's teachings were shaped by the whims of corrupt, despotic, and fanatical popes. Historians now see that ignorance is a fertile soil for evil. The doctrinal fallacies of the church during this period of darkness were nourished by the ignorance of the times.

The cross. In the beginning of the Christian church, the cross was never represented in art or sculpture. Constantine's armies, contrary to popular opinion, did not bear the cross on their insignia – rather they used the first two letters of Christ's name in the Greek language. Artists began to depict the cross as the symbol of Christ's suffering when thousands of Christians died on crosses all over the Roman Empire. But it was an empty cross. Who would dare recrucify Christ? In the fifth century artists began to paint a cross with a lamb next to it. Christ was not shown on the cross until the sixth century. More and more the Church of Rome yielded itself to the fascination of art depicting Christ on the cross. Now, it is overdone. Artists depict Christ in agony-deep wounds, agony in every limb, dereliction in his eyes, and naked except a loincloth. The cross is a symbol of the death of Christ. However, in the Church of Jesus Christ of Latter-day Saints, we believe in a living Christ.

In conclusion, it appears that present-day Christianity is the result of gospel interpretations made by those who were strong enough to suppress differing opinions. It is as German poet Johann Wolfgang von Goethe states – that the history of the Christian church is a mixture of error and force.

The Restoration of the Gospel gives Christianity a fresh start, for we are to make the love of Christ the strongest power in the world. We need to be aware of the tragedy of Christian history. But we should not create ill feelings or pass judgement. Latter-day Saints need to understand that for the first time since shortly after the death of the early disciples of the Savior, we finally have the gospel in its entire purity, undefiled by human ambition and without human interpretation.

CHAPTER NOTES

The History of Christianity in England is a fictional work of the author, based on several sources, and was not actually written by Theodore Turley. Chief sources are: *Christianity in England* by Elizabeth Proud (Pitkin Unichrome, Hampshire, England, 2002), *Vicars of Christ* by Peter de Rosa (Crown Publishers, Inc. New York, N.Y. 1988), and *The Great Apostasy* by James E. Talmage (Deseret Book Company, Salt Lake City, Utah 1968).

44

THE WORDS reverberated in Wilford's mind like an afternoon thunderclap. *Go south. Go south.* He was on the last leg of his journey, a fourteen-mile walk from Worcester to the John Benbow farm. In faltering daylight, he squinted at his surroundings: Rolling hills that William called the Malverns. Naked elm, poplar, oak, and willow trees. Leafless hedges, lining the muddy road. Here and there a granite Anglican house of worship. Stone cottages with thatched roofs. Smoke curling lazily from chimneys. Fields with cattle lowing. Barnyards with chickens clucking. Farmers in carts and wagons, wearing their frocks and wool coats.

Wilford was deep in thought about what his final destination might be. Was it the Benbow farm? William had told him that his brother belonged to a religious order called the United Brethren. That a man named Thomas Kington had started the order, and worked for his brother. Was there something special about the United Brethren? About John Benbow? About Thomas Kington?

Go south. Wilford was dizzy with the possibilities. And impatient. It seemed that the trip had taken forever: An omnibus pulled by six horses from Hanley to Wolverhampton. Train to Worcester. Now the last fourteen miles on foot.

"I apologize for the long walk," William said. "In rural areas like the Malvern Hills there are no stages yet to link the small parishes. But we'll be there shortly after dark."

Wilford shrugged off William's concern with a smile. "I'm used to walking. It's just one of the requirements of being a missionary. When I was called to serve in the Southern States Mission I had to travel from Missouri to Tennessee, several hundred miles. I walked most of the way."

Unconsciously, Wilford picked up the pace as the walked through a lower vale where wisps of fog were beginning to form. Melodious birds sang in the quiet of the approaching night.

"You're a better walker than I am," William responded from a weary frame.

Wilford laughed. "In Tennessee someone gave me a horse to cover my hundred and thirty mile circuit after we got things going. But soon the horse died. I think I overworked him. Or enemies of the church poisoned him. After that I walked again most of the time."

"What's it like in America?" young Johnny Benbow asked, intrigued with Wilford's stories. He looked forward to seeing his older cousins, Thomas and Ellen, John Benbow's adopted children.

"Big," Wilford stated. "Lots of space. Lots of places to walk."

"What's Commerce like, and Kirtland, and Missouri?" William asked.

For the next hour, as darkness settled in, Wilford told them, beginning with Joseph Smith experiences in the Sacred Grove in New York, and the history of the church leading to the settlement in Illinois, now called Nauvoo. He related how sick with the ague he had been when he left his wife there.

"I suppose you miss her very much," William said.

"Yes, I miss Phoebe. We haven't been married for very long. I'm looking forward to getting a letter from her."

"How long will you be in England?"

"At least a year."

William's face registered no surprise. He beamed a smile at Wilford. "You are a very dedicated man."

"It is nothing compared to the dedication of the Savior. He gave his life for me. His gift of immortality and eternal life is priceless, and when He calls I have to respond."

"Do you think it was His voice that came to you the other night, and told you to go south?"

"Yes." Wilford answered the question emphatically.

"I hope this trip to my brother's place is the answer to your prayer."

"I have a feeling it will be."

The English moon beamed brightly as William Benbow led two other shadowy shapes along a dirt road and instinctively found Bishops Frome, Castle Frome, and turned left through a thin layer of fog into the lane that led to the Hill Farm. Wilford could see a large white stucco house at the end of the lane surrounded by barns and corrals. The Benbow mansion was well lit by lanterns. The two men and one boy walked down the lane and knocked on the door, then stood there as a cold breeze throttled through the porch. A young servant who doubled as a butler and farm worker answered the door, letting them into the large parlor where they found John Benbow sitting at a paper-cluttered desk, reading by a lantern.

"William! Johnny! What a surprise," John said, rising quickly, giving them strong bear hugs. He picked up his nine-year-old nephew and swung him in the air. "My, how you've grown."

"John, I would like you to meet a friend," William interrupted, gesturing toward his companion.

Wilford stepped forward and offered his hand to a man slightly taller than himself with sturdy shoulders, a chin that thrust ever so slightly forward, long triangular nose, rosy cheeks, and a forehead that sloped back to reveal a slightly receding hairline, full of brown hair with strands of gray. He wore black pants, a white shirt and a brown vest. Wilford stood erect as he grasped Benbow's hand, and spoke rapidly in a warm but firm voice.

"I am a missionary from America, Mr. Benbow. My name is Wilford Woodruff, and I am an elder of the Church of Jesus Christ of Latter-day Saints. I have been sent to your home by the commandment of God as a messenger of salvation, to preach to you and your household and the inhabitants of the land."

Blinking twice, his eyes locking onto the visitor, John Benbow was startled by the words. At first sight, he was taken back by this weary looking, travel-stained man with the short stocky frame, penetrating eyes, and stern face. He was not the legendary American he had built up in his mind – no George Washington, Thomas Jefferson, or Benjamin Franklin. The man was an inch or two shorter that he was, brown hair, bull necked, thick-shouldered, emanating a feeling of disciplined strength and profound spirituality. John looked at his brother William as if to say, *Who is this man, really?*

John did not recognize the name of the church, but the words seemed to flow out of the American's mouth with ease. He liked the fact that he heard the name of the Savior in the name of the church. He had often thought that a church ought to carry the name Jesus Christ, especially if it purported to be His church. The handshake was firm and friendly, although the hands were icy cold from the long trip. Turning to the stately woman at his side, he said, "I would like you to meet my wife, Jane."

Wilford bowed deeply and took her by the hand, shaking it. "Pleased to know you. Thank you for allowing me in your home." A warm feeling came over Wilford, a feeling of peace, and a feeling of the Spirit that confirmed to him he had arrived at the place where he was supposed to be. He began to relax.

Curtseying, Jane responded, "Not at all...Reverend?"

"Elder. Just call me Elder Woodruff."

"Very well. Won't you sit down please? I'll have refreshments here presently," she said, contemplating the American.

"Thank you," Wilford said, his eyes bright and full of confidence.

Sizing up his brother's traveling companion, John was curious as to why his brother had brought Elder Woodruff to Castle Frome unannounced, arriving so late in the day. The man must be important, or his message must be important. Or both. He had no idea William had joined another church. "Have you been in England for very long?"

Wilford made a cheerful face. "Just long enough to be directed here. I arrived January eleventh in Liverpool and preached the gospel in your brother's area until yesterday. I was told to travel south and we left early yesterday. Your brother was gracious enough to bring me to you."

With an arch-questioning look, cocking his head, John asked, "Who told you to travel south, to my place?"

"The Lord Jesus Christ."

John Benbow again blinked several times and took a step backward, not knowing quite how to respond. A look of surprise came over him and he gave Wilford another curious survey, eyeing him head to foot as though, indeed, he might be a special messenger. After a few seconds he said, "Well, this is going to be an interesting evening." He stole a glance at his brother.

Returning a smile to his brother, and feeling a gush of warmth through his veins, William nodded and said in a calm voice, "That is an understatement."

Wilford smiled too, and tried to remain relaxed as he took a seat in a cushioned red velvet armchair in the Benbow parlor. He wanted to begin telling the story of the restoration, but knew he had to be patient and learn more about William's brother and his wife, the family the Lord had led him to. His eyes took in his surroundings. He was impressed with John Benbow's home. In his mind it was more like a mansion compared to the homes he had stayed in previously. He complimented Jane on its cleanliness and orderly appearance. Wilford had already learned from William that John was a yeoman, leasing two hundred acres, which included the house, from Jane's relative, a Mrs. Anne Freeman. He also knew that he leased another hundred acres from the Castle Frome parish glebe. Wilford asked John to tell him about his farm. He learned that the patchwork of small fields, enclosed by hedges that he had seen on approach to the Hill Farm, raised various corns – wheat, barley, rye and oats – as well as hops, clover, and turnips. There were also orchards of apple and pear trees, and livestock.

Wilford began asking questions as John stirred the fire in the hearth, sending a shower of sparks spiraling upward. He placed two large logs on it, anticipating an evening of conversation. Wilford arose and stood by the fire, warming himself with William and Johnny, listening to John's answers. He learned that John would be forty years old on April first, and that he was born in nearby Grenden Warren, Herefordshire. Jane voluntarily disclosed that she was forty-eight, also born in Herefordshire. They had been married thirteen years and had lost two sons, both dying as infants. However, John and Jane had adopted two of John's brother's children, Ellen and Thomas, both in their teens. Wilford knew there were things he could say in his discussion that would bring them tears of happiness regarding those lost children.

Over a display of yellow and orange cheeses, dried beef and biscuits, cakes, apple cider, pear juice and English tea, the conversation soon turned to the United Brethren. John Benbow, looking bright-eyed as though it were mid-day instead of late evening, making broad gestures, began telling Wilford about Thomas Kington. He explained that he provided Superintendent Kington with a part-time job and room and board, but that the rest of the time he was out of the circuit, as he was at this particular time. Wilford dove into the food with enthusiasm, yet listening with intense curiosity as John explained that one of the main purposes of the United Brethren was to wait for additional "light and truth." The words seemed to echo inside Wilford's eardrums, ringing familiarly, settling comfortably. Suddenly, he knew with more exactness why the Lord had sent him to Castle Frome and the Hill Farm.

"We've told you about us," Jane said, giving Wilford a pleased, flattered look. "Please tell us about you. I would like to know where you are from. Are you a celibate priest or do you have a wife?"

Wilford, looking a little surprised yet thoughtful, chuckled, downed a big bite of cake, then patiently and with zest told them about his own life, his marriage, and his new home in Nauvoo. He gave them the short version, detecting that John appeared anxious for him to get on with the reason William brought him to Castle Frome, all the way from Hanley. Wilford felt like a boiling cauldron anyway, ready to erupt with the story of the restored gospel. It was not his nature to be patient and listen to chatter. He said an opening prayer himself, asking everyone to get on their knees. He wanted to make certain that the most important element of his presentation – the Spirit – would be present.

A warm spirit was radiating through the soul of John Benbow as he knelt for the prayer. It had started the moment John Benbow met Elder Woodruff and heard the bold declaration that "Jesus Christ had sent him" to his home. As he listened to the American's prayer, John wished Thomas Kington were there with them. But he knew that Kington was somewhere in the Malvern Hills doing the work of his own ministry, training preachers, meeting in members' homes on every night of the week, and opening new places to generally strengthen the cause of the United Brethren. He didn't know exactly when

Kington would be back.

John Benbow's feeling of warmth was reconfirmed as he gradually heard the message of the restored gospel. Deep inside, John knew this had to be the "additional light and truth" that he, Thomas, and the other members of the United Brethren were waiting for. It was a fantastic message, filled with wonderment and common sense. God had a plan of salvation for all mankind, authored by the Savior himself. In previous ages prophets such as Adam, Noah, and Moses had revealed the exact same plan to his people. Now, there was a prophet on the earth once more who had actually seen and talked with God. His name was Joseph Smith. Just twenty years ago this man, then a young boy, went into the woods to pray, prompted to do so by a passage of scripture in the book of James. John Benbow hung on every word that the American missionary said: The description of the pillar of light. The words from God the Father introducing his Son. And how the Savior answered Joseph's question on which church to join.

He was even more fascinated by the story of the Angel Moroni: How he appeared to Joseph Smith three times in one night. How Joseph received the ancient record written on golden plates. How they were translated and became the Book of Mormon. He held the book in his hands when Elder Woodruff gave him a copy. He promised to read it and test the challenge of Moroni, to ask God if it were true.

Oh, how John Benbow wished Thomas Kington were here.

After two hours of discussion, answering a myriad of questions from the Benbows, Wilford was worried that his hosts were beginning to tire. He could answer more questions tomorrow. It was not to be. John wanted Wilford to "unload the whole load" in one sitting. Wilford continued by telling the Benbows about the Lord's plan of salvation, the physical resurrection, overcoming both physical and spiritual death; about faith, repentance, baptism by immersion for the remission of sins, the gift of the Holy Ghost; how the true church of Jesus Christ was restored, that the Aaronic Priesthood was conferred on Joseph Smith by John the Baptist, that the Melchizedek Priesthood was conferred upon him by Peter, James and John; that all necessary gospel ordinances necessary for the salvation of man can now be performed; and how the Lord commanded Joseph to reestablish the Church of Jesus Christ on the sixth of April 1830.

Feasting on every word, John Benbow knew he had to be baptized. When Elder Woodruff asked him if he would like to be baptized, it was two o'clock in the morning, Friday, March the sixth. Answering with an enthusiastic "yes," he turned to look at his wife. Filled with emotion, she merely nodded her head up and down.

"Is there a pond around here?" Wilford asked.

"Yes," John said, "just less than two hundred yards downhill from the house." Despite the hour, he wished the dreamlike quality of the evening would never end.

"I'll see it in the morning," Wilford said softly. "Let's get some rest."

45

NEXT MORNING, promptly at seven thirty, Wilford appeared from the upstairs bedroom to find Jane Benbow bent over her stove cooking tender sizzling steaks and ham. Rubbing his bloodshot and baggy eyes, he managed a happy "good morning" and drank a glass of apple juice. He had only slept five hours but the smell of the food and the first light of dawn had awakened him. He had been in England for nearly three months but he had never had a breakfast like the one served by the Benbows, the meats with eggs, cheese, bacon, and muffins. It was the beginning of a bright winter day, and the sun was glistening off the frosty fields surrounding the Hill Farm as he dug into the breakfast, expressing his deep gratitude to Jane. He knew there were many people here waiting for his message, people now organized into the United Brethren. There was no time to waste.

"I would like to preach the gospel to as many people as possible, and as quickly as possible," he said to his host, pausing to wipe his mouth with a bright yellow napkin. Wilford didn't know what was more important at the time, talking or gulping down his sumptuous food.

"You haven't seen it yet, but attached to the house is a separate building we call the Great Hall," John responded, pointing his finger to the north end of the parlor. "We have been using it for a meeting place for the United Brethren for our members that live close to the farm. It will hold around two hundred and is properly licensed. Will that do?"

Wiping his mouth again, overwhelmed at what was turning out to be a perfect setting, Wilford nodded up and down. "I'll look at it when we finish eating."

Hunched over a warm cup of tea, sipping it meticulously, John smiled at the American and at his brother and nephew, all of whom appeared famished. He was pleased that he could be of so much help so quickly. "I'll have my farm servants ride out this morning with word there will be a special meeting tonight featuring an American missionary. We should be able to gather up a few people for you to preach the gospel to, and the word will spread from there."

"How many members do you have by now? William told me four or five hundred."

"Membership has grown to around six hundred," John answered. "Here is a copy of Superintendent Kington's preachers plan for the Fromes Hill Circuit." As he handed him the piece of paper he explained that they trained both men and women and had a system for training and advancing them from "trial" to "full" preacher status, as well as a systematic way of adding and dropping meeting places throughout the Malvern Hills area where they were organized the strongest.

A pleasant surprise flashed on the face of the American apostle. "How will your members feel about the message I am preaching about the restored gospel?"

"I think they will respond the same as I did. If they take the matter to prayer and feel the Spirit as I did, they will know it is true. I have no hesitation about inviting them to hear you."

As Benbow's farm servants began scouring the nearby countryside, Wilford, feeling stuffed and a little dizzy after the incredible breakfast feast and a lack of sleep, walked to the small pond south of the house with William Benbow and his son. There was a little ice formed on the edges, but he determined it would suit the purpose perfectly. People had been baptized in cold water before. He hoped Thomas Kington could be reached. He would like Kington to hear the gospel message and be one of the first to be baptized. He could ask Kington and Benbow to be his assistants to help him find and teach the other United Brethren members. However, the farm servants returned without making contact with Kington. Nevertheless he spent a pleasant day teaching John and Jane Benbow more about the fullness of the gospel.

Sunday was approaching and Benbow surmised Kington was somewhere in the three-shire area and may not return for more than a week. Nevertheless, a small crowd showed up for a Friday evening meeting. Wilford preached his first group gospel sermon in the Malvern Hills. Six persons were baptized: John and Jane Benbow, Mary Rowberry, Charles Price, Ann Boum and John Cheese.

Later in the evening, Wilford caught up on his journal.

MARCH 1. Sunday. This is my birthday. I am 33 years of age today. It being Sunday, I preached twice through the day to a large assembly in the City Hall, in the town of Hanley, and administered the sacrament unto the saints. In the evening I again met with a large assembly of the saints and strangers, and while singing the first hymn the Spirit of the Lord rested upon me, and the voice of God said to me, "This is the last meeting that you will hold with this people for many days." I was astonished at this, as I had many appointments out in that district. When I arose to speak to the people, I told them that it was the last meeting I should hold with them for many days. They marveled, for they

306 Light and Truth

expected, as well as myself, that I should spend months in their midst; but the ways and thoughts of God are not like our ways and thought in every respect. At the close of the meeting four came forward for baptism, and we went down in the water and baptized them. [Editor's note: The March 1 journal entry, and some of the other days immediately following, is a compilation of Elder Woodruff's original entry, plus three other sources: (1) his letter to the Times and Seasons written in Manchester, England, October 7, 1840; (2) his book entitled, Leaves From My Journal, 1881; and (3) Matthias Cowley's book, Wilford Woodruff, published in 1909.]

MARCH 2. Monday. In the morning I went in secret before the Lord, and asked Him what His will was concerning me. The answer I got was, that I should go to the south, for the Lord had a great work for me to perform there, as many souls were waiting for the word of the Lord. I walked to Burslem, and returned to Hanley. Elder Turley returned from Birmingham; we counseled together, he thinking it best for me to go to Birmingham and try to open doors and establish the work in that city, and leave the Potteries in the hands of Elder Turley. But believing it to be my privilege and duty to know the will of the Lord upon the subject, therefore, I asked my Heavenly Father, and as I asked, the Lord gave and showed me that it was his will that I should go immediately to the south of England. I conversed with brother William Benbow upon the subject, who had lived in Herefordshire and had friends still residing there, and much wished me to visit that region of country, and generously proffered to accompany me to his brother's house and pay my fare, which I readily accepted.

MARCH 3. Tuesday. I walked to Stafford and called at the Kings Inn. I had an interview with Mr. Coleburn, the rector of the Church of England. I then called upon the clerk of the peace about a license, but he could not give me information upon the subject. I then had an interview with Mr. Alexander Stewart, a preacher, but he rejected my testimony, and brought a railing accusation against me and turned me from his door. In fulfillment of the directions given me, in fulfillment of the word of the Lord to me, I took the omnibus in company with Brother William Benbow, and his son, and rode to Wolverhampton and spent the night, distance of 26 miles.

MARCH 4. Wednesday. We took the coach, rode through Dudley six miles, Stourbridge five miles, Kiddeminister seven miles, Stourport four miles, Worcester twelve mile. Then we walked to Mr. John Benbow's Hill Farm, Castle Frome, Ledbury, Herefordshire. Mr. Benbow was a large farmer. Cultivated about 300 acres of land. I spoke the word of God unto him and his house, and he received my testimony, and we had a good time. I spent the night at his house.

MARCH 5. Thursday. I spent the day at the John Benbow mansion and continued to teach him and his wife the gospel. He told me that there were many waiting in the area to hear the word, and he predicted that they would join the church.

MARCH 6. Friday. I preached at John Benbow's Hill Farm in the evening and a number received the word and I baptized six, including John Benbow and his wife, Jane, and four preachers of the United Brethren, of the Methodist order: Ann Boum, Mary Rowberry, Charles Price, and John Cheese.

46

THE GREAT HALL attached to the Benbow home was indeed massive. The rough-hewn stone building shimmered in the rain, and doves cooed in the roof overhead on this Sunday, the eighth of March. Inside, more than two hundred curious Castle Frome residents, both United Brethren and Anglican Church members, were crammed together, curious, anxious to hear the American missionary speak. They were surprised that he was speaking for the third time. He had preached in the Great Hall earlier, and also at nearby Frome's Hill.

Wilford Woodruff did not care that the architecture of the hall was course and simple. Or that the building looked nothing like a church. Or that his audience was composed of both United Brethren congregation and Anglican Church members. He was ready to preach the restored gospel of Jesus Christ. As he was introduced by his new convert, John Benbow, he felt the physical world fade away.

"Friends, the Lord has sent Elder Woodruff to us," Benbow said, his eyes looking restful. "I believe with all my heart that the purpose of the United

Brethren movement was to gather and prepare a group of people to hear and respond to the message that Elder Woodruff brings to you tonight."

Wilford felt a biting warmth spread over him.

"When Elder Woodruff arrived just four days ago, we invited as many as we could in a short time and he preached to us the most wonderful message I have ever heard. As you know by now, I accepted the invitation to be baptized and my wife and I were baptized the next day, as were four others. Elder Woodruff, who just turned thirty-three years old a week ago today, said that it was the best birthday present he had ever received. But I say to you, my baptism was the greatest gift I could have received. Thank you, Elder Woodruff."

Benbow turned to his new American friend, arm extended. "May I introduce Elder Woodruff, a member of the Quorum of Twelve Apostles, from the Church of Jesus Christ of Latter-day Saints."

As Wilford stood, the main door burst open and the imposing presence of an instantly recognizable man wove through the crowd toward the rostrum.

It's the constable, Benbow gasped.

The man approached with the strides of an attacking bull. His mouth was curved downward. There was a serious, chilling look on his face. He placed his body directly in front of Elder Woodruff. "Sir, I am Roger Mortimer, the parish constable. The rector sent me to arrest you. I have a warrant." He fumbled at his coat, and drew out a paper.

Wilford exchanged appalled looks with John Benbow, whose jaw had dropped in shock. Wilford backed off awkwardly and abruptly, his eyes popping wide open. The crowd murmured, then quieted, waiting for a response from the American preacher.

Regaining his composure and his confidence, Wilford cleared his throat under a constant stare. "For what crime?"

The crowd noise rose again, and then fell. Wilford stood contemplating Mortimer, remembering what he had been told over and over again, that constables in England were under control of the Anglican Church. John Benbow had already disclosed to him that there were several members of the Castle Frome parish in the audience, and that earlier in the day almost the entire parish had skipped Anglican services to hear about the new religion from the American missionary.

Reaction to Wilford's question was swift. A smirk appeared on the constable's hard, smug face and he said in a cold, acid tone, "For preaching to the people without a license."

Slightly irritated, Wilford thought of the Ministerial Certificate signed by Joseph Smith, the prophet of the Dispensation of the Fullness of Times. The only man on the earth authorized by the Savior to hold all priesthood keys. "I came to England with a license to preach. Please sit down and I will wait upon you after the meeting." He pointed to a chair. It was the one he had sat in while Benbow introduced him. It was the only empty chair in the room.

Again, noise from the crowd.

The constable winced, and lost his imposing look. He glanced at the chair. The crowd fell silent, watching. For a few seconds, the constable weighed whether he should merely walk out of the Benbow hall or comply with the American's request. He coughed, clearing his throat. He stammered, as though he were going to lodge a protest. Then, quietly, meekly, he sat.

Elder Woodruff raised his arms in a gesture to calm the crowd, restoring order. He planted his feet behind the rostrum and began his presentation again, speaking in a warm, commanding, aristocratic voice. With every eye in the hall fixed on the American preacher, Elder Woodruff began to unfold the story of the restoration, emphasizing the coming forth of the Book of Mormon. Speaking for more than an hour, he finished with a simple declaration and explanation of the four main principles of the gospel of Jesus Christ, which he declared to be the doctrine of Christ: Faith. Repentance. Baptism.

And the gift of the Holy Ghost.

Keeping the constable and the crowd in the palm of his hands with his infectious gospel teaching ability and mannerisms, Wilford concluded by bearing his testimony. "I testify in the name of Jesus Christ that the things I have taught you this evening are true. There is a simple test that each one of you can apply to know that my message is true. If you will in prayer ask your Heavenly Father, in the name of Jesus Christ, with a sincere heart and real intent, I promise that each of you can come to the same testimony that I have – and that Brother Benbow and his wife have. God's true church is on the earth again. His true church is the Church of Jesus Christ of Latter-day Saints. In the name of the Savior, Jesus Christ, Amen."

The hushed quiet that had overcome the audience of Anglicans and members of the United Brethren was broken only when each and every person answered Wilford's amen with an amen of their own. The sound echoed throughout the room.

Wilford now surveyed his audience, trying to look into each pair of eyes. He asked those to stand who wanted to be baptized, tonight, this very evening.

The sound of a chair emptying behind Wilford startled him. He turned to find Constable Mortimer on his feet. "Mr. Woodruff, I would like to be baptized."

In shocked silence John Benbow stared at the constable, the man who had come to arrest Wilford Woodruff. John knew Constable Mortimer as one of the most die-hard faithful Anglicans in the Castle Frome parish, and he had known him for many years. But there he was, standing in humility in front of an apostle of the Lord, asking for baptism. Gone was the smirk from his face, the smugness, and the acid tone of his tongue. For a moment Benbow watched as the constable began weeping, begging for forgiveness. John's heart melted as he saw Elder Woodruff embrace the man, shake his hand, and tell him that he would be baptized by immersion for the remission of sins.

Less shocking to John Benbow was when two of the United Brethren lay preachers, Joseph and Margaret Pullen, stepped forward. John looked over the crowd of more than two hundred persons jammed into the Great Hall. He could hear husbands and wives debating whether or not they should get baptized tonight, or wait to hear more, or wait until relatives had heard the gospel message. He could see two more lay preachers of the United Brethren walking forward, James Hill and John Parry. They were followed by Jane Gailey, who leaned over and whispered into Benbow's ear, "I wish my husband were here. I hope he'll forgive me for being baptized without him. But I can't wait."

John gave her a faint smile and whispered back, "I'm sure he'll understand." Another lady came forward without her husband; he recognized her as Charlotte Clark. Then John saw his brother walking forward with his eight-year-old son. "Johnny said he wants to be baptized tonight, too," he said to his brother.

"Fine, lad. Stand up straight, John William Benbow."

MARCH 8. Sunday. I preached at Fromes Hill in the morning, at Stanley Hill in the afternoon, and at the Hill Farm in the evening. I had a large congregation. The Lord of Hosts was with me. I baptized seven persons, four of which were preachers. Joseph Pullen, Margaret Pullen, James Hill, John Parry, Jane Gailey, John William Benbow, and Charlotte Clark.

MARCH 9. Monday. I preached at Stanley Hill and baptized seven persons, two of which were preachers: Ann Benbow [John Benbow's mother], Prestwood Benbow [John's 53-year-old brother], Sarah Benbow [young Thomas Benbow's wife; Thomas, an adopted son of John Benbow, was baptized March 28.], Helen Benbow [probably Ellen Benbow, adopted daughter of John Benbow], Ann Perry, Robert Holmes, and Elizabeth Holmes. [Jane Benbow's maiden name was Holmes, so Robert and Elizabeth were probably her relatives. Clarifications in brackets are from A History of John Benbow, by Arthur B. Erekson, 1988, Provo, Utah.]

MARCH 10. Tuesday. I preached at Brother Benbow's Hill Farm and baptized twelve persons, three of which were preachers: Hannah Badham, Mary Hill, Ann Rowberry, Ann Smith, James Barnes, James Benbow [John Benbow's 56-year-old brother], Mary Ann Holmes, Robert Hill, Thomas Jenkins, Hannah Williams, Sarah Tumkins and William Evins.

MARCH 13. Friday. I visited the sick and walked to Stokes Lane six miles and preached and baptized William Davis, Jonathan Davis, Caroline Gaston, Francis Birch, Ann Birch and Richard Hall.

MARCH 15. Sunday. I preached at Fromes Hill. I met with the saints in the afternoon and confirmed 22 persons. I preached in the evening to a congregation of about 800, but some of the baser sort made much disturbance. There was a number of persons that wished to be baptized but returned home without it in consequence of the people. This was a laborious day to me.

MARCH 16. Monday. I called on Squire Johnston, a magistrate, and obtained a license for preaching in any part of the English government. On my return I visited a number of persons and found them believing. I preached at Fromes Hill and baptized three persons, one of which was a preacher: Mr. Jenkins, John Williams and Mary Cheese.

CHAPTER NOTES.

Wilford Woodruff does not give the name of the constable who came to arrest him while preaching at the Hill Farm that first Sunday. Elder Woodruff recorded the names of all those persons he personally baptized. Perhaps John Benbow or one of the other early converts baptized the constable. So the author has given the man a fictitious name. But the incident in based on fact.

47

ABRUPTLY WAKING in the middle of the night, his limbs jerking, Bobby found himself in a cold sweat. The sheets were soaked on his side of the bed. In the eerie silence of the dark night, with only the breathing of Hannah making a dim noise, he thought about the ugly nightmare that had troubled him, haunted him, until he had suddenly sat up in bed, eyes wide open. Rarely did he dream, and when he did they were not troublesome dreams. Rather they were dreams either of his childhood, his family, or the way he had fought a fight. This dream had been different, and it had a remarkable, chilling effect on his mind. He put his hands to his head, wiping away rolls of sweat, then frustratingly dug his fingers toward his fogged brain, trying to erase the dream from his memory. It had been a fight dream again, but with a disastrous ending. His opponent had no face and no name, but it had been for the championship. Whenever he had struck out at the opponent, it had been like hitting thin air, a vapor, or a ghost of sorts. In the end, the no-name, no-face opponent had been declared the winner. Any chance for fortune and fame for himself had vanished, disappeared, slipped away. But an odd feeling had swept over him at the end of the dream. He had lost the British championship, yet, in his dream, he had not cared, and that was troubling to him now. There had been no feeling inside his heart of personal devastation, as he would have imagined. Now that he was awake, sweating, breathing hard, confused, he wondered what the dream meant.

He glanced at Hannah, barely visible, her face dimly lit by rays of moonlight flitting through the window. He slowly let out all his breath and again stretched out beside her, trying to control the anxiety he felt. He wanted to wake her and tell her about the strange dream, but decided against it. He had never shared a personal, middle-of-the-night dream with her before. She would think he was strange, especially this time of the night. A long time passed while he contemplated the dream, all the while listening to his wife's breathing. He lay there that way until morning, not sleeping. Just before Hannah woke up, he rose, dressed, and left the house.

At the sparring room in Gloucester, Bobby struggled to maintain his normal focus. He was sluggish on the heavy bag. His timing was off as he sparred against two different fighters. For the first time ever, his sparring partners felt they were getting the best of the young butcher. After sparring, he ran. His feet felt heavy during his roadwork.

Following his training session, he slogged through a cold, miserable rainstorm to the Ferret's Folly, to share his dream with his two brothers. William and John enjoyed a hearty round of laughter, telling him not to put much stock in the weird dream. As far as they were concerned, their brother was still going to be the champion.

Bobby's brothers were further astonished at Bobby's complaints about Hannah, that she was unwilling to live in London for even a few weeks. In William's view Hannah was ungrateful, insensitive, and unappreciative of her husband's abilities.

"Just look at what you have provided Hannah," William said, nursing a nasty cough. "You have a hundred-acre farm, with more promised. A rather nice cottage to live in. You're making more money as a fighter than I am as a butcher. And you'll be earning big purses in the future. What does she have to complain about?"

Inwardly, William was insanely jealous of his youngest brother. Everyone in the pub recognized Bobby when he had walked in. Since Bobby's victory over Sam "The Man" Gregory in London, he was viewed as a celebrity of sorts. Bobby had seen all the famous spots in London. He'd never been to London. Bobby was a yeoman. He was a low-class butcher. Bobby had a strong, athletic body. His was thin and wiry, susceptible to sickness.

John scoffed. "Just bring Hannah in here for a few weeks. I'll put her to work waiting on tables, carrying trays of food and drink to my customers. It wouldn't be long until she tired of the monotony and the drunks. Every married woman in Gloucestershire would happily trade her places. If she were my wife, I'd tell her to button up. She doesn't know when she's well off."

Bobby gripped his mug tightly with both hands and smiled awkwardly at his brothers. Now that his parents were gone, his two older brothers, in some strange off-handed way, seemed to take the place of his father. Like his father, they were highly opinionated, independent, assertive, spontaneous thinkers, and a bit arrogant. Tonight, however, for a strange reason that confused him, his brothers seemed inconsiderate, self-serving, and out of touch with what he had tried to explain in his dream.

"After you're champion you'll be able to buy my butcher shop, the Nightingale Dairy and anything else you want," William said. "Tell Hannah to bite her tongue and just go to London with you. John and I can help Daniel with some of the farm work." His cough was guttural, from deep inside his lungs.

Bobby pensively rubbed his chin and gave William a concerned look.

"Sound's like you ought to be home in bed, brother. Maybe it's me who ought to be offering to help with your work. Maybe you ought to take a few days off and get better."

"Nonsense, I'm fine." William answered, coughing again. "If I had a chance to live in London and be the champion my wife would do cart wheels all day long. Hannah is too independent and strong-minded, just like her father was."

"And your friend Henry," John teased.

"Don't remind me," Bobby said, asking for another ale. "Do you really think I ought to just put my foot down and tell her what we're going to do?"

"I wouldn't let her ruin your life and your chance to make a lot of money," John advised. "Just pack her up and move her to London."

A nervous spasm swept Bobby and he hung his head. Up until his confusing dream, he would have agreed with everything his brothers were saying. Now, he didn't know. His upcoming fight with Ben Caunt, just like London, seemed so far away. And the Hannah-bashing was beginning to seem a little awkward.

48

THOMAS KINGTON came clip clopping into the Hill Farm on the old hack that he had named Beggar on Tuesday, the seventeenth day of March. He gingerly dismounted and began unsaddling when he saw John Benbow emerge from the mansion and walk toward him in hurried steps, with an unusually excited look on his face.

"Good morning," Thomas said, untying his leather satchel and pulling the saddle off Beggar's steaming back. He wondered why Benbow had such a quick pace about him. He also wondered why he was dressed like it was Sunday, why his eyes were lit like they were, and why he had not waited inside the mansion like he normally did when they were to meet together.

"You haven't heard?" John asked, buttoning his coat, following Superintendent Kington to a shed where the saddle was placed. A chilly breeze was blowing from in gray clouds from the southwest.

"Heard what?" Thomas asked, returning to Old Beggar and leading the gelding to a corral.

"About the American preacher, Elder Woodruff?" Benbow calculated that Kington might already know, depending on where his travels had taken him.

Thomas gave his employer a quizzical glance. "No, I sure haven't. An American preacher, you say? What's an American preacher doing in these parts?"

"He represents a new church that has been organized there. He's been staying here for the past few days, teaching the gospel."

Kington felt a rising uncertainty about Benbow's tone. "What church?"

"The Church of Jesus Christ of Latter-day Saints." The yeoman farmer straightened his tie, letting the long name of the church sink in. The thought popped into his mind, *just tell him.* "Thomas, I've been baptized into that church."

The remark caught Kington off guard. He stopped in his tracks, turned his back against the wind, dropped his jaw, and stared into his employer's face. "What did you say?"

"It's true. I'm now a member of another church. There's a lot I need to tell you."

The look of Benbow's face told Kington it was no joke. Agonizing bewilderment came over Kington's face. He stood there for a moment, chest heaving, gripping the leather satchel still in his hands.

"You're joking of course." He was still trying to digest Benbow's words.

"No, I'm not. The American missionary will be back soon. You better come in. Jane has lunch prepared."

Kington's mood drifted from perplexity to bordering on anger.

John placed a hand on Kington's shoulder, helping him absorb the shock. "Don't worry. Everything will be fine."

As Thomas followed John toward the house, his heart stirred with a certain pain, his thoughts tormented by the words he had just heard. Below the

Hill Farm, in every direction, in the English countryside of the Malvern Hills, lay the many parishes within Gloucestershire, Herefordshire, and Worcestershire. These were the communities where eight years of ministry had yielded much satisfying fruit. In the leather satchel he was carrying were many of the records of the religious organization that he and his employer had built: Names of six hundred members. Names of dozens of lay preachers. Locations of United Brethren branches. Circuit teaching schedules. Sabbath preaching schedules,. Weekday preaching plans. Committee names. Licenses for holding religious services in more than forty private homes. Preaching licenses. A deed of conveyance for ownership for the Gadfield Elm chapel. A receipt from a man named Thomas Shipton in the amount of twenty-five pounds for purchase of the Gadfield Elm property. Less important items such as sheets of paper with the words of popular hymns.

The record represented a good portion of Kington's life and soul. Was John Benbow really abandoning this effort? Had he really joined another church? Did his employer expect him to do the same? Was his future employment dependent upon following John Benbow into another religion? These were questions that rained upon Thomas Kington's mind as he entered the familiar kitchen, greeted Jane Benbow, and sat in his usual chair.

After a certain measure of leisurely small talk, after John's pronouncement of grace, and over the first few mouthfuls of stewed loin of veal and macaroni and cheese, John Benbow began. "The further light and truth has come, Thomas."

Thomas stopped chewing his food, blinked twice, and stared hard at his employer and good friend. With imploring eyes and a half-opened, gaping mouth, he reflected on the familiar words, words that both he and John had used hundreds and hundreds of times as they had built the United Brethren organization. He glanced at Jane. She smiled as if to confirm her husband's statement. The room seemed charged with a deep intensity. Kington's emotions alternated between confusion, elation, and amazement over John's first choice of words. He reeled in disbelief, yet a peaceful calm began to come over him, fueled by John Benbow's bold statement.

"I'm sure you're going to tell me what you mean by that," he said in a meek voice.

John leaned forward, letting his emotions come to the surface. His eyes misted, but they became points of light that locked firmly onto Thomas Kington. Then John began the amazing story of the night Wilford Woodruff showed up at his home with his brother and nephew, the message that he bore, and the teachings of the restored gospel. Benbow related how they had stayed up practically all night asking questions, had learned basic beautiful principles, and how he and his wife had been baptized in the icy pond just below the mansion. Thomas listened, not eating any more food, not drinking any more drink, but digesting every word. He began to understand why John and Ann had joined the American's church. And why, only a few days after Elder Woodruff's arrival to the Malvern Hills, several other United Brethren members had already been baptized into the Church of Jesus Christ of Latter-day Saints, including many key lay preachers.

As Benbow unfolded the story, Thomas studied him intently. Benbow seemed like a new man, a man possessed with a new spirit, a calm, inviting spirit. The mention of a prophet named Joseph Smith, a book called the Book of Mormon, and an angel called Moroni, intrigued and fascinated Thomas. Was it true that a series of heavenly messengers, including ancient apostles, Peter, James and John, and the man who had personally baptized the Savior, John the Baptist, had come to the earth to help restore the true church of Christ? And that other heavenly messengers had come as well? Moses? Elijah? Each restoring portions of the lost gospel back to the earth, to a living prophet, who now had the proper keys to administer saving ordinances to earthly people? It was either the most fantastic lie perpetuated upon the face of the earth, or it was the most glorious truth he had ever heard.

John and Jane Benbow obviously believed it. Wilford Woodruff, who had gone to Green Yeal to talk to another group of investigators, was scheduled to return to the Benbow home later that day. Thomas Kington, his emotions still alternating back and forth, wanting to believe, but harboring some doubts, not wanting to let loose of his organization, was determined to find out for himself.

"Thomas! Hey, Thomas!"

Thomas Kington jerked his head out of the Bible, went rigid as a stretching cat, and opened both eyes widely. For five long, strung-out hours he had been pacing back and forth in the mansion parlor, visiting with the Benbows, meeting with three farm servants about the coming duties of spring work, walking outside, reading scriptures, munching on cheese and biscuits, sipping tea, reviewing papers from his satchel about the United Brethren, praying, thinking, and weighing what John had told him during lunch.

"Huh?"

"Elder Woodruff, is here. I see him walking up the lane."

"Good!" Thomas fluttered his eyes and sat up out of his chair. He closed his Bible and jumped excitedly to the front window, where John stood peering out. A short stocky man came striding toward him, his coat wrapped tightly around him to protect him from the cold rain that was falling. He held his neck forward, his shoulders hunched, with his hands in his pockets, and a black American beaver hat pulled over his tousled brown hair.

Woodruff's plain appearance shocked Thomas. He had expected a tall man in long, flowing red robes and a red hat, similar to that of a Catholic cardinal or the Archbishop of Canterbury. Wilford Woodruff from America had been described by John Benbow as an apostle of the Lord Jesus Christ. He was reportedly a member of the Quorum of Twelve Apostles, a man answering only to a living prophet, and that living prophet the earthly link to God.

So where was the flawlessly decorated blue and white royal coach drawn by six matched white horses, that should be delivering him to the doorstep? Surely an apostle would be entitled to a coach equal in stature to that of the King of England. And where were his trumpeters, his footmen, his armed guards, his calvary, and his personal secretary?

Squinting through the glass, eyes gawking, then standing back as Benbow opened the door to the humble, muddy-footed man who approached, Thomas Kington's first reaction was to sag his shoulders in disappointment. Then he quickly thought of his own words, words that he had used with Daniel and Elizabeth Browett when he had compared the pope to the Savior, in dress and demeanor. A true apostle would not come in flowing red robes or richly embroidered vestments. Just as the original apostles would have done in their day, an apostle would wear the clothing of a common man, nothing more. Thomas threw back his shoulders, repented of his thoughts, cleared his throat, and prepared to meet Elder Wilford Woodruff, the apostle.

A puff of cold air burst into the Benbow mansion as John Benbow opened the door to admit Elder Woodruff, who looked a little frazzled, tired, and weather-beaten. As soon as Wilford saw Thomas Kington, he guessed correctly that he was the man who had organized the United Brethren. He thrust out his right hand. "You must be Thomas Kington. I've been most anxious to meet you. I can't tell you how much love and respect the people around here have for you."

The apostle's rapid words and friendly smile were disarming. Kington's mouth quickly curled into a returned smile. "So, I finally get to meet the man who is decimating my congregation."

Elder Woodruff blinked.

"Sorry, I meant that as a joke."

"Brother Benbow must have been talking to you," Elder Woodruff said, smiling again, taking off his large beaver hat. "I guess we've got a lot to discuss. Sorry not to have arrived sooner, but the interest in the gospel in these parts is almost overwhelming." What Kington had said in a joking manner was true. More than three-dozen members of the United Brethren had already been baptized, more had been taught, and many more were discussing the possibility of baptism with their families.

Benbow closed the door and motioned for the two men to step toward the hearth. "I've got a good fire going. Come in, Elder Woodruff, and warm yourself. I suspect we're in for another long night." He chuckled to himself.

Kington recalled what Benbow had said about his all-night vigil with the American.

Benbow asked his wife to pour some hot tea. He turned to Kington and boomed a laugh. "I think we're going to have a repeat performance."

The United Brethren superintendent managed a laugh of his own, and tolerantly shook his head in approval. "As you can imagine, I have a lot of questions. I hope you have a lot of answers, Elder Woodruff."

Wilford smiled, his eyes darting alternatively between his new friend and convert, John Benbow, and the new arrival, Thomas Kington. He scanned the sectarian preacher and superintendent up and down, judging him to be as intelligent, organized, hard working, energetic, studious, and God-fearing as everyone had told him. Kington was twelve years older than Wilford, recently married, but at forty-five years of age still possessed a youthful charisma, a masculine charm, and magnetic personality, in Wilford's view. Tonight's challenge was simple for the American missionary – to make certain Kington not only learned the truthfulness of the restored gospel through what he would hear and see, but also through what Kington would feel. After an hour of sampling Jane's vegetable beef soup and freshly baked bread, chitchatting, building a relationship of trust, Wilford retired with the other two men to the parlor where all three offered up a prayer, one at a time, each asking for the Spirit to attend them.

To Thomas Kington's British eyes, the American apostle's face took on a spiritual countenance of its own: the clear brown eyes, the firmly set jaw, a smooth triangular nose sticking out of a weather-beaten but mild face, all under locks of jostled brown hair. His voice was medium low, resonant, and only slightly guttural. His style of preaching was different than Kington was accustomed to, no abnormal gesturing, no raising of the voice, no shaking. But it was the message that struck Kington as most unusual. He was fascinated by the story of Joseph Smith. It reminded him somewhat of his own life. He had become confused about which church to affiliate with, just like the fourteen-year-old American boy. He had prayed about what to do, just like Joseph Smith. He had disassociated himself with all other organized religions and started his own. Joseph Smith had sought light and truth. So had he. But Thomas Kington knew there was a major difference. God the Father and his Son, Jesus Christ, had not manifested themselves to him as they had done to the young New Yorker, Joseph Smith. Kington was astonished at the Book of Mormon story, the angel Moroni, the translation process, and the organization of the church in 1830. The book made sense to him. Certainly God could have spoken to other people on the earth. Certainly they could have kept a record. Certainly other prophets could have lived. Kington had heard of the "Urim and Thummim" in the Bible. Certainly a prophet would need a tool like that to translate an ancient record.

At two in the morning Thomas Kington made an agreement with Wilford Woodruff. As leader of the United Brethren, he wanted to be able to tell his members that he understood the "full gospel message," then he wanted to assist Elder Woodruff in finding and teaching the other members. And he wanted his wife to hear the message, also. Then he would be baptized. The American missionary agreed.

As Elder Woodruff retired to his bedroom, he knew Thomas Kington had felt the Spirit and would be baptized. He dropped to his knees and thanked his Father in Heaven for sending him to the Malvern Hills and opening the door to a prepared people. He knew he would be busy for the next few weeks. Go south, the voice had told him. Now he knew why.

True to his word, Thomas Kington was baptized the following Friday with his wife. In addition to recording the names of those he baptized, Elder Woodruff wrote these words in his journal: "Glory Hallelujah, the work of God rolls on!"

MARCH 17. Tuesday. I walked to Green Yeal and preached in the home of Philpotts to a large congregation. I was exceedingly hoarse at the lungs. Later, I had an agreeable interview with Thomas Kington, the superintendent of the United Brethren. I laid the whole work of the fullness of the gospel before him and he seemed to receive my testimony.

MARCH 19. Thursday. Visited Sister Ann Bourne who was sick and prayed with her. Walked to John Fidoe's at Bishop Frome, and from thence to Hopton's Corner and preached at the house of Richard Davis. I spent the night at the home of James Gurney. Baptisms: Francis Birch, Ann Birch, James Gurney.

MARCH 20. Friday. I baptized three persons, one a preacher, and preached at Bridger and Smith, and some of the baser sort armed themselves with rotten eggs and flung them at me. One hit me in the head but did not break until it struck the ground. I walked to Hill Farm and spent the night.

MARCH 21. Saturday. I walked to Ledbury and found a letter from W. Richards. I returned to Brother Benbow's and baptized four persons (Thomas and Hannah Kington, George Brown and Ann Teague). Two were preachers, one of which was Thomas Kington, the superintendent of the preachers of the United Brethren. Glory hallelujah the work of God rolls on.

MARCH 22. Sunday. I preached at Frome's Hill. In the afternoon I preached at the Hill Farm to a large congregation. I also met with the saints in the evening and confirmed six persons. I ordained Thomas Kington to the office of an elder and William Jenkins to the office of a priest.

49

BOBBY WAS ASTONISHED when William died in his sleep at age thirty-five. The cold had settled obstinately in his lungs, worsening to a crisis stage the day after Bobby and his brothers met in John's pub. Bobby could not believe that his brother was gone. Now there were just the four of them left—John, Dianah, Elizabeth, and himself. Within a year and a half he had lost his mother, his father and his oldest brother. Why was God doing this to him? Who was next? One of his sisters, Dianah or Elizabeth? His wife? One of his children? Death was such a mystery. Why did a few people live to their seventies and eighties? Why did some die as babies? Why did some, like his brother, die at only thirty-five? He couldn't understand why a heart could beat one minute and not the next. Where was his brother William now? Was he with his father and mother? Didn't anyone believe families had a right to be together in the next life?

Bobby had feelings of guilt when it came to the butcher shop. Who would keep it running? Who would keep the family tradition alive? He couldn't do it. He had a fighting career and a hundred-acre farm to manage. He would talk to John. Maybe he could manage both a pub and a butcher shop. Maybe Dianah's husband Thomas Bloxham could help. Maybe Daniel and Elizabeth could help.

He vowed to dedicate his next fight to the memory of William. When his father died, he did the same thing and it secured him a victory. Bobby felt he could do it again.

At William's funeral, Bobby avoided talking to the Anglican priest, the Reverend Spencer Hobhouse, who had ministered to his family for the many years they lived in Deerhurst. He didn't care. Reverend Hobhouse didn't have any answers.

It was Sunday morning. After only a few hours of troubled sleep, Bobby raised up and rubbed his eyes. He was exhausted from the previous day's workout at Squire Hastings' sparring room in Gloucester. He was numbed over the death of his brother. He was angered at the lack of comforting words from the funeral. And he was still confused at his odd dream.

He dressed, yawned several times, and grimaced from his splitting headache. He slumped down the stairs expecting a breakfast that would revive him and give him enough energy to begin another long training day. As he pulled up a chair and sat in it without saying "good morning" to Hannah, who was standing over her stove with her hands on her hips, he stared at an empty table. Without conversation, Hannah slid a plate in front of her husband. On it were seven raw chicken livers and a raw cow's tongue.

Bobby glared at the raw food, and glared at his wife. He spoke through clenched teeth, his blood boiling. "What is this supposed to mean?"

Hannah had not slept well, either. Four-month-old Willie had a bad croup, and had cried nearly all night. She had spent most of the evening downstairs with him. When the baby had finally gone to sleep, and Hannah had finally slumbered off, Lizzy awakened her for a drink of water. Yesterday, the housemaid had not worked because of sickness. Joseph had fallen down playing outside, and scraped his elbow. To top it all off, her two sisters, Nancy and Jane, and her mother, had visited yesterday. They had argued about whether or not Hannah should continue to stiffen her neck about going to London with Bobby, with her mother telling her that, in her opinion, she should go. But Nancy and Jane sided with Hannah. When Ann Eagles asked if Bobby had been attending church with Hannah, Hannah told her the hurtful truth. Ann recommended that Hannah confront her husband immediately.

Confronting was what Hannah was doing now. "If you're not going to attend church with me on Sundays, I'm not cooking on Sundays. I hope you like raw chicken livers. There's one for each day of the week."

Bobby put his hand to his forehead and rubbed the spot where his head was throbbing. "And the cow's tongue?" he growled.

Hannah let her face come to a mutinous smirk. She grabbed a small iron frying pan and held it across her chest, thinking how she would like to make his headache worse. "I'm not holding my tongue anymore in our marriage. I'm going to tell you what I think."

Bobby snorted in male amusement. "I've never known you otherwise."

"If you don't go to church with me today it will be six Sundays in a row you have missed."

Bobby rose out of his chair and poured himself a cup of tea. It was cold. He sipped on it anyway, trying to rid the morning stale taste that clung to his mouth. At least the room was warm. Hannah had a blazing fire going in the hearth. Outside, it was another cold, rainy, windy spring day.

"I don't have a choice, Hannah. You know that as well as I do." He glanced at his wife, and at the frying pan. Her eyes were red, her eyebrows furrowed. It troubled him that she was so angry, so detached, so demanding. Besides, he was still experiencing a deep sense of loss over William's death. Again and again, the image of William working at the shop, sparring with him, and holding the weight bag as he pounded it, flashed through his mind.

Hannah considered Bobby's answer. She had expected him to come back with something more irrational, words that belayed his intolerance of religion. But it didn't matter. Her reply was curt and stinging. "It's Sunday. Don't you understand the importance of keeping the Sabbath day holy anymore?"

As she waited for her husband's reaction, Hannah thought about her own religious commitment. Although she knew very little about the United Brethren, their teachings, precepts, beliefs, sacraments, and catechisms, she still had a deep abiding faith because of her strict Methodist upbringing. She felt that the Sabbath was a day when one went to a chapel or a church, sang hymns, uttered and listened to prayers, paid attention while the minister preached, and learned about Christian principles as taught from the Bible. By mutual agreement with her husband, she was a member of the United Brethren congregation now. She felt guilty about not participating every Sunday. She wanted to demonstrate to her Methodist mother that she had a religion of her own, that things were okay in her family, that Bobby and she were active, God-fearing members of the new religion. She was tired of feeling guilty. She was tired of her husband's slipping commitment to a faith-based religion. She wanted to change, and she wanted Bobby to change.

Bobby opened the cupboard door and found a loaf of bread. Instead of slicing it, he broke about a third of it off and stuffed a portion of it in his mouth. He chewed furiously while his eyes narrowed in anger.

"Where's the butter?" he asked sharply, yanking her back.

"If it was a snake it would have bitten you. Look in the cupboard where you found the bread. Answer my question. Don't you believe in the Sabbath anymore?"

He strode toward the cupboard again, giving her a cynical look. "You're starting to sound like the Sabbatarians. Are you against trains running on Sunday? Are you against the poor using bakehouses on Sunday? Are you going to close down John's pub? Don't be so radical, Hannah!"

Hannah took a strong grip on the frying pan, and raised her voice. "Radical? You think radical is keeping the Sabbath day holy? All your friends have joined the United Brethren and some of them are even lay ministers already! Daniel and Elizabeth are preaching nearly every Sunday now."

Bobby buttered his bread with quick, angry strokes. "It'll just have to wait until I retire from fighting."

"Mama!"

Lizzy came scooting down the stairs backward, her two-year-old legs carefully considering each steep step. Joseph was right behind her, and he asked, "Why are you and papa yelling at each other?"

Hannah glanced at her children then at her husband. "It's because your father doesn't have the backbone to stand up to Squire Hastings."

Bobby threw his head back in a cynical laugh. "So now it's the squire's fault."

"Just tell him you are not going to train on Sundays!" She threw the frying pan on the table, making a clatter. The noise startled Lizzy, and she began to cry.

Hannah glared at Bobby, not wanting him to rehearse again all the reasons why he had to train on the Sabbath. She knew them well: Bobby's next fight was against the highly regarded Ben Caunt. If Bobby could defeat Caunt, then he would automatically be considered for a shot at the British heavyweight championship against William "Bendigo" Thompson. Squire Hastings had hired London's best and most expensive trainer to work with Bobby. The training fee demanded that he work every day including Sunday. The purse for the championship might be as much as a hundred pounds.

Hannah shuddered to think of the several hundred pounds Hastings would bet on her husband, and the anger he would have if Bobby lost.

Bobby took his still-sobbing daughter into his arms, then returned a defiant glare to his wife. "We've been over this before. I need every available day to get ready for this fight. I'm going into Gloucester, and that's that." He thrust Lizzy into Hannah's chest and grabbed his coat.

Realizing that her aggressive tactics had failed, Hannah began to beg. "Bobby, stay home. Please! Go to church with me."

Lizzy began to sob again. "Don't cry. Mama's all right," Hannah told her, clutching her daughter to her bosom.

"Hannah," Bobby said, reaching for the door latch, "you've already got Lizzy crying and you're going to wake up the baby."

"Oh, I'm surprised you care," Hannah said, wiping at her tears.

"I'm doing this for you, Hannah. Think of the money we'll have after I am champion. We'll be set for life. The squire will lease us more land after I retire. We will pay off our debts on our livestock. I'll be one of the wealthiest tenant farmers in all England!"

"I don't care anymore, Bobby. This is consuming you too much. I don't like the crowd at the London fights. I don't want to live in London, and that's where we'll be if you win."

Bobby shook his head, fuming. "Just for a few years, until I retire from fighting, Hannah. You know that. We've talked about this time and time again."

"Bobby, listen to me," she said, taking a free forearm to wipe at more tears. "I don't need all that money to be happy. I don't need anything except you and my children. I would be happy if you were the village butcher again. We don't even need a farm to lease. I just want a quiet life in the country, read the Bible every day, go to church every Sunday, and raise a good family. I thought that's what you wanted when we first married."

Bobby unlatched the door and opened it. "Hannah, you know that I love you and the children. But sometimes you are too selfish. Please don't deny me a chance to fight for the championship. You know it's my life's goal and practically has been ever since we met. You are very fortunate to have this nice cottage and to be wearing nice clothes. It's more than just coincidence, you know."

The words ate at Hannah. She was feeling anything but fortunate, and coincidence was a concept she did not entirely trust. She stomped on the floor. "Selfish? Selfish? Bobby, it's all you. You're doing this for you. Not me, not for the children. Just you."

Bobby glanced outdoors, put his hand out to feel the rain coming down, and looked at the barn and the corrals where he had yet to saddle his horse. "Don't you want me to be the champion? You said before you wanted me to. Why have you changed, Hannah?"

"Because it has consumed you, Bobby."

"After I am champion, you'll see. You'll be happy. I've got to go."

He left without kissing her goodbye.

The rain had quit when a creaking, clattering phaeton carriage pulled by a bay mare and a gray gelding arrived in front of Hannah's home. "I see Hannah with her baby and the children, but I don't see Bobby," Nancy told James, pointing.

James Pulham jumped out to assist Hannah into the carriage. Her new baby was wrapped in a bundle of colorful blankets. "How's little Willie?" She had named the baby after Bobby's brother, William.

"Doing well," Hannah said, handing the baby to the nursemaid. Hannah gave last minute instructions and boarded the carriage with Joseph, her oldest, soon to turn three.

"Still no luck with Bobby?" Nancy asked, her skin tone and facial features looking remarkably like Hannah. Just more slender.

Hannah shook her head and made a sad face. "He's in Gloucester already. Seven days a week. I hate it." A draft of air from the Cotswolds to the south gushed through the hamlet, sending a chill through her.

"Sit here by Uncle James," Nancy's fiancée told Joseph. In another month, he and Nancy would make it official. Then he really would be Joseph's uncle. "Don't you look dandy? You get to go to church with us."

"You've been crying," Nancy said, observing her sister's red eyes. "I'm sorry."

"You can't say I didn't try. Bobby wouldn't stay and go to church. He's married to pugilism it seems, not to me. He left the house upset."

James tapped the lines on the rumps of the two horses and the carriage jolted to a start. "Where are Daniel and Elizabeth today?"

"I don't know," Hannah answered. "I can't keep up with them anymore, they are so busy. They could be anywhere from Dymock to Twigworth to Crowcutt to Old Starridge. Who knows? I'm just happy that Daniel is doing so well with the United Brethren, and Elizabeth, too. She was just made a lay preacher, too."

Joseph sat wide eyed, fascinated by the horses. Nancy said, "Maybe Uncle James will let you take the lines, Joseph. Would you like that?"

The boy nodded.

James placed the lines in Joseph's hands. "You're such a big boy now. How old will you be on your birthday?"

Joseph held up three fingers.

"And what do you want for your birthday?"

"A puppy," Joseph said, his eyes lit up.

50

THE CARRIAGE arrived at the Gadfield Elm chapel just before ten o'clock. James flinched when he saw a larger than usual crowd.

"I've never seen so many people going into the chapel," he said, blinking hard and feeling a rising anxiety. "And look at all the carriages. I wonder what's going on?"

"Twenty, twenty-one, twenty-two," Nancy counted, her jaw dropping.

"I knew our congregation was growing fast, but this is unbelievable," James said, his face incredulous. He quickly tied the horses to a hitching post and approached two couples, the Roberts and the Greens. "Why so many people today?"

"I thought everyone had heard by now," Levi said with a grim sigh. "John Benbow and several of our United Brethren preachers have joined another church."

Hannah reeled, numb with shock. "What? You're kidding!"

Levi looked sheepish, as though he had lost his best friends. "It's true," he said. "A preacher from America came to Farmer Benbow's home only last Monday. John and his wife and four others were baptized Tuesday evening."

"Including Reverend Kington?" Hannah asked, uncertain how to respond.

"I heard he was out on the circuit, but was baptized yesterday," Levi's wife, Harriet Ann, explained, hardly believing her own supposition.

Hannah's heart sank. Was the United Brethren congregation falling apart? What would Daniel and Elizabeth think? Or did they already know?

"I'm surprised you hadn't heard before," Hyrum said. "I'm sure someone was assigned to tell you about the special meeting today."

"We've been in Gloucester every available minute to watch Bobby train, at his insistence," Hannah said, still in disbelief. "If he had his way, we would be there today. Have you seen Daniel lately? He's bruised all over. Bobby's pounding on every sparring partner he can find."

Nancy's body language was stiff. "What's going to happen in today's meeting?"

"Edward Phillips has already listened to the American preacher," Levi said. "He's going to make the best explanation he can. Let's go in. The meeting is about to start."

Hannah, Joseph, Nancy, and James found a seat next to John Davis and Mary Ann Weston. There was no song, and no prayer. Instead, Edward took the stand and made a terse announcement.

"I do not wish to occupy much of your time today," he said. "As most of you know, both Superintendent Kington and John Benbow have been baptized into another church. My purpose is to give you an invitation from them to come to a special meeting this afternoon at the Benbow farm. They will give you all the details. They apologize for not being here today. They are giving the same information right now at the Great Hall."

There was a rumble throughout the chapel as the overflow crowd absorbed the impact Edward's statement.

James raised his hand. "What are you going to do, Edward?"

Clearing his throat with an emotional burst, Edward answered. "John Benbow and Thomas Kington are convinced that the American's church is the further light and truth they have been waiting for. So am I. I'm going to the meeting because I want to hear more about it."

"Who is this American?" John Davis asked.

"Elder Wilford Woodruff from Nauvoo, Illinois, United States of America."

"What is the name of Elder Woodruff's church?"

"The Church of Jesus Christ of Latter-day Saints."

"Why did Benbow and Kington get baptized so quickly?"

"That's the purpose of the meeting today. Go and find out for yourself."

"Does that mean you have been baptized, too?"

"No, but I soon will be," Edward emphasized. "Those of you who wish may stay here and talk about how you want to reorganize the United Brethren. Those of you who are going to the meeting, you better leave soon."

A loud buzz was heard throughout the building. One by one, everyone stood up and began an orderly exit. No one stayed in the chapel.

Nancy's face was full on intrigue as she stepped into the mid-morning sunshine. "I want to go meet Elder Woodruff," she said.

"Not without Bobby," Hannah said, still confused.

"When will he be home?" James asked.

"Last Sunday it was early in the afternoon."

James pulled out his pocket watch. "Let's see. It's fifteen miles to the Hill Farm from your place. That means we'd have to leave by one thirty at the latest."

"Do you think Bobby will go with us?"

Hannah hung her head. "I hope so."

Shirt soaked with sweat, out of breath, his face bruised from the sparring session, Bobby ended his roadwork when he reached the Ferret's Folly. For the first time in a long while, he noticed how quaint the pub looked – large mullioned windows, tile roof, and honey-colored Cotswold stone.

"Afternoon," he said to John's wife, on her knees preparing a flowerbed that would soon grace the entry. "Going to plant Wisteria again this spring?" He remembered how beautifully they had bloomed.

She responded, not looking up, "I suppose when they come up you'll be one step closer to being the heavyweight champion of the British Isles, won't you?"

'That's the plan," he answered.

John was standing at a serving hatch at the end of a small corridor. "Ah, good to see you again, brother. Doesn't look like you have been to church today out at the Gadfield Elm chapel. Or did you go early this morning?"

"I didn't go. Sunday is just another training day nowadays."

John poured his brother a drink. They sat down at the only vacant table, the one nearest the old grandfather clock that never told the correct time. The other tables were surrounded by gusty groups of local lower-class working men, farmers, tradesmen, and laborers. All of them recognized Bobby. There were compliments, backslaps, and wishing him well on his next fight.

"Hannah go to church today?"

"I'm sure she did."

John reacted with a huff. "My wife won't let me open the pub on Sundays until we've gone to church first." He sipped his ale slowly.

Bobby sat with his head thrust down, his jaw muscles twitching. "We had an ugly argument this morning about religion. She just doesn't understand. Squire Hastings has paid a lot of money on my new trainer. Both of them insist that I train seven days a week. We'll move our training camp to

London in a few weeks. It's the most important fight of my life. But I don't think Hannah supports me anymore, the way she acts."

"What are you going to do then?"

Bobby took a drink and shook his head. "I don't know."

"You could always get a divorce."

"I've thought of it. But you know how hard divorces are to obtain."

"Just think of all the women who would be after you if you become champion."

"I know."

James and Nancy had waited inside Hannah's home since noon, nervous as cats. They paced the floors, glanced out the windows, nibbled on cold cuts and cheese, and stared at the clock. The nursemaid tended to the children.

"I still don't see him coming," James said, sending Hannah a blank stare. "We can't wait any longer, or we'll be late."

Nancy put on her coat. "Are you coming with us, Hannah?"

Hannah sighed and shrugged her shoulders. "I want so much to hear what this American preacher has to say. But I want Bobby to hear him, too."

"It's up to you," Nancy said. "I wouldn't want to go without James. If this leads to another change in our religion, it's something a husband and wife should do together."

"We'll give you a full report when we get back," James said, with a tingle of anticipation. "See you tomorrow."

Frustrated, Hannah watched James and Nancy board the carriage.

"Wait," Hannah screamed, opening the door and putting on her coat. "I'm coming with you."

51

A SENSE OF LOST TIME haunted Hannah as she listened to Elder Woodruff's concluding remarks to a packed crowd at the Great Hall in the Benbow mansion. Why couldn't this "light and truth" have come into her life five years earlier, about the time she married Bobby? It would have prevented so much turmoil, heartache, and discontentment. There was only one thing left to do: get Bobby in front of Wilford Woodruff. It would be a life-changing experience for him. She just knew it.

Her entire life seemed to flash before her: Her childhood, raised on the dairy farm. Strict Methodist parents. Falling in love with Bobby. Daniel's idea for a double wedding. The controversy that caused. Bobby's dislike of religion. His career. Three children. And now this, the gospel of Jesus Christ. She felt so good she wanted to cry.

No wonder John Benbow and Thomas Kington had been baptized into the American's church.

Nancy's sharp elbow broke Hannah's thoughts.

"James and I both want to be baptized," she said, her eyes glazed with tears.

"Tonight?" Hannah asked, looking both startled and pleased. She closed her eyes for a few seconds, recalling Elder Woodruff's invitation. All those who desired baptism were asked to raise their hands and walk forward. People were chattering throughout the hall, their volume low and reverent.

"Yes, tonight. What about you? Don't you feel the same?"

Hannah wiped at a tear with a silk handkerchief. "Yes. Of course I do. But I want to wait for Bobby. But what if he won't come to listen?"

"He will," Nancy said as she grasped James by the hand. "I'm sure of it."

Nancy followed her husband to the front of the Great Hall where Elder Woodruff was beginning to explain how the ordinance of baptism would be performed. White clothing was issued. Soon a great procession followed the American missionary to the little pond near the Benbow mansion.

Hannah found herself staring idly into the rapidly darkening farm fields as she rode in the carriage back to her comfortable stone cottage Squire Hastings had provided for her and her family in Apperley. All because of Bobby's fighting ability. She remained in a near trance as she pondered how to approach Bobby about the experience she just had. A possibility of outright rejection? Yes. A possibility that he would listen to the American? Slim.

Hannah stared at the faint light from the upstairs window of the cottage as she bid James and Nancy goodnight. She felt rigid as she contemplated the confrontation that was coming. She fought the reflex to shiver. She had been full of confidence as she watched James and Nancy be baptized hours earlier. Now, that confidence had eroded. She feared the man inside the stone cottage. For a moment she stood in the doorframe, wondering. Was he in bed, asleep? Or ready to spring an accusation against her? Not once in her married life had she come home late. It had always been the other way around.

The planks of the floor creaked annoyingly as she walked across them and laid her coat on the blue cushioned sofa. She poked her head into the kitchen to find that the fire had been banked for the night, casting faint, garish shadows across the room. Except for a breeze that seeped through cracks in the window, the cottage was silent. She removed her shoes and began climbing the stairs, one step at a time.

An imposing figure intercepted her at the top of the stairs, holding a small candle. Bobby shoved the candle into Hannah's face, frightening her.

"*Where* have you been?"

Hannah contemplated the gruffness in her husband's voice. She tried to swallow, but her mouth was dry.

"Did your hear me?"

She nodded, heaving a ponderous sigh. "I've been with James and Nancy," she said in a very soft voice. A chill raked her flesh.

"I heard their voices," he responded, his anger brimming. "I asked you *where* have you been."

"There was a special meeting tonight at Farmer Benbow's place. I wish you could have been there."

"What kind of special meeting?" he snorted.

"We listened to an American missionary. We found out why John Benbow and Thomas Kington joined the American's church."

There was a cruel laugh. "Benbow and Kington joined another church? Sounds like your precious United Brethren organization is falling apart. So much for *that* religion."

Hannah brought her hands to her face. "Bobby, please don't make fun of what is happening. James and Nancy were baptized, too."

There was a moment of silence. "I suppose you're going to tell me you were baptized, too."

"No. Not without you."

"This is just what I need, a distraction. You should have stayed home with the children, where you belong."

"Bobby, I want you to listen to the American missionary."

"Go to bed."

Hannah began to undress. "His name is Elder Wilford Woodruff."

Bobby shot his wife a smoldering gaze. "You are not going to be baptized into an American church."

"It's not an America church. It's the Church of Jesus Christ of Latter-day Saints. Please, Bobby. This is the most important thing you'll ever do."

"The most important thing I'll ever do is win the championship. Shut up and go to bed. Not another word."

Minutes later, as Bobby lay beside Hannah, he thought of his dream again. Then he drifted off into a troubled sleep.

52

ELIZABETH HAD ALWAYS seen in Daniel a man who had a plow horse work ethic, a deep sense of purpose, highly disciplined, stable, dependable, sincere, and a high achiever. That's exactly how he regarded his position as lay preacher in the United Brethren. While Hannah, Nancy, and James were fortunate enough to hear about Wilford Woodruff's visit to the Castle Frome area, Daniel and Elizabeth had been off doing their circuit work, organizing stronger branches, assisting members in need of spiritual guidance, and, in general, being faithful workers. But when Daniel heard that Thomas Kington and John Benbow had been baptized into another church, Elizabeth saw a different side of her husband. She was astonished at how betrayed, angry, guilty, and frustrated he felt. He had been busting his back building up their organization while they, the leaders, totally and completely abandoned the United Brethren in favor of a foreigner's religion.

Daniel heard the rumor from Elizabeth's cousin, John Gailey, a fellow United Brethren lay preacher, on Sunday evening. From then on, Elizabeth found her husband to be a bundle of nerves, engaging her in an almost all-night conversation in which he flitted from one emotion to another. He belittled Kington and Benbow for abandoning their own church without calling a general meeting. He saw the whole thing as illogical and it depressed him. He became sarcastic, questioned the two men's integrity and sensitivity, and almost seemed, in Elizabeth's opinion, that he never would be able to forgive Kington and Benbow. He even talked about confronting them about it first thing in the morning.

In her own mind, Elizabeth remained optimistic that Kington and Benbow had a good reason for changing to another religion, that perhaps they had found something better and took a daring leap to embrace it. She told Daniel not to jump to conclusions until they could listen to the American preacher named Woodruff, and tackle the problem on their own in a careful, analytical consideration of the new religion. She began thinking about what to wear, what outfit she had that might impress an American.

It was well past three o'clock in the morning when they finally agreed on something – that they should pray about it. Their prayer brought an end to their lengthy conversation and they slept until six thirty. Daniel threw back the covers and said, "Let's go get Bobby and Hannah and find Mr. Woodruff."

Elizabeth jerked awake, rolled over, put a finger to her lip without opening her eyes, and muttered, "Shhh. Let me *sleep*." Outside, the first gray of dawn was barely separating the earth from the black velvet of night.

"I want to talk to Bobby before he leaves for Gloucester."

Elizabeth moaned and crawled deeper into her covers. Even with a tired, muddled mind, she could think of a lot of sassy things to say, but she didn't. Daniel washed, dressed, and began heating water for hot tea. "Let's go!" he yelled from downstairs.

"He's probably left the house already," she managed to say, rolling her tongue through her dry mouth.

Daniel stuffed some bread and cheese into his mouth, hitched his horse to his two-wheeled gig, then paced back and forth waiting for Elizabeth while she half hurriedly sorted through her wardrobe, picking out a dark blue carriage dress that she thought looked somewhat American. She tied her bonnet while they bounced along the road to Apperley, still heatedly discussing Benbow and Kington's baptism into the new church, and found Hannah still in her nightclothes nursing her baby.

"Where's Bobby?" Daniel asked, bursting through the door.

"Where do you think?" Hannah answered, covering herself and burping the child.

Daniel stared at the road leading to Gloucester. "Have you heard about John Benbow and Thomas Kington? They were baptized into another church."

"I was at the meeting in the Great Hall yesterday afternoon."

Elizabeth's mouth dropped. "You've *already* listened to the American preacher who baptized them?"

"Yes," Hannah stated, her eyes brightening. "And I want to be baptized, too."

"You, too?" Daniel asked with an incredulous look on his face. "What about Bobby?"

Hannah frowned. "That's another story." She launched into a recap of her eventful Sabbath: The trip with Nancy and James to the Gadfield Elm chapel. Edward Phillips' announcement. Waiting for Bobby at the cottage. Listening to Elder Woodruff. Watching James and Nancy be baptized. And her frightful encounter with Bobby late at night.

"I was hoping to catch Bobby before he left," Daniel said.

"He left early, angry. He'll be angry when he gets home, too."

"We've been up most of the night, Hannah," Elizabeth said, sitting on the sofa with Hannah and her baby. "We couldn't *sleep*. We're on our way to the Benbow farm right now. We want you to go with us."

"I'm tempted to ride into Gloucester and get Bobby," Daniel said, shifting his weight from one foot to the other.

"You'd be wasting your time."

"Then let's ask John Gailey to go with us," Daniel said, shifting his attention to his wife.

Elizabeth gave her sister-in-law a hug. "Are you still having a birthday party for Joseph on Wednesday?"

Hannah smile was sort of enigmatic. "Of course."

"Do you think my bull-headed brother will take time out of his training to attend his own son's party?"

Hannah's eyes dropped. "Your guess is as good as mine."

The trip to the Hill Farm was uneventful. The midmorning sun was a ball of dim yellow as it bore through scattered layers of high clouds. Elizabeth dozed a little. Daniel went over the same concerns with John Gailey as he had done with Elizabeth the night before. Unnoticed were fields alive with farm workers dressed in loose smocks, plowing, digging, mending hedges and fences, and hoeing fields.

Daniel felt himself bristle instantly when he pulled his horse to a halt in front of one of the weathered barns at the Hill Farm. Benbow and Kington were walking toward the pond with two other men. He recognized one to be William Jenkins, a twenty-one-year old lay preacher. He was dressed in white clothing.

John Gailey pointed. "Do you suppose the other man dressed in white is the American?"

"Let's go meet him," Elizabeth said, bouncing out of the gig.

Daniel just sat there, taking in the scene with a broad sweep of emotions. He desperately wanted to understand why his mentors, Thomas Kington and

John Benbow, would be happily engaged in assisting this foreigner in baptizing yet another United Brethren lay preacher. This is not how Daniel envisioned things were going to be in the future; rather he envisioned his whole life wrapped up in building up the United Brethren, not seeing it decimated by another force. Daniel shifted his eyes to Elizabeth, who seemed ambivalent to the situation. During the nearly five years of their marriage, he had always looked to her to keep things in perspective, to help him facilitate social relationships, to help him foster optimism and hope, to remind him that there was a reason for everything, a time to laugh, a time to cry. He felt like crying, but she looked like she could break out in laughter at any time and it confused him.

Elizabeth assumed that there was a good reason why Kington and Benbow turned and waved, flashing big smiles, looking happy and fulfilled, accompanying two men dressed in white, as they saw the horse-drawn gig pull into the yard. As Daniel's confused face bore into hers, she touched him on the chin and said, "Don't just *sit* there. Come on. They're *all* here together, aren't they? Lucky us. Let's go find out what's going on."

She smiled at him intently and refused to let him turn away until he smiled back. As they walked hand-in-hand, Elizabeth squeezed Daniel's hand tightly. She was thinking how grateful she was to be married to him, for the sense of direction he had given their lives, the compassion he had for others, the stability, and his leadership qualities. She sensed they were walking into a situation that would bring them a measure of happiness not yet achieved, and she relished the moment. While Daniel remained stone-faced, she was smiling.

John Benbow and Thomas Kington stopped in their tracks when Daniel, Elizabeth, and John Gailey started toward them.

"Who are those people?" Elder Woodruff asked.

"Three more of the United Brethren preachers," Kington answered.

"They probably want to talk to you."

A wave of guilt swept over Thomas as he watched them approach. A part of him whispered that he should have looked up every member of the United Brethren congregation to give them an explanation for his actions. Especially his lay preachers. But he had felt so good about the message of the restored gospel that he had reacted on the Spirit. Strong emotions had propelled him into the waters of baptism. If the three approaching lay preachers wanted to accuse him of betraying the loyalty to his own cause, so be it. Once they heard Elder Woodruff's message they would be baptized, and all would be forgiven. Those were the thoughts that crossed Kington's mind when he saw Daniel, Elizabeth, and John.

As Wilford Woodruff watched three strangers approach, two thoughts went through his mind. He wanted to proceed with the baptism of William Jenkins, but he felt that the two men and one woman who had just arrived wanted to hear the gospel. He quickly took those thoughts into consideration and made a decision. He began walking back up the hill, away from the pond. "Let's take a minute so that I can be introduced to them," he said, "then if they want to they can watch Brother Jenkins be baptized."

As Daniel watched the three men turn around and walk toward him, he began to collect his thoughts. He still felt angry toward both Thomas Kington and John Benbow, but those feelings were beginning to give away to a frantic urge to investigate the religion of the American. Right before his eyes a fellow lay preacher was dressed in white for the obvious intent of being baptized. Perhaps Elizabeth was right in her assessment of the situation.

Kington was the first to speak. "Good to see you, Daniel. You too, Elizabeth, and John. I can just imagine what you're thinking. I'll bet you have a million questions on your mind." He thrust his right hand toward Daniel, whose optimism remained darkened.

"Maybe just one question," Daniel said, accepting the handshake. "And that would be this. Why?"

Kington refused to let the question shake him. He stepped aside to introduce the American. "This is Elder Wilford Woodruff. He can tell you why we are now members of his church."

Before Daniel, Elizabeth, or John could say anything, Elder Woodruff stood directly in front of the three of them and made a bold statement. "In the name of Jesus Christ, I testify that the Lord's church has been restored on the earth. Have you come to be baptized into that church?"

The words struck Daniel like a bolt of lightning. He dropped his jaw and stared at the American, the words ringing in his ears. Normally, he shunned spontaneity and pressure for immediate action. At first the words made him uncomfortable, but strangely, he began to feel warm and peaceful. His smugness melted.

Elizabeth, however, was immediately at ease with the American's commanding presence and bold challenge. She felt an irresistible spine tingle that gave her the urge to say "yes" without regard to what Daniel may or may not be feeling, but she patiently waited for a response from her husband. It came when Daniel glanced at her and they locked into each other's eyes. With his mouth still open, Daniel gave a faint nod to Elizabeth, and she nodded back with an excited smile.

Daniel heaved a big sigh and stared at the American again. Then he answered Elder Woodruff's probing question with a simple, "Yes."

"And you, Sister Browett? I suppose you would like to make your own answer," Wilford commented.

Elizabeth did not hesitate and broke into another smile. "My answer is yes, too."

John Gailey merely nodded in the affirmative when Elder Woodruff looked in his direction.

"Very well," Elder Woodruff said as he shook each of their hands again.

"Let me baptize Brother Jenkins and then we'll go back inside and I'll teach you about the restoration of the gospel." With that statement he began walking down the hill toward the pond.

For a few seconds Daniel stood motionless, and it took a tug on the arm from Elizabeth to get him to move. The bright smile was still on her face. Daniel's mouth was still open in astonishment. He had just committed to be baptized into a church that he knew nothing about. Although he still felt that it was the right thing to do, because of the warm feeling that had come over him as the American spoke his few powerful words, he marveled that he had done it. He had to ask himself, *is this the way Thomas Kington, John Benbow and all the others had been converted into the American's church?* He recalled how carefully he had contemplated the United Brethren religion before making the decision to join. What he had done was so unlike him. In one instant he was ready to confront Kington and Benbow, and in another instant he had thrown those feelings away and was ready to follow the man named Wilford Woodruff anywhere. It struck him as odd. But he felt good about it.

Elizabeth was a raging inferno of curiosity. She pulled on Daniel, wanting him to catch up so they could see how the American baptized another person. She wanted to watch every detail, and she wanted to hear what Elder Woodruff would have to say about the new religion. She wondered what new doctrines they were about to embrace, how they would be different than what she already believed. This was the beginning of a new adventure for her, and she was enjoying every minute of it.

Both Daniel and Elizabeth could not help but reflect back to the day they sat under the huge oak tree by the pond where they were now standing. It was the exact place they had listened to Thomas Kington explain why he had organized the United Brethren, his perspective of all the other religions in England, and his religious background and training. Now here they were again. Birds chirping from the same tree. Cattle lowing nearby. Peaceful weather. And a great event happening before their eyes.

The American led William Jenkins into the pond. Both men stepped gently and carefully until they were more than waist high in the water, drawing short breaths as they got used to the cold temperature. Daniel and Elizabeth could picture themselves standing in the water with Elder Woodruff. The words to the baptismal prayer struck them as simple, to the point, and powerful. They wondered if the American was going to pour water over William's head, or immerse him in the pond, but they did not see any kind of water container. The question was quickly answered for them when William bent his knees as though on cue, fell backward, trusting the American to hold him in control. William Jenkins was totally immersed under the water.

William came out of the pond, wiping water from his eyes. He looked happy and peaceful, and gave the American preacher a hug as John Benbow held towels to dry them off.

Wilford Woodruff then turned his attention to his curious bystanders. "That's the way Jesus was baptized by John the Baptist. The total immersion of the person receiving baptism is symbolic of the death, burial, and resurrection of the Savior. Baptism is the introductory ordinance of the gospel and now must be followed by baptism of the Spirit in order to be complete. We will do that inside by the laying on of hands."

John Benbow motioned for everyone to follow him back to his house. "Let's get you two inside quickly so you can get your warm clothing back on."

As they walked, Wilford continued his teaching. "You are probably curious about why we dress in white. We do it simply as a sign of purity. Brother Jenkins presently is as pure as he was the day he was born. His sins are washed away."

Thomas Kington wedged himself between Daniel and Elizabeth, gently holding their arms as they walked. "I suppose you're wondering what's going to happen to the United Brethren."

"The thought has crossed my mind," Daniel admitted with imploring eyes.

Kington gave him a warm smile. "I'm no prophet but I will make a prediction. I think that virtually every one of our United Brethren will be baptized. When that happens – poof! No more United Brethren. We'll all be members of the only true and living church on the face of the earth. You'll understand what I mean as soon as you listen to Elder Woodruff's message."

"I have a simple question," Elizabeth said as they approached the house.

"Feel free," Kington responded

"Do Elder Woodruff's teachings have anything to do with the additional *light and truth* you have been waiting for?"

Kington tugged at their elbows, stopped walking, looked into Elizabeth's eyes, then Daniel's, and said, "Yes." His eyes misted.

Benbow opened the door. "Come in and make yourselves at home."

As they stepped in, Jane Benbow pointed to a table filled with teacups, biscuits and, cheese. "I have some refreshments for everyone." Her two adopted children stood there smiling.

"I'll dry off, change clothes, and be with you in just a few minutes," Elder Woodruff said, dashing up the stairs, followed by William Jenkins.

Kington said, "The three of you are in for a real treat. You are going to learn that there is a living prophet on the earth today, that the Savior's church has been restored to the earth – organized exactly the same as it was in olden times, and that Heavenly Father has a divine plan for each of his children."

Daniel's forehead wrinkled in thought. "Organized the same as in New Testament times? Like you always preached?"

"Precisely," Kington said with a beaming smile. "And you will especially like hearing about the Book of Mormon."

"Book of what?"

53

DANIEL WAS ASTONISHED at how good he felt during Elder Woodruff's presentation of the restored gospel. The feeling only intensified following his baptism and confirmation two hours later. His compared his decision to become a member of the United Brethren with his decision to be baptized into the Church of Jesus Christ of Latter-day Saints. The first had been mostly intellectual, the latter totally spiritual. When Elder Woodruff asked him, for the second time, to be baptized, his answer was overwhelmingly in the affirmative. He immediately felt deeply committed to his new faith, ready to make any personal sacrifice he might be asked to make. He was ready to become a lighted beacon of goodness and truth, loyal to the gospel and to its leaders, to build his life around gospel principles. More than at any time before, he felt his life had a purpose, and that purpose was to serve, to help others, to be productive in the cause of righteousness, to make a contribution to building up the Kingdom of God on earth. He looked to those things as a way to bring him the satisfaction that he sought in his personal life. He felt like a sponge, wanting to hear more from Elder Woodruff. He began thinking of ways to arrange his schedule so that he could hear more of the apostle's teaching in the coming days and weeks. He knew he had a lot to learn, and the sooner the better.

Elizabeth, on the other hand, regarded their quick conversion into the church as though fate had smiled on her again because she regarded "lady luck" as a close friend. After all, "lady luck" had brought her Daniel. Wasn't it true that he had moved to Deerhurst and opened his shop right next to her father's just at the right time, at the time she turned twenty-one years of age? "Lady luck" had introduced both her and her husband to John Benbow. That led to the barrel orders. That, in turn, ensured the success of her husband's new business. "Lady luck" had brought them the unexpected lease of a farm through her brother's athletic ability. "Lady luck" had brought them into the United Brethren church, where the most important premise was to wait for "additional light and truth." Now, that light and truth had come. These were her main thoughts following her baptism and confirmation at the hands of Elder Woodruff as they walked out of the Benbow house and prepared to leave for home.

The conversation turned to stories surrounding Elder Woodruff's first days in the Malvern Hills: Arriving at Benbow's farm. The meeting in the Great Hall. The constable that had come to arrest Wilford.

"Whatever happened to the constable that came to arrest you on that night?" William Jenkins asked.

"Constable Mortimer? Oh, he was baptized; didn't we tell you that?" Elder Woodruff responded.

"Yes, but what I mean is, what happened after that?"

Elder Woodruff flashed one of his biggest smiles. "He went back to the rector at the Castle Frome parish and told him that he had been baptized into the Church of Jesus Christ of Latter-day Saints."

Elizabeth couldn't help but laugh. "I'll bet the rector was *frightfully* upset!"

"He was," Wilford nodded, "and furthermore, the constable told him that if he wanted me 'taken up' or arrested for preaching the gospel, he would have to serve the writ himself. That's because Brother Mortimer said that he had heard me preach the only true gospel sermon he had ever listened to in his life."

"So that was the end of that, hey?" John Gailey commented.

John Benbow shook his head. "Not quite. The rector immediately sent two clerks representing the Church of England to investigate."

"When?" Gailey gasped.

"Just the other night."

Elizabeth's mouth dropped, and blood drained from her face. "What happened?"

John Benbow paused for a few seconds, smiled, shrugged his shoulders, and said, "They were baptized, also."

Elizabeth joined in the laughter, finding the story laced with irony. "I'll bet the rector doesn't dare send anyone else."

Daniel, Elizabeth, and John Gailey were still chuckling about the incident with the constable and the rector as they began their trip back to Deerhurst. The gig was bouncing merrily along the rutted road, and the world suddenly seemed more alive than before: Birds flitting in the trees, landing on branches that were faintly manifesting evidences of newly formed buds. The broad sky, slowly building puffy white clouds in the southwest. Farm laborers in the fields, spreading manure and plowing. For a while they talked about their eventful day: The concern they had earlier that morning that the United Brethren organization seemed to be falling apart. The impressions they had in their minds when they first saw Elder Woodruff walking toward the pond dressed in white. What went through their minds when the American bore his short, powerful testimony to them. How they felt watching William Jenkins being baptized Listening to nearly two hours of gospel teaching at the hands of an apostle of the Lord. Each of them agreed that they had learned more about the gospel and the nature of God in those two hours than they had learned and understood in their entire lives.

Elizabeth was the first to recall the letter Daniel had received from his uncle in France, connecting the prediction of the old Catholic priest, Father Gratius. The words from the letter seemed to suddenly flash into her mind.

The old true gospel and the gift thereof is lost, false doctrines prevail in all the church on the face of the earth. All we can do is exhort the people to be just, fear God, shun evil and pray. Prayer and purity may cause an angel to visit a deeply distressed soul, but I tell you, God will have spoken within a hundred years. He will restore the old church again.

She brought the subject up as they passed through Ledbury, which caused an instant discussion with John. He had not heard of the letter before. As they talked about it, Elizabeth thought about her rock-headed brother and Hannah, and the night Daniel had first brought the letter to their attention. Bobby had dismissed the letter as nonsense, but Elizabeth at once became excited and restless. She wanted to go home, find the letter, and immediately thrust it into the face of her brother and say, "See this? It's happened! The old true gospel is on the earth again. God has spoken." Her pulse went up as she thought about it. She contemplated what her brother's reaction might be, all the way home, arriving well after sundown, just as the sky filled with orange. She wanted Daniel to take her to Bobby's house right then. Exhausted, he thought about it as the evening approached, and then talked her out of it. They would go there early in the morning, before Bobby left for Gloucester and the sparring room.

MARCH 23. Sunday. I received my trunk that was sent to me from Hanley. In it, I received three letters, one from Elder John Taylor, one from Willard Richards, and one from Alfred Cordon. Elder Taylor informed me of his baptizing 17 persons in Liverpool. Elder Richards wished to inquire of the Lord his will for himself and his wife, for they are in deep affliction. Elder Cordon informed me that Elder Theodore Turley was taken with a warrant and cast into jail by the instrumentality of John Jones. A man took him from Birmingham because of a certain debt which was contracted 15 years ago before he left England, which was supposed to be wholly settled. But it is the work of the devil to put him in prison to stop his preaching. But God will yet turn this work for good, and if it is stopped in one place it will burst out in another place. May God open the prison doors and soon let Elder Turley free. I preached in Stanley Hill and baptized 12 persons, one of which is a preacher. The names are: John Fidco, Lydia Fidco, J. Benbow, Elizabeth Benbow [probably John Benbow's cousin, also named John, and his wife], Elizabeth Woodyatt, Mary Cole, Mary Jones, Harriet Tyler, Hannah Jones, Rebecca Tyler and Harriet Hill.

MARCH 24. Monday. A preacher, William Jenkins, called upon me and after I conversed with him a while, he requested baptism at my hands. I changed my clothing and as I got ready to go to the pool, three other preachers – Daniel Browett, Elizabeth Browett, and John Gailey-rode up in a gig or chariot to see me. The fame had gone out into all the county of the speedy work that God was performing. They had not heard me preach or any other Latter-day Saint, but had come more than 20 miles to see me. They came down out of the gig and walked where I was. Notwithstanding there were ministers yet, I stood up and boldly declared unto them Jesus, and testified unto them of the great work of God in these last days, and the power of God rested upon us. They bowed down and prayed and gave glory to God, and we all rose up and the gig stood still, and we all went down into the water at the same hour and I baptized them, and laid my hands upon them that they might receive the Holy Ghost. They went their way rejoicing. I then walked to Moorends Cross and spent the night, and preached at Brother William Parsons, and baptized five more persons, making nine baptized during the day. I also confirmed eight persons. Names of those baptized: Daniel Browett, Elizabeth Browett, William Jenkins and John Gailey; later in the day, John Shepherd, William and Mary Parsons, James and Hannah Hadley.

54

❧

ELIZABETH THOUGHT of Bobby and Hannah all night long. She talked about them with Daniel as they stepped into the house, fixed supper, did dishes, cleaned house, filled the tub and took baths, and even as they lay in bed, until they finally fell to sleep after one of the most eventful but exhausting days in their lives. Elizabeth's sleep was light and restless. Her mind raced with thoughts about what she could say to her brother to convince him to listen to the gospel message, how to get it through his thick head that the key to true happiness and peace was now truly within his grasp.

Bobby and Hannah were not the only people occupying Elizabeth's mind. She thought of her sister, Dianah, whom she had grown up with. Because she was three years older, and probably because of her personality characteristics, Dianah had always been the older, wiser, quiet, reflective, patient, kind sister; setting an example of always being calm under pressure. Dianah had always taken time to think about things. She never rushed to judgment. Rather she flowed with the various crises of life and was nondemanding, and had always been willing to accommodate Elizabeth's every wish, no matter how superficial, inconsistent and irresponsible those wishes and demands may have been. Elizabeth positively knew that Dianah would be receptive to Elizabeth and Daniel's suggestion that she investigate the church because, if nothing more, she would do it out of kindness. Dianah had always wanted to feel included in anything that attracted the attention and commitment of her younger sister, and her willingness to carefully consider anyone else's feelings and beliefs. In all likelihood, Dianah would take a lot more time to respond to an immediate challenge to be baptized, because that was her nature. She had been hesitant about everything in her life. Her husband, Thomas Bloxham, had courted Dianah for a long time until he convinced her to marry him. She was nearly twenty-two when she got married back in 1831.

Elizabeth couldn't begin to guess what her brother John's reaction might be to the gospel message. He seemed to be the odd-man-out of the family, withdrawing from the butchering business, leasing and managing a pub because, in her opinion, it was more self-serving and self-gratifying. He loved listening to the personal problems of the people who frequented the Ferret's Folly, and instead of trying to solve those problems, he seemed to stir things up. No matter the situation, he always seemed detached and insensitive, using whatever means he could get to forge an advantage and get ahead in business. She remembered John in their childhood as someone who always expended a high degree of energy trying to manipulate his parents to get his own way, and he, more than anyone, engaged in sibling rivalries for control and power. While her father was alive, Elizabeth feared John some, but through her own charm and charisma learned how to get along with her father, persuading him to do things that normally were against his nature. An example was the time she talked her father into allowing the first double date between her and Daniel and Bobby and Hannah.

Her thoughts turned back to Bobby and Hannah as Daniel drove the gig through a light, chilly rain from Deerhurst to Apperley. The sky had turned a gloomy gray in the early morning light. It was a sharp contrast to Elizabeth's bright optimism that surely, and most certainly, Bobby would be reasonable and listen to the marvelous experience she had yesterday at the Hill Farm with Elder Woodruff. Her bubble burst with the first words out of Bobby's mouth as they found him saddling a chestnut horse loaned to him by Squire Hastings, his hat dripping with rain.

"This is a bad time to visit," he said, his voice ringing sharp and crisp. "I'm already ten minutes late. Hannah has been nagging at me all morning about the American preacher and his wonderful message, so don't you start on me, too. I know you went to see him yesterday."

Daniel rolled his eyes. Elizabeth considered breaking the tension by teasing him about anything she could think of-his intensity, his rigorous training, his next opponent, his rudeness, the ugly old squire, or even the water dripping off his hat and into his face. She decided against it. Rather, she came right to the point.

"There's not a human being alive who's too busy to visit with his own kin, Bobby, so calm down." She paused for a few moments, speaking from her sitting position in the gig, letting the biting words sink in. "But it's *true*, and we won't deny it. We're here to tell you that the absolute *best* thing for you to do in your life is to hear Elder Woodruff's message."

Bobby laughed at the proposition. As he thought of it more seriously, he took in a deep breath and slowly exhaled. "Squire Hastings doesn't want me to have any distractions right now. This next fight is the most important, by far, of any fight I've ever had. So the answer is no. Get out of my way, I don't want to be late." He tested the cinch for tightness, and mounted the chestnut gelding.

Elizabeth got out of the gig and grabbed the gelding's bit, holding it tightly. "There are some things more important than fighting, like your *own* salvation. Bobby, I love you. I don't want you to miss out on this. Why don't you be *nice* and invite us inside?"

Daniel gasped at his wife's boldness. She seemed not to care about her brother's commitment to his training, trying to make him feel how she felt. Bobby's eyes glared with a determination that Daniel sensed he would not want to test himself.

"I've told you," Bobby hissed, "and I've told Hannah, a thousand times, that right now I am not interested. Let go of the horse."

"But Bobby. This is the true gospel. It can answer all the questions that have troubled you before. You can't just turn your back on this."

"Oh can't I? Watch my back." Bobby jerked the reins toward him, buried both heels into the horse, and galloped away.

Angry, hurt, frustrated, her hands stinging, Elizabeth stood there in the drizzle and watched the chestnut carry her brother down the muddy lane, around the corner, and disappear into the gray gloom of the morning. She glanced at Daniel, then slowly walked toward Bobby's house to see Hannah standing at the door.

"Did you hear everything?" Elizabeth asked as she stepped into the house where Joseph and Lizzy sat at the kitchen table eating a breakfast of porridge and bread.

Hannah hung her head. "Sure did. He was that way with me this morning, too, as you can guess. He has a one-track mind right now. It doesn't include religion, apostle or not, 'further light and truth' or not. Frustrating, isn't it?"

Still seething, Elizabeth shook her head up and down. "Yes, it is. But we shan't give up. We'll find a way, *believe me.*"

Daniel grinned, admiring his wife's tenacity.

Elizabeth glanced at the children, still dressed in their nightclothes. "Surely you're still having a birthday party tomorrow afternoon for Joseph?"

"Oh, yes," Hannah said, finding a reason to smile. "I've decided to throw a party for both Joseph and Lizzy, since their birthdays are so close together. Dianah told me that she and Thomas and their children would be here. So with you and Daniel we can have a nice party, even without Bobby."

"You're kidding," Elizabeth gasped. "Bobby is not going to be here for his own child's birthday party?"

Hannah's eyes misted. "He keeps telling me that he is too close to his fight and needs every minute at the sparring room and doing his road work. He says we can have a party for both Joseph and Lizzy sometime after the fight."

MARCH 26. Thursday. I walked from the Hill Farm to Stokes Lane and preached at the house of Joseph Evins and spent the night with William Davis. I had the following dream. I saw by night a river in which there were many fish. I cast a hook and caught some of them, and while fishing I saw some large ones near shore. I put the hook to their mouth. They bit it and I caught them, and one very notable one exceeding all other fish that I had caught. And as I was taking care of them, I saw a still larger river. It appeared like the Farmington River In the USA, at the mill that my father is tending. On the other side of the river was a boat to which was tied many fish lines. On one hook was a fish so large that the captain of the boat, Israel Dorman, could not bring him into the boat. He sailed the boat across the river where I was, and the fish were taken out and a bellman was called for to divide the fish. After the bell was run each man took a part, and while dividing the fish, one man said to another man I saw baptizing last night, "Was not you baptized?" I also saw a truck representing to be Elder Turley's trunk, and it ought to be taken care of for he is cast into prison. What this dream means time will soon determine. There is to be much baptizing done soon somewhere. Some of our brethren will soon come from the USA to be divided among the people, and I shall baptize many and some noted persons.

MARCH 27. Friday. I walked to the house of Mark Davis and baptized two persons, Richard Hall and William Williams, one a preacher. I then walked to Shucknell Hill, a very noted and sightly place. The plains looked beautiful in the valleys around it, and notwithstanding it is a country place, yet I could count 21 churches from the top of the hill. I preached in the evening to a large congregation, and although it was the first time that they had heard of the gospel, yet if there had been water convenient, there would have been 20 baptized. But as it was a great distance to the water, most concluded to omit it until another day. However, some would not take no for an answer, and they followed me until two o'clock in search of water. We finally found a stream and baptized five persons in a place where we had to let them down eight feet perpendicular by the bank before we reached water. Three of this number were preachers. One was an aged woman who had followed us the whole time, leaning upon her staves. Philip Green, Jane Green, Ann Graves, John White, Francis Brush.

MARCH 28. Saturday. I confirmed one and walked to the Hill Farm and baptized two persons, George Allen and Thomas Benbow, one was a Primitive Methodist preacher. [Thomas Benbow was the adopted son of John and Jane Benbow. Thomas's sister, Ellen, was baptized on March 9.] Spent the night at the Hill Farm and dreamed of being with several others in a small boat in a storm on the river. We had to paddle ashore with our hands having no paddles. There was a serpent, which crawled into the boat and I flung him out with my hands, and reached the shore in safety.

MARCH 29. Sunday. I have much to do today. I preached at Fromes Hill at half past 10 o'clock, and at the Hill Farm at half past two. Baptized 14 persons, two of which were preachers. I met with the saints in the evening at 6 o'clock at the Hill Farm, and confirmed 35 persons. Names of those I personally baptized: Thomas Smith, Elizabeth Davis, James Watkins, William Morris, Mary Prosser, Susanna Morris, John Dyer, Benjamin Williams, Mary Williams, Ann Dutson, Harriet White, Thomas Hope, Eliza Parry. Broke bread unto about 80 saints, which closed the business of the day. Oh how much strength and wisdom I need in the midst of much labor. Bur surely the Lord does give me grace according to my day, for which I feel very thankful. I am informed this day that the ministers of the Church of England are holding meetings and councils to petition Parliament to stop my preaching, and to cause our religion to cease out of the land. But may the Lord order all things right, I pray.

55

SUDDEN FEELINGS of insecurity swept over Daniel in the days following the birthday party. No longer was he a lay preacher of the United Brethren. He was a novice in his knowledge of the restored gospel. Aside from telling his mother, sister and brother, and a few others, about his conversion and baptism, he didn't feel qualified to teach the doctrines of his new religion because, in fact, he didn't know much about them. He had been baptized because of his feelings. There was no doubt in his mind that it was the Spirit of the Holy Ghost that had confirmed to him that the brief, powerful message delivered by Elder Woodruff was true. But he was gripped with his usual strong desire to know more, to know all that there was to know, and to use that knowledge to spread the word and improve the lives of others. He moped around his farm, giving his farm servants direction for their spring farm work: plowing, fertilizing, tilling, and planting. He kept tabs on his barrel and furniture business, telling James Pulham and John Davis about his experience with Elder Woodruff, checking orders, supplies, workload, and the efficiency of his shop.

He made another trip to the Hill Farm to find out where Elder Woodruff was teaching, and if he could spend some time following him around and listening to him, helping, supporting, and doing whatever he could to help.

On a breezy but otherwise mild Friday afternoon he found Thomas Kington at the Hill Farm, hard at work organizing his own farm servants, still in Benbow's employ, happy, smiling, hands dirty, shirt soiled, and glad to see Daniel. Feeling a little lost and awkward, Daniel exchanged small talk about farming, wives, weather, and their new church, and then asked him a question. "Now that we are not members of the United Brethren anymore, what do you want us to do?" In a way, though the feeling was diminishing every day, he still regarded Kington, the former superintendent of the United Brethren, as not only his friend but also his mentor.

Kington gave Daniel an odd look, as if to say, *Don't you already know?* Daniel did not realize it, but Kington was relieved to be free of the heavy duties that had piled up over the years: Training lay preachers. Organizing circuits. Being gone away from home. Preaching, teaching, and building up an organization declared to exist for one main purpose, to "wait for further light and truth." That purpose had been fulfilled. Now Kington was content to be a member of the Church of Jesus Christ of Latter-day Saints. Just a lay member. Gone was the glory of being the superintendent of the United Brethren; but he stood ready, willing and able, to assist the missionary effort in whatever capacity he was asked. He had already spoken to Elder Woodruff about it, so he made a calculated response to Daniel's question. "The most important thing we can do right now is help Elder Woodruff convert the rest of the congregation."

The answer didn't surprise Daniel. In fact, it was exactly what he thought Thomas would say. He just wanted to know how to do it. "What specifically should we be doing? How can I help?"

Kington's response was instant, as was his smile. "Elder Woodruff told me to just keep telling the other United Brethren people about the gospel and help set up teaching appointments. I think by now just about all of our people have heard about my conversion, and John Benbow's conversion. By now, they've probably heard about you, John Gailey, and William Jenkins. So they'll be very curious."

"I have done some of that, but I can do it some more."

"Good man. Tell your family, your friends, and anyone else you are acquainted with."

"Do you think it would be possible for Elder Woodruff to come to my home and teach some members of my family?"

"Sure do," Thomas said, chuckling. "That's what he's doing now, over in Herefordshire, teaching at a member's home. And he is scheduled to be in Ledbury on Monday."

Daniel got a gleam in his eye. "Really?"

"If I were you, I would take your wife to Ledbury and follow Elder Woodruff around all day. Listen to everything he says. He's the gospel fountain of knowledge. There's so much more to learn."

"That's exactly how I feel."

The most striking scene in Ledbury on Monday, the thirtieth of March, was not the timber-framed Tudor and Stuart buildings that lined its cobbled streets. Neither was its collection of shops: saddlers, glaziers, carpenters, masons, plumbers, banks, business agents, doctors, legal advisors. Nor its seventeenth century black-and-white Market House that stood rigid on its sixteen oak stilts. Nor the magnificent Feathers Hotel, the Royal Oak Hotel, or the medieval St. Michael's parish church, founded before the Norman Conquest and mentioned in the Doomsday Book. It wasn't even the home of poetess Elizabeth Browning. No, none of that. Instead, the most striking scene in Ledbury on that particular day was the sight of thirty to forty natives, mostly from the beautiful borderland called Herefordshire that separates England from Wales, following a short, plain-looking American into a simple Baptist chapel, on the Homend between Belle Orchard and Orchard Road.

That's where Daniel and Elizabeth Browett found Elder Woodruff, with John Benbow and Thomas Kington at his side. He was having a conversation with the Baptist minister, Reverend G. H. Roper-Curzon. The chapel reminded Daniel of the simple red brick Methodist chapel back in Apperley, where he and Elizabeth had been married.

Wearing the modified green dress she had been married in, eyes open wide, smiling, and squirming through the crowd so that she could hear what was being said, Elizabeth glued her eyes on Elder Woodruff. He had just asked the Baptist minister for permission to speak in his church.

"Who are all these people with you?" Elizabeth heard the gray-haired, round-shouldered reverend ask Elder Woodruff, his inquisitive eyes scanning the crowd that had followed the American to the church's steps. The crowd was swelled by the fact that it was an unusually warm, partly cloudy, beautiful spring day. Birds sang gaily from overhead tree branches, and a gentle breeze was blowing. A few curious Baptists, on their way into the building, had joined the crowd. Carriages with well-dressed men and women were still arriving. *Amazing*, Elizabeth thought. *It's not even Sunday.*

Thomas Kington answered for Elder Woodruff. "Most of them are members of the United Brethren congregation, and some of them are members of Elder Woodruff's church."

In a nervously merry mood, Reverend Roper-Curzon paused, still scanning Elder Woodruff's followers, trying to hide the fact that he was counting them. Elizabeth knew better. The more he counted the farther out he stuck his chest. "Elder Woodruff you say? An American?"

"Yes," Kington responded. "He's the best speaker I've ever heard. Your congregation will enjoy him."

Overcome with curiosity, weighing the advantages and disadvantages, and directing his question to the American, the reverend asked, "What would you talk about?"

Elder Woodruff locked eyes with the Baptist minister. "The gospel of Jesus Christ."

The minister could see no harm in that. He broke into a sly grin. "Please come in," he said, doffing his hat and using it to point the way, flattered that he could expand his audience by some thirty to forty persons.

Daniel and Elizabeth sat on a pew in the middle of the chapel, holding hands. Elizabeth regarded the experience as a unique treat. A Mormon elder preaching to a Baptist congregation, with several not-yet-baptized United Brethren members. The Baptist minister spoke first, using the thirty-fifth chapter of Isaiah as his text. To Elizabeth, the message was too complex and therefore muddled.

The minister introduced Elder Woodruff. "I don't know really who you are except that you are a preacher from America. I am as curious as the next man to hear your message. The time is yours."

As Daniel listened to Elder Woodruff for the second time, he felt an immediate, warm connection. He appreciated the apostle's knowledge, dedication, and commitment to his calling. He knew that when Elder Woodruff's speech was over, it wouldn't be enough and he would want to know more. He was going to have a difficult time paying attention to his work, because he knew he would have a natural tendency to do as the disciples of Christ had done in Biblical times when the Savior had said, "Follow me." Daniel knew that if Elder Woodruff asked him to walk to the edge of the earth and jump off, for the sake of the gospel, he would do it gladly. He was fascinated with the simple but eloquent explanations of basic gospel doctrines. At the end, when the apostle bore his witness of the divinity of the Savior, Daniel found himself teary-eyed.

And so at the end of this unusual day in Ledbury, a large crowd of people got into their gigs, coaches, and carriages to follow Elder Wilford Woodruff, a member of the Quorum of Twelve Apostles of the Church of Jesus Christ of Latter-day Saints, five miles northwest to the Benbow Hill Farm. There, they watched nine persons, including Edward Phillips, taken to a small pond where they were baptized by immersion for the remission of sins. Four were previous members of Reverend Roper-Curzon's congregation.

As for the reverend himself, he walked home slowly, thinking of the American's sermon, knowing that it was probably true, but too weak to respond to it. In fact, he had told Wilford that he believed everything that he had said. However, his salary and position in his church were too important for him to make a change. After all, what else could he do to make a living? He had found out that all Mormon ministers traveled without purse or scrip, just as Jesus had taught, and that the Mormon lay preachers were unpaid as well. The reverend perceived that without a way to replace his salary there was no room for him at the inn.

Following the baptisms, Daniel, Elizabeth, and Thomas Kington followed Elder Woodruff to the home of Francis Pullen, where they learned the latest religious "gossip" surrounding the Mormons and Elder Woodruff. Someone earlier in the day had relayed the news from London that several Malvern Hills Anglican ministers and rectors had just sent a petition to the Archbishop of Canterbury, requesting Parliament to pass a law prohibiting Mormons from preaching in British dominions. The petition claimed that one Mormon missionary – namely Elder Woodruff – had baptized fifteen hundred persons, mostly members of the Church of England. Everyone at the house laughed at the exaggeration.

Suppressing his annoyance at what he had just heard, Daniel thought of the Baptist minister in Ledbury, who had just lost four of his congregation. He shrugged his shoulders at Thomas Kington and remarked, "I was surprised that the reverend let Elder Woodruff speak to his congregation." He glanced at the apostle, who was busy talking to his recent converts. Daniel resolved that he was going to express his desire to assist in whatever assignment, large or small, that Elder Woodruff would give him.

"I was too," Kington said. "I think that before the week is over quite a few people from his congregation will end up being baptized. I suppose the next thing that will happen is that we are going to get even more opposition from some of the reverends, maybe not from the Baptist reverend in Ledbury, but certainly from others."

"I hope all the other church people don't start hating Mormons like the Anglicans hate the Methodists, and visa versa," Elizabeth said, shuddering.

As the crowd began breaking up, Daniel made a last comment to Elder Woodruff. "We want to help. Let us know what we can do."

"That's easy," Elder Woodruff said in a cheerful voice, although looking a little weary after another long day. "I believe that after a person is baptized into the church he or she now has a responsibility to help the missionary effort by finding others to teach. I'll give you some examples."

Daniel's face was lit with happiness.

Wilford said, "After Jesus called John the Beloved and Andrew, the Bible tells us in the first chapter of John that Andrew found Peter. *He first findest his own brother Simon, and saith unto him, we have found the Messiah.* A second example is found in verse forty-five, which tells us what Philip did when he found the gospel. *Philip findeth Nathanael.*

Daniel quickly understood. *And Daniel findeth Bobby.*

Wilford was not done. "And again, after the Savior taught the woman of Samaria, what is the first thing she did? She went to town and told everyone she could. I challenge you to do the same thing. Tell everyone you know, your friends, your relatives, everyone. We must spread out from the Benbow farm and find and teach in the other villages near here."

Elizabeth was energized by Wilford's suggestions. She whispered into Daniel's ear. He nodded. "Elder Woodruff," she said, "would you come to Deerhurst and stay in our home and teach our friends and relatives?"

"Of course, Sister Browett," he said with a cheeky grin. "That's the spirit. Let's make it Thursday, because I'm going to be in The Leigh anyway, on Wednesday, staying at the home of William Jenkins."

MARCH 30. Monday. I walked to Ledbury, six miles, and had not been in town an hour before many flocked to see me and gave me the hand of fellowship. The Baptist minister opened his chapel for me to preach in, and he went into the pulpit with me and opened the meeting by reading the 35th Chapter of Isaiah, and praying mightily for me. I then arose and preached to the largest congregation (it was said) that ever met in the chapel. The minister was believing and bid me God speed. After the meeting many offered themselves for baptism. I baptized John Morgan, Mary Powell, Elizabeth Hill, Elizabeth Tringham, Ann Benbow, Thomas Clark, Edward Phillips, Edward Jenkins, Malina Prichard. I spent the night with Francis Pullen. I received three letters, one from W. Richards, one from Cordon, and one from Mulliner. MARCH 31. Tuesday. I walked to the Green Way and baptized 13 persons, 4 of which were preachers. I then walked to the home of Thomas Kington, and preached at his house in Dymock, and spent the night there. I wrote four letters, one to W. Richards, one to Turley, one to Wm. Benbow, and one to Clayton. Names of those baptized: John Preece, Mary Ann Preece, Hannah Pullen, Mary Pitt, Hannah Pitt, James Palmer, Henry Palmer, James Palmer Jr., James Bishop, Elizabeth Bishop, Elizabeth Smith, Rosanah Bayliss, Lydia War.

CHAPTER NOTES

The incident in Ledbury is true, taken from the Wilford Woodruff journal. The author also looked up the web site connected to the Ledbury Baptist Church, where it is acknowledged that during that period they lost membership both to the "Brethren" and to the Mormons.

56

ELIZABETH HAD ALWAYS revealed a knack for being just terrifically organized for any kind of social engagement. She seemed to have a sixth sense on how to everything work out perfectly. She had a zest for living that Daniel admired, and it showed in her preparations for Elder Woodruff's visit. She saw to it that their house was cleaned top to bottom, working vigorously with her housemaid, and even using a couple of the farm servants. All the bedding was washed. She stocked the house with food, shopping at the butcher shop, the dairy, the bakery, and drawing out anything that looked eatable from the root cellar.

Daniel worried about a much different aspect of Elder Woodruff's visit – filling the house with investigators. His sister, Rebecca, now twenty years of age, and his three younger brothers – Thomas, twenty-five, John, twenty-one, and William, nineteen – responded with a measure of enthusiasm. But it frustrated him that his mother, Martha, was bull-headed and would not commit.

It was on Monday afternoon, another warm spring day, that Daniel sat

Elizabeth down to tell her that she needed to take time away from her house cleaning to invite members of her own family. "Everyone is not like you, Elizabeth," he said. "You drop everything at a moment's notice, but other people are not as spontaneous as you. They need a little time to respond to your invitation."

The reminder worked, and soon the two of them were sitting in the gig, traveling around to invite Elizabeth's sister, Dianah, and her husband Thomas, then Elizabeth's cousins, Margaret Crook and Susanna Margarett; and her friends Mary Hill, Eliza Jenkins, and Elizabeth Lambert. But the person who was most on their mind was Bobby.

Elizabeth and Daniel found Hannah at home in a sagging spirit, alone with her three children, fretting from the moment she saw the gig coming down the road toward her house. Before they said a word, Hannah knew why they were there. For the sake of peace in the house, she had temporarily given up talking with Bobby about Wilford Woodruff and shuddered to think that the turmoil was going to begin all over again. That's because Bobby's sister and her husband were knocking on the door to announce some kind of plan to convince Bobby to explore the Mormon religion.

"I suppose it's too much to hope that Bobby might be home," Elizabeth said as she walked in, almost knocking over little Lizzy, who came toddling up in the little purple dress Elizabeth had given her for her second birthday, just days earlier.

Hannah's smile was indulgent. "He's either still in Gloucester or sitting at the Ferret's Folly, telling his brother what a nagging wife he has. Move out of the way, Lizzy."

Elizabeth patted Lizzy on the head. "You do look *cute* in your new dress." Lizzy looked at her aunt with big, playful eyes, smiled, and went into the other room, looking for Joseph. Elizabeth touched her sister-in-law on the arm and said, "Hannah, we have some *really* good news."

Hannah doubted that the news would cheer her up, and she said with a straight face, "What kind of good news?"

"Wilford Woodruff will be at our home tomorrow night."

Hannah's doubt turned to a sliver of mistrust, initially refusing to believe such a thing were possible. The American apostle, the man who had so much charisma, and who taught with so much power – he would be at the Browett home? How did that happen? She paused for a few seconds before she responded. Then the rationale of it came to her. Daniel had been one of Kington's most trusted and most ardent lay preachers. It would follow that Daniel and Elizabeth would have the connection to get Elder Woodruff to come to their home. To her, it did make sense.

"Oh? That's wonderful," Hannah said, still with a hint of doubt.

Elizabeth was a little chagrined at Hannah's hesitancy, expecting her to bubble over with enthusiasm like she would have done if the situation were reversed. "We've already invited all of Daniel's family, and Dianah and Thomas, plus some other friends. This is the *perfect* opportunity to invite Bobby."

Hannah was at once apprehensive. "Bobby won't come. You know that as well as I do. You've already tried. The most important fight of his career is just two weeks away. If I ask him to sit in on any religious meeting, especially right now, he'll just get mad again. All he thinks about is his fighting."

Daniel glanced at Hannah's sad eyes. He perceived that Bobby had verbally beaten her down so many times recently that she had almost given up on trying to bring some spirituality and religion into his life.

"Answer this question honestly, Hannah," Daniel said. "After hearing Elder Woodruff and the message of the restored gospel, do you think Bobby ought to quit fighting, join the church, and change his way of life?"

Hannah breathed deeply, and her eyes misted, feeling grateful that Daniel had finally come to the crux of the matter. Until now, she perceived that she was the only one in the world who felt that boxing was a cruel sport, un-Christian, and uncivilized. "Yes, I do. You know I've never liked his fighting career, especially since our experience in London."

Elizabeth was surprised that Daniel had made the statement suggesting that Bobby actually quit fighting, because they had never discussed it together that way. She had always regarded herself as her brother's most vocal supporter of his fight career. But listening to Hannah's response, and thinking about it, she was surprised that she felt the same way. The thought of her brother actually attaining the heavyweight championship of all Great Britain had, up until this point, always intrigued her. However, eternal life was much more important than the heavyweight championship. There had to be a way to get Bobby to listen to Elder Woodruff.

"How shall we go about inviting him to our house, then?" Elizabeth asked Hannah, rubbing her chin, and plopping into the sofa.

"I would appreciate it if you would invite him personally," Hannah said. "But to do it you'll have to come back later tonight, or early in the morning before he leaves for Gloucester. Either that or try to catch him at the Ferret's Folly, but I wouldn't recommend it."

"No, I won't do that," Elizabeth agreed. "That would be the *worst* place to try and talk my brother about Elder Woodruff."

Daniel pulled his wife out of the sofa. "Come on, then. We've got some other people we can visit yet this evening."

"We'll be back in the morning, Hannah," Elizabeth said.

"Better come early."

Before the sun rose over the Cotswolds, Bobby was already sitting alone at his breakfast table in his usual squalid mood when he heard his dog bark at the clip-clop of a horse outside. The spaniel quit barking when he recognized the person driving the gig to be a friendly face. Bobby got out of his chair to see a woman wearing a blue riding dress with a dark blue mantle, trimmed in white, tying a horse to a post and walking toward the house. She admitted herself through a gate that was part of the white picket fence surrounding the cottage. He recognized the woman through the gray dawn to be his sister, Elizabeth, so he yelled for her to come in before she knocked at the door.

Elizabeth found Bobby alone, slumped over at the table eating leftover ham, cheese and bread. He was unshaven, a black cap already covering his unruly brown hair, and staring at her with a restless, half-angry look that startled her.

"I'm glad you named your spaniel 'Duke,' but it makes me think of the dog Henry killed," she began with an off-guard remark. "I hear Joseph wants a puppy of his own."

His comeback was icy and accusatory. "You could have bought a puppy for Joseph for his birthday, or did you forget that he just had a birthday?"

The words pierced Elizabeth's heart, revealing the fact that her brother not only had missed the birthday party, but also had not even taken the time to learn who was there and what went on. Elizabeth sank into despair, knowing that their early morning conversation was already off to a rocky start. Bobby hadn't asked her to sit down or even invited her to take off her mantle and visit. He continued to stuff his mouth full of ham and cheese, and wash it down with big gulps of milk.

"What are you doing here so early?" Bobby asked in an icy tone.

Refusing to let her brother's morning grouchiness depress her, she collected her thoughts, dispensing with small talk. She dropped into a chair beside him and waited until he looked at her. "I've come to give you a *special* invitation."

"To what, dinner or something?" He turned his eyes from her to his empty plate. "You know how busy I am. It's out of the question."

Elizabeth leaned forward and put her arms on the table. "I'm sure there will be a dinner afterward. I want to invite you to our home to hear the American missionary speak."

Bobby drew a big breath, expressing his frustration. "No thanks."

"I didn't expect to be turned down so *quickly*, so..."

"Rudely?" Bobby allowed himself a rare smile.

"Yes. Rudely."

"I don't have time for religion right now, dear sister. Not even from that American. Woodruff?"

Elizabeth pressed the issue. "Bobby, this will be the most *important* thing you will do in your life."

"The most important thing to me right now is to win my next fight."

"What salvation will that gain you?"

Abruptly, Bobby stood. He towered over his sister. "What has happened to you? You used to be my biggest fan. Can't you understand the importance of winning this next fight? A chance to be booked against the champion? Think of the money I'll earn. Think of my future. Religion can wait. It will be there when I retire in a few years."

Elizabeth sat back and stared at her older brother, longing for a return to the good times of their youth, when they had nothing serious to argue about. "I still am a big fan of yours, Bobby. I really would like to see you win the championship. But just slow down a bit and think of your spiritual life. You need some *balance*, dear brother."

Bobby sat back down in his chair. "Why is this American in your home? Did you get baptized, too?"

"Yes, and so did Daniel."

A feeling of defensiveness stole over Bobby as he played with his utensils. "That's your life. You do what you want, but don't push it on me."

Elizabeth quickly shot back a response. "But Hannah wants a *religious* upbringing for your children. Tomorrow may be too late. You *know* how quickly children grow up."

Bobby made a face. "She can take them to church, I don't object. You can help her. You don't have any children of your own yet."

As far as Elizabeth was concerned, that was the worst thing possible her brother could have said. As the words bit into her, sensations of both hurt and anger flooded her mind. More than anything in the world, Elizabeth wanted to be a mother like Hannah. With tears welling up in her eyes, Elizabeth bit her tongue.

The sight of his sister welling up caused Bobby to assess his words, and the room went stone silent. It made him uncomfortable. He rose from the table and reached for his coat. "I've got to go. You're just like Hannah. You cry too easily."

Elizabeth took a series of deep breaths and wiped at her eyes with her sleeves. "Bobby, listen. I *know* that you have had a lot of concerns about religion, and that there are a lot of things that have troubled you over the years, and a lot of unanswered questions. I *guarantee* that Elder Woodruff can answer all those questions and resolve *all* your concerns."

"I've heard that before."

"Elder Woodruff is different..."

"I've heard that before, too."

"Please, one last time, Bobby. Come and meet Elder Woodruff..."

"I don't have time." Bobby walked toward the door.

Elizabeth had one weapon left. "Remember the letter Daniel has with the story about the Catholic priest?"

"Yes, of course."

"This is the church. It fits the description. It is led by a *prophet* instead of a pope or an archbishop."

"You can't trick me, little sister." Inwardly, he was flabbergasted by her bravado.

Sighing in frustration, Elizabeth reached out and took her brother by the hand. "You've got to believe me, Bobby. The letter said a church was going to be restored – and that's exactly what happened. God himself and Jesus too, appeared to this prophet. The restored church has apostles, prophets, teachers, deacons, just as the Catholic priest predicted. Elder Woodruff is one of the apostles."

"Not interested..."

"Come to the meeting, please."

"I don't have time."

As Elder Woodruff taught the gospel message to a large crowd stuffed into the parlor of the Browett home in The Leigh, Elizabeth stood in the doorway that separated the parlor from the kitchen and wove herself through a wide loom of emotions. Her house was clean, and crumpets and cakes were sitting on the kitchen table ready to be served whenever Elder Woodruff finished his teaching. A spare bed with clean sheets had been prepared for the American so that he could stay overnight. All those things made Elizabeth feel proud and happy.

Because her home was part of the farm lease with Squire Hastings, it was larger than the ordinary cottages of the common laborers: the farm servants, the butchers, the carpenters, the cobblers, and the watchmakers. That was a source of pride, too, and it showed on her face as she surveyed the room. But her survey revealed the fact that a few people that she and Daniel had invited had not shown up, including Daniel's mother, and her brother Bobby, and that irritated her. They had robbed her of a chance to feel that her "cottage meeting" was a complete success instead of a partial success. As she glanced at her sister, Dianah, she felt the same way because her husband, Thomas Bloxham, had not shown up. With those three exceptions, however, everyone else was seated in the parlor, eyes glued on Elder Woodruff, mouths dropped in a sort of spiritual wonderment, soaking up the message of the restoration. Daniel's sister, and three brothers were all there. And so were Frederick Evans, Joseph Bayliss, Mary Hill, Eliza Jenkins, Margarett Crook, and Susannah Margarett. Plus James and Nancy Pulham, and John Davis and Mary Ann Weston.

Elizabeth reflected on her early morning visit to Bobby and the frustration she felt as she had pleaded with him to respond to her invitation. She remembered her anger as she watched him storm out of the house and take off for Gloucester to please his gods – pugilism and Squire Hastings. She recalled her short conversation with Hannah afterward, the sadness, the insecurity, and the frustration.

Elizabeth contrasted her visit at Bobby's house with that of her later visit to her older sister, Dianah, when they had stood in Dianah's house and talked and giggled. That had revived her spirits, even though the sight of Dianah's five happy, lively children and the fact that Dianah's sixth child would be born any day, normally brought on the old feelings of jealousy. As Elizabeth watched Dianah sitting uncomfortably in her chair not too far from where Elder Woodruff was standing, she wondered what would happen at the end of the day if her sister felt the same way that she and Daniel had, and want to be baptized. To her, it would look funny for a heavily pregnant woman to walk into a pond to be baptized by total immersion. She chuckled to herself at the thought of it. Even when Dianah predicted that Thomas probably wouldn't come to the meeting, it didn't depress Elizabeth like it did over the thought that Bobby might not show up. Of course, Bobby was her kin and Thomas was a brother-in-law.

Worrying about the comfort of her guests, Elizabeth paced back and forth as Elder Woodruff concluded his story of the restoration. He said, "I want to leave you with a challenge to read this book, the Book of Mormon. There are two basic purposes of the Book of Mormon. The first is that we may know the covenants of the Lord to the House of Israel – which is you – and the second is to teach you, to convince you, that Jesus is the Christ. I promise you that you will become closer to the Lord by reading the Book of Mormon than by reading any other book."

Daniel was pleased that the words seemed to impact the members of his family. He gained the strong impression that they would want to be baptized right away.

Elder Woodruff's concluding remarks caused Elizabeth to think of Bobby and Dianah's husband, Thomas, again. The gaiety of the occasion energized her, and she felt like hitching the horse to the gig, grabbing Daniel by the arm, and riding immediately to find Bobby and Thomas again, to literally drag them to the presence of Elder Woodruff. She would gladly risk Bobby's sarcastic attitude again just to have a chance to give him another invitation to hear the gospel. She continued to feel that way as the apostle concluded his remarks.

"I invite you, and all men everywhere, to read the Book of Mormon, to ponder in your hearts the message it contains, then ask your Heavenly Father in the name of Christ if the book is true. If you will do this, if you ask in faith, I promise that you will gain a testimony of its truth and divinity by the power of the Holy Ghost. By this same power you will also come to know that Jesus Christ is the Savior of the world, that Joseph Smith is his revelator and prophet in these last days, and that the Church of Jesus Christ of Latter-day Saints is the Lord's Kingdom once again established on the earth, preparatory to the second coming of the Savior."

Hugging Elizabeth at the conclusion of the meeting, Dianah was in tears. "Thank you for inviting me tonight," she sobbed. "I want to be baptized tonight." There were no giggles, no laughter. Elizabeth knew her sister felt the same way that she did the day she was baptized.

Expressing the same feelings as Dianah, Mary Ann Weston told Elder

Woodruff and Daniel she wanted to be baptized. Daniel heard the same joyful request from every member of his family. As the baptismal candidates changed into white clothing, Daniel approached his business partner, John Davis.

"What about you, John?"

"There's nothing I would like better," John said with a friendly but apologetic smile. A sad look came upon his face. "But you know my mother. She's already upset that I've been attending the United Brethren meetings. I've got to think about how I can approach her."

Feeling sorry for his friend, Daniel proposed a later date. "Elder Woodruff is coming back in a few days. Try for then." With that, the group left for a nearby neighbor's pond where, after securing permission from the owner, a baptismal service was conducted. Daniel baptized his sister and three brothers and Elder Woodruff baptized Dianah Bloxham, nine months pregnant, and several others.

APRIL 2. Thursday. I walked to Twigworth and preached at the home of John Hill, then returned to The Leigh and preached and spent the night with the Browetts. I baptized today: Frederick Evans, Joseph Bayliss, Mary Hill, Eliza Jenkins, Mary Ann Weston, Elizabeth Lambert, Dianah Bloxham, Margarett Crook, Susannah Margarett.

57

OVER A BREAKFAST of bacon and eggs the next morning at the Browett house, Elizabeth studied Wilford Woodruff, his mannerisms, his likes and dislikes, his personality traits, the unique solid core that reflects the unique essence of any particular human being. It was a habit of hers to do this, and she often suspected she got it from her maternal grandmother Mary Gardner, who died in 1816. Elizabeth could not really remember her, but her mother, Sarah, often told Elizabeth that she reminded her of Mary, and that Elizabeth had a unique ability to characterize people and compare them one to another.

As Wilford and Daniel discussed other people that might be invited into the Browett home to be taught, Elizabeth was amazed at the similarities between the two men, and she was equally astonished at their differences. First of all, she discovered that she had never met someone who was so deeply committed to doing his Father in Heaven's bidding as Elder Woodruff. In listening to him, she concluded that the title of apostle must have been given to him because of his devotion to the Savior. As she listened to Daniel's conversation with Elder Woodruff, she was taken by how much Daniel appeared to want to emulate the apostle, to have some kind of apostolic insight. She heard Daniel make statements that he felt just as obligated as Elder Woodruff to raise the warning voice, and to propagate the gospel.

Elizabeth was impressed by Wilford's explanation of his earlier life, and the similarities between his personal search for the true church and theirs. The prophecy of Old Prophet Mason. The letter from Daniel's uncle containing the prophecy of the old Catholic priest in Switzerland.

Wilford said that he didn't join any church as a young man, but that at age twenty-three, some ten years ago, he began to explore religion. "But I couldn't find any body of people, any denomination, or any church that had faith as its basic doctrine. It seemed to me no one was practicing the principles, ordinances and gifts that constituted the gospel of Jesus Christ as taught by the Savior and his apostles in Biblical times. Nor could I find anywhere the manifestations of the Holy Ghost with its attendant gifts and graces."

"Didn't you talk with some of the ministers?" Daniel asked.

"Yes," he answered. "But when I did, they would always tell me that prophets, apostles, revelations, and so forth, were given only to establish Jesus Christ and his doctrine, back in the days of the New Testament, but in their opinion those things were done away with because they were no longer needed. I could never believe such a thing."

"So you went through your own struggle about religion," Daniel said, scratching his chin.

"Definitely," Wilford commented. "My belief back then was firmly fixed in my mind. From my personal study of the Bible, I found that the principle of cause and effect was the same in all ages, and that divine promises were made to all generations. I found no changes in the gospel in the days of Christ and the apostles, or no evidence that there would be any change in the plan of salvation in the last days. I learned from the scriptures that many of the ancient prophets, including Christ and his apostles, foresaw by inspiration and revelation that the gentile nations would apostatize and turn away from the true faith, just as the ancient Jews had done, and that there would be a falling away; that other systems, manmade, would arise."

Daniel's eyes brightened as he remembered what Thomas Kington had told him that day under the oak tree, by the pond where he and Elizabeth were baptized. "It's amazing that Brother Kington knew a little bit of these things, without knowing about the restored gospel."

Wilford nodded. "Yes, it is. He and I have talked about it. The Lord truly raised him up to prepare people like you for the gospel."

As Elder Woodruff told more about himself, Elizabeth compared his thirst for knowledge to that of Thomas Kington's. Wilford said that even before he joined the church he began to have a voracious appetite for knowledge, and that he began to devour books that contained the histories of the United States, England, Scotland, Greece, and Rome.

"I find that by perusing history we converse with men of judgement, wisdom, and knowledge." Wilford continued. "Later, I took up the Bible as a study of history, and I never found any history equally interesting until later on when I read the Book of Mormon. Reading those two books, the Bible and the Book of Mormon, we converse, as it were, with the Lord and his holy prophets and apostles, and we learn truths that cannot be acquired from any other source. So now I am of the opinion that we ought to keep our noses in those two books as opposed to any others, because they contain the revelations of heaven and they are of far more interest than books containing merely the opinions, theories, and doctrines of men."

"The Book of Mormon is now my favorite," Daniel said, beaming.

"And mine," Elizabeth said.

As their conversation returned to missionary work, Elder Woodruff told

Daniel and Elizabeth that he could return to their home as early as Friday. Until then, he was scheduled to work with Thomas Kington in the Ledbury and Gadfield Elm areas for a couple of days. Daniel and Elizabeth then began to express how disappointed they were that Bobby and Hannah had not shown up last night.

"Why is it that your brother seems to have lost an interest in religion?" Wilford asked.

Elizabeth drew a big breath. "Two reasons. First, he's involved in pugilism and he's *very* good at it. So good, in fact, he may have a chance to fight for the British championship in London this year or next year. It's taken over his life even to the point of *training* on Sundays. He gets very defensive when confronted by it. He cuts me off, he cuts Hannah off – anyone who tries to talk to him about religion."

"And what's the second reason?" Wilford asked, picking idly at the remaining bits of scrambled eggs.

Elizabeth continued. "That would be religion itself. If anyone could have given him answers to gospel questions-the answers you have brought to us with the restored gospel – it would be different. But Bobby *withdrew* from religion altogether. We think if it were not for that frustration he would find the time to attend church with his family. It's true that the man holding his fight contract wants him to train on Sundays, but that's not the *real* issue. The real issue is Bobby's feelings about religion." Seeing her guest's empty plate, she dished out more scrambled eggs.

Elder Woodruff leaned forward and pressed for more information. "What kind of questions?"

"Our parents lost three children in infancy," Elizabeth answered. "Bobby refuses to believe those babies are not in heaven. Churches, except for ours, teach that they aren't, you know. It bothers Bobby that no one teaches that families can be together in the hereafter. Basically, he just doesn't know the plan of salvation. If he would just listen to you, listen to the full gospel message, he would be the happiest man on earth! What shall we do, Elder Woodruff?"

Wilford was deeply stirred. "Let me tell you about a dream I had last night. I have this same reoccurring dream every once in a while. As you might know, I love to fish. I keep dreaming that I am fishing and that just about every time I put my line in the stream I pull a fish out."

Elizabeth went blank. What did fishing have to do with her brother? Was her new church leader being flippant or light minded? Until now, she had not seen that trait in his personality, and she hoped that she was misjudging him.

Noting Elizabeth's surprise at his dream, Wilford asked, "Now what do you suppose the Lord is teaching me in that recurring dream?"

Elizabeth was silent but after a few seconds, Daniel spoke. "Does it have something to do with the New Testament?"

Smiling in approval of Daniel's astuteness, Wilford nodded. "Jesus taught his disciples to follow him and be fishers of men. My missionary effort here in the Malvern Hills is turning out to be one of the biggest fishing trips ever in the history of the church. My dreams confirm that. I testify to you that the gospel hook will eventually catch your brother, too. Just be patient. Say your prayers for him. There's lots of fishing left to do."

"Of course," Elizabeth said, letting a feeling of peace settle into her heart. "I say my prayers for Bobby every day. I'll continue to do that."

"I'll include him in my prayers as well."

"Do you think he will come to the meeting?"

"Maybe, maybe not. No need to rush him. Have patience. I'll be in this area for many more weeks."

The hearth at the Browett home was cold, but Wilford Woodruff paced before it a few days later nonetheless, giving Daniel and Elizabeth a caution that astonished them. "It is the pattern in missionary work that as soon as success is given by the Lord, the Adversary immediately steps in. So when and if trouble happens, don't be alarmed."

Stopping in his tracks with a grimace of incredulity, Daniel sensed he was about to learn a new principle. "What do you mean?"

"How quickly were you baptized?" Wilford asked, eyes narrowing.

The answer was easy for Daniel. "We heard your message and were baptized the same day."

"We didn't give Satan much time, did we?"

After a pop-eyed pause, Daniel shook his head. "No, I guess not."

Throwing his arms apart in explanation, Wilford continued. "Many of the baptisms in the Church of Jesus Christ of Latter-day Saints follow the example of Philip in chapter eight of the New Testament. Remember that an angel directed Philip to the eunuch and Philip joined him in the chariot and taught him along the way, stopping shortly thereafter and going down into the water to baptize him. Know the story?"

Elizabeth nodded. "Yes, we've read it *many* times."

"My coming here has many similarities. A voice, the voice of the Savior, told me to come to this part of England. Ever since I arrived most people have been taught and baptized the same day or just a few days afterward."

"When the Spirit tells you the message is true I guess that means you're ready for baptism, even if it does seem quick," Daniel acknowledged.

"That's exactly true. Now, to the next point. Satan is quickly mustering his forces. He does not want to lose people to the true church of Jesus Christ because in that church, the Church of Jesus Christ, there exists all of the saving ordinances, once again restored to the earth.

"I understand, totally," Daniel said, stunned at the simplicity of logic.

"Several days ago Anglican ministers sent a petition to the Archbishop of Canterbury that calls for the banishment of myself and all other American missionaries of our church from British soil."

"You're kidding."

At Daniel and Elizabeth's concerned look, Wilford elaborated. "We have been praying fervently that the petition would not be granted, and it wasn't. Brother Kington just gave me the report. But that won't be the end of it. Now I hear that John Benbow's farm lease is in jeopardy because Mrs. Freeman has received pressure from the rector of the Anglican Church in Castle Frome. The rector is upset that so many people have joined the church and he has lost a few of his members as well."

Recalling the beautiful white mansion, the Great Hall, the outbuildings, the green fields, the livestock, and the pond where Daniel and she were baptized, Elizabeth shuddered. "Oh, no! What will Brother Benbow do if he loses his farm?"

"People have sacrificed more than just a farm to embrace the truthfulness of the gospel. I tell you these things so that when more of the unknown happens – trials and tribulations – you can be strong enough to remain faithful. Surely we're not wrong to be bothered by trials."

With shades of deep concern, Elizabeth asked, "Do you expect trouble right here, around Apperley and Deerhurst, and The Leigh?"

"Just don't be surprised when it happens. I don't think Satan is too happy right now."

APRIL 4, Saturday. Yesterday I wrote two letters, one to Willard Richards. I walked to the Gadfield Elm chapel and preached to a large congregation, and spent the night at Mr. Hill's at Turkey Hall. Today, At Gadfield Elm, the following were baptized: Ann Brooks, Jane Brooks, Sarah Smith, Mary Smith, Mary Packard, Susan Packard, Sarah Embary, Elizabeth Bubb, Mary Hanes, Margarett Turner, Mary Roberts.

Leading a group of baptismal candidates, including Levi Roberts, to his neighbor's pond following a Sunday meeting in his home, Daniel was disheartened to see a crowd of ruffians collecting. He was still digesting the sickening surprise when he was struck by a rock. Trying to shield the women, he walked between the ruffians and his wife and the other women, Levi Robert's wife and two of his cousins. Next, rotten eggs were thrown. One narrowly missed Elder Woodruff. Recalling the warning he had heard from Elder Woodruff in front of the Gadfield Elm chapel, Daniel wondered what to do. He counted nearly a hundred persons in the unruly mob. Suddenly he recognized two of the ruffians – Henry's friends, Alex and Richie. Thankfully, he could not see Henry. Daniel wished Bobby were here with him. Just the sight of Bobby would frighten them away.

As they arrived at the neighbor's pond, the ruffians grew bolder. With his pitted face twisted in anger, Alex yelled at Wilford. "You American! Where are you going to wash your sheep?" Daniel and Wilford looked at the crowd, then at each other. The owner of the pond emerged, expressing his concern. The jeering and rock throwing continued.

Wilford drew an audible breath and whispered to Daniel. "Let's go back to your home and try again later. Maybe Satan will go home, too."

When things had quieted down after Wilford walked to Norton and back, and at the insistence of the baptismal candidates, Daniel went back and talked to the owner of the pool who once again gave his permission to use it. The baptismal candidates were brought back and although most of the crowd had dispersed, a few remained. They continued the jeers. Between baptisms a dog was thrown into the pool. One ruffian, Richie – Henry's friend, yelled: "I'm coming in the pool to baptize the dog!" The group of persecutors laughed boisterously. The dog swam out and the service continued. A few rocks were thrown, one hitting Wilford on the head.

Daniel felt totally spent as the group walked back to his house in The Leigh. As they approached, a lone figure strode out into the street and walked toward Elizabeth.

"Bobby! What are you doing here?" she asked. Even in the dark, Elizabeth could see a pained look on her brother's face.

"Dianah just had her baby."

Still puzzled by her brother's look, Elizabeth replied, "That's good news. I think I'll get my things and go to her house and see what I can do to help."

"That would be a good idea. The baby was born dead."

APRIL 5. Sunday. I met for a prayer meeting in The Leigh. After meeting we went to Brother Daniel Browett's for the purpose of baptizing ten persons. Got ready. But before we got ready or closed praying and singing, a desperate mob gathered together, about 100 in number, and the owner of the pool would not let us baptize while there was such a mob present, fearing that serious consequences would ensue. I then went in search of water in other places for about an hour, with the mob following and calling out, "You American, where are you going to wash your sheep". But as I could not find water we had to omit it until afternoon. The mob commenced fighting among themselves and the people sent for constables to clear the crowd. I went to Norton and preached, and then returned to The Leigh immediately, and the man gave his consent to the water, and as I commenced to baptize, the mob began to gather again. But I baptized nine persons, three of which were preachers, while surrounded by the rabble. But I performed the ordinances without any injury or insult excepting the tongue of slander, and throwing a dog into the pool where I was baptizing. I also preached in the evening at The Leigh to a vast congregation, and the power of God rested upon us. I bore testimony unto them of the judgements of God that would rest upon them if they did not repent. I spent the night at Brother Browett's. Names of those baptized by me: Thomas Oakey, William Simons, Levi Roberts, Nathan Roberts, Charles Hayes, Harriet Roberts, Sarah Roberts, Harriet Ann Efford.

APRIL 6. Monday. I walked to Eldersfield and preached at Turkey Hall at Benjamin Hill's, and baptized five persons, one a preacher, and one a clerk of the Church of England. Names are: Daniel Colette, Thomas Smith, John Spiers, Mary Robbins, and Harriet Hayes. Elder Kingston is with me. I received three letters, one from Elder Taylor in Liverpool. He informed me how the work is with him; and one from Elder Richards and one from Elder Turley.

APRIL 7. Tuesday. I walked to Apperley and preached to a large congregation. Many were believing. I then walked to The Leigh and spent the night at Brother Browett's. We spread the case of Elder Turley before the Lord, and plead before God for his deliverance out of prison. The Lord testified unto us that he would speedily do it, and I say in the name of Jesus Christ it shall be done and his enemy shall fall, and the weapons formed against Him shall be broken.

APRIL 8. Wednesday. I wrote a letter to Elder Turley and sent him half a sovereign. I preached at The Leigh to a large congregation and baptized seven, four of which were preachers. John Vernon, Thomas Smith, John Harlick, Ann Robins, William Bayliss, Henry Bayliss, Mary Gaskin.

58

THE REMORSE THAT gripped Elizabeth over the death of Dianah's baby was powerful, a deep sadness laced with guilt. In her viewpoint, there were two things tragically wrong with the death of her sister's baby. First was the death itself. Her sister had carried the baby boy full term, and Dianah had known the baby was alive right until the moment of birth. But something had gone dreadfully wrong during birth. The cord was wrapped around the baby's neck, strangling him during the birth process. The other tragedy was that Dianah's husband somehow connected the death of the baby to Dianah's baptism into the church. Thomas saw the death as an omen of some sort, a sign that she should not have been baptized. As for her sister, Dianah did not feel that way, and she hoped that her husband would get over it. It was proving to be an awkward time for the Bloxhams, for Elizabeth and Daniel, and for Bobby as well. Bobby announced that he agreed with Thomas.

On Thursday, a letter was delivered to Elder Woodruff as he was preparing to leave the Browett cottage for a teaching appointment at the home of William Simmons near Haw Cross, not far from the Gadfield Elm Chapel. A farm servant working for John Benbow brought the letter.

The letter, marked "urgent," had been posted from Manchester and directed to Elder Woodruff in care of the Benbow farm, then forwarded to The Leigh. It was from Elder John Taylor. There were two items of note. His former companion, Elder Theodore Turley, was still in prison in Stafford. And it was time for conference.

"Other members of the Twelve have arrived in England and there has been a conference called for April fifteenth in Preston," Wilford said. "I've been expecting this letter. Usually we have our spring conferences as close to April sixth as we can, to commemorate the organization of the church on that date."

Elizabeth's olive eyes gleamed. "I remember what year," she said. "It was in 1830, in the state of New York."

"Yes," Wilford responded, teaching again. "But do you know why the Savior commanded that his church be organized on that specific date?"

"No," she said, puzzled.

"Because that's his birthday."

Elizabeth raised her eyebrows. "You mean he *wasn't* born in December?"

"He was born in the spring of the year, when shepherds were in their fields. The Savior revealed his birth date in the first verse of Section Twenty of the Doctrine of Covenants, the revelation on church organization and government, received by the prophet in April the year the church was organized."

"Are we supposed to celebrate Christmas in April from now on?"

Wilford laughed. "No. We celebrate it in December along with the rest of the world. But the Savior was born in April."

Nodding his head as he absorbed the information, Daniel had a question of his own. "Tell me the names of the other apostles you were expecting."

"Brigham Young, Heber C. Kimball, Orson Hyde, Parley P. Pratt, Orson Pratt, and George A. Smith."

"After your conference, will you come back?"

"Wild horses couldn't keep me away. There's still a lot of work to do."

Flushed with relief, Daniel added, "Good. We want you to teach Bobby and Hannah and a lot of other people."

Wilford grinned. "Brother Kington and Brother Benbow have a lot more people for me to teach, too. I'll be back."

"Is he actually losing his farm lease?" Elizabeth asked.

"Last I heard he was," Elder Woodruff answered, giving the farm servant a morbid look. The servant nodded up and down.

"What will he do now?" Daniel wondered.

Wilford shrugged his shoulders as he shook Daniel's hand goodbye. "I don't suppose he knows just yet. But he is a talented man. I'm certain the Lord is listening to his prayers. Something good will happen."

APRIL 9. Thursday. I received two letters, one from Elder Richards and one from Elder Taylor, informing me of the arrival of five of the Twelve and that they have appointed a conference in Preston on Wednesday, the 15th of April, and wish for me to attend. I preached at Wm. Simons at Haw Cross to a vast mass of human beings, and not a quarter of the people could get into the house. There were many of the baser sort present, and the house was much disturbed by the crowding of the people. The people did not break up for several hours. Many wished to be baptized, but could not because of the crowd and the mob. But some wishing to be baptized notwithstanding the persecution, I repaired to the pool about 12 o'clock at night, but we were still surrounded by a desperate mob of the gentiles. I went down into the water and baptized five persons in the midst of a shower of stones flung at me by the mob. While they were pelting my body with stones, one of which knocked me down into the water with the man I was baptizing, but the Lord saved me from falling and I continued until I had closed my baptizing and my mind was stayed with God. Those baptized: Mary Bunday, Elizabeth Rook, Bobby Rook, Elizabeth Collett, Benjamin Hill. I spent the night with Thomas Kington.

It wasn't until Friday, on a spring day tinged with warmth, that Wilford found John Benbow staying at a friend's house in nearby Frome's Hill. It was an airy house, three stories high, and gleaming with a new coat of white paint. The landscaping had been neglected, however. Weeds choked the flowerbeds and surrounding vineyards; dead limbs disfigured the trees. A low brick wall surrounding the property needed mortaring. Wilford sensed that the yeoman farmer missed the meticulously kept Hill Farm. With a wave of troubled emotion, they embraced.

"I've come for my luggage," Wilford began, explaining the coming conference he had to attend.

"It's here with my things," John said.

"I'm sorry you lost your lease," Wilford said, fighting back tears. "Any details you can share with me?"

John shook his head in disappointment. "Mrs. Freeman sent me a note that she was terminating the lease so my wife and I went to see her. She told me that she did not agree with the Mormon doctrines and all the religious activity going on in the area. At least she was honest. Apparently the rector at Castle Frome put a lot of pressure on her because I joined the church. Legally, if I wanted to fight it, I could win the case against her. But it would just create more friction and bad feelings."

Wilford grimaced. "Are you going to find another farm somewhere?"

"I'm actually thinking about emigrating to America. I'm already in the process of selling my personal farm equipment, and my livestock."

The remark jolted Wilford. There was a moment of silence. It was premature for him to share information he had received in letters from the other brethren about encouraging members of the church to gather to Nauvoo. Yet he knew that thousands of people in Great Britain were leaving in record numbers, seeking a new life in America.

John pressed for a reaction. "What do you think, Elder Woodruff? Shall I leave England?"

The smile that grew on Wilford's face was almost revealing. He placed a hand on John's shoulder. "My friend, let me respond to that after I return from the conference. I may have some information to share with you."

"Hold out your hand," John said, giving Wilford a warm smile.

Wilford complied. John pressed a two-pound note into it. "To help with your travel expenses. Come back soon."

APRIL 10. Friday. I walked to Greenway and baptized three persons, Margaret Morgan, Hannah Palmer, Mary Cleft. Walked to Ledbury, and from thence to Fromes Hill, visiting with saints along the way. I found Brother John Benbow, and that he had sold his possessions and had taken up his abode at Fromes Hill. I called upon him and spent several hours. He gave me two pounds to bear my expenses to and from the conference. I then walked to Stanley Hill and spent the night.

APRIL 11. Saturday. I rode in a horse cart to Worcester 16 miles, then took a coach to Wolverhampton 35 miles, and took the railroad to Stafford the last 18 miles. I started to go to the jail to visit Brother Turley, and I saw a large congregation of people of about 10,000 gathered together at the jail, and on inquiring the cause I was informed two men were to be hung. I came as near as I could to the jail. I soon saw the gallows erected and in a few moments James Owen and George Thomas were taken onto the scaffold and a rope put around their necks, and in an instant they were dropped into eternity for murder, precisely at one o'clock, and the rope was cut and their bodies dropped at two o'clock. The gallows were removed at three o'clock. I then went into the jail and had an interview with Elder Turley, who was unlawfully put into prison. I spent an hour with him. I carried him some provisions, and read the letters to him which I had written. I left him in good health and walked to Stone. From thence to Stoke Upon Trent, 15 miles. Stopped and spent the night with Brother Hulme. I was weary in body. Have been traveling 20 hours. The whole distance 84 miles.

Riding in the second-class railcar from London back to Gloucester, Elizabeth stared at the cut under Bobby's left eye, the cut on his right temple, and his bruised, swollen chin. His fight against undefeated Edward "The King" Tringham had been close for the first six rounds with each fighter being floored three times. But Bobby had finally won in fourteen rounds.

"I was *worried* about you early in the fight," Elizabeth said, drawing a heavy breath. She listened to the click-clack sound of the rail for a few seconds, contemplating both Bobby and Hannah. "I thought you were going to *lose* for the first time."

Bobby snorted. "Then you'd have to agree that my training paid off, wouldn't you?"

Elizabeth knew what her brother was driving at. It was hard to disagree with him. "I suppose so."

Bobby's tone did not soften. "When my trainer says to work out on Sunday and every other day of the week, I'll do it, without question."

"I think you were motivated by one other thing," Elizabeth commented, her mood softening. "Perhaps we can attribute your victory to that, more than anything else."

Bobby drew his face into a puzzle. "What do you mean?"

"You dedicated the fight to the memory of William, or did you forget?"

He sat in reverent silence for a few moments. "I didn't forget."

Hannah had feigned happiness over Bobby's win ever since they had boarded the train. For the most part, however, she sat on the seat, hugging her legs in a heavy checkered skirt, looking out over the English countryside. She had hated London all over again. Now it appeared Bobby was certain to be matched against Ben "The Torkard Giant" Caunt by the end of June. The winner of that match would probably be guaranteed a fight with the British champion, William "Bendigo" Thompson. That meant two more trips to London. There was even the possibility that the squire would force them to move there. She plunged into a horrid gloom at the thought.

Several minutes passed. Bobby nudged Hannah in the ribs. "Two more fights and I'll be champion."

"Then you'll retire?" There was a note of sarcasm in Hannah's voice.

"Retire?" Bobby scoffed at the thought. "At my age? I'll be able to hold the championship for five or six years, maybe longer. Five fights a year at three hundred pounds a fight. That's fifteen hundred pounds a year. Retire? Hannah, you're crazy again."

Elizabeth's fingers slipped into Daniel's as Bobby lectured Hannah. For a moment she put her cheek, cool and bony, and yet soft, against his. She thought of how she appreciated Daniel's spiritual strength, and the fact they now had the true gospel in their lives. Her heart hurt for Hannah.

Patience. That's what Elder Woodruff had told her. Keep praying for Bobby and have patience. She worried about having too much patience. What if he won the British championship? He might not listen to the gospel for years if that happened. Elizabeth almost wished he had lost the fight against Tringham in London. The cuts on Bobby's face would heal up either way. She didn't know whether or not Bobby would heal up over the fact that Dianah had lost her baby so close to the day she was baptized. It was a problem for her brother, and it was a problem for Dianah's husband as well.

Arriving home, Bobby took two days off to heal, but at the insistence of Squire Hastings he began to train for his fight against Caunt.

CHAPTER NOTES

Ben Caunt and William Thompson were actual British fighters.

59

WILFORD WOODRUFF twittered with excitement, even feeling a tinge of pride, as he bounced along the road from Dudley to Worcester in a crowded coach pulled by two spans of matching bay horses. He had every reason to be excited and proud. Seated on cushioned seats next to him were fellow apostles Brigham Young and Willard Richards, assigned to assist him in the work in the Malvern Hills. At the recently concluded conference in Preston, Wilford had reported that after laboring in the Malvern Hills for only one month and five days, he had baptized a hundred and sixty former members of the United Brethren congregation, including forty of their preachers. More than thirty licensed locations for holding church meetings, including the Gadfield Elm chapel, had been turned over to the Church of Jesus Christ of Latter-day Saints.

"I can't wait to see this Malvern Hills area you've talked about so much," Brigham said as they left Dudley. He had arrived in Liverpool April sixth with brothers Parley and Orson Pratt on the *Patrick Henry*, paying eighteen dollars each for steerage passage, furnishing his own provisions and bedding and paying the cook a dollar a day. Brethren in New York had donated straw ticks for them to sleep on. But Brigham had arrived sick and emaciated. To Wilford, he still didn't look good. His narrow eyes looked too narrow, his face gaunt, his skin off color, and his weight down from normal.

"Most beautiful part of England, they say," Wilford said, beaming. Once they arrived in Worcester, they planned to catch another stage to Ledbury and continue their missionary work. "I'm going to have the saints fatten you up when you get there. Mark my word on that."

"I won't resist at all," Brigham said, his sagging spirit lifted somewhat. "I'll match Elder Richards pound for pound when we're done." He took a quick glance at Willard, who, to Brigham's relief, laughed heartily. Already during the trip they had exchanged a few stories. Willard had told stories about teaching school in Columbia County, New York, and in Berkshire, Massachusetts, then later devoting much of his time to the study of the healing art, learning the Thompsonian practice of medicine from Albert P. Rockwood.

"We'll start the fattening up process when we get to Ledbury," Wilford said, chuckling. "My guess is that Sister Pullen will have a big meal waiting for us."

As their conversation dwindled and his traveling companions closed their eyes for a nap, Wilford reflected on the conference that had been held in the Preston Temperance Hall, originally built forty years ago for cockfighting. Counting the success in the Malvern Hills that Wilford reported, overall Great Britain church membership had now swelled to 1,671 with thirty-four organized branches, thirty-four Melchizedek priesthood holders, and an even one hundred Aaronic priesthood holders. Following the conference, Wilford had met the next day with members of the Twelve and had supported an effort to obtain a British copyright for the publication of the Book of Mormon and

The Doctrine and Covenants. He hoped that within a few months both books would become available to his Malvern Hills converts as well as to all the new saints in the British Isles.

John Benbow was particularly on Wilford's mind. The thought that Benbow had lost his lease haunted him, but Wilford was ready to propose a solution. He knew that Benbow was thinking about emigrating to America. The two apostles riding in the stagecoach were bearers of good news. They were authorized, by letter from the Prophet Joseph Smith, to begin announcing the doctrine of the gathering of Israel. Up until now the Prophet Joseph Smith had instructed them to remain silent on the matter. The call was going out for as many converts in Great Britain as possible to gather to Nauvoo.

A tall black hat jostled on Brigham's lap, ready to teeter to the floor. Wilford reached over and settled it without disturbing Brigham. Brigham was wedged tightly between Willard and a young athletic looking man that reminded Wilford of Bobby the fighter. He wondered how Daniel and Elizabeth were progressing with Bobby, and if Bobby had won his last fight in London.

When Bobby crossed his mind, Wilford thought of another dream he had while in Preston. It was about catching fish. Bobby remained a fish to be caught. He prayed daily that the young fighter would forsake the ways of the world and embrace the saving truths of the gospel.

To Wilford the fisherman, all men were catchable in the gospel net. He had even talked to the coach driver, a man with a fun-filled personality who wore several layers of mud-encrusted clothing with a stylish box-cloth coat and a beaver hat. When the coach stopped to change horses and the passengers had lunch at an inn – choosing between an endless selection of York hams, Banbury and Shrewsbury cakes, Bath buns, Everton toffee and Wymondham cheeses – Wilford talked to everyone about the gospel. Even after a brief breakdown of the coach, when the guard was required to repair a wheel, Wilford complimented the guard on his assortment of tools and spare parts, and turned it into a gospel discussion.

By the time the three apostles were seated in the Pullen home in Ledbury in front of a rabbit stew dinner, Wilford had been proven right in his forecast that they would have to wait in Worcester for another coach. To pass the time they visited the Worcester Cathedral, which dated back to 1084. Inside, they had seen King John's Tomb, Prince Arthur's Chantry, the early 12th century Chapter House and St. Wulstan's Crypt. They even had time to attend the afternoon service.

"Give Elder Young another helping of stew," Wilford said to Sister Pullen.

Brigham pushed his chair away from the table. "Excuse me, no thanks. You've filled my plate three times. One more time and I'll be sick from overeating."

"You are going to be working hard, so eat up," Wilford added. He had plans to introduce Elder Young and Elder Richards to John Benbow and Thomas Kington tomorrow, then split up and do some preaching in Morehead Cross, Crowcut, and Stanley Hill. "You're going to see the Malvern Hills first hand."

"I've been meaning to ask," Elder Young said, "but what does the word 'Malvern' mean?"

Wilford's eyes came alive, anxious to explain what he'd learned. "Malvern is a Welsh word meaning bare or balding. The Malverns are the 'bald hills' that divide two counties, Herefordshire and Worcestershire. For my sake, I think, the Saints here have been using the term Malvern Hills to describe the total area where the old organization, the United Brethren, was organized. But as we get down toward Apperley and Gloucester, we'll actually be in Gloucestershire, and south of that is the hilly area we call the Cotswolds. It all looks similar. All beautiful."

The next morning, once the two missionaries had walked the four-mile distance to Frome's Hill in the crisp April air, Brigham Young met the United Brethren organizers for the first time. Once the introductions had been made, John couldn't wait to ask Wilford an obvious question. John said, "The last time I saw you I mentioned that I was thinking about leaving England. You told me you might have some information that would help make my decision."

Wilford beamed. He had good news. "When Elder Young and the other apostles arrived in England on April sixth, they brought the official word from President Joseph Smith that I was expecting. We are, from this time forth, authorized to encourage members of the church living in the British Isles to emigrate to Nauvoo. Nauvoo is a new settlement in the state of Illinois that is now a safe haven for the members of the church."

A sigh of temporary relief came over John. He looked both pleased and bewildered. "Shall I arrange my own transportation?"

"We will work with you," Wilford said quickly. "Before we left Preston, we had a series of meetings. We are going to start organizing companies of Saints, each with a leader, to make the trip across the Atlantic to Nauvoo. We want to send the first group by July. Perhaps you could be ready by fall?"

Benbow's eyes lit up. "I'll discuss it with my wife. But I think we would be very interested."

APRIL 22. Wednesday. We walked to Fromes Hill and called upon Brother John Benbow and had an interview with him and Elder Kington. In the evening we had a church meeting at Stanley Hill to formally organize the Stanley Hill Branch of the church. Brigham Young was called to the chair and John Benbow chosen clerk. President Young opened the meeting with prayer. It was motioned by Elder Woodruff and seconded by Elder Kington that James Hill, James Barnes, Charles Price, and John Parry, be ordained to the office of a priest, and John Benbow to the office of a teacher. They were then ordained.

Charles Price was chosen clerk of the Stanley Hill Branch. Spent the night at Fromes Hill.

APRIL 26. Sunday. Notwithstanding I was quite ill, I walked five miles to Ashfield and preached at Mr. Bailey's. In the afternoon I went to Crowcutt and preached and baptized ten persons: George Brooks, Mary Brooks, Edmund Wattis, Hannah Wattis, William Beard, Elizabeth Johnson, Ann Baylis, Susan Baylis, Mary Baly, Mary Haywood. Ordained Edward Phillips to a priest. I then returned to Moorend Cross and spent the night with Brother Jenkins. Elder Young baptized four at Fromes Hill.

APRIL 27. Monday. I arise quite ill with my cold. I preached at Moorend cross and baptized three persons, Mary Phillips, Ester James, Mary Jinkinson.

MAY 5. Tuesday. I preached at Crowcutt, and later walked to Bowery and baptized five, John Meeks, William Johnson, James Williams, Ann Beard, Elizabeth South.

MAY 6. Wednesday. This is the driest spring that has been known in England for many years. The ground is parched yet all nature is covered with verdant green while the fruit trees send forth their perfumes from the smiling blossoms with which they are clothed. I baptized five persons at the Bowery and confirmed them, Susan Williams, Rachel Jinkins, Ann Rowley, Ann Jones, Hannahh Prichard. Walked to Tapperdy and preached at Smith's and baptized and confirmed four persons, Henry Jones, Susanna Barrup, Henry Griffits, Hannah Weaver.

MAY 10. Sunday. I met a company of saints at Colwall at Lucy's at 9 o'clock in the morning and baptized four, two were preachers: Samuel Jones, Jonathan Lucy, Melina Cook, Hannah Hill. I confirmed 12 persons. I then preached at Brother Lucy's, dined with Mr. Holmes, then walked over the top and across Malvern Hill, and preached at the Pale House, then back again and preached at Benjamin Holland's on the north side of

Malvern Hill.

MAY 11. Monday. A visit to the Herefordshire Beacon, which is the south part of Malvern Hill. Meditated by reading Parley P. Pratt's "eternal duration of matter." I preached at candlelight at Brother John Allard's at Windpoint, had the Spirit of God, and baptized four: Ann Steed, May Symons, Ann Bartlett, and Phebe Davis. Spent the night at Joseph Symons'.

MAY 12. Tuesday. A member of the Wesleyan Methodist Church came to see me and inquire what she would do to be saved. I told her that she must be born of water and the Spirit, repent, and be baptized for the remission of sins. She received my testimony and wished me to baptize her. I also called upon a woman that tended the gate at Chaney's Pitch, and preached the word unto her, who received the word gladly and wished to be baptized. I then called upon Mrs. Sarah Stanton, the overseer and keeper of the splendid mansion house by the name of Brand Lodge. This lady was a Wesleyan, but received my testimony and I baptized the three females above spoken of in a convenient pool, or bath, enclosed in the lodge. Held a meeting with the saints and confirmed 19. Spent the night with William Hills.

MAY 13. Wednesday. Baptized one more, then walked to Ledbury and received two letters, one from Elder Turley and one from Parley P. Pratt. I then walked to Stanley Hill and had an interview with John Cheese and Brother Barnes. Brother Cheese had baptized 15 persons since I last saw him. Also John Parry had baptized three. Elder Turley says in his letter that he will be liberated from prison tomorrow. I walked to Frome's Hill and baptized three, Mary Patoe, Ann Davis, Hannah Thomas. Met in company with Brigham Young, and broke bread with the saints. Ordained John Cheese an elder, and William Parsons and Joseph Pullen to the office of a priest, and Thomas Jenkins a teacher. Elder Cheese baptized two more, and Brother Clark baptized two more. I spent the night at John Benbow's.

MAY 14. Thursday. I received 200 pounds from John Benbow for the printing of the Book of Mormon. I walked to Ledbury with Elder Brigham Young. From thence to Keysend Street and preached, but amid much disturbance and as the meeting was about to break up the congregation was besmeared with rotten eggs. Spent the night with William Hill.

MAY 15. Friday. I walked to Dymock and spent the day with Elders Young, Richards, and Kington. I baptized Francis Hill. I found out that Elders Richards and Kington had baptized 50, confirmed 100, ordained 10 priests, and one teacher since I last saw them. Elder Young preached at Brother Kington's house. Blessed the household of Elder Kington and laid on hands for the healing of the sick.

60

BRIGHAM YOUNG was in a delightful mood. After a few days in the Malvern Hills, true to Wilford's prediction, he felt rejuvenated. His health was improving daily. On this sunny Sabbath day he was walking with Wilford, Willard Richards, and Thomas Kington, toward the Gadfield Elm chapel for two meetings. Everywhere he looked, the English countryside was soothing: Budding trees and blooming wildflowers. Farms with fertile soil. A landscape dotted with sheep, goats, cows, pigs, and chickens. Farmers bartering goods, eggs for wheat, geese for barley, milk for apples. A village wheelwright making new wooden wheels. Crops and gardens being planted.

"I feel better just being here," Brigham told Wilford as a wagonload of wheat passed by on its way to a nearby miller. More than the beauty of the countryside, Brigham was impressed with the people he had been meeting. They were less argumentative and more spiritual than any people he had met in England. "You were right, Elder Woodruff. These are a prepared people. Brother Kington and John Benbow obviously did a marvelous job gathering together the United Brethren. I believe, like you, that the Lord had a hand in it."

Wilford smiled an enormous smile. "We are going to be busy the next few days. We need to get down to The Leigh so we can work with Brother and Sister Browett again."

"The Browetts?" Elder Richards remarked. "Isn't it Sister Browett who has a brother that's a fighter?"

"Yes, that's the one," Wilford replied somberly. "While I was in Preston for the conference he won an important fight in London. Now I hear his promoter has him lined up for a fight with another leading contender. The winner of that fight is virtually guaranteed a bout with the champion."

Brigham Young raised both eyebrows. "We might have a member of the church as the champion of all England?"

"He's not a member. That's the problem. I would like all of you to include Bobby Harris in your daily prayers. His wife, Hannah, and the Browetts are praying that Bobby will listen to the gospel message. His wife wants to be baptized, but she is waiting for her husband."

"Be happy to."

Two hundred people were jammed into the Gadfield Elm chapel. It was built to seat only a hundred. Pews had been pushed to the front, and most of the people were standing behind them. The crowd consisted of newly baptized Mormons, and United Brethren people who had committed to baptism.

The announcement of the gathering was being made, unexpected, by Brigham Young in his talk. Daniel Browett, who had just been approved by the congregation to receive the Melchizedek Priesthood and be ordained to the office of an elder, was caught off-guard. Now he sat on the front row, his jaw gaping, and his mind racing.

"We need you in America," Brigham was saying. "The saints can accomplish more to build the Lord's kingdom on earth through combined efforts as a gathered people than they could in their scattered condition."

He quoted from the Doctrine and Covenants, Section twenty-nine, verse seven: *And ye are called to bring to pass the gathering of mine elect; for mine elect hear my voice and harden not their hearts.*

Daniel turned his eager hands to that section, read it, and pondered.

"The first group of saints will leave on June sixth on the *Britannia*, under the direction of a convert named John Moon," Wilford went on to say. "And there will be others. More companies will be organized. More company leaders will be chosen. We are working with agents in Liverpool for the best prices possible for steerage passengers."

The words struck Daniel like a thunderclap. An impression came to his mind: *Sailing across the Atlantic with Elizabeth, Bobby, and Hannah.*

"We ask as many of you as possible to gather out of Babylon, the world. Do not partake of the world's sins. Gather to Nauvoo. There, you will have greater economic opportunities than anywhere in Europe where the continuing depression hampered progress."

Daniel's head was still reeling as Elder Young sat down. *What about my mother? My brothers, and my sister? What will they think? What about our farm leases? What will Squire Hastings think?*

Elder Woodruff began speaking: "The principle of gathering to Zion is as old as the history of the earth. The Lord has always asked his people to gather together so that gospel ordinances can be administered. A temple will soon be built in Nauvoo. We need your help to build the temple, but more importantly, you need the saving ordinances that will be administered in the temple."

The long meeting was interrupted periodically by anti-Mormon ruffians, who pelted the roof with rocks. Afterward, Daniel and Elizabeth struck up a conversation with Elder Woodruff.

"You can use our home any time you want for your work," Elizabeth said. "We want you to know that."

"How is your brother doing? Is he ready for the gospel?" Wilford asked.

"We keep asking. He keeps saying no."

"I still regard him as one of the big fish we need to catch" Wilford said. "I include him in my prayers every day. Elder Young is praying for him, too. I think I'll be able to come to your area within a couple of weeks. So invite Bobby again."

MAY 17. Sunday. This is the anniversary at Gadfield Elm, at which place I met with the saints in company with Elder Young and Elder Richards. I preached in the morning and Elder Young in the afternoon, and while he was preaching opposers made much disturbance and they were determined to break up the meeting. Elder Young rose up in the power of the priesthood, and in the name of the Great God and according to the laws of the land, commanded order. Two of the brethren went to the door to keep order. Elder Richards was one of them, and they were able to overcome the enemy and peace was again restored. Baptized Joseph Evans, Thomas Saunders and J. Cheese at Creek Green. Four were ordained priests: Thomas Brooks, William Simmons, Thomas Smith, and Warren Samuel; and one teacher, James Baldwin. I then walked to Dymock, spent the night at Kington's.

61

THOMAS KINGTON stepped out of his front door and peered up and down the main street of Dymock, a hamlet located two miles south of Ledbury. He could not see any ruffians. He pulled a piece of paper out of his pocket and looked at it again. He had found it on his doorstep yesterday. The warning was clear. *If you entertain Mormons at your house there will be trouble.* Thomas folded it and returned it to his pocket. He suspected that because his yard was filled with so many people, it more than likely was an idle threat. No one would think of making trouble to such a large gathering on this beautiful afternoon. Returning to the party, a sumptuous affair spread on the back lawn of his home, Thomas decided not to share his concern with the others who had come to what his old religious organization had come to call "Feast Day."

As he walked back to his table, Thomas forced a smile. Tables that had been piled high with sausages, kidneys, roast beef, roast goose, mutton chops, cheeses, vegetables, pies, fruits, breads, and puddings were now filled with empty plates. The buzz of talk continued at a steady drone as guests, eyes bright and gestures animated, argued British politics, economic conditions, and discussed religion, laughing about their experiences in leaving their old lives behind and joining the church. His special guests, Wilford Woodruff, Brigham Young, and Willard Richards were in a good mood, enjoying the hospitality of nearly a hundred Malvern Hills members of the church. Thomas's sister-in-law, Mary Pitt – a sister to William Pitt – was in a good spirit, the best he'd ever seen. Tonight she was going to be given a special blessing by the three apostles. For the past eleven years she could not walk without crutches, due to a mysterious ailment the doctors could not identify. Thomas said another prayer in his heart. Please, God, let poor Mary be healed tonight.

Thomas was about to sit at the table with Mary again when Wilford stepped atop a chair. Wilford had been sitting next to Daniel and Elizabeth and John Davis. John had just been baptized a few days earlier. Holding his arms in the air and clanging a fork against a glass, Wilford had something to say. "May I have your attention please. As you know, you all want your own copies of the Book of Mormon and Doctrine and Covenants."

Thomas joined a chorus of "Amens" and applause.

Wilford was pleased with the reaction of the banquet guests. He spoke in a deep, authoritative voice, eyes twinkling, surveying his audience, and sweeping one arm across the panorama of people. "It is one thing to obtain a copyright, which we are doing, but it is another to finance the printing costs. I am pleased to announce the church has been blessed with an adequate donation to make the printing of those two books possible."

More applause.

Wilford pointed to a table at his left. "Brother John Benbow has donated two hundred and fifty pounds, and Brother Thomas Kington has donated fifty pounds."

A full smile broke out on his face as Wilford watch the audience respond with a round of applause. "Just think of how many people would get baptized if we had copies of the Book of Mormon to give to investigators of the church."

Elizabeth felt tears sting her eyes. "If only we could get Bobby to *read* it. The book is so powerful." He remained a fish not yet caught in the gospel net.

As excitement over the Book of Mormon waned, Mary Pitt, under the watchful eye of Thomas Kington, struggled to a chair set in front of Wilford, Brigham, and Willard. With the aid of crutches she hobbled to the chair, then half collapsed in it. Having been baptized by Elder Woodruff at the end of March, Mary had not yet been confirmed. Thomas joined the three apostles, John Benbow, and Daniel Browett in the circle as hands were laid upon Mary's head. Wilford acted as voice, confirming her a member of the church, giving her the gift of the Holy Ghost, and concluding with a special blessing. By the power of the Melchizedek Priesthood and in the name of Jesus Christ, he commanded Mary Pitt to be made whole, to throw down her crutches, to walk, and to have her muscle memory restored.

As the blessing concluded, Mary straightened her spine, sat more erect in her chair, carefully recalled and contemplated every word she had just heard, hesitated, bit her lower lip, wiped away tears streaming down her face with a brush of her forearm, then slowly arose. Without the aid of crutches and without a limp, with every eye following her every step, with hushed murmurs of surprise and adulation, she returned to her seat. Thomas Kington was the first to give her a warm hug, then stood aside while everyone else gave her similar hugs.

With an appraising look, eyes still watering, and a wide smile on her face, Mary picked up her crutches and fondled them. "I won't need these anymore."

She threw them on the ground in a final gesture of triumph. The healing was an affirmation of her faith. She felt a deep appreciation to the church authorities who had given her the blessing, but even a deeper appreciation to the Savior, through whom the healing had actually come. No more feeling sorry for herself. No more dependency on others. She was set free from the physical affliction that had plagued her body.

Having never seen someone healed so quickly, Elizabeth was touched with a sense of envy. As the closing hymn was sung, she wrinkled her nose and leaned over to Daniel's ear. "Daniel, I would like one of the apostles to give *me* a special blessing tonight."

"Are you not feeling well?" he asked in surprise, taking both her hands in his and caressing them.

She shook her head impatiently. "It's not *that*. Do you know how long we have been married?"

"Of course I do, Elizabeth," he answered with a puzzled look, speaking above the singing voices.

Elizabeth contemplated Daniel's reaction, wondering how best to explain her feelings. Now that they were members of the Church of Jesus Christ of Latter-day Saints, she had even stronger feelings about raising a family. She desperately wanted to participate in the Lord's plan by helping to provide bodies for Heavenly Father's spirit children. She flickered her bright green eyes at him. "We've been married six years and we still have no children. I would like to be blessed to have children."

Daniel met her words with silence and a returned glance. As the singing ended and a voice began uttering a closing prayer, Daniel weighed his wife's request to have a special blessing. He clasped both of her hands again, and then let one finger rub the skin on her hands and her arm. Her request seemed to pierce heavenward, even though Daniel was hesitant and unsure about approaching Elder Woodruff and the others. He did not know if church protocol warranted this type of a priesthood blessing. He drummed out an excuse as the prayer ended. "It's getting late. The brethren probably want to get their rest." He was just as concerned about Elizabeth's failure to become "heavy with child" as she was. They talked about it many times. But should he trouble three apostles of the Lord with such a trivial matter?

Elizabeth gave Daniel a stern look, pushed her lips to a dry pout, and nudged him with a sharp elbow. "Please ask them."

"Yes, dear." Obviously his wife did not feel the matter was trivial.

Relaying the request to Elder Woodruff, Daniel was surprised at the positive enthusiasm displayed by all three church authorities. In just minutes Elizabeth was sitting on a chair with three sets of hands on her head, those of Elders Woodruff, Young, and Richards, assisted by Daniel. She listened carefully as Elder Woodruff gave her a blessing: Her concern for motherhood. Her desire to have a family. An assurance that she was loved by her Heavenly Father, that the Savior loved her, and that her testimony was firm. Then the best part. *I bless you that you will become a mother in Zion.*

As Daniel visited Elder Woodruff about his new missionary assignments and arranged for a time that the apostle could teach in their home again at The Leigh, a large hand grabbed Elizabeth by the shoulder. It was Willard Richards. As Elizabeth turned around and sized him up she wondered if his tailor had to charge him additional for the gray suit he wore. It was extra, extra large to fit an extra, extra large man, standing there with his broad forehead, kind eyes, and curly hair.

Speaking in a soft voice, looking up and down at the woman who had just received a special blessing, Elder Richards said, "Sister Browett, I think it would be wise to remember Brother Woodruff's carefully chosen words." A concerned smile made its appearance on the apostle's face.

Startled at what Willard had just said, but ruefully impressed, Elizabeth was almost speechless. "What do you mean?" she asked. As far as she was concerned, the blessing was just exactly what she had wanted to hear. She could almost see a baby's face partially hidden by a blanket, laying on her bed in her home at The Leigh, surrounded by gifts from family and friends: layettes, blankets, toys, a rocking horse.

"The wording of the blessing," Elder Richards said, his tone apologetic, "was that you would become a mother in Zion."

Elizabeth nodded in agreement, not taking the hint. "I remember *exactly*. That's certainly what I wanted to hear."

Elder Richards placed a hand on Elizabeth's shoulder in a despairing gesture, and peered at her with soft eyes. His knew his next words would become a sort of haunting burden to her. "But remember Elder, Woodruff said nothing in the blessing about *when* you would become a mother in Zion. Nor did he say anything about having several children. I just want to caution you with the impression I felt during the blessing. The Spirit told me you will eventually become a mother, but you may have only one child. You will have to be both patient and understanding about what the Lord has planned for you in this regard."

Staring at Willard in disbelief and involuntarily putting her hand over her mouth, Elizabeth did not know how to respond. One child was not acceptable. In her mind, she would become pregnant within a month or two after tonight's special blessing, not a year or two. Or three or four. Her dream was to be the mother of a whole house full of children. With a peevish toss of her head, she lapsed into silence for a few moments, unusual for her. Thinking about his words, she finally forced a few words out of her mouth. "I'll *try* to be patient, Elder Richards, and understanding, as you say." She could not conceal the puzzled, disappointed look that remained on her face.

Smiling and patting her on the back, assessing the damage his truthful statement had made, Willard tried to make it up with some other pleasantries. "Daniel has told me all about you, Sister Browett, how helpful you are to others. I feel impressed to give you some advice that will go along with your personality and personal attributes."

Dazed but perking with curiosity, Elizabeth was in awe of the oversized man. In one instant he had knocked her off a spiritual high with a statement of unwanted reality, now he might say something to elevate her to the previous high. Her mouth was dry and her knees quivered. "I'm listening," she replied.

After an excruciating pause while he gave Elizabeth another appraising look, Willard said, "I feel you could be of great benefit to others in your natural desire to help people if you would study midwifery and botanical cures."

Elizabeth's right hand automatically returned to cover her mouth as she began to think. She was stunned. She could remember that Daniel had already told her about Elder Richards, that both he and his brother, Levi, had joined the church four years ago and Elder Richards was regarded by the Prophet Joseph Smith as a personal, trusted physician. Now here he was, transplanted to British soil, seemingly inviting her to join his profession. Rubbing her hand across her chin, thinking with her mouth wide open in abstracted silence, and staring upward into Willard's face for several seconds, she asked, "How will I do that?"

"Unfortunately I don't have time to teach you what I know, but I can recommend a few things. Buy yourself a copy of a book called Aristotle's Works: *Containing the Master-piece, Direction for Midwives, and Counsel and Advice to Child-Bearing Women.*"

"I've heard of it," she said, trying to keep a cheerful face, "but *reading* a book won't make me a midwife, will it?"

He dried up for a moment, seeing her amused look. "It will if you combine it with practical experience. Just volunteer to help other midwives. They will be glad to teach you."

"What else?"

"Learn all you can about the Thomsonian theories of botanical cures. You won't be able to get a diploma in it like I have, but you can learn the basics from others and read the manuals."

This time Elizabeth's eyebrows wrinkled. The weight of his suggestions made her feel like sinking into the damp grass of Kington's yard. "What is it? What are these theories?" she asked incredulously, her face half-vexed and half-titillated.

"Simply stated," Elder Richards said, his tone eloquent and confident. "Thomson believed that heat is a manifestation of life and cold is a manifestation of disease. We advocate cleansing the sick body with the herb lobelia, which is an emetic, and with enemas. We restore heat with cayenne pepper, taken internally. And we carry away the residue of 'canker' with doses of things like bayberry, sumac, red raspberry and so forth."

"Sounds *complicated* to me," Elizabeth responded, dropping her voice and shaking her head.

Willard pursued his course. "A bright woman like you can learn it. If you end up emigrating to Nauvoo, you can help the Saints that way. Especially if you are not tied down by a lot of children."

"Tell me what it is like in Nauvoo," she said.

Before Willard could answer, he saw a group of angry men approaching the Kington house. There were six, seven – no, more like ten, twelve, or was it twenty? They seemed to appear from nowhere, instantaneously cursing and uttering mad threats, their arms swinging wildly at the house. Some were banging pails and pans, others were making noise by beating drums and sticks together.

Crash!

A rock shattered the parlor window in Kington's home.

Crack! Crack!

Two more rocks broke an upstairs window. The women in the group of Kington's guests began screaming. More rocks rained against Kington's home.

Thud! Thud! Thud!

Elizabeth retreated, assessing the men who appeared ugly, half-mad, obsessed with anger, vulgar, drunk, fiery-eyed, tense, and fanatical.

Running toward his house, Thomas Kington screamed, "Everyone get back. Get out of range of the rocks! Don't let them hit you!" Almost frozen in horror, Thomas thought again of the note in his pocket and kicked himself. He should have warned everyone at the party instead of keeping the threat to himself, despite the fact that it would have created a low mood over the proceedings. A wave of guilt swept over him as he shouted the warnings.

Dragging his wife, Hannah, and his sister-in-law, Mary Pitt, away from the house, Thomas pointed in the direction of the mob, all of whom were still throwing rocks, shaking fists, beating their breasts, and uttering threats and obscenities.

"Who are these men?" Wilford asked.

"See the man in the black frock coat with the streaky light gray beard?" Thomas said, pointing. "That's the local vicar of the Church of England. I heard he was upset because a few of his congregation were in the crowd tonight, but I didn't think he would organize a mob against us."

Both Wilford and Thomas were amazed how sprightly Mary moved without her crutches. He wanted to smile but the situation was becoming more critical by the second. As rocks continued to rain against Kington's house, other ruffians barged through the front door.

"They're destroying our furniture and our house," Hannah Pitt Kington cried as she looked through the windows at the propensity of evil, her face turning blood red with anger and concern. She watched a big redheaded man take a knife and slash the cushions on her chairs. Others were smashing dishes against the walls and on the floors. Hannah buried her head in the chest of her husband and sobbed. How ironic, Thomas thought. A short time ago he felt so elated over Mary's miraculous healing. Now he felt like part of his world was being torn from him.

Protecting Elizabeth from the rocks, Daniel retreated to the spot where Thomas was consoling his wife and Mary, soon joined by Elder Woodruff. "I wish Bobby were here."

"Bobby the fighter?" Elder Woodruff asked in shaky tones.

Daniel's voice trembled with concern over the safety of the women, and with anger at what he was witnessing. "Yes. He could whip fifty of them at a time."

Wilford held up both hands in a gesture of caution. "I think it best to keep standing back out of the way and not fight with them. They'll be done in a few minutes and then they will go. We don't want them to hurt any of our group, and we don't want to hurt them."

Quickly, Daniel and Kington spread the word: Stand back, don't engage the mob. Have patience, the mob will leave soon.

At his point Daniel noticed something that made his blood boil with anger. Among the crowd of mobbers he could pick out the definite images of Henry Eagles and his two ruffian friends, Alex and Richie. They were breaking vases, tearing furniture with their knives, smashing dishes, scattering the contents of cupboards, and causing general mayhem. He was stupefied at the sight. Daniel muttered a wishful prayer, hoping that Bobby would suddenly ride up on his horse, jump off, and attack the attackers, breaking every jaw, every rib. In a strange way, the prayer seemed to be answered in part because as suddenly as the mob stormed into the Kington home, just as suddenly they left, running, cursing, prancing away, disappearing into the sullen dusk of the approaching evening, through the rutty streets of Dymock.

An eerie silence followed. A few birds sang their final evening lullabies in the overhead trees, unaware of damage done to the Kington home and to the confidence of those attending the party. A rooster crowed. A cow bellowed. Women could be heard crying, in increasing intensity.

His pulse still jumping, Daniel exchanged glances with Elder Woodruff. "What shall we do now?"

"Let them go. Let's go help Brother Kington clean up his house."

MAY 18. Monday. This was an interesting day. I met some friends at Mr. Joseph Hill's in Dymock at five in the morning, and I baptized Bobby Clift, Elizabeth Clift, James Morgan and Mary Pitt. From thence we walked to William Hart's. Elder Kington baptized seven. Elders Young and Richards confirmed them. In a few moments I baptized five others, who were confirmed as they came out of the water: John Davis, John Smith, Mary Ann Clark, Elizabeth Rowberry, William Hall. Then we returned to Elder Kington's and while on the road we met another person who wished to be baptized, and Elder Kington baptized her. This was FEAST day. Elder Kington made a feast for the saints, which had been a custom among the United Brethren. But as they were now all receiving the fullness of the gospel, they had become saints. The saints began to collect at 2 o'clock. By 4, we had nearly 100 saints together to the feast. Elder Young addressed the saints, clothed with the power of God, and then asked a blessing upon the food prepared. We then sat down to the table and ate and drank with nearly 100 saints, possessing glad hearts and cheerful countenances. Elder Richards remarked that he did not believe there had ever been such a company of saints prepared in so short a time and bid fairer for the Kingdom of Heaven than the company now before us, at least since the Church of Jesus Christ was organized. I truly felt grateful to my Heavenly Father for his mercy, when I reflected back upon the time only two and a half months since I first proclaimed the fullness of the gospel in this region, and began to baptize such as received my testimony. Now there are nearly 400 souls standing in the New and Everlasting Covenant, and the prospect of the work constantly increasing. After the feast, Sister Mary Pitt, who has not walked for the past 11 years except on crutches, was healed. We also ordained Daniel Browett an elder, and the following were ordained priests: John Smith, John Davis, James Morgan, Robert Clift, John Gailey, and William Evans.

MAY 19. Tuesday. I walked in company with Elders Young and Richards to Keysend Street in Berrow where Elder Young preached. Afterward I baptized four, Mary Webb, Charlotte Walters, Eliza Shinn, Caroline Trehern. Received the hundred pounds from

Elder Kington for the Book of Mormon.

From the top of Herefordshire Beacon at Hill Point on a rare clear and rain-less day, Wilford could easily see Ledbury parish only three miles to the south-west. Pointing to the west, he tried to describe to Elder Young and Elder Richards the setting of the Hill Farm near Castle Frome, where Wilford had first met John Benbow two and a half months ago on March fourth. Just south of Ledbury, they could see Dymock, where the church party at the Kington home had been interrupted by mobbers only a few nights ago, where members of the church were still working to repair the damage and trying to console Sister Kington in her tragic losses. Turning to face the southeast, Wilford shaded his eyes with his arm and could barely see where Daniel Browett lived at The Leigh, nearly ten miles away. He hoped that the Lord was softening the heart of Daniel's brother-in-law, who lived a mile from The Leigh in south Apperley. From atop one of the highest peaks in the Malvern Hills, Wilford felt at peace as he knelt in prayer with his two companions. They had much to discuss – assisting members of the church in their emigra-tion efforts, selecting leaders of companies to lead British saints to Nauvoo, printing three thousand copies of the Book of Mormon, printing a collection of hymns, just to name a few items.

Aside from growing opposition and concern about future mobbing action, the work in the Malvern Hills was proceeding beyond Wilford Woodruff's wildest expectations. He gave thanks to his God.

MAY 24. Sunday. We walked to Old Starridge Common to attend a camp meeting. I preached in the morning and Elder Richards in the evening, after which we broke bread unto the saints. Ordained three priests, George Allen, James Williams, John Meeks, and one teacher, William Williams. Baptized three at Tapperdy: William Smith, George Eddins, and William Rowley.

MAY 25. Monday. We spent the day looking up the aged and infirmed, baptizing as many of them as would receive our testimony. I baptized six and Br. Richards confirmed them: Susanna Higgins, Joseph Haywood, John Field, Hannah Field, Elizabeth Meeks and Ann Jones.. Spent the night with William Rowley. We walked to Little Batchfield. Ordained John Fidoe a priest, stayed over with him.

MAY 27. Wednesday. Yesterday we walked to Little Batchfield. Ordained John Fidoe a priest, stayed over with him. Today I baptized Charlotte Hannah Pullen. She had been a cripple from her birth and she received a blessing by receiving the ordinances of the gospel. We walked to Stokes Lane and preached at Joseph Evans'; confirmed 10 persons, ordained two priests, William Davis and Thomas Sanders, and one teacher, Thomas Vernon.

MAY 28. Thursday. Baptized four at Cricks Green -Eliza Gurney, Elizabeth Davis, Hannah Even, Ann Sanders. We then walked to Hope Rough and preached at William Hall's, baptized five, Jane George, Elizabeth Hall, Mary Rowberry, Elizabeth Rowberry, and William Hall. Visited an evergreen farm called Hopton in the Hole, parish of Much Cowen, Herefordshire, owned by Richard Gardner.

MAY 29. Friday. Baptized two at the creek, Ann Daniels and Ann Banister, then walked to Shucknell Hill and preached, then baptized John Powell, Elizabeth Powell, and Sarah Rock. Ordained Benjamin Williams a priest.

MAY 30. Saturday. At Shucknell Hill, Elder Richards baptized two and I confirmed them (Ishmael Phillips and Elizabeth Pitt). We then walked to Fromes Hill and spent the night with John Benbow. Brother Fidoe came and brought us six letters, three for me. One from Sister Mary Packard at West Bromwich, one from Elder Milton Holmes, Georgetown, Massachusetts, and the third one from PHOEBE W. WOODRUFF, Montrose, Lee County, Iowa, USA. Yes! Glory Hallelujah, I have now got a letter from

Phoebe. It is the first letter I have received from her since I have been in England. Her letter contained much intelligence of interest. She informed me she was blessed with the birth of a son, on the morn of the 22 of March 1840, at 6 o'clock. His name is WILFORD WOODRUFF, JR. May he be preserved blameless unto the coming of the Lord Jesus Christ, for which I will ever pray. One letter was from Elder Brigham Young at Manchester, informing us that the first number of the Millennial Star was off the press, and that the hymnbook and the Book of Mormon would soon be in type.

MAY 31. Sunday. According to appointment we met at Fromes Hill to attend a camp meeting. I preached in the morning on the authenticity of the Book of Mormon, after which I went to the pool and baptized 12, which we confirmed at the water's edge. Elder Richards preached in the afternoon. We then broke bread unto the saints, about 100. Then went to the pool and Elder Cheese baptized two. Spent the night at Benbow's. Those that I baptized: Samuel Badham, Francis Holmes, Hannah Holmes, Elizabeth James, Elizabeth Birch, Elizabeth Went, Hannah Bishop, Mary James, William Embry, John Birch, Elizabeth Embry.

CHAPTER NOTES:

The incident at Thomas Kington's home is taken from Kington's personal history, which states a mob damaged his home in the month of May. However, Wilford Woodruff does not include the incident in his journal until September 16. The account listed in this chapter of the book is taken, therefore, from the combined resources. Perhaps the home was damaged on both occasions. Following is Elder Woodruff's September 16 account: Elder Kington had been faithful in warning the inhabitants of Dymock and had gathered together about 50 Saints which had much stirred up Mr. John Simons, Rector of the Church in Dymock, manifested much of the Spirit of the Devil by stirring up mobs against the Saints, which had disturbed the meeting of the Saints in several instances. On this occasion as we began to gather together the beat of drums, pails, pans and sticks was heard through the street. The mob soon collected and paraded in the streets in front of the house. We closed the window shutters and doors in the room where we were, and I opened the meeting by singing and prayer. No sooner had we commenced than the mob armed themselves with eggs, bricks, rocks, and everything else they could lay their hands upon, and began to throw them upon the house like a shower of hailstones for nearly an hour. They dashed in the windows, scattered stones, brick and glass through the rooms, broke the tile on the roof, and continued such depredations until the close of the meeting.

The blessing given to Elizabeth is fictional.

62

A VASE OF FRESHLY cut flowers in the nearby windowsill diffused the late afternoon sunlight as it shined through the etched window of the Ferret's Folly onto the flagstone floor. In a distant corner a man who had supped heavily on mutton roast and potatoes slumbered on his chair, dust motes dancing above his head. John Harris picked up the man's empty glass, wondering if he should fill it again. Seated at an oak table in the opposite corner, Squire Hastings put on his wire-rimmed, half-moon spectacles and unfolded some legal papers handed to him by his attorney.

"This is the contract for your fight with Ben Caunt, Bobby," the squire said, his heavy gray eyebrows raised high. His tone was serious, but with an awkward trace of warmth. "My attorney, Mr. Brown, has drawn it up and he assures me everything is in order. It has already been signed by Mr. Caunt and his people in London."

Bobby sat forward, elbows on the arms of his chair, and fingers interlaced, trying to read the document. The few pages of paper in front of him represented his ticket to the British championship. He wondered if Lawyer Brown, a stoop-shouldered, squat, ordinary man of about forty, in a gray suit with a red tie, balding, light brown hair, had ever drawn up such an important document. Bobby felt a trifle intimidated under the squire's scrutiny.

"You see the head of the stag with the impressive set of antlers above us here?" Hastings asked in a curt voice, pushing away plates that had been emptied of spicy sausages, cooked cabbage, slices of bread, and orange cheeses. His jowls hung above a waddled throat, his eyes wild, darting all around the pub.

Bobby gave a short nod, turning his head to see the stag's head he had seen a hundred times. "Yes, sir."

The squire's little red eyes narrowed and his face turned serious and hard. "How much effort would it take for you to knock it off the wall?" A bony finger pointed upward.

"Not much, sir," Bobby answered. He knew the stag's head was hung precariously by a single bent nail. He had helped John hang it himself. An accidental bump would send it crashing to the floor. He shrugged his shoulders, wondering what the old man was getting at. "Not much, sir."

Hastings leaned forward in his chair, pitching his voice above the combined conversations of eight other tables crowded with eating, drinking, talking, and singing Ferret's Folly customers. "That's right, young man. Not much effort at all. But how difficult it is going to be for you to defeat Ben Caunt?"

"It's going to take my very best effort," Bobby replied, laughing to himself at the squire's weak attempt to make a point. "I hear he's a ruddy good fighter."

"I've seen him fight several times and he is *very* good." The squire picked up a newspaper and rolled it tight. "You'll have to be in better shape than you were in the last fight, and you were probably in the best shape of your life. You'll have to improve your fighting skills to an even higher level."

"I understand," Bobby nodded, wishing for the conversation to end. "I'll do my best, sir."

"Now let me tell you about 'Big' Ben Caunt," the squire said as his face darkened. He leaned back, twisting the newspaper roll. "He's two inches taller than you and weighs eighteen stones, so he outweighs you considerably, even though you have gained weight yourself during the past few months. He was a blacksmith before he started fighting and he's tougher than nails and twice as mean. Last year he beat 'Bendigo' Thompson in seventy-six rounds. They were fighting for three hundred pounds a side.

"Early in the fight, when Bendigo came at him, Caunt would put a strong bear hug on him, and they would crash to the ground together. Bendigo insulted Caunt time after time with things I can't repeat. Caunt tried to crack Bendigo's skull against a ring stake but Bendigo retaliated with a well-aimed kick. Caunt grabbed Bendigo by the throat and pushed him over the ropes. At this, the spectators in Nottingham were cutting the ropes and invading the ring, but by that time Bendigo's face was black.

"The officials restored order and revived Bendigo with a noggin of brandy. Finally, in the seventy-sixth round, at the point of sheer exhaustion, Bendigo fell to the floor without being hit, crying 'foul.' But he was disqualified, making Ben Caunt the winner. The Nottingham 'Lambs,' as they were called, stormed the ring again and attacked Ben with sticks and stakes and whatever came to hand. Ben's own friends had to protect him and he was forced to try to flee in a coach. But the ruffians held the coach, so Ben finally managed to escape riding bareback on a stolen horse."

Bobby swallowed hard, scanning the squire's intense face. His dark eyes flickered back at him, causing a silence of several seconds. He had heard the story about Caunt's fight with Bendigo several times before, but not exactly the way the squire described it. For the first time in his life Bobby was unnerved and wondered if he had the stomach to resort to such mean tactics. He looked across the smoke-filled pub trying to find his brother, a gesture of temporary escape from the squire's watchful eyes. John was carrying a tray full of steaming potatoes and roast beef to a table of hungry customers. Customers at another table begged him for more ale. Bobby slumped glumly into his chair.

The squire, wearing a tweed coat far too heavy for the weather, eyes still glaring, took off his glasses and coughed. "The fight is scheduled to take place July twentieth. I've made all the arrangements with the London Pugilistic Society. I want you to train in London this time. If the fight goes as long as the one I just described, the man who is in the best shape will win. You will go to London on the fifteenth of June. All the accommodations have been arranged."

Bobby absent-mindedly bit on his lower lip. "What about the farm? If I am gone, who will take care of things?" He was also thinking of Hannah, and her hatred of London.

The squire's answer came quick and abrupt. "You can ask your friend Daniel Browett to do it. He owes me a big favor anyway for allowing him to lease land from me."

A condescending smile appeared on Bobby's face. "I suppose he'll do that for us."

"Good!" The squire rolled the newspaper tighter and used it to strike the table, almost spilling the glasses of ale. "I want you to win this fight, Bobby. It's important. I'll have a lot of money bet on you. Right now you are still not too well known in the fight business. If you beat Ben Caunt, you'll be instantly recognized all over Great Britain. You'll surprise everyone in London. I think you are fast enough, clever enough, and tough enough to beat Big Ben Caunt. But you'll have to train harder than you've ever trained in your life. You'll make a hundred pounds for the fight. If you win you'll start making double and triple that every time you fight. Thousands of people will want to see you. Do you know how many people watched the fight last year between

Burke and Bendigo?"

Bobby shook his head no.

"Fifteen thousand."

The words pierced Bobby's sense of ambition. No wonder fighters like Caunt, Bendigo, and Burke were so famous and so rich. The most he had made on any previous fight was sixty-three pounds. Now he was up to a hundred pounds. The next plateau was two hundred or three hundred pounds. Bobby sipped his drink, wondering how Hannah would respond to living in London for a month with their three children. He was afraid to ask but it would have to be done.

When Bobby told Hannah that the squire was going to require them to move to London for a while, she exploded in humiliated anger. She ran up the stairs and threw herself on the bed. She sobbed and beat on the pillows. How could she live in London with three young children? Was this proof that Bobby loved his sport more than he loved her? Could she trust him if he went there alone?

Bobby slowly trudged up the stairs behind her, a knot in his stomach. He regretted he had told her. Perhaps he should have waited for another day or two, thinking of a better way to approach the subject. He could have arranged a meeting and let the squire and the lawyer her. He could have sent her a note first, let her read it, then come home and face her. He could have delayed telling her until a day or two before they had to move.

"It won't be for long," he said, sitting on the bed, and then touching her on the neck. "We'll be back home in no time."

Still sobbing, she cringed at his touch. "That's what you say. But win or lose, there'll be more fights in London. The squire will demand more and more. Bobby, I don't want to raise my children in London." She put a pillow over her head and turned away, sobbing again. *Why hasn't God answered my prayers?*

"I don't either, Hannah," he agreed, trying to control his irritation. "But it will be just for a short while. Please be patient and understand this."

"I just can't do it." Her voice was barely audible, muffled by the pillow.

Bobby's mood darkened. "Yes you can," he scowled. "Think of me for a change. You're always thinking of yourself."

That remark jolted Hannah. She gritted her teeth, threw the pillow on the floor, and sneered at her husband. They began to argue, their voices rising, falling, then rising again. They rapped out reasons why each was right in terse sentences, some unfinished, some filled with misunderstanding, some with seething accusations. She rehearsed all the reasons it was such a bad idea to live in London, even temporarily: The evil she had felt there. The squalid living conditions. The hordes of people. The smoke-filled air. The fog. The lack of morality. He had his reasons for going: The importance of the fight. The squire required that he train in London. The move would be temporary. He didn't want to go to London alone.

"How can you be so insensitive?" she said, rising to her feet, giving Bobby her worst evil look, and wiping away more tears. "If you loved me, you wouldn't even think of leaving us just to train in London. In my opinion, the squire is exploiting a desperate man. And that desperate man is you."

"You are crazy, Hannah."

"I'm going outside with the children," she said, throwing up her hands in a despairing gesture. "Don't follow me."

She went down the stairs.

63

SPRING IS A BUSY time for farmers in England. At his leased ground near The Leigh, Daniel made a list of things to do: Plant wheat, barley, rye, and oats. Fertilize fields, shear sheep, and wash the fleeces. Trim hedges, sharpen scythes and get ready for the hay harvest. Make new pitchforks. Fix a wheel on a broken wagon. Set beehives out. And buy a bull at the Tewkesbury cattle sale.

He looked at his list and knew he had to double the work effort, despite all his church responsibilities. He had promised to care for Bobby's farm in Apperley. Bobby would soon be off to London to train for his next fight. Were it not for a few farm servants, it would be impossible to get all the work done. His appointment with Bobby was for eight o'clock this morning, before Bobby left for the Gloucester sparring room. A separate list would be made of all the work that needed to be done in Bobby's absence.

Daniel's stablehand in very dirty clothes was grooming three neighing, stomping horses in the early morning dampness. When he brought Daniel a saddled chestnut gelding called Stormy, Daniel adjusted the stirrups and mounted, grinning as Stormy flattened his ears and jumped into a gallop.

"Fine, if you want to gallop all the way to Bobby's farm, have at it," Daniel told the horse. In another year or two of good training, perhaps Stormy would understand a little of what he was saying. A few minutes early wouldn't hurt anything. It would give him more time to review what needed to be done on Bobby's farm. Daniel also planned to talk to Bobby about something else. It was time to try to land the "big fish" again.

Streaking along the narrow road leading to Bobby's farm, aboard the free-spirited gelding, Daniel thought about John Benbow's decision to emigrate to America. Daniel had mixed reactions about it. True, the door was open to go to Nauvoo. A clarion call had been issued to gather to Zion. Impulsively, Daniel counted the blessings he had here in England: A wife that loved him. A hundred-acre farm. Membership in Christ's church. Holder of the priesthood. A personal friendship with Wilford Woodruff. A hundred-acre farm. A thriving barrel and furniture business. A chance to lease more ground from Squire Hastings as Bobby's fighting career progressed.

Although the squire had financed everything on his farm and the animals and crops were not truly Daniel's, someday they would be. John Benbow had lost his lease. There was good reason for him to go to Nauvoo and start over. But for him, Yeoman Daniel Browett, it was a hard thing to consider. There was a lot to give up. If only Bobby and Hannah would join the church. Maybe he would feel differently about it.

Darting through the winding lane lined with hedges, Stormy galloped the three-quarter mile to Bobby's farm where he stopped quickly, head down, blowing like a whale. Exhilarated, Daniel hopped off just as Bobby appeared from the house and grumbled his hello.

"Are you trying to train a race horse?" Bobby asked, noting the lather on Stormy.

"No. I think he just wanted some exercise," Daniel said, patting the gelding on the neck and tying him to a rail. "When do you have to be in London?"

"Middle of June."

As they sat talking side by side on the top rail of the corral overlooking a field of clover, Daniel detected no concern from Bobby that he was going to move Hannah and his three children to London for several weeks while he trained for his next fight. Daniel knew that Hannah was in the house worrying about where she was going to live and how the children would fare. He decided to broach the subject of the gospel before reviewing the double farm duties that were coming. Without giving it further thought, he blurted out the words. "It's time you let Elder Woodruff teach you the gospel, Bobby. He's going to be at our home again. It would be nice if you were there."

Bobby's face showed little reaction, just an abstracted stare with a little negative headshake. But in a stern voice he said, "Don't start that again."

Daniel looked over at his brother-in-law solemnly, pensively rubbing his chin. "The reason I will keep asking, Bobby, is because I love you. You need this in your life."

"Well, I appreciate your concern, but not now," Bobby said in a disgusted tone. He jumped off the rail, a signal that he was uncomfortable. "I've got lots to do. Let's talk about the farm work, then I need to go."

Daniel paused, then tried again. "If you would just listen to Elder Woodruff and read the Book of Mormon, you would gain so much peace in your heart. It would change your life."

"I don't need that book. I've heard it is a farce written by a false prophet."

"It was translated by a true prophet of God."

Bobby pursed his lips tightly. "I don't believe it."

"What if Moses walked up to you right now, would you tell him you didn't need the Ten Commandments?"

"Of course not. Let's talk about the farm."

Daniel and Bobby exchanged odd glances, but Daniel wasn't through. "The problem with people like you is learning to accept the fact there is a living prophet on the earth today."

"Your Joseph Smith claims to be a prophet, but that's all, he just claims."

"Listen, Bobby," Daniel said, feeling preachy. "If ancient revelations are true, surely modern revelations and heavenly visitations must follow. If we are to believe that God appeared to Moses and the ancient prophets, what is wrong with believing that he is a God of the same kind of miracles today? If God could speak anciently both by a voice of thunder and by the voice of perfect stillness, could he not do it today as well? The Anglicans and Methodists that you are familiar with all profess to accept Moses, Abraham, Isaac, and Jacob as prophets, yet they cannot accept a modern prophet. You're just like them, blinded. Surely the announcement that such a prophet again walks the earth ought to be received with rejoicing among people of faith and goodness."

There was a long and painful silence as Bobby shuffled his feet. He stared at the ground, then shifted his stare to the fields that comprised his farm: the grain crops, the hay fields, the pastures, the cattle grazing; these things were going to be his. He had yet to actually earn them, but they were going to be his, except for title to the land. Bobby knew he had a defiant, one-track mind about it, but further exploration of religion was untimely right now. His experience with religion thus far in his life had not been good.

"Bobby, Joseph Smith is a prophet. I know he is. I testify that he is."

Feeling a little confused, with the smirk gone from his face, Bobby replied, "I wish I had your faith." He forced a slow inhalation, relaxing his muscles.

"I think you do," Daniel said with an appraising look. "At least you have a little seed of faith. I know you well enough to know that's a fact."

"Well, maybe there is a little seed down there somewhere, Daniel, but down there is where it's going to stay. I'm going to concentrate on winning my fight with Ben Caunt, and running this farm. Right now there's nothing more important. Do you know how much money Squire Hastings says I will earn in this fight, win or lose?"

Daniel gave Bobby an empty stare. "I don't want to know."

"Well, it's a lot," Bobby chortled. His eyes went from dull suffering to a bright puckish gleam.

"I'm not going to quit asking, Bobby."

"I'm not going to quit saying no, Daniel. I don't want your Book of Mormon or your Elder Woodruff."

"Never?"

"Ask me in three or four years."

JUNE 1. Monday. At Frome's Hill I baptized nine and Elder Richards confirmed them: Sarah Loggin, Elizabeth Cole, William Cole, Susan Simmons, Elizabeth Dutton, Mary Phillips, Sarah Morris, Richard Perry, Ann Parks. Stayed in Ledbury.

JUNE 2. Tuesday. I wrote a letter to Elder Taylor from Ledbury. We received our first copies of the Millennial Star. Elder Young ordained John Preece of Ledbury a priest, and Phillip Green of Lugwardine an elder. We walked to Dymock and spent the night.

JUNE 5. Friday. I preached at Bran Green and walked to Haw Cross and spent the night at William Simons. I was accompanied during this day's walk by Brother Job Smith. He was but 11 years of age, but he had the longest head I ever saw upon a boy, and the most in it. He had a great mind and it was well stored with knowledge and understanding. He is almost a Proverb among the people where he is known, and I think he will be a useful character in his day and generation.

64

BY THE LIGHT of a late afternoon sun on a Sabbath day in June, Daniel and Elizabeth were in their home reading the "pass along" Book of Mormon that Elder Woodruff had brought from America with him, when they heard footsteps. An open door revealed the figure of Hannah. "I've got to talk to you," she said in a somber voice.

Daniel was surprised to see Hannah. He motioned for her to enter the parlor. "Where's Bobby?" he asked, knowing the obvious answer. He was either training late or at his brother's pub.

"He won't be home for a while," Hannah said with a note of worry, sitting on a cushioned chair that Daniel set before her. "I need to get back before he gets there, but I want to run an idea past you. You might think I'm a little out of my head, but I want your opinion."

Elizabeth felt her face muscles tighten as she sat down. She knew Hannah was unhappy about the prospect of taking her children to London and wondered if she was thinking about separating from her brother. That would be unthinkable. Not knowing what to expect, Elizabeth nodded. "Go ahead, we're listening."

Hannah took a deep breath. "What if you invited Elder Woodruff to speak at my home this time instead of yours?"

Daniel blinked several times in deep thought. Inwardly, his first reaction was to say no. "Bobby won't like that one bit, Hannah. He'll be angry when he finds out."

Daniel and Elizabeth exchanged puzzled, worried glances.

"I won't tell him." Hannah's tone was resolute.

"How will you keep it a secret?" Elizabeth asked. "It would be next to *impossible* to keep him from knowing."

"Not in his circles," Hannah charged. "Who would hear it at the training camp. Or at the pub? I've thought about it for a long time. It's the only way I can think of to get him in a meeting with Elder Woodruff."

"You mean let him stumble into the meeting?" Elizabeth said, dumfounded.

Daniel's face brightened. He touched his wife on the arm. "Elizabeth, wait. Maybe Hannah has a good idea. In fact, the more I think about it the more I like it. Hannah, you're a genius."

The open compliment caused Hannah to smile. "Do you think it will work?"

"I really do," Daniel answered. "It's worth a try."

With a new vision sweeping her mind, suddenly Elizabeth was brimming with optimism. "I do, too. Let's see now. We need *several* people for Elder Woodruff to teach, so let's invite some family and friends to your home. That way we can ask them not to tell anyone. And when we arrange it with Elder Woodruff, we'll tell him the situation and ask him to be sensitive to the matter, also."

"None of this guarantees Bobby will be there," Hannah cautioned. "It may not work at all. He's not even planning to attend the funeral for Nathan Roberts. Nathan was Levi's brother, and Levi is one of Bobby's best friends. The whole thing makes me sick."

"What time does he usually get home?" Daniel asked.

"He is either home by seven in the evening or at John's pub. If he's there, he's home by eight because he always wants to get to bed early so he can get up and get into Gloucester to the training camp on time. We've got to get this done in the next few days, before they end the training camp there and move it to London."

"Perfect," Elizabeth bubbled on. "We'll start the meeting at seven and when he comes home... oh, dear! What will he do when he comes *home* and finds your house full of guests?"

Realizing that setting the trap was the objective, Daniel chuckled to himself for a moment, then turned his brows into a furrow as he wondered about the repercussions of Bobby seeing a room crowded with people in his own home. "What if he gets mad and tells everyone to leave?"

Hannah set her jaw. After her long experience with her husband, wary of his selfishness, and his sometimes blatant and harsh dealings with her, she said, "The whole thing is risky but I want to try. We just have to hope we see Bobby's good side. He has one, you know. We haven't seen it for a while, but he has one. If we can just get him to feel what we have felt. The Holy Ghost can work miracles and we need a miracle."

"I'll speak with Elder Woodruff," Daniel said. "There will be quite a few people who will want to hear him teach the gospel."

"I want my mother there, too," Hannah said, her face beaming now. "And as many members of my family as possible."

"I don't think I'll invite my brother John because he might tip off Bobby," Elizabeth laughed. "But I *will* invite Dianah and her husband. I just hope Thomas will come with Dianah. He's not the problem that Bobby is, but he's being stubborn about joining the church also."

"We'll make sure that John and Lizzy get a chance to hear Elder Woodruff another time," Hannah injected. "But you're right. It wouldn't be smart to invite them right now."

"Oh, and Hannah, you better not invite Henry."

Hannah laughed. "Don't worry. I don't want to guarantee failure."

Elizabeth wondered if Hannah knew Henry was part of the mob that almost destroyed Thomas Kington's home.

She doubted it.

JUNE 8. Monday. I walked to Deerhurst and preached. Blessed two children and spent the night at the house of William and Thomas Smith. I dreamed I saw a large church on fire. The steeple, which was high, was in a flame. Several men were in the belfry with ropes, pulleys and chains, trying to save some part of the building, but were soon obliged to flee for the safety of their own lives, for much of the surrounding country was on fire. I was on a large horse and rode out of the way of it.

65

HANNAH GLANCED at the mirror, surveyed her slightly sagging figure in the altered green dress that she had worn on her wedding day, drew a deep breath, and opened the door to welcome the apostle from America, who had just arrived with Daniel, Elizabeth, and Dianah. As the coolness of the outside air washed over her, she said, "Elder Woodruff, I am so honored to have you in my home this evening."

Humble, charismatic, smiling superbly, but appearing slightly weary from his busy schedule – which earlier in the day had included speaking and singing at the funeral of Nathan Roberts – Wilford accepted Hannah's dainty hand. "Thank you for inviting me into your home. It's an honor." He was in a new gray suit that John Benbow had paid for, made by a tailor in Ledbury. He came bouncing into the house, gesturing to others who followed him.

"Oh, it's my honor, I can assure you," Hannah gushed, her eyes alive and glittering.

With a countenance that was open and hearty, Wilford said, "I want you to know that I totally understand your precarious situation this evening. I told no one where I was preaching this evening, even though many asked. Two people followed me here so I'm afraid your parlor will be crowded with people you did not personally invite."

A pleased look crossed Hannah's face. "We have lots of room. Bring them in." She met the two men who had followed Wilford, Daniel, and Elizabeth to Apperley hamlet, then said, "I am sorry to hear about Brother Nathan Roberts. My husband is a good friend to Nathan's brother, Levi. Bobby should have been there." A slight shudder went through her.

"I'm sure your husband was missed, but perhaps after tonight things will change."

Elder Woodruff's words seemed to relieve the tension Hannah felt. "I hope so," she said with a genuine smile, leading the men toward the parlor. As she surveyed her guests she thought about all the preparations she had made, and how quickly the time had passed since the afternoon Hannah had walked to the Browett home and revealed her plan. She had been a bundle of worry since then: Hoping that Bobby would not find out that a missionary meeting was going to be held in his home. That her mother would not divulge the secret. And that neither Dianah nor anyone else invited would divulge it. Then there was the matter of the house. There was a side of her that had wanted to repaint it, buy new furniture, spruce up the yard, and clean the windows. It had been a vain thought anyway because doing too much would have aroused Bobby's suspicions. But as usual he had left for the sparring room early, and afterward she had busied herself and her house servant with sprucing things up the best she could.

"Your home looks very nice," Wilford said.

"Thank you," Hannah answered, her face blushing. "But I'm afraid not everyone we invited is going to be here."

"No apology necessary," Elder Woodruff said quickly. "You will have to learn that not everyone in the world responds to an invitation to hear the gospel message. But I must say that here in this part of England the number of people that are accepting baptism exceeds any experience I have had, and I have preached the gospel for several years to a good number of persons."

Hannah's shoulders sagged. "I suppose you are curious to know when I will be baptized."

"Daniel told me you are waiting for your husband, and that is perfectly understandable."

Tears brimmed in Hannah's eyes, and she fumbled for a moment. "We're hoping and praying that he will be here." She had almost forgotten how good she felt around Elder Woodruff. Those feelings were coming back.

"Do you believe God answers prayers?"

Hannah wiped at her eyes. "Yes, I do, Elder Woodruff."

"Then he will be here."

Exchanging a quick glance with Daniel and Elizabeth, Hannah again reached for Elder Woodruff's hand and gave it a tight squeeze. She managed a soft, "thank you."

Wilford's eyes glowed with a deep sincerity, and he gave her a warm smile. "I'll depart from my usual procedure tonight, Sister Harris. I'll use up a little time and tell about how I was converted to the church; is that okay? Perhaps by then your husband will be here."

"Whatever you think is best," Hannah shrugged. "I would love to hear your story."

"Your home does look lovely tonight, Hannah," Elizabeth said in her usual excited tones, her chatter constant as she strode into the parlor with Wilford, Daniel, and Dianah. Spread before her was a mixture of people she knew, and some that she did not: James and Nancy Pulham; William Loveridge, Sarah Bail, Eliza Davis, and Elizabeth Clark from the parish of St. Mary de Lode. Elder Woodruff introduced Richard Cole and John Rowberry, the two men who had followed him.

Daniel said the opening prayer. Hannah took a determined breath as she watched Elder Woodruff take over the meeting. Inwardly, however, she remained a bundle of nerves, wondering what Bobby would do when he came home. In the recesses of her mind she could envision either a disaster or a miracle. Despite Elder Woodruff's words of encouragement, she didn't know which. In a chair that gave her a view of the window, she peered out for a few seconds then hung her head and said another silent prayer, her chin trembling. *Please, God. Soften my husband's heart.*

Every eye in the house was fixed on Elder Woodruff as he began his remarks. "I have often been asked how I joined the church. Everyone has a unique conversion story, and telling of those experiences always invites the Spirit. You may think this strange, but I never made a profession of religion until I was twenty-three years of age."

Hannah's shoulders remained slumped, her face clouded.

A reverent silence gripped the room as Elder Wilford related that when he was eight years old a strong religious revival took place in his hometown of Farmington, Connecticut, conducted by the Baptist Church. He said that the Baptists baptized his stepmother and several other relatives but Wilford, even though he had attended several of the meetings, did not feel impressed to be baptized himself. At age fourteen, when he was living with and working for a Mr. Cowles, Wilford again attended a series of revival meetings conducted by the Presbyterians.

"I tried to get religion by effort and prayer, but my efforts created darkness instead of light and I was not happy in the attempt. They wanted us to give our hearts to God without telling us what to do or explaining any principle in a comprehensive manner. There were many young people at that time of my age who made a profession of religion. I did not wish to make a mockery of sacred things by professing light when I had received none, so I kept aloof from all religions."

As Wilford paused to order his thoughts, he could see the deep sadness that filled Hannah's face because there was still no sign of her husband.

"My conversion to the church happened in late December, a little more than six years ago, in 1833, after my brother and I moved to the state of New York and bought a hundred and forty acre farm in Richland. On the twenty-ninth of that month, two humble elders of the church, Zera Pulsipher and Elijah Cheney, came to my home. We were out working but my brother's wife received the elders kindly. It always seems that women are a little more spiritual than men, don't you think?"

The words were directed at Hannah. She looked up and gave Wilford a warm but worried smile.

"My brother's wife and others gave out an invitation to hear the two missionaries preach that evening at the local schoolhouse. When I heard of the meeting, I immediately turned out my horses and started for the schoolhouse without waiting for supper. On my way I prayed most sincerely that the Lord would give me his Spirit and that if these men were the servants of God I might know it, and that my heart might be prepared to receive the divine message they had to deliver.

"When I reached the place of the meeting, I found the house already packed. I crowded my way through the assembly and seated myself upon one of the writing desks where I could see and hear everything that took place. Elder Pulsipher opened with prayer. He knelt down and asked the Lord in the name of Jesus Christ for what he wanted. His manner of prayer and the influence which went with it impressed me greatly. The Spirit of the Lord rested upon me and bore witness that he was a servant of God. After singing, he preached to the people for an hour and a half. The spirit of God rested mightily upon him and he bore a strong testimony of the divine authenticity of the Book of Mormon and of the divine mission of the Prophet Joseph Smith. I believed all that he said. The Spirit bore witness of its truth. Elder Cheney then arose and added his testimony to the truth of the words of Elder Pulsipher.

"Liberty was then given by the elders to anyone in the congregation to arise and speak for or against what they had heard as they might choose. Almost instantly I found myself upon my feet. The Spirit of the Lord urged me to bear testimony to the truth of the message delivered by those elders. I exhorted my neighbors and friends not to oppose these men, for they were the true servants of God. They had preached to us that night the pure gospel of Jesus Christ."

Elder Woodruff went on to say that he began at once to read the Book of Mormon and "as I did so, the Spirit bore witness that the record which it contained was true. I opened my eyes to see and my ears to hear, and my heart to understand. I was baptized two days later."

Hannah Eagles Harris looked at the clock, stared out her window again and at her interlaced fingers, said another silent prayer, and fought back the tears. She was beginning to feel that her plan was doomed to failure.

A heavy wooden door creaked on its rusty hinges as Henry, Alex, and Richie barged into the Ferret's Folly. They stormed toward Bobby's table.

"I'll bet you have no idea what's going on at your home, do you?"

Revulsion crossed Bobby's face as his eyes shot upward. "What do you mean?" he asked, taking stock of his old enemy.

"I just came from there," Henry said, his face drawn into a smirk. "There's a Mormon missionary in your parlor preaching to Hannah. Daniel and Elizabeth are there. There's so many people that some are sitting on the floor."

Bobby's eyes narrowed. Suddenly his plate full of sliced ham, boiled vegetables, baked apples, and hot bread lost its appeal. So did the ale.

"Are you certain it's my house?"

Thirty pairs of eyes locked on Bobby. Thirty pairs of ears had been listening to his blow-by-blow account of his last fight in London – for the hundredth time.

Henry nodded. Yes.

A snicker came from a man seated at Bobby's table, a lanky, sandy-haired cobbler named Geoffrey. "I wonder if my wife is there, too. She likes religious meetings. I never know what she's doing when I'm at the pub."

Low laughter was heard for a few moments. It stopped when the leading contender for the British heavyweight championship glared at the thirty sets of eyes, one by one.

Bobby burned at the inference. "Shut up, Geoffrey. Henry's not telling the truth. Hannah wouldn't dare have a meeting like that in my house without telling me." His suspicions forced him to stand up. Without realizing it, his back straightened and his fists went into a ball.

"Go see for yourself," Henry said with a curt nod in the direction of Bobby's home. An audible gasp could be heard from the pub patrons.

Bobby grabbed Henry by the shirt, and shook an index finger in his face. "If you're wrong, I'll break every bone in your body." He shoved Henry into Alex and Richie.

"I'm not wrong," Henry replied, wilting.

A controlled rage was visible in Bobby's walk as he stormed out of the Ferret's Folly. He was numb with anguish and embarrassment. He regretted that he didn't have a horse tied to the hitching post. One of Squire Hasting's servants had dropped him off at the pub, following his workout at the training camp in Gloucester. He broke into a run.

He covered the half-mile in just over two minutes. Bright lantern lights gleamed from his stone cottage. The sight of carriages and gigs, and horses tied to posts, shocked him. His chest heaving, he looked through the parlor window. It was just as Henry said. Hannah was beaming.

A short man dressed in a dark suit was gesturing, talking. He looked confident. Bobby quickly concluded the man must be Wilford Woodruff.

With tiny beads of perspiration trickling down his forehead, Bobby crept to the back door. In stealth, he opened it. *How could Hannah do this to me? Doesn't she respect me anymore? I'll grab Woodruff by the neck and throw him from here to Deerhurst.*

Without warning, a feeling of dizziness bordering on nausea struck Bobby. He paused to brace himself, dumbfounded. *What's happening to me? I only ran a half-mile.*

All eyes swept to him as he stumbled into the parlor.

"Bobby!" Hannah exclaimed. She cupped her hand over her mouth to muffle her surprise.

Stopping in mid-sentence, Wilford took a step backward. An eerie silence fell into the room.

Bobby pulled his face into a twisted contortion. The failure of his body to respond to his brain stunned him. Words would not come from his constricted throat. *Why can't I move? Why can't I talk? What unseen power is protecting this man?*

The American missionary remained motionless, waiting for Hannah to introduce him to her husband.

"Bobby?" Hannah said, puzzled. "Are you all right?"

A groan hissed from Bobby's mouth. He turned around and vanished in the direction he had appeared. The back door slammed.

Hannah licked her dry lips. "That was my husband," she said to Elder Woodruff. "He didn't expect this tonight. I'm afraid he may be a little upset."

Tears welled up in her eyes, and her shoulders sagged in disappointment.

"He'll be back," Wilford said in a confident tone. "Let's continue."

Bobby slogged back to the Ferret's Folly, his strength returning. A dark feeling engulfed him and a devious plan came into his racing mind. The American would pay for the embarrassment he had just suffered. He dashed into the pub, sweating, cursing, and pointing.

"John, give me all the eggs you have. Rotten ones if you have them."

Caught off guard, the manager of the Ferret's Folly considered his brother's erratic behavior. "Why?" John asked, "What are you going to do?"

"We're going to rotten egg an American preacher," Bobby yelled, gasping for breath. He pointed a finger at Geoffrey the cobbler. "Untie your team. You and you, help John with the eggs. Let's go. Hurry!"

An amused Henry Eagles rose to his feet.

"Not you Henry," Bobby said, glaring. "You and your friends are not invited."

Bobby pulled four other men to their feet. "Come with me," he ordered.

Within seconds Bobby's mob had boxes of eggs loaded into Geoffrey's wagon. Bobby ripped the lines from Geoffrey's hands and whipped the horses into a gallop. With white knuckles, the mob clung to the wagon as it bounced toward Bobby's home.

Bobby's orders continued in sharp clips. "When we get there, hid outside. I'll go in alone. They'll think everything's fine. When I raise my arm, storm the house. We'll take the American outside and rough him up. Use up all the eggs, every one of them. Then we'll dump him outside of town. He'll never come back, that's for sure."

Bobby spied a whip. He used in the on the terrified horses. "Hyaa! Hyaa!"

With the cool evening air swirling by as the wagon made a mad dash toward Bobby's house, John wondered why the next British pugilist champion needed help to rotten-egg and rough up a preacher. True, it would give customers of the Ferret's Folly something to laugh about for weeks and months ahead, but John thought it was curious. He also thought it was curious how easily a group of drinking men could be coaxed into organizing themselves into a mad mob.

As the lighted windows of his house became larger and larger with each galloping lunge of the brown horses, Bobby repeated his instructions. Closer to the house, he wisely slowed the horses to a walk, and almost silently slipped the wagon into the barnyard. Putting a finger to his rounded lips, Bobby made a "shhhh" sound. He jumped out of the wagon, crept to the back door, and entered his house. As the door closed behind him he paused momentarily, wondering if the dizziness would return. Relieved that it did not, he walked into the parlor feigning a smile.

His face clouded in puzzlement, Daniel watched as Hannah rose again to greet her husband, wondering why Bobby appeared to be relaxed and comfortable this time. Ever since he had walked out, appearing mad and confused, Daniel had wondered whether or not Bobby would return. With Wilford continuing his story telling, he had no chance to discuss how Hannah or Elizabeth felt about what had happened. The meeting had continued almost as though there had been no incident at all.

Wide eyed, apprehension written on her face, Hannah gestured to Wilford. "Elder Woodruff, this is my husband, Bobby."

"It's a pleasure to know you," Wilford said, letting Bobby's big hands wrap around his. "I appreciate being in your home. We have been waiting for you. I've told a few stories but now I am ready to begin. Please sit there, by your sweet wife."

Again, a strange sensation overcame Bobby. He stood on unsteady legs, powerless to do anything but obey. His attempt to acknowledge Daniel and Elizabeth was weak. As he meekly sat down, he could barely make out the forms of the men he left outside. The stood a few paces from the parlor window, staring, waiting for his signal. Bobby struggled to remember his own instructions: *When I get in the house, I'll raise my right arm. That's when you'll burst through the door.*

Bobby tried to raise his right arm. It didn't move.

Outside the cottage, Geoffrey leaned his body toward the window. "He hasn't raised his arm. He's just sitting there by his wife, listening to the American."

Several minutes passed. John sobered at the remembrance of Bobby's instructions, feeling more and more like he should go back to the pub.

With Elder Woodruff talking now, brilliantly animated, gesturing, Bobby sat as though he were spellbound.

"...Joseph Smith said that after he had retired to the place where he had previously designed to go, having looking around, and finding himself alone, he kneeled down to offer up the desires of my heart to God. Joseph had scarcely done so, when immediately he was seized upon by some power which entirely overcame him, and had such astonishing influence over him so as to bind his tongue so that he could not speak. Thick darkness gathered around him, and Joseph said that it seemed to him for a time that he was doomed to sudden destruction."

"What shall we do?" Geoffrey whispered.

"Wait for the signal," John said, still confused. Bobby seemed to be hanging on every word that came out of the American preacher's mouth.

"But Joseph Smith said that he exerted all his powers to call upon God to deliver him out of the power of the enemy that had seized upon him. At the very moment Joseph was ready to sink into despair and abandon himself to destruction, just at that moment of great alarm, Joseph saw a pillar of light exactly over his head, above the brightness of the sun, which descended gradually until it fell upon him. The light no sooner appeared than Joseph found himself delivered from the enemy which held him bound. Joseph said that when the light rested on him, he saw two personages, whose brightness and glory defy all description, standing above him in the air. One of them spoke unto Joseph by name and said, pointing to the other, 'This is My Beloved Son, Hear Him!'"

Geoffrey pulled a face. "Maybe we missed Bobby's sign. Too much time has passed. Let's go in."

Silas nodded his approval.

Geoffrey reached for the latch. The door opened.

Full strength gushed into Bobby's body, giving him control of his five senses. He suddenly stood up, his body rigid. He held his arms out, straight from his body, palms up, and pushed against Geoffrey's chest "Stop! Go back. I don't need you. There's something to this religion. Please – go back to the pub."

Geoffrey's mouth dropped in bewilderment. He retreated.

"I'm sorry I got you into this," Bobby whispered to his brother. "I'll explain later. Get these men out of here. Good night."

Hannah sat speechless.

Closing the door, Bobby made apologetic gesturing motions. "I don't know what to say," he muttered. "But they're gone now. Sorry for the interruption. It's my fault."

Daniel placed an arm around Bobby. "We understand. Shall we have Elder Woodruff continue?"

"Yes. By all means."

Elder Woodruff flashed a warm smile.

With his eyes misting, Bobby said, "Tell me about the pillar of light again."

An hour later, with a renewal that filled every fiber of his being, emotions in his throat, and his eyes glowing with a new sincerity, Bobby watched as his home emptied of guests. Only Hannah, Daniel, Elizabeth, Dianah, and Elder

Woodruff remained. Years of bitterness, confusion, and doubt had been swept away by a short, simple gospel message that was sweet to his soul, and he wanted more. He passed a nervous hand through his dark hair, and then touched Wilford on the arm.

"I feel awkward in asking, but would you have time to stay for just a few more minutes?" Bobby asked the American, his voice cracking. "I have a lot of questions."

"Bobby, I've invited Elder Woodruff to stay as our guest overnight," Hannah interrupted, a broad smile on her face. "I hope you don't mind." She was mesmerized by the soul-shaking realization that the gospel message had changed her husband forever, and the feeling left her reverently stunned.

"That's a pleasant surprise," he said. He pointed to the chairs. Visions of his past life swept over him: his pride, arrogance, stubbornness, and insensitivity. He had a lot to apologize for.

"I appreciate your hospitality," Wilford said. "I'd be happy to answer your questions.

Ashen faced and in a nervously merry mood, Bobby cleared his throat. "I owe everyone an apology for what I tried to do tonight. I apologize to you, Elder Woodruff, because I intended to do you harm. I apologize for not going to the funeral of Levi's brother. I apologize to my wife for the way I have been acting. I am truly sorry, Hannah."

Hannah began to weep.

Bobby hung his head and paused, groping for words. "I can't tell you how sorry I am, Hannah. And to you, Daniel, my best friend, and Elizabeth. Both of you. And you, too, Dianah. I apologize to you also for the way I have been acting. Please forgive me."

For the first time in a long while, tears came to Bobby's eyes.

Ruefully impressed during this tender moment, Wilford remained silent. He, too, wept.

Bobby faced Elder Woodruff. He felt as though an anvil had been lifted off his back. The good news of the gospel tinged his soul from top to bottom. He felt reborn. "I have so many questions, I don't know where to start. I just wanted to apologize tonight, but I have a feeling that you will be able to answer a lifetime of questions I have had."

Wilford unfolded his legs and sat forward in his chair. With a sort of paternal smile he said, "My mission is to preach the gospel of Jesus Christ and I am at your disposal. I have spent many hours in the middle of the night explaining the details of the restored gospel to many people. I remember my first evening at John Benbow's home – it was two in the morning before we retired."

The smile, the words, the tone, all disclosed the sincerity of the man to the former anti-religious, humbled father of three. Bobby's skin prickled as he considered Elder Woodruff's words and spirit. Gnawing his lower lip, he said, "You mean you are willing to preach more tonight?"

"Certainly, if that is what you want."

A horrid thought came to Bobby. "But I have to get up early and go into Gloucester to train tomorrow." He lapsed into silence for a few moments, thinking about the consequences of not showing up at the squire's sparring house. Then Bobby's eyes brightened again. "No, I don't. I don't have to do that if I don't want to. Suddenly, it doesn't seem as important as it did."

Wilford peered at Hannah. Her eyes were shining and enormous. He turned back to Bobby. "Shall we get started?"

"Yes, but where?"

"Ask your first question."

"My parents had young children who died in infancy..."

JUNE 9. Tuesday. I attended the funeral of Brother Nathan Roberts. I sung a hymn and prayed before the body was conveyed to the grave. I blessed her children, and endeavored to comfort the widow. I baptized six there and confirmed them: Samuel Roberts, Elizabeth Roberts, Ann Hopkins, Hannahh Hopkins, Hannah Hopkins, and Mary Ann Smith. Blessed II children, laid hands for the healing of four that were sick, this at Deerhurst. Then I walked to Apperley and preached at Brother Robins, then went to the home of Robert Harris and preached.

CHAPTER NOTES:

The story of Elder Woodruff teaching in the home of Robert (Bobby) Harris is taken from an original family history written many years ago (no date is on the document) by A. Wayne Harris with information researched by V. Ben Bloxham. The account is embellished here, of course, to suit the purposes of the novel, but it is based on a true story. Robert Harris, who had a background in pugilism, was restrained by the Spirit from harming Elder Woodruff. He did return to the pub to get friends to help him, and the Spirit did restrain him from raising his arm to give a signal to his friends. Robert Harris was baptized shortly thereafter. It is not known for certain if Wilford Woodruff personally baptized Robert and his wife. Their names are not listed in Wilford's journal as personal baptisms, but Elder Woodruff spoke at Robert's funeral in Utah and stated that he had baptized Robert Harris while in England. However, it is possible that Robert and Hannah were baptized by Daniel Browett, but taught by Elder Woodruff.

66

WEARING A NEW black silk hat he had bought just because it was spring weather, Squire Hastings showed up at the Gloucester sparring camp at noon in a jovial mood to have lunch with Bobby. His mood quickly turned sour when neither the manager nor any of the trainers knew where his star prize-fighter was. It was the first time Bobby had not shown up for training. Taking off his hat the squire wiped at his brow, revealing a bald forehead corrugated with worry lines. "Is he sick?" he asked, pulling on his long mutton-chop side-burns.

"We don't know," replied the manager, a short, barrel-chested former fighter named Higgins, with a nose that looked like it had been broken five too many times. Higgins had spent the morning working with two other young fighters he was trying to groom, instead of with Bobby. In the back-ground they and other fighters were skipping rope, punching heavy bags, doing push-ups with weights tied to their shoulders, practicing footwork, and getting ready to exit the camp for running exercises.

"What do you mean you don't know?" the squire squealed, grinding his teeth together. He bore his deep-set blue-gray eyes into the manager. "Did you send anyone to his home to find out where he is? What's the matter with you? It's only four miles from here. Surely that's not too far to send a training stable servant. Why doesn't anyone around here have any common sense but me?"

"No, sir," Higgins answered, with a lump in his throat. He had known the squire to fire people over lesser frustrations.

"If you want to keep your job, find out where Bobby is. Right now. Do you have that clear?"

"Yes, sir," was the answer.

Squire Hastings turned on his heel and stormed out of the sparring room, leaving the frustrated manager standing there with a dropped jaw. The squire boarded a bright blue barouche, pulled by matching white horses, and rode off with a suspicious-looking young lady half his age, her golden hair streaming in the sunlight. Higgins had seen her before, but did not know her name. He knew better than to ask.

By noon, Daniel had baptized both Bobby and Hannah in the same pond at The Leigh where hecklers, a few days earlier, had disrupted a baptismal service by throwing a dog in the pool. Today, there were no hecklers. The service was conducted in privacy with Wilford and Levi Roberts acting as witnesses. Later, Wilford blessed Bobby and Hannah's children.

Bobby had kept Wilford up until three in the morning, asking questions about the gospel. Is there really a physical resurrection after death? Will everyone be resurrected? How can I be forgiven? What is the atonement? How can I properly repent? What covenants do I make at baptism? How can I spiritually be reborn? How did the original church disappear from the earth? Why did the priesthood need to be restored to the earth? Where did I come from?

Why am I here on earth? What is the purpose of life? Am I really a child of God? Was I created in his image? Can I really become like my Father in Heaven? Just like Him? Why is heaven divided into three parts? What is the Celestial Kingdom like? Will we live there as families?

All through the evening, and again as he woke up the next day, Bobby knew his life had to change. No longer could he toss aside the serious matters of life and the gospel and continue to be self-centered and uncommitted about religion and his family. He knew he had made a mistake in the goals he had sought for himself. He had wanted to become heavyweight champion of England for personal, prideful reasons, and that made his life unbalanced. He recalled everything Hannah had said about the importance of his children and the quality of life in Deerhurst and Apperley as opposed to what it would be in London. From now on, he would be more caring, more responsible. He would seek to do things that would be pleasing in the eyes of God rather than the eyes of men. From now on, he would keep the Sabbath day holy. He would study the scriptures every day. He would attend church every Sunday. He would live his religion every day, not just on Sunday.

Elder Woodruff explained to him that when he was baptized he would make a simple covenant with God – to keep all the commandments and to serve others. If he would do his part, he knew God would do his part. God would allow him into his Kingdom, the Celestial Kingdom – the highest part of heaven – living forever in the presence of God, his Heavenly Father, and his Son, Jesus Christ. If he were faithful, *all* that the Father hath would be given to him. It was unfathomable to think of, but glorious nevertheless. There was so much to learn.

Bobby knew he would be missed at the training camp but didn't care. He was going to achieve the championship, fine, but religion had come into his life and he was going to keep it as a high priority. As he began mulling it over in his mind, he suspected that if he could win the championship and keep the principles of the gospel it might be possible. He thought about going to the training camp tomorrow and talk with Squire Hastings. Perhaps they could work it out. But no more would he train on Sundays. He did not want to live in London. He would set limits on the controls the squire had placed on him. Like it or not, the squire had to let him have a personal life. And the personal life had to include the gospel and his new religion. There had to be a way to achieve balance. He could be the heavyweight champion of England, and embrace his new religion at the same time.

After the baptismal service, Elder Woodruff left for Twigworth where he had an appointment to teach a United Brethren member named William Loveridge, and some of his friends. Bobby and Hannah stayed at Daniel and Elizabeth's home for lunch and to discuss the gospel some more. They had promised Elder Woodruff to read and ponder the thirty-first chapter of Second Nephi in the Book of Mormon.

"Are you worried about the training camp?" Hannah asked with a thoughtful glance as they opened the book.

For a few moments there was no response, not even a twitch from Bobby. He finally said, "I guess I should be, but this is such a special day. I would just as soon forget about my training for at least one day. I want to learn about and contemplate the gospel all day. The training camp will still be there tomorrow."

"What if they come looking for you?" Hannah asked, her tone worried.

"Then they'll probably find me – the new man," Bobby smiled, still feeling a springtime quickening in his veins. Remembering Elder Woodruff's spirit, charm and magnetism, he gave Daniel an eloquent look. "Teach me what is in this special chapter of the Book of Mormon that Elder Woodruff is so keen about."

With an easy knowing grin, Daniel turned to Second Nephi and began. "The Prophet Nephi explains the gospel in such plain and beautiful language.

Several hundred years before the birth of the Savior, Nephi, in a vision, sees the Savior get baptized by John the Baptist. Then he goes on to explain that having faith, repenting of our sins and changing our lives, being baptized by immersion for the remission of sins, and receiving the Gift of the Holy Ghost is the doctrine of Christ – which is also the doctrine of the Father."

"Which, of course, is why it is the doctrine of Christ," Elizabeth added, clutching her brother's arm. She had already decided that she liked the new Bobby better than the old one. She contemplated him while he read chapter thirty-one out loud. She could tell that her brother was enchanted by the simplicity of the words, and in the depth of the meaning.

"Now here is what Elder Woodruff thinks is the key, after we have accepted the doctrine of Christ and have been baptized," Daniel said. "Read verse twenty, very carefully." He paused while Bobby, Hannah and Elizabeth pondered the words, then he continued. "The key is faith, hope and charity. Faith – press forward with a steadfastness in Christ; hope – having a perfect brightness of hope; charity – and a love of God and of all men."

A look of overpowering spirituality enveloped Daniel. He enjoyed this teaching moment. "There are just two other things. One is to press forward, feasting upon the word of Christ. We are so fortunate to have not only the Bible, but the Book of Mormon and Doctrine and Covenants as well, so we have a lot to feast on. Then the final thing, endure to the end."

A feeling of warmth spread over Hannah. She touched her husband's hand and looked at him with a renewed affection. "I sincerely hope I can do all those things," Hannah said.

"Me too, Hannah," Bobby agreed, touched by her words and stirred by the scriptures he had just read. He marveled how easily the words came out. Until last evening, he would not have been caught dead in this kind of discussion.

"If we do, what is the promise?" Daniel asked. He paused as the others read the very last portion of the verse.

"Eternal life," Bobby answered, with a fresh resolve in his heart.

"Do you now want eternal life?" Daniel asked.

"More than anything in the world."

"Are you willing to sacrifice anything to have eternal life – which is to gain the Celestial Kingdom."

"Yes."

"Do you remember Elder Woodruff talking about temples?"

"Yes."

"Eventually, Elder Woodruff feels, there will be a temple built in Nauvoo, where the church is now located. Like the one built in Kirtland."

"Really?"

Daniel paused for a few moments, considering his next question. "How would you like to go to America, Bobby? To Nauvoo?"

"To visit?"

"No. To live."

"What are you saying, Daniel?" Hannah asked. She blinked and pondered. *Leave England? Live in America?* It sounded too good to be true.

Bobby's eyes widened in disbelief.

"It's called the gathering. Leaders of the church are inviting new converts to gather to the headquarters of the church, in Nauvoo. In America."

"You mean now?" Bobby asked. His eyes betrayed a trace of uneasiness.

"Elder Woodruff and other members of the Quorum of the Twelve have been instructed to arrange transportation on sailing ships as soon as possible. The first one left June sixth from Liverpool."

"Are you suggesting that we give up everything and go to America?" Bobby's voice was tormented. He clearly was not prepared to entertain such an idea.

"It's not mandatory by any means," Daniel explained, repeating what he had learned from Elder Woodruff. "And certainly I don't mean to infer that eternal life and going to America have anything to do with each other. But church leaders are asking as many gather to America as possible to help build up the church there. Think of it – what an opportunity. We can go to America. We can meet the Prophet Joseph Smith and live in the same city as him."

Bobby riveted his gaze on Daniel. "What about my fighting career and our farms?"

"What about them?" Daniel shot back, caught up in the moment.

"Do you just want me to walk away from an opportunity to be the champion of England? And walk away from my farm lease? And you walk away from your farm lease?"

"John Benbow lost his farm because of the gospel."

Hannah was startled. "He did? How? Why?"

While Bobby was absorbing the impact of his proposal, Daniel answered Hannah's question. "It's a complicated story. After he joined the church some of the local members of the Castle Frome Anglican Church put pressure on his landlady, Mrs. Anne Freeman, to terminate the lease."

"Just because he joined with the Mormons?" Hannah asked.

"Yes, the rector of the church, I think his name was either Harper or Hopkins, pressured a young man by the name of Richard Oakey, one of his parish members, to talk Mrs. Freeman into giving the lease to him. Of course he had to tell Mrs. Freeman a lot of lies about our new church."

"Richard Oakey? He might be a distant cousin of mine," Elizabeth said. "Really?"

"Yes. Remember, my mother's maiden name was Sarah Oakey."

"Maybe you'll want to disclaim him after this," Daniel said with a hint of a smile.

"And I suppose his lies about the church served their wicked purpose,"

Hannah stated with a quelling look.

Daniel nodded in the affirmative. "Yes, it did. Mrs. Freeman told Brother Benbow to renounce Mormonism or lose his lease. He's going to America on the next ship."

Bobby's mouth was open. "So he really did walk away from his lease. What did Elder Woodruff think about that?"

"He told me he wrote in his journal that Mr. Oakey would soon feel the weight of the Almighty because of the underhandedness of the way the lease was transferred."

Elizabeth blinked hard at the answer.

"What do you think about going to Nauvoo, Bobby?" Daniel asked, pressing.

"Give him time to think, Daniel," Elizabeth said. "This is so *sudden* to all of us."

"Can we talk about this with Elder Woodruff?" Bobby asked, deep in thought.

"No problem. He's staying at our home tonight," Elizabeth said."

The conversation was interrupted by a knock at the door. Bobby instantly recognized the figure there, a young servant with a long face and a narrow nose that worked at the training camp.

"The squire is worried about you," he said, huffing.

"I'm fine," Bobby said. "Just tell them I will be there tomorrow. I had to attend to something very important today, a personal matter."

"Yes, sir," the servant said. Then, bowing, he departed.

JUNE 11. Thursday. I spent the day at Twigworth. I baptized four: William Loveridge, Sarah Bail, Eliza Davis, and Elizabeth Clark. I preached at night at Brother Hill's. A Quaker from Gloucester attended the meeting. I blessed four children, and walked to The Leigh and spent the night at Browett's.

67

AN EXHAUSTED Elder Woodruff, still wearing the gray suit bought for him by John Benbow, sat in the Browett home at a simple dinner consisting of vegetable-marrow soup with macaroni and cheese. The service was on new china, maroon and gold. Elizabeth pictured a meal in Nauvoo, on the same china.

"Our farm lease has brought us so many blessings," Elizabeth said, filling Wilford's plate again. "A year ago we would never have been able to afford china."

Wilford drew a breath, not responding to her comment. Old crockery would have been fine.

"It's exciting to hear Brother Loveridge was baptized," Daniel said, shooting Wilford an ardent look. "It won't be long until all the old United Brethren members are Mormons."

Wilford weighed Daniel's words. "I guess that would be a worthy goal, Daniel. Before our work is finished here, let's try to reach, teach and baptize every single one of them. Agreed?"

Daniel filled his mouth with macaroni and cheese and spoke around it.

"Agreed. We'll have Bobby and Hannah help us in this area."

Bobby peered at his new American friend from under arched eyebrows. In his view, Elder Woodruff seemed to have an uncanny ability to read his innermost thoughts. It was the strangest sensation Bobby had ever experienced. "First, we have some questions about going to America." Ever since Daniel brought up the subject, it had haunted him. *Do I really want to give up a chance for the championship?*

"Let me give you a little background," Wilford began. "Everywhere the missionaries have gone so far, we have counseled the converts to gather to Zion. Earlier we had a lot of persecution in Kirtland and in Missouri, but things are settled down now and we have a new settlement in Nauvoo, Illinois. President Joseph Smith has things really well organized there. Plenty of land for homes and farms. The prophet feels strong about the need to gather there, to build up the church."

"Maybe more than a question or questions, I need some advice," Bobby said with an appraising look. His normal obstinate will had given way to a mingling softness.

"Go ahead, brother."

Bobby's blue-gray eyes widened and he cleared his throat. "I have a contract with a man named Squire Hastings. He has arranged an important fight for me in London next month. I'm fighting the other leading contender for the championship, and the winner gets to fight the champion later this year. I feel I can win that fight, and I also feel confident that I will end up being the champion. But if I go to America..."

"How does your wife feel about this?"

Bobby sighed. "I'll let her answer."

An amused surprise flashed on Hannah's face, and her enormous dark eyes flickered. "To tell you the truth, Elder Woodruff, I have been uncomfortable with my husband's fighting career for a long time. In the beginning it was okay, but then it got too serious." She went on to relate their courtship, marriage, and Bobby's struggle with religion. "I wanted to go to church, but Bobby quit going because of his frustration with the doctrine or the lack of it, pressure from my parents and his parents, and because he began training on Sundays. If he wins the championship I fear Squire Hastings will require that we live in London permanently. I know you have never been to London, but I do not have a good feeling when I am there. I don't like the people who go to the fights there. I don't like the promoters and those who wager. It's just a bad feeling I have. I know there are probably many wonderful people who live in London, but I felt evil there. I don't like it and I don't want to be part of it."

"You're certainly not bashful about your feelings, Sister Harris," Wilford said, chuckling mechanically and raising his eyebrows.

"No, she's not, Elder Woodruff," Bobby smiled, sticking his tongue out of the corner of his mouth to make a point. "See what I've been living with all these years?"

"See what she's been living with *all* these years?" Elizabeth countered in a voice tinged with irony, but in a loving tone.

"Bobby has another problem, which is also my problem, Elder Woodruff," Daniel added, spreading his hands in a graceful, resigned gesture. "We both lease farms from Squire Hastings."

"Oh, yes," Wilford sighed with a grim little smile. "I understand those farm leases now. It was disheartening when Brother Benbow was ejected from his farm at Castle Frome. But it is not unusual for people to make great sacrifices when they hear the truthfulness of the gospel and join the church."

Daniel nodded in agreement. "We have been talking about our options and want your advice."

"I know what I would do," Wilford said forcefully. "I would do everything I could do to go to Zion."

"Do you expect all the new saints to go to America?" Hannah asked, reflecting on the fact that this day, as yesterday, was turning into one of the most delightful days of her life. Outside she could hear birds singing in Elizabeth's sunny yard and garden. A mild breeze, passing through the hedges and fields of the farm and flowerpots set on the porch, brought in a heavy, sweet odor of flowers through the open windows.

Wilford cocked his head thoughtfully. "Gracious no. But we encourage it; highly encourage it, even though we advise you to do it with as little public notice as possible. No, we don't want all the saints to leave England. But here are some of the reasons why immigration is a good idea. First, you have accepted not only traditional Christian values and the Bible as the word of God, but also the Book of Mormon and Joseph Smith's revelations as scripture. You now have a testimony of the pre-existence, man's eternal progression, a knowledge that man is a spiritual child of God, inheriting his Parent's divine potential; that salvation and exaltation comes through knowledge and personal development, and that the heavens are open. God speaks today as in times past. You know about the work that is to be accomplished during the millennium, about baptism and temple ordinances for both the living and the dead. That sets you apart from the rest of the world, doesn't it?"

"Yes, it certainly does," Hannah answered, feeling ruefully impressed. She glanced at her newly baptized husband, who held his head at an attentive tilt and seemed glued to every word coming from the apostle's mouth. "We're very different people, aren't we?"

Wilford's voice took a decidedly serious tone. "You are very different from your neighbors, and you will be persecuted for it. The principle of gathering is as ancient as the earth itself. Believers of the gospel have always gathered together. Moses gathered the children of Israel. It's a concept rooted deeply in the Old Testament, in the dreams of the ancient Hebrews. The Lord redeems his people and he gathers his people. Even though the saints in

America have been persecuted in Missouri and driven out, our dream is to find a place where we can gather and live in peace and freedom. The Prophet Joseph Smith has asked that as many converts as possible gather to Zion – which is Nauvoo, the headquarters of the church. He needs your help to build the Kingdom of God on earth. We must strengthen the church then send out more missionaries. The message of the restored gospel must penetrate every nation."

Dizzy with the thought of gathering to this place in America that Elder Woodruff referred to as Zion, Hannah began to daydream. Her skin prickled at the possibility of going there, but cringed at the thought of being separated from family and friends that would be left behind. She rose in her chair then dropped into it again, sitting on her legs with her red frock spread over them.

"Do you like the thought of going to Nauvoo?" Wilford asked Hannah.

"Nauvoo. It sounds so far away. But it sounds enchanting, too. You say there will be a temple in Nauvoo soon?"

"Yes there will," Wilford said. Then after a long pause, and in an entirely different tone, he added, "Someday, although it may be many, many years away, there will be a temple in England. We have several thousand members here now and only a portion of them will go to Nauvoo. But if I were you, I would go. I would gather to Zion. That is my counsel to you. I feel, and know, that the United Brethren congregation – you four included – were a prepared people, a people who were seeking further light and truth. Go to Zion. That is where you will learn even more. That is where you are needed."

The words had a remarkable effect on Bobby. He pursed his lips, scratched his chin, rounded his eyes and tilted his head. He appeared stimulated at the possibility of going to America, yet confused. "If you were me would you fight for the championship, be the champion, then go to Nauvoo in a year, or two, or three?" His face went pale as he waited for a response, his eyes darting from Wilford to his wife, and back to Wilford again. He hardly resembled a chin-jutting, hardened contender for the British heavyweight championship.

"Would you be a rich man by then?" Wilford asked, examining his convert with a new shade of curiosity.

Bobby fixed his eyes on the apostle and answered quickly. The words made him desire the championship all over again. "Oh, yes. Very rich, I think." He couldn't help breaking out in a slight, prideful smile. *Three hundred pounds per fight.*

"Then I would go to America right now and give up fighting before it infects you more than it has done."

"What?" Bobby dropped the smile off his face. He shifted his weight in his chair and uncrossed his ankles. He stole a glance at Hannah, who gave him an innocent shrug of the shoulders.

Wilford's face toughened. "If you wait a year or two or three you'll never go. You will be so entrenched in the 'world' you could never give it up."

"Really?" Bobby asked, plunging himself into a cold gloom.

"Take a good look at the people who are converting to the gospel in England," Wilford answered, his face remaining stern. "Who are they? The common people. Humble people. We have not converted a duke, or an earl, or a baron – not an aristocrat in our bunch. What would happen if you tried to preach the gospel to Squire Hastings?"

"He would tell you to get lost," Hannah said in an acid tone.

"Probably – and that's the point. The Savior converted common fishermen. We've converted farmers, shoemakers, carpenters, and butchers. What would have happened if Brother Harris were already the champion of England, and we tried to teach him the gospel – would he listen?"

"No," Hannah said, being as blunt as she could. That brought chuckles from Daniel and Elizabeth.

"I get the point." Bobby slumped his shoulders and sat back in deep thought. He was so close to fame and fortune he could taste it. But another taste had entered his senses, a new taste that came only yesterday. The taste of the gospel. It tasted better than anything he had ever encountered. But couldn't he have both? Apparently not. Not according to the apostle. Wealth had the potential to jeopardize spiritual prosperity.

"When you have time," Elder Woodruff continued, "look up some of the scriptures that contain the phrase *set their hearts on riches*. Then compare them with scriptures that say *if ye keep my commandments ye shall be saved*. That will help you in your decision.

"What are you going to do?" Daniel asked Bobby with a worried look, trying to hide his own insecurity over the matter. If Bobby gave up pugilism, the squire would want to boot them off their farms. It would be a big letdown. Feelings of guilt swept over Daniel, and it puzzled him. If they lost their farms, he would tend to blame himself, which was silly, he knew, but that's the way his mind worked. As a minimum, he knew it would be best to keep their leases intact until they actually emigrated.

For a few moments Bobby sat in reflective silence. Then he peered back at Daniel and asked awkwardly, "What are you going to do?" He was far less worried about losing his farm than Daniel was, simply because he knew he would be resourceful enough to think of another angle to be successful in life, something that both he and Hannah would feel good about. He wondered if his brother-in-law had already made up his mind about emigrating. However, he was worried about the legality of the contract with the squire, and he quickly made that point with Daniel.

"I've already looked into the farm lease with a lawyer," Daniel replied, a remark that surprised Bobby. "It's year-to-year. I can give up the lease at the end of the year and go to America in January or February. You can too."

"But what do you think Squire Hastings will do if I end my fight contract?"

"I asked the lawyer about that too."

"And?"

"If you quit, there's nothing he can do. All your contract stipulates is that the squire gets a percentage and you get a percentage – a small percentage compared to what he gets, by the way. He'll be mad, but that's it. You can whip him, can't you?"

Hannah and Elizabeth giggled like little girls.

Wilford reached for his chin and tugged at it thoughtfully. "I have one final piece of advice, and obviously the most important. Take this matter to the Lord in prayer. He will tell you what to do."

Daniel nodded. Spoken like a true apostle of the Lord. Take the matter to the Lord in prayer. So simple. So full of common sense.

Wilford pushed his chair away from the table and stood up. "If the rest of you will excuse us, I need to speak with Daniel." He motioned Daniel to the door and together they stepped out into the warm breezes of a delightful June day and strode toward the barns, leaving Bobby, Hannah, and Elizabeth wondering why he needed to speak to Daniel in private.

"You've been a very faithful member of the church, Brother Browett," Wilford said, sizing up his friend of only three months. But in those three months Wilford had been impressed with Daniel's dedication, intelligence, and willingness to assist the missionary effort. "After much prayer and deliberation, on behalf of the Lord I have a calling in the church to extend to you. Actually, two callings if you will accept."

Daniel's face reddened slightly at the compliment. "I guess I'd do anything you ask me to do."

"That's the spirit. But remember, in church callings, I am just an extension of the desires of the Lord. The Spirit has directed me to issue you these calls."

"I understand. What do you want me to do?"

"With all the love I possess, I call you to the position of district president. In this calling you will be over all the branches south of the River Severn. Another brother will be over the branches north of the river in the Malvern Hills area. Your job will be to train the branch presidents. When you are set apart in the coming conference, you will be given priesthood keys. Those keys give you the right to preside over and direct the church within that specific jurisdiction, under the direction of members of the Twelve Apostles." He went on to explain all the duties Daniel would have. At the conclusion, he asked, "Do you accept?"

"Of course I do," Daniel replied.

"Thank you. The other calling is that of clerk. I want you to function as the clerk at the upcoming conference of the church for all the branches south of the River Severn. It will be held in the Gadfield Elm chapel. That means you would keep the minutes of the conference and we will send the proceedings to church headquarters in Nauvoo. Would you accept?"

"Do you really think I could do that?" Daniel asked.

"Certainly. Your handwriting is exceptional, as is your intelligence. And you have had some good experience in the church already. You'll make a fine clerk."

68

FOR TWO DAYS, Bobby fasted and prayed and studied the scriptures, just as Elder Woodruff recommended. He returned to his training, but nothing was the same. His heart wasn't in it. His manager and trainers continually asked him if he were sick – they detected that something was different, something was wrong. They thought it suspicious that Bobby declined eating lunch with them. He told them, no, that he was not sick, and it was an honest answer. He was well. He felt better than he ever had before. He was weakened from his fast, true, but he could still batter his sparing partners around with ease. However, he didn't feel good about hitting them. It didn't seem like the Christian thing to do.

Bobby did not have to face Squire Hastings, who was off to London on business. The squire had received a message, however, that Bobby had returned to the camp and everything appeared somewhat normal.

Just as Elder Woodruff predicted, as a result of his fasting and praying, Bobby suddenly experienced a compelling desire to leave England and travel to Zion. He knew the Spirit was beckoning him to abandon his past and start new in a Promised Land. He had a testimony that Zion was a sanctuary for the "pure in heart." He wanted to physically be in Nauvoo or wherever the church may be. He wanted to work out his own salvation without distractions. He wanted to escape the world and its temptations and evils. He wanted to help build a temple and perform sacred ordinances. He wanted the discipline of true Christianity. He wanted to be a disciple, a follower of Christ. And there were other attractions that he could not get out of his mind: America was an abundant land, living costs were far less than in England, and land was cheap and fertile. Perhaps the biggest attraction of all, for Daniel at least, was the delightful thought of living in Nauvoo where he could hear and see for himself the man he accepted as God's living spokesman on earth, the Prophet Joseph Smith.

Making the decision was easier than facing Squire Hastings. He dreaded it, but it had to be done.

On Friday afternoon, Bobby took Daniel with him to meet with the squire at the Ferret's Folly, the first opportunity after the squire's return from London. Had Bobby judged the squire's reaction better, he would have arranged the meeting in the woods beyond anyone's ears.

Bobby explained what had happened earlier in the week, why he had missed the day at training, filling in with as much detailed as he could about his conversion.

The squire was seated on the window side of a round table, and the squire's face remained a comic one to Bobby's eyes; the chubby cheeks, the bulbous nose, an oval defiant mouth, a white homely face, and glaring eyes. And John's pub took on a different appearance. To Bobby, it looked and felt garish. The smell of beer and ale and tobacco smoke was sickening, especially when the squire lit a fat cigar and began to lecture him, concluding that he was a fool.

"Young man, you are making a horrendous mistake. You can't quit now, not after all I have put into you. I have trained you, I have paid for your expenses, I have arranged for your fights and I have brought you to a position that I can have you fight for the championship after this next fight. Have you thought about that? Have you thought about what I have done for you?" He pulled at his mutton-chop sideburns with chubby nervous fingers, poking out from a hand that was beginning to show faint freckling and old age.

"Yes, sir, I have. Really I have." Bobby said the words apologetically, hoping the squire would quickly understand his resolute desire to change his life and quit the sport that he had previously loved so much. He stared at the squire eye-to-eye. Seen this close the squire's deep-sunk eyes were pale, puffy and somewhat glassy, and his down-curved mouth was rigid and tense.

The squire touched his sweating forehead with a handkerchief, and then spoke in sharp, curt tones. "Nonsense. If you have really thought about it you wouldn't even consider quitting now. I have you lined up for the most important fight of your career. If I keep you in training, you might win every fight I get for you. I will make you rich. I will make you famous. I will let you lease more land. I will have you set up for life." He returned his handkerchief to his pocket and drummed his fingers on the table, invoking the impression that he could turn on terrifying anger at will.

Bobby had consciously counted the number of times the old squire said "I." A dozen or more. Suddenly he knew this was all about the squire and his lust for money. It was as though the squire were the king and Bobby the pawn.

Bobby slumped glumly in his chair trying to sum up his courage and his thoughts. "Sir, with all due respect, I thank you for what you have done. I appreciate it very much. But my mind is made up. My family and my religion are the most important things to me right now, and they should have been all along." Bobby paused and cleared his throat. "As of right now I quit. No more training. No more fights. It's not important. I'm going to America and live in a place called Nauvoo."

Large beads of sweat collected on the squire's forehead again. His face became a reddened inferno, his personal devastation total and complete. He opened and shut his fists and began to breathe heavily at first, then in a constricted manner. The muscles in his face tightened. Then he began to yell and curse. The things he said embarrassed even the most hardened patron of the pub. Everyone, including Bobby's brother John, stopped talking and turned their attention to the table where the squire continued his rage and where Bobby and Daniel began to retreat toward the door.

"Your lease is ended," the squire yelled at the top of his lungs. "Get off my land! Go back to where you came from! Be a bloody butcher! Be a bloody Mormon! Get out of my sight. You'll be sorry for this. You'll regret this the rest of your life. You'll never amount to anything!"

As Bobby and Daniel escaped through the door, with dogs barking, the squire threw his glass, full of ale, toward them. John quietly grabbed a washcloth, and began cleaning up the broken glass.

A light rain was falling along the Cotswolds as Bobby and Hannah returned home from the Gadfield Elm conference. Hannah was grateful for the covered carriage she was riding in, protecting the bright blue promenade dress Bobby had bought her with the money he had made from his last fight. Today was the first time she had worn it, with its short silk pelisse robe and matching bonnet.

"I am so proud of you," Hannah said, spontaneously leaning toward her husband and kissing his cheek. "I feel better about you holding the priesthood in the true church than I did about you winning any of your fights."

"Thanks sweetheart," Bobby replied, switching the lines to one hand and putting his arm around his wife. "I feel good about it, too. This is quite a change. No more fighting. Just a farmer, for at least this season." The horse leaned against its collar, its iron shoes digging into the earth, as the carriage followed the incline of a hill leading toward home. Ahead of them the sunshine broke through the gray clouds, and the road took on a fairyland appearance, continuing into the leafy woods.

"Then to America and Nauvoo," Hannah exclaimed, dazed with a happiness beyond imagining. "It sounds so exciting. I think Joseph is beginning to understand that we are going to have a new home in a new country." Bobby and Hannah had left their three children at home with their nursemaid. The couple now planned to concentrate on harvesting their crops and filling their farm lease obligation until the end of the year. They would leave for Nauvoo shortly after that. They now faced the daunting task of telling Hannah's mother and family.

"Are you disappointed you won't get to live in London?" Bobby asked with an abashed grin.

"Oh, please. Don't even make me think of that. I am so relieved."

Bobby left the main road and turned into the lane that led to their home. As they came closer they could see something piled up in front of the house. It was their personal belongings – children's clothing, dishes, food...

"Bobby!" Hannah gasped, biting her lip in disbelief.

His face blood red, Bobby jumped out of the carriage, past the piles of personal belongings and ran to the door. It was locked. He banged on the door and yelled, "Joseph!" For a moment he stood on the front step with emotions that alternated between confusion, anger, and frustration.

"Where are the children?" Hannah cried. Tears brimmed her eyes and there was a torment in her voice. She ran to Bobby and clutched at his chest. "Where are my children?" No one was in sight, not even the nursemaid.

A lone rider on horseback appeared out of the trees. It was the Gloucestershire constable, riding a big black gelding with a bolly face and one stocking foot. He galloped towards them. Bobby fixed on him with cold eyes.

Plain features but bull-necked and thick-shouldered, the reddish-haired constable was brief and to the point. Sitting rigid in the saddle, he stated, "I am required to tell you that you are not to set foot on this property any more. You are to remove your own belongings as soon as possible. Right now, in fact."

A smoldering rage formed in Hannah's chest. "Where are my children?" she yelled hysterically. "Please! Where are my children?" She tensed, waiting for an answer.

The constable's back stiffened, but his voice softened. "They are quite safe, Mrs. Harris. I was ordered to have them removed from the house. They are being held in the Apperley Methodist chapel with your nursemaid. You may go there now and get them, but first, do something with your personal belongings."

Bobby's eyes continued to narrow. "They better be safe, constable, or..." There was a threat about to break from Bobby's lips, newly baptized Mormon or not.

"Or what?" the constable growled.

Bobby glared at the constable, thinking what he would have done to him prior to his baptism. "Come on, Hannah, let's hurry," he said, grabbing her arm and walking toward the carriage. So the squire owned the constable, too. He owned the reverend. He had owned Bobby. But no more.

"By the way," the constable added. "That carriage you are in, and the horse, belong to the squire. Leave them here, with me."

Bobby turned, appalled. "How am I supposed to haul our things away?"

"That's your problem."

Barely hanging onto his patience, Bobby wanted to grab the constable, jerk him off the horse and let the old Bobby, the "natural man," break his jaw. If he found his children harmed, he would do it anyway. "Let's go, Hannah, the church is not that far away. Let's check on the children, then we'll come back."

They began a hurried one-mile walk toward the church they had been married in, Hannah's blue dress dragging in the mud.

Shoulders slumped, still sobbing, her face clouded with doubt and concern, Hannah walked at a brisk pace trying to keep up and wondered if her husband now had any regrets. Vivid negative thoughts passed through her mind. Not only had he lost his profession, a profession that was going to make them extremely wealthy, but their house and farm as well. What would they do for the next several months until they emigrated? How would they provide for their children? Where would they live?

"What are we going to do, Bobby?" she cried. "It's all my fault." Inside her heart she felt totally devastated. It was turning out to be one of the darkest days in her life.

"Nonsense, Hannah," he countered. "Don't talk like that. What could we expect from the squire?"

"Isn't he legally bound to let us live in our house and lease the farm until the end of the year?" she gasped, nearly out of breath.

Bobby's voice was pained but realistic. "Technically, yes, but he will tie us up in legal harassing maneuvers for the rest of the year, and by that time we will be on a ship headed for America. So what's the use?"

Suddenly, both of them thought of Daniel and Elizabeth.

"Do you think the same thing has happened to the Browetts?" Hannah asked, a new concern striking through her.

"Yes."

As they saw the redbrick chapel, they broke out into a run. As they burst through its door the sight of their children wilted their emotions.

"Joseph! Elizabeth! William!" Hannah screamed as they ran to their children and embraced them.

The sight of her mother gave Hannah a poignant tug at her heart.

"Thank the Lord you are here, Mama." Ann Eagles returned a sad, concerned look, and embraced her daughter.

Bobby found himself face-to-face with the man who married him, Reverend Crooks. He walked up to the bent over form of a man and extended his hand. "Thank you for being here. It's good to see you."

The high-pitched voice was the same. "Congratulations on having such beautiful children. This is the first time I've had the opportunity to be with them." Bobby interpreted his remarks to be filled with a whole-hearted warmth.

"Now tell me, what is going on?" Hannah's mother demanded. "The constable dropped the children off without any explanation."

Bobby turned to Hannah. "Tell her everything, all the details. I think Daniel and Elizabeth are going to show up here after awhile, then we can borrow a wagon and get our things together."

There was a lot to tell: Both Bobby and her had been baptized into a new religion. Bobby had been ordained a priest, receiving the Aaronic Priesthood. He had decided to give up his profession as a pugilist. An angered Squire Hastings had booted them off their farm. Their belongings lay in a heap.

The face of Reverend Crooks turned sour at the story. He excused himself and left.

Hannah felt a deep chill as Daniel and Elizabeth walked into the chapel moments later. She arose from a pew and ran toward her sister-in-law, sobbing. "Oh, Elizabeth! What are we going to do. We've lost everything."

The pallid women clutched each other, crying.

Bobby's dark eyes settled on them. "Get control of yourselves. What did you think the squire was going to do when I decided to give up the sport? Give us more land to lease as a reward?"

Daniel faced the two sobbing women, and grunted. "He's right. We're just back to square one. I'm just 'Daniel the carpenter' again. Bobby is 'Bobby the butcher' again."

Hannah looked more troubled now, as if somehow she preferred her old life. "But there is no such thing as the Harris Butcher Shop anymore." When William died, the shop closed.

"There will be, by tomorrow," Bobby said with a resolute grin.

As Hannah stood in the old Methodist chapel and squinted in the harsh light, she reminded herself to her amazement that Bobby was right. A few days ago she had been begging for him to change his life. He had, drastically. Quickly now, she repented of her thoughts.

"Then Bobby the butcher it will be," said Hannah, wiping at the tears streaming down her reddened cheeks.

Bobby embraced his wife. He didn't know where he could get the money to buy the first steer to slaughter, or the first ram, or the first hog. But he was going to find his old bloodstained leather apron and tools and find a way to support his family and earn enough to buy passage on the ship that would take them to America.

As they embraced, Hannah couldn't tear her eyes from her mother. *Why not take her to America with us? But will she join the church?*

69

ANN EAGLES had acted like a perfect angel ever since Bobby moved his family in with her: Insisting that Henry move into a vacant servant cottage owned by Farmer Nightingale. Loaning Bobby money to rent a shop for his butchering business. Even loaning him enough to buy some livestock.

As Bobby mounted a bay gelding, owned by the dairy, and rode off to the Tewkesbury cattle market, Hannah had no idea that she would begin making demands that they could not meet. Her elderly features set in an icy mask, Ann began in a docile, placating tone. "I haven't asked anything in return for allowing you to live with me and loaning you the money for your husband to start his business. But I do have one condition."

"And what condition would that be?" The word "condition" startled Hannah. She stopped nursing her baby and laid him down.

"This new religion of yours, Mormonism, I don't think you realize what you have done, Hannah." Visibly shaking now, Ann walked to the window so that she did not have to look her daughter in the face. "You need to give it up, renounce it. It is the work of the devil. You need to return to your Methodist roots, and live here in Apperley the rest of your lives. It's the least you could do for me."

Hannah stood stone silent in shock. *Who planted this idea in my mother's mind? Henry? Reverend Crooks? Members of her congregation?*

"Did you hear me, Hannah?"

Hannah arched one of her dark, narrow eyebrows. "Mama, who in the world put into your mind that my church is the work of the devil?"

"That's not important."

"I have never felt more at peace than I have the past few weeks since my baptism. And you can see the change in Bobby. If he hadn't been baptized, we would be in the process of moving to London, permanently."

"He's a changed man, alright," Ann said stiffly. "He's lost everything – his career, his farm, your home, the chance for financial security forever. All for what? An American religion that is a tool of Satan to lead people away from Christianity."

"Mama, our church is not an American church. It is not even the Mormon Church. It is The Church of Jesus Christ of Latter-day Saints. It is the Savior's church. It is named after Him."

"Nonsense, Hannah," Ann countered, still full of venom. "Whoever heard of such a thing? Reverend Crooks said that the Bible has all the answers. You need to come back to your Methodist roots, and study just the Bible."

Oh, no! thought Hannah. *It was Reverend Crooks. What else had he told her?*

"And you and your people think you are so doughty, predestined to be selected to be baptized into the only true church. Now I hear that Joe Smith wants all his English Mormons to go to America to be indoctrinated with more false teachings. Oh, it's the church of the devil all right, Hannah. And you better not be thinking of leaving England."

Hannah recoiled in disbelief. "Mama, I hate to tell you this. But, yes. We are thinking about emigrating to America. Maybe as early as January or February."

Ann began to shriek in convulsing tones. "Out of the question! You cannot do this! I forbid it!"

"Mama, I love Bobby and I will follow him wherever he goes. Both of us want to go to America."

"Why? Why? Why?" Ann put her hands over her face and began to sob, sinking into a horrid gloom.

"Because that is where the saints are gathering. That is where the prophet is. Besides, in America, we can own land. Think of it, Mama. We can own land. Not lease it, but own it. And it is inexpensive. Think of the future of our children, too."

"Your children are better off staying here in England."

Hannah scoffed at the thought. All of Great Britain was going through perhaps the grimmest period in the history of the nineteenth century. A depression had been racking the Empire for at least three years. Serious rioting between Whigs and Tories might lead to revolution and social upheaval. Thousands were leaving the country.

"Mama, I love you. You need to come with us."

"And become a Mormon? No. Never."

70

DANIEL BROWETT had shaken his blonde head in concern the evening he heard that Ann Eagles was giving Bobby and Hannah fits over their conversion. The concern quickly melted into fear about his relationship with his own mother. Just as Bobby and Hannah had done, he and Elizabeth had moved in with his mother.

"Your new church has proved to be a curse to you," Martha Browett told Daniel a few days after he and Elizabeth moved in with her. For days she had whined about the loss of their farm lease, and Bobby giving up his chance to fight for the championship.

"Not a curse, but a blessing," Daniel said, laughing at his mother's misunderstanding heart. "Sacrifice yes, but I've never been happier." He thought of the blessings: His personal relationship with an apostle. His calling as a district president. The opportunity to go to America. And he still had his cooper shop.

Elizabeth sat quietly in a chair, reading her Aristotle book.

"How can you say that?" Martha quipped, her blue eyes lashing out.

"One day you're a yeoman, next day you're just a common barrel maker again. And I never see you on Sundays anymore. You're gone all the time."

"Next Sunday come with me. You'll enjoy our meetings."

Martha frowned. "I'm just getting so that I enjoy Reverend Hobhouse at the Anglican Church. I'm too old to change my religion again."

"You're never too old to do what's right, Mother."

"Daniel," Martha said, her voice turning soft. "I've heard a rumor that some Mormons are leaving England, for America. You are not planning anything like that are you?"

"I've been meaning to talk to you about it, Mother. Yes. We are thinking about it. Nothing official, yet."

Martha sank to her knees. "I knew it. I knew it. Mormonism is going to destroy our family."

When Wilford Woodruff heard Daniel's report that both Daniel and Elizabeth and Bobby and Hannah had literally been forced off their leased farms by Squire Hastings, he had shrugged his shoulders in the same resigning manner as he had done hundreds of times. *True conversion brings much sacrifice.*

Taking a drink of water, Wilford sat on his bed at the home of Thomas Kington in Dymock and read through his journal entries of the past month. He marveled at how fast the Lord's work was progressing among the United Brethren, how they truly were a prepared people, a people that had sought further light and truth. He chuckled to himself as he thought about Bobby's conversion that night in Apperley: How Bobby had tried to throw him out of the house. How the spirit had protected him. Bobby's conversion had been miraculous, true, but so had been the entire experience that had led him to the United Brethren.

With pen in hand, Wilford caught up on his journal entries, closed the journal, snuffed the lantern, and settled into a deep, peaceful sleep.

JUNE 12. Friday. I walked to Dymock and had an interview with Elder Richards. He had just returned from the south part of Herefordshire where he had built up a church of 11 members and ordained one teacher, John Castreo. We preached at Elder Kington's, confirmed two and healed one that was sick. Elder Richards wrote a piece for the Millennial Star.

JUNE 13. Saturday. I held a council with Elder Richards and Elder Kington preparatory to the coming conference. We received a letter from Elder Young at Liverpool, stating that 40 of the saints had left Liverpool on board a ship, for America, and that they had taken my letters to Phoebe and Brother Holmes. We spent the evening at Brother Hill's at Turkey Hall. [William Pitt was baptized by Thomas Kington on this day.]

JUNE 14. Sunday. [Editor's note: This is a brief summary of a two-session conference held this day for the United Brethren converts at the Gadfield Elm Chapel. Elder Woodruff's journal contains much more detail, which is omitted.] When the meeting was called to order by Elder Thomas Kington, Elder Willard Richards was chosen president and Elder Daniel Browett was chosen clerk. It was moved by Elder Kington, seconded by Elder Browett, and this meeting be hereafter known by the name of the Bran Green and Gadfield Elm Conference of the Church of Jesus Christ of Latter-day Saints. William Jenkins was ordained an elder. The following were ordained priests: William Coleman, William Pitt, Joseph Ferkins, and Robert Harris. And George Burton, James Palmer, and William Lavendge were ordained teachers. All were ordained under the hands of Elder Richards and Elder Woodruff. Assignments for the care of the church in twelve different branches were given [branch presidents and their counselors]: Dymock, Robert Clift; Kilcott, James Palmer; Twigworth, John Hill; Haw Cross, William Simonon; Bran Green, William Coleman; Ryton, Thomas Brooks; Lime Street, John Smith; Deerhurst, Charles Hays, assisted by Thomas Smith; Apperley, John Vernon, assisted by William

Bayliss; North, John Arlick; The Leigh, John Spires, assisted by John Davis; Gadfield Elm, Thomas Oakey. Elder Daniel Browett was assigned to take charge of the churches on the south side of the River Severn [similar to today's calling of district president or stake president]. Elder William Jenkins to take charge on the north side of the river. Elder Thomas Kington was assigned to be the presiding elder over all the churches composing the conference [similar to today's calling of a stake president or Area Seventy Authority]. Daniel Browett was assigned to represent the conference at the next General Conference of the church in England to be held at Manchester on July 6.

JUNE 15. Monday. We walked to Dymock, then to Ryton and preached, then returned to Dymock and spent the night; confirmed two persons. I received a letter from Elder John Taylor.

JUNE 16. Tuesday. Walked to Lugwardine. Preached at the house of William Green, father of Elder Phillip Green. Afterward, three were baptized by Elder Green. Elder Richards and myself confirmed eleven. John Powell and John White were ordained priests.

JUNE 17. Wednesday. I baptized six at Lugwardine – Charles Powell, John Tyler, Hannah Gibbs, Susan Tyler, Jane Dutson, Mary Gibbs, one of them a preacher. Elder Richards confirmed them. Four others were baptized at Marden after preaching at the home of William Jay. Blessed four children and healed seven that were sick. Spent the night with Brother Jay.

JUNE 18. Thursday. I baptized five at Marden: Ann El, Thomas Jones, Ann Edwards, Rebecca Tew, and Susan Tew. We ordained Francis Burnet to a priest. Blessed six children and administered to two that were sick. Walked to Shucknel Hill and preached at Brother William's. The church minister in the parish sent a spy to attend the meeting, to carry him word what we preached. As soon as the meeting closed I put my hand upon his shoulder and asked him what he thought of our doctrine. He replied, "I think it is of God." He appeared astonished when he left the house. Ordained Ishmael Phillips to the office of a priest, blessed seven children.

JUNE 19. Friday. I arose early in the morning and baptized and confirmed one. A number of others soon came to us and wished to be baptized. We immediately walked to the River Lug, being hindered a short time looking for a suitable place for baptizing. A man by the last name of Pitt came to us, filled with the devil and wrath at the head of a mob, and commanded us not to be baptizing in that river, and threatened us much if we did so. Elder Richards preached to Mr. Pitt and warned him to repent and be baptized, or he could not be saved. But the devil raged to such a degree in this man and his company we thought it wisdom to omit it on this occasion. We did so, and retired and went our way, with this wicked man and the rest of the mob following us, shouting, hooting, and yelling as though a part of hell had at least broke through. The saints were strengthened, seeing that they were not part of the world, but the world hated them. We went our way rejoicing that we were counted worthy to partake of these things. We cleansed our feet by the wayside as a testimony against Mr. Pitt for rejecting our testimony, and forbidding, and hindering others from entering the Kingdom of God. We walked to Fromes Hill and found Brother and Sister Benbow both in better spirits than I have ever seen them before. Baptized John Tiler and Mary Henbury today. Spent the night with Benbows.

JUNE 20. Saturday. I spent the day in company with Elder Richards and Elder Kington is making arrangements for the Stanley Hill Conference. It was an exceedingly busy day. We had a great variety of business on hand. I baptized eight persons: Ann Jennings, Jane Tyler, Mary James, Sarah Wall, Sarah Cole, James Cole, Ellen Clark, and Eliza Clark. A total of 14 were confirmed, and we administered to two persons that were sick. The power of God is among the people. The Lord is making short work in this part of the land. The churches in this part of the vineyard now number more than 500 souls, where a little less than four months ago there was not one to be found, or the fullness of the gospel heard. Spent the night with Benbows.

JUNE 21. Sunday. [Editor's note: Again, minutes of the conference have been shortened.] Minutes of the Stanley Hill Conference of the Church, Castle Frome, Herefordshire, England, held at the home of Elder John Cheese. Called to order by Elder Thomas Kington. Elder Wilford Woodruff was chosen president of the conference, and Elder John Benbow, clerk. Decided that hereafter the conference would be known as the Fromes Hill Conference. Moved that the following be ordained: as elders, Thomas Clark, James Hill, Charles Price and Samuel Jones; as priests, John Jones, John Morgan, Joseph Shinn, Samuel Badham, Henry Jones, John Dyer, and James Baldwin; as teachers, Robert Hill, James Shinn, George Brooks and James Watkins. Assignments for the care of the branches [branch presidents and their counselors]: Stanley Hill, John Parry, assisted by John Morgan, James Hill and Joseph Pullen; Ridgeway Cross, James Barnes; Moorend Cross, William Dossons, assisted by William Jenkins and Thomas Jenkins; Colwall, Jonathan Judy; Pale House, Thomas Jones; Ledbury, John Preece, assisted by Joseph Firkins; Keysend Street; Samuel Warren, assisted by Joseph Shinn and James Shinn; Wind Point, James Baldwin assisted by John Allard; Wofferwood Common, George Allen. The hamlets of Rough Leasowe, Birchwood, Tunbridge and Duns Close were united into one branch called Duns Close, with Samuel Badham in charge. Ashfield and Crawcutt, Edward Phillips, assisted by James Williams and George Brooks; Old Starridge, John Meeks, assisted by Henry Jones; Hope Rough, John Gailey; Shucknell Hill, Benjamin Williams, assisted by Ishmael Phillips; Lugwardine, John Powell, assisted by John White; Mardon, John Dyer assisted by Francis Burnett and James Watkins; Stokes Lane, William Evans assisted by William Davis, John Sanders, and Thomas Vernon; Bishop Frome, John Fidoe. The following elders were given assignments to be over groups of branches [similar to today's calling of District President or Stake President]: Samuel Jones, Phillip Green, John Cheese, Charles Price, James Hill and John Benbow. Thomas Kington received the assignment to represent the

Fromes Hill Conference at the upcoming Manchester conference [similar to today's call-ing of Area Seventy Authority]. It was determined that at this time 534 members of the church comprises the two conferences in the Malvern Hills area. I baptized the follow-ing: Hannah Jones, John Baily, Margaret Dovey, and John Rowberry.

JUNE 22. Monday. Elders Richards and myself spent the morning in arranging the min-utes of the conference at John Benbow's. Confirmed one and blessed four children I baptized five and confirmed them: Ann Cole, daughter Ann Cole, Richard Cole, Sarah James, and Martha Clark. Baptized one at Ledbury, Robert Gomery. Started on my jour-ney for the conference at Manchester. I never before left a field of labor with as much satisfaction as on this occasion, and I felt to render up the gratitude of my heart to God for his goodness to me by giving me many souls as seals of my minister, for being led to this country by the Spirit of God. Since stopped at John Benbow's on the fifth day of March, traveling 80 miles from Hanley, I am this day blessed with the privilege of leav-ing a fruitful field in this land with 33 organized branches, now numbering 541 mem-bers, 300 of which received the ordinance of baptism under my hands. The others have been baptized by Elder Brigham Young, Elder Willard Richards, Thomas Kington, John Cheese, C. Price, Daniel Browett, T. Clark, S. Jones, P. Green, John Parry, J. Barnes, T. Oakey, J. Morgan, W. Jenkins, J. Spires, B. Williams, W. Parsons, W. Evans, and J. Gailey.

JULY 22. Wednesday. [Editor's note: Elder Woodruff departed the Malvern Hills and his work among the United Brethren June 23 to attend the Manchester conference. Elder Thomas Kington and Elder Daniel Browett met him there at the Millennial Star office on July 4. They attended the conference, representing their areas, and received addi-tional training. Kington and Browett had positions similar to today's Area Seventy Authorities. Kington was ordained to the office of a High Priest at the conference. Elder Woodruff stayed in and around the Manchester for nearly a month, preaching, teaching, ministering and baptizing. One month later, on July 22, he returned to the Malvern

Hills, so we pick up the activities mentioned in his journal once again.] We took the coach and rode to Worcester, and from thence to Ledbury. I walked to Dymock and held a meeting and spent the night.

JULY 23. Thursday. We walked to Fromes Hill and found the saints strong in the faith and increasing fast in numbers, and preparing to emigrate to be with the saints in the United States.

JULY 24. Friday. I received a letter from Father and Mother, and Sister Eunice Woodruff, which I was glad to get. I found Brother and Sister Benbow strong in the faith and willing to make every sacrifice in their power for the gathering of the saints. Had an interview with Elder Kington. We spent the day at Benbows.

JULY 26. Sunday. I walked to Ridgeway Cross and preached and confirmed eight, and bless eight children, and laid hands upon many that were sick. I walked to Moorends Cross and preached, and confirmed two. I returned to Ridgeway Cross and communed with the saints and had an interesting time, which will be the last time I break bread with many of those saints, as they are about to emigrate and gather with the saints in Commerce, Illinois, and Montrose, Iowa. A company of about 50 is about to start for America from Herefordshire, England, about 40 of whom will go by free charity and philanthropy of Elder John Benbow.

JULY 28. Tuesday. I wrote a letter to Elder John Taylor and wrote a recommend for Elder John Benbow and Jane Benbow to emigrate.

71

ON A PLEASANT Sunday in July, Elder Woodruff preached at the Gadfield Elm chapel about the gathering, covering these thoughts: Christ's converts left all and followed him. The Kingdom of God, although as small as a mustard seed currently, could someday fill the earth prior to the Second Coming. Moses had restored keys relative to the gathering to Joseph Smith in the Kirtland temple.

Daniel hung on every word, letting the Spirit confirm to him that he must join in the gathering. Afterward, Elder Woodruff talked to him in private in the upstairs office.

"Are you committed to go to Nauvoo, Brother Browett?" Wilford pressed, his tone firm. He slid his chair next to Daniel.

"I still have concerns about my mother," Daniel answered. "But yes. Elizabeth and I have discussed it thoroughly."

Wilford stared at him a moment, and smiled. "The church needs a few faithful men to lead companies of church members to Nauvoo. You are being considered to be one of those leaders."

Daniel's face colored at the suggestion. "When?"

"Probably within the next six or eight months. You would function as company captain, but also as their spiritual leader. You would need to choose six assistants, giving us a seven-man presidency, of sorts."

"How many members of the church would be in our company?" Daniel asked, his heart thumping. He shed his jacket and wiped his brow.

"Hard to say at this point. But I would guess between fifty and a hundred."

"What about my mother?"

"Let's get her baptized and invite her to go with you."

"She's being very stubborn," Daniel said, trying to overcome his trepidation. "So is Hannah's mother."

"Bring Brother and Sister Harris up here for a few moments."

As he found them and had them follow him up the stairs, Daniel sensed that Elder Woodruff was going to give them suggestions that would help with both his mother and Hannah's mother. It didn't surprise him how quickly the apostle came to the point.

"Brother Browett, when you try to interest your mother in the gospel, how do you do it? And what happens? You be thinking about this, too, Sister Harris."

Daniel scratched his head. "We try to find common ground, using the Bible."

Hannah nodded. "My mother constantly refers to it, and to what her minister has told her."

"Let me suggest something," Wilford said with a glint in his eye. "Missionary work is more effective when we cling to those things that have been revealed through the Prophet Joseph Smith. Use the Book of Mormon, and declare everything that has been restored in the latter-days such as the priesthood, temples, and the nature of God."

Hannah pursed her lips, still skeptical.

"The message of the Restoration centers on the idea that it is not common ground we seek in sharing the gospel," Wilford said, his eyes now riveted on Hannah. "There is nothing common about our message. The way we answer questions about our faith ought to be by finding the quickest and most direct route to the Sacred Grove, meaning the story of how God and Jesus Christ appeared to Joseph. That is our ground. It is sacred ground. It is where testimonies are born and the greatest truths of heaven are unveiled."

Hannah reached for Bobby's hand. He squeezed it, as if to say he knew the apostle was a hundred percent right.

"We claim no priesthood, keys, power, authority or doctrines that do not trace themselves directly to heaven," Elder Woodruff continued, his thoughts churning. "We have not built upon the theological rubble of the past. All that we have has come by direct revelation in the latter days. I testify that the heavens are open once again, and that there is a living prophet on the earth. The quicker both of you convey that message to your mothers, the sooner they will be baptized."

Hannah smiled. "My mother thinks she has all the gospel knowledge she needs. And she thinks Reverend Crooks is the only one qualified to keep spoon feeding her more knowledge. When I told her about you, she wanted to know about your formal training for the ministry. She laughed when I told her you had none."

"I had about the same experience with my mother," Daniel said, looking amused.

Wilford laughed. "It is the degree of understanding one has received from the Spirit, not the degrees awarded by the understanding of men, that prepares an individual to teach or receive the gospel. We live in a world of information and knowledge. But the knowledge of the world has no power to save mankind, inspire faith, or encourage repentance. Only that which comes from God will bring men to God."

"I certainly found that to be true," Daniel admitted.

"It could be worse," Bobby said. "Both my father and Hannah's father passed away a few short years ago. Neither Hannah's mother nor Daniel's mother are as narrow-minded as they were about the religious traditions of both the Methodists and the Anglicans."

Wilford chuckled again as he loosened his tie. "I've been bold and direct with you today, and will remain so. Religious traditions can be a major stumbling block to receiving the restored gospel of Jesus Christ, whether it's here in England or in America. Many doors are closed to us in the name of loyalty to another faith or church. The true test of discipleship lies in receiving the message of the Savior, especially when it entails forsaking former false religious principles. It is self-deception for individuals to say that they have received Jesus into their lives if they then reject the restored gospel. If they had lived on earth at the time of Jesus, would they be one of his disciples? Our message is the same today as it was in the time of Christ."

"I just hope Mama will listen," Hannah said, her expression uncertain.

Wilford opened his Bible. "Listen to what the Savior taught, about who will listen to the message of the gospel: *My sheep hear my voice, and I know them, and they follow me.* The four of you are the Savior's sheep. The gospel was taught, you listened, you accepted, you were baptized. You are what we call the elect of God."

"That makes me feel good," Elizabeth said, her tone faintly gloated.

Switching books, Wilford opened the Doctrine and Covenants. "Furthermore, the Savior said that *the elect hear the Lord's voice and harden not their hearts.*"

Bobby slumped his shoulders. "I guess you could say my heart was hardened for a long time."

"Until you heard the message of the restored gospel," Wilford shot back.

"See my point?"

"Do you think my mother is one of the 'elect,' that she will respond to the gospel?" Hannah asked with a lump in her throat.

"You'll never know until you try," Elder Woodruff said in a firm tone. "Our responsibility in missionary work is to seek the elect of God. The elect are people just like you and your husband. You elect – you choose – by virtue of your freedom of choice, which we call agency, to keep the commandments and have a goal to reach heaven."

"We've got to get our mothers in front of you, Elder Woodruff," Daniel said. "When can we do it?"

Bobby thought of John, his brother.

Wilford pulled his appointment book from his vest pocket. "I can be in Apperley the end of next week."

72

IN THE CRAMPED, stuffy Browett cottage in late July, Martha Browett, swelling in blue gabardine, looked over the guests that had been invited to hear Elder Woodruff. She had approved the meeting without much comment to Daniel, but she appeared to her son be self conscious and ill at ease. Martha had tried to smother her surprise that Ann Eagles had accompanied Bobby and Hannah to the meeting, riding in a Nightingale Dairy wagon pulled by a team of black horses, shiny and bathed in the late afternoon sunshine. Also stepping out of the wagon had been Hannah's younger brother, Elias, and younger sister, Jane, a sight that further disconcerted Martha.

Letting her mood continue sour, Martha sat between her daughter, Rebecca, and Elizabeth. With her lower lip pulled in as a protest of being in the same room with so many Mormons, Martha whispered to Elizabeth, "Where's your brother, John? I thought he was going to be here."

Until now, Elizabeth's face had been brilliantly animated. She had been basking in open pride at the thought of another successful missionary meeting, albeit in her mother-in-law's cottage this time. She turned a bit gloomy to answer Martha. "I guess he can't leave the Ferret's Folly even for *one* night." The admission brought an almost suppressed smile to Martha's face. She wished she were at John's pub, avoiding the preaching that was about to take place out of the mouth of the short, serious-faced American missionary. She still blamed Woodruff for trying to break up her family. She did not want Daniel to go to America, although she agreed that there were more economic opportunities there than in England. But she did not think anyone else in her family would be interested, least of all herself. She was too old to pull up roots, board a creaky sailing vessel and tackle an Atlantic crossing. And she was certain her daughter and other three sons would not want to go.

Martha glanced at Ann Eagles and the two elderly ladies exchanged distorted grins, their faces stiff with a resolve to resist whatever the American had to say. Martha took her lower lip into her teeth and sank deep into her chair.

Ann Eagles sat patiently, eyeing the man Hannah seemed almost to worship, and made a skeptical face. She still felt pressured to even be in the Browett home. Had she to do it all over again, she would not agree to come to the meeting. How would she explain it when Reverend Crooks found out? Certainly he would. Everyone knows everything in small parishes like Apperley and Deerhurst. Ann was relieved that Henry had turned down the invitation. She feared another fight would break out between him and Bobby.

But Ann Eagles' greatest fear was that her daughter, Nancy, would join the Mormon Church. Her fiancée, James Pulham, was too closely associated with Daniel. Both Nancy and James were seated near her. Ann was determined to take the lead role – if no one else did – to point out the fallacies in Mormon doctrine. She had studied the Bible all her life, had attended church every Sunday, and felt confident that she would be able to recall just about every sermon that Reverend Crooks had preached. Especially those he had preached against Mormonism. Proving the falsehood of the American religion would thwart Hannah's desire to leave England.

Ann's concern shut her mind to reason. She was confident that Elder Woodruff would not say anything that would cause her or Martha Browett to change their minds about religion. What she was not prepared for, however, was how she was about to feel.

Through the closed bedchamber door it sounded like crying, but Bobby did not know if it was Hannah or her mother. They had returned from the meeting with Elder Woodruff without much conversation. Bobby could not tell if Ann Eagles had responded to the gospel message or not. Ann looked worn and listless. She had sat silent during the meeting, not saying a thing or asking any question. Once, however, she had wiped her eyes with a tissue. Bobby had been afraid to ask if the tears had come because she had been touched by the spirit, or out of concern that Hannah was certain to emigrate. After they had arrived home, Ann had gone straight to her bedchamber. After Bobby and Hannah had talked softly together for ten minutes in the parlor, Ann had called for Hannah. He could hear muffled conversation, then the crying. He walked to the door.

"Hannah?"

No answer. The sounds ceased.

"Hannah – is everything all right?"

Whispering. Then Hannah's voice. "I'll be right out, Bobby."

Bobby retreated to the parlor then watched as the light in Ann's bedchamber dimmed. Hannah emerged in her oyster-white nightdress, blinking and dabbing a handkerchief at swollen red eyes.

"Was it you crying or your mother, or both or you?" Bobby asked.

"It was both of us," she answered as she began brushing her hair.

"Anything I can do to help?"

"She wants you to baptize her."

"What?"

"The Spirit hit her hard in the meeting, darling. She told me how she was going to disrupt the meeting and cause as much mischief as she could. But she believed everything Elder Woodruff taught her in the meeting. For a while, at least until after we got home, she was in self-denial. She knew the gospel was true but was still struggling inside with her pride. She didn't quite know how to tell me, and to apologize for what she said earlier. While I was in the bedchamber with her she broke down completely. She asked me to forgive her, and said she wanted to be baptized."

"I guess she knows how I felt the first time I heard Elder Woodruff," Bobby admitted.

"There's one slight problem, however," Hannah said, continuing to brush her hair in familiar charming gestures.

"What's that?"

"After you baptize Mama, she wants you to introduce the gospel to Henry."

Daniel stood in the small pond at The Leigh, near the home he and Elizabeth had lived in while they leased the two hundred acres from Squire Hastings. It was the same pond where Bobby and Hannah had been baptized and where, just minutes earlier, Bobby had baptized Hannah's mother. Amid towering white poplars and oak trees and typical late-blooming summer wildflowers, a hushed reverent crowd had also watched several other baptisms – James Pulham, Nancy Eagles, Elias Eagles, and Jane Eagles.

Daniel, who had obtained permission from Elder Woodruff to conduct the baptismal ceremony, raised his arm to the square, glancing quickly at Rebecca, who stood at the edge of the pond, dripping wet in her plain white dress. Now it was their mother's turn. "Martha Pulham Browett. Having been commissioned of Jesus Christ, I baptize you in the name of the Father, and of the Son, and of the Holy Ghost. Amen."

As she arose from the water, her hair plastered to her head, Martha wiped her face and said with exuberance: "Thank you, Daniel. We're going to Zion together!"

AUGUST 2. Sunday. I preached twice in Dymock and Elder G. A. Smith preached in Ledbury. I am happy to learn on our return to the churches in Herefordshire and adjoining country, the Malvern Hills, that the work of God is rolling on rapidly upon every hand. The elders and priests are universally blessed in their ministry in this part of the vineyard. They are baptizing daily. Elder Richards has baptized about 40 since his arrival and Elder Kay about 20. Elders Kington, Browett, Benbow, Cheese, Clark and others have baptized many. We have baptized 40 this day in different parts of the vineyard in this region. There have been 250 baptized in this region since the conference which we held in this region. The membership in the branches here now numbers about 800. We are looking for Elder Kimball every day, and as soon as he arrives we shall take our leave of the saints here and go to the city of London and preach the gospel there. I spent the night at Kingtons.

AUGUST 3. Monday. I walked to Ledbury and met with Brother Smith. Wrote two letters, one to Elder Young, the other to Turley. I forwarded two blank licenses to Elder Young for licensing rooms to preach in.

AUGUST 5. Wednesday. I wrote a letter to the Millennial Star and one to Young and Richards. Elder Smith and I preached at Fromes Hill and confirmed three. We have had warm or hot sunshine for several days, which is almost the first good weather we have had. It appeared like summer, for we have had a cold, wet season.

AUGUST 8. Saturday. One year ago this day I left my family in Montrose to take a mission to England. I started with Elder Taylor, and crossed the Mississippi River in a canoe, sick with ague and without money. But I am now in the south part of England in company with Elder G. A. Smith, and enjoying good health, and I pray the Lord to give good health to my wife and children.

AUGUST 11. Tuesday. Elder Benbow loaned Elder Turley 20 pounds and gave me 15 for my London mission. We took the parting hand with Elder Turley, who started for Liverpool to prepare a ship for about 80 saints to emigrate to America, 40 of which John Benbow takes with him and pays their expenses to America, out of mercy to the poor saints. He gave Elder Turley 100 pounds to secure the passage for those saints. We took the parting hand with Brother and Sister Benbow and the saints at Fromes Hill, to see them no more until I meet them in Nauvoo.

AUGUST 12. Wednesday. We walked to Dymock and found Elder Kimball at Elder Kington's. He had come from Manchester to meet Elder Smith and myself for the purpose of going to the city of London. Elder Kimball had two letters direct from America, one from his wife and the other from father John Smith to his son, George A. Smith. Elder Kimball informed us of the death of Bishop Edward Partridge. His loss will be greatly felt by the church.

73

THE TWO-STORY cottages surrounding the Nightingale Dairy were all similar in their appearance: stone walls, thatched roofs, few windows, and a dreary hearth. They looked their best when the late afternoon sunlight cast a pleasing array of colors on them from the west. Henry's cottage, however, was in disrepair: cracked windowpanes, sagging timbers, and loose door hinges. As Bobby knocked, he wondered what the interior would be like. Henry was almost thirty, unmarried, and still frequented the pubs nearly every night. But at the dairy, no one could outwork him.

The door opened.

"Hello, Henry."

The intense dark brown eyes of Hannah's brother at once seemed distrustful. "What do you want?"

Bobby felt himself go rigid. He wanted to offer a hand of friendship, but knew it would probably be rejected. "Your mother sent me."

"What about?"

Uninvited to go in, Bobby peered inside. He saw clothing strewn about on the furniture and dirty dishes scattered throughout the parlor and the kitchen. "I suppose you heard she joined the Mormon Church."

"What has that got to do with you and me?"

"She wants you to join it, too." A stale, musty smell reached Bobby.

A wry little smile crossed Henry's face. "I'm going to marry a Mormon."

There was a long silence. "What do you mean?" Bobby asked, throwing a challenging look at his brother-in-law. He almost laughed at the absurdity of it.

"Just what I said. I'm getting married next month. Then my wife and I are going to America. Just like you and Hannah."

Bobby stared into Henry's square blocky face in disbelief. "Who is the lucky girl?"

"Katherine Hill. Are you coming to my wedding?"

Bobby recognized the name. She was a cousin to Joseph Hill. "I suppose all of us will be there. When are you going to America?"

"Whenever you do. We'll travel together. Sounds exciting, doesn't it?"

"Have you told your mother?"

"I was fixing to."

Bobby rolled his eyes and decided to leave. "I'll give her the news. She'll be pleased to know."

Henry's decision to marry a Mormon girl, like the elephant, resembled a rope, a wall, a snake, or a tree, depending on where the blind took hold of it. A howl went up from Ann Eagles, who faced the prospect of losing not only Hannah and Nancy to the emigration process, but Henry as well. She cautioned everyone to not press Henry about being baptized, that he would submit as a natural order of things after his marriage. Hannah jeered at Henry's gassy rhetoric, claiming that he already embraced Mormonism despite his status as a non-member. She clung to the hope that her mother would emigrate as well, but was ambivalent about Henry's desire to go to America. Bobby's reaction was to stay out of the controversy altogether.

There was the same quiet look to the parish of Deerhurst in mid-August when Elizabeth hosted Bobby and Hannah to an evening dinner to discuss their emigration plans in more detail. Only a few people had visited the shops that lined the main road earlier in the day because of the heat, rare for England. It was late in the afternoon when farm servants returned to the fields, harvesting second crop hay.

The Browett cottage was a maelstrom of activity, with Martha helping Elizabeth dice vegetables, fry meat, and check the oven to see if the bread had browned. Rebecca was sewing on Katherine Hill's wedding dress. Daniel's youngest brothers, Johnny and Willie, were changing their clothes after another day's work in the cooper shop. Elizabeth's Aristotle book lay open on a chair, waiting for her to take it up again.

Elizabeth came to the door wearing a yellow satin dress that she had bought three days before they lost their farm leases. Her long blonde hair was piled on top of her head, held in place by a matching yellow ribbon. "Come in, come in. Daniel's not here yet. He took Elder Woodruff to Cheltenham to catch the train to London. He'll be back anytime."

"London?" Hannah gasped. "What on earth for?"

"The mission president asked him to take his missionary work there," Elizabeth answered. "I guess his work is done here. He's baptized *every* single one of the United Brethren except one."

Bobby squinted with one eye. "You mean he let one get away?"

"One, and only one. A former lay preacher named Phillip Holdt. Elder Woodruff also expressed frustration over one other person. And you know who that is."

Bobby nodded. "Thomas Bloxham."

"He's turning out to be a hard-headed Anglican, just like your father," Hannah chided.

"Either that or he still blames God for the death of their baby," Bobby added, "because it happened right after Dianah was baptized."

"I suppose Daniel enjoys his calling as district president," Hannah said.

"It has kept him busy," Elizabeth said. "In addition to helping Elder Woodruff and others in the missionary work, he has to recommend brethren for advancement in the priesthood, and for the emigration process."

"Who went to London with Elder Woodruff?" Hannah asked.

"Heber C. Kimball and George A. Smith. Aren't you proud of me? I only met them once and I remembered their names. Daniel was going to introduce them to his brother, Tommy, before they boarded the train. You knew that Tommy moved to Cheltenham, didn't you? Oh, Hannah – aren't you getting excited about going to America? Have you decided which dresses you are going to take and which ones you will have to leave behind?"

Hannah was about to answer when Daniel arrived with his horse and carriage. He appeared in the house rubbing the road dust from his eyes. He drank a big glass of water and sat at the table, famished. His guests were hungry for any news about the emigration process.

"I found out during our trip to Cheltenham that John Benbow is leaving next month," Daniel began after the blessing of the food. "September eighth to be exact."

"So soon?" Hannah asked.

"The ship is called the *North America*. They think there will be around two hundred members of the church on board. Elder Theodore Turley is returning to America and will be their leader."

"It seems so risky," Bobby said. "Who in Nauvoo knows John Benbow? Here he was such an important man. There..."

Daniel chuckled. "Elder Woodruff has written him a very impressive letter of introduction. And the apostles here in England are in charge of issuing everyone a written recommend to make the trip."

"When will the next ships leave?" Hannah pressed, her large brown eyes dancing with excitement. "Do you have any idea when we will go?"

"The brethren have arranged for another ship in October, but that has been assigned to converts from Scotland," Daniel answered, his eyes prowling the table. "Pass the mutton, please. The earliest we can go is January or maybe even February."

"Who do you think will go with us?" Bobby asked.

A slow, gratified grin spread across Daniel's face. "So far, Levi Roberts, John Cox, Williams Jenkins, John Cheese. There will be a lot by the time the list is made." He took another bite of the roast. It was moist and fragrant, especially to a hungry, tireless worker.

"I know that Dianah wants to go, if she can talk Thomas into it," Elizabeth said.

"I hope so."

"And don't forget about Rebecca and me," Martha grinned, showing sparse teeth in an elderly mouth. "What about your mother, Hannah?"

Hannah wiped her mouth. "I'm still trying to convince her. She says she's too old, and she can't stand the thought of leaving some of her grandchildren behind. But then, she can't stand the thought that three of her grandchildren are going with us. She's in a quandary."

"And Henry?" Daniel queried.

Bobby slumped in his chair, dreading the upcoming marriage. "He claims he's going." He wondered how Henry would survive the recommend interview. He would have to lean on the merits of his new wife.

"Do you have any idea how long the trip will take?" Hannah asked.

"About a month, depending on weather," Daniel answered between bites of mutton. "If we leave in the middle of the winter, it could take longer. The winds blow west to east, and we're going west, against the wind most of the time. The brethren are talking about booking a ship that will take us to a southern port in the United States called New Orleans. From there we'd go up the Mississippi River. By the time we get to Nauvoo it will be spring."

Bobby's eyes were alert, searching. "What do you know about Nauvoo?"

"It's right on the banks of the Mississippi in a northern state called Illinois, in a beautiful spot. They're even calling it Nauvoo the Beautiful. Around a thousand acres have been divided into lots eleven by twelve rods in size and distributed to new settlers. Think of it! We'll actually be able to own land – not lease it from some kind of American squire, but actually own it. We'll have room to build a home, have a garden, plant fruit trees and everything."

"Best of all we'll be neighbors to Joseph and Hyrum Smith," said Elizabeth with girlish gratification.

Hannah put her hands together in a wishful look. "Oh, Bobby! Let's get a lot right next to Joseph Smith."

Bobby scoffed. "I'm sure those lots will be gone by now."

"Nauvoo is a small town," Daniel said, his face registering a satisfaction that everyone seemed pleased with his report. "You'll get to see the prophet many times, I'm sure."

AUGUST 13. Thursday. We walked to The Leigh and held a meeting with the saints. Elders Kimball, Smith and myself all spoke to the people. After the meeting I baptized four and helped confirm seven. We spent the night at Elder Browett's.

AUGUST 14. Friday. I spent the day at the Leigh. In the evening we met the saints at Elder Browett's for a council meeting. We had an interesting time. Elder Smith spoke first, and recommended the saints to spent five minutes each day in getting an idea in their minds from the scriptures, and in one year they would have 365 new ideas in their minds which would form a fountain of intelligence and knowledge, which would benefit themselves and mankind. After the meeting two were baptized. We spent the night at Elder Browett's.

AUGUST 16. Sunday. We held a camp meeting at The Leigh. Elders Kimball, Smith and myself spoke both in the forenoon and afternoon. A large congregation was together. We baptized four and confirmed seven, and ordained John Horlick an elder, and George and William Horlick were ordained priests. They came from 12 miles away to the meeting.

AUGUST 17. We took the parting hand with the saints at The Leigh and rode in company with Elder Browett to Cheltenham, and called upon Sister Clark at Mrs. Smith's, No. 3 Union St. We then called upon Brother Thomas Browett, at No. 11 Hanover St. We then called at the Temperance Hotel and spent the night. We leave for London by coach in the morning.

74

AS BOBBY WATCHED Elder Woodruff descend from the pulpit at the close of the Frome's Hill Conference of the church, held at Stanley Hill in Herefordshire on September fourteenth, he wondered where the American got his stamina. The apostle had been in England less than a year but had converted six hundred persons in the Malvern Hills area and was likely to do something similar in London. Bobby compared him to a champion fighter, keenly trained, armed with knowledge, knowing nothing but success.

"I enjoyed your talk," Bobby told Elder Woodruff after waiting in line with Hannah, Daniel, and Elizabeth to greet him. He had preached about baptisms for the dead, in response to a communication he had received from the Prophet Joseph Smith. "It makes me feel good to know people like my father and my brother can be baptized, and that unbaptized little children literally can be saved, despite what my old ministers used to teach."

Wilford contemplated the man whose conversion had been somewhat of a miracle. "Thank you Brother Harris. You need to do that work for your father and brother after you reach Nauvoo. I have some news for you, by the way. While I was in London I heard about a great fight that took place there. A man by the name of Ben Caunt won the British championship. Isn't he the man you were scheduled to fight at the time you joined the church?"

"Yes, sir. And I could have beat him, too."

Wilford smiled at Bobby's playful allusion. "Are you going to give up the gospel and go back to fighting just to prove it?"

"No, sir," Bobby said, drawing his wife to his chest with a powerful arm. "I am not. I have never been happier in all my life. Hannah and I are going to America within a few months. I have peace in my heart and that is worth more than all the money in the world or the honors of men. And Hannah tells me we are going to have another baby."

"Your fourth?"

"Yes, their fourth," Elizabeth said. "And you don't know how *jealous* I am, Elder Woodruff."

"Thanks again for serving as clerk, Brother Browett," Elder Woodruff told Daniel.

"You're welcome. I'll make certain the minutes get forwarded to Nauvoo."

"Do you like working in London, Elder Woodruff?" Hannah asked.

"Yes," Wilford said. "But I have often thought about your personal feelings about London, that you were so uncomfortable there. I feel the same way. I don't think Satan wants the Lord to gain a foothold in London."

Hannah returned a perceptive smile. "Thanks. But if anyone could be successful in converting people to the Lord's true church in that city, it would be you, Elder Woodruff."

Shortly after Henry's marriage in October, when Bobby personally baptized a new convert by the name of James Robins, Hannah felt her husband was firmly entrenched in the gospel. Bobby and Daniel had even taught James, the son of Richard and Ann Robins of Apperley, along with his parents and brother Thomas. After Bobby and Daniel baptized James, Richard, and Ann, they began to teach James' other brother, Edmund, who was baptized a short time later. Soon, the entire Robins family was making plans to emigrate to Nauvoo.

In Hannah's opinion, Bobby made a much better missionary than a professional fighter.

Elder Woodruff returned to London with his companions and on October eighteenth he recorded the following experience in his journal:

> "We retired to rest in good season and I felt well in my mind and slept until 12 at night. I awoke and meditated upon the things of God until near 3 o'clock and while forming a determination to warn the people of London and overcome the powers of darkness by the assistance of God, a person appeared unto me which I considered was the Prince of Darkness, or the Devil. He made war with me and attempted to take my life. He caught me by the throat and choaked [sic] me nearly to death. He wounded me in the forehead. I also wounded him in a number of places in the head. As he was about to overcome me, I prayed to the Father in the name of Jesus for help. I then had power over him and he left me, though much wounded. [Then] three personages dressed in white came to me and prayed with me and I was immediately healed and [they] delivered me from all my troubles."

CHAPTER NOTES

Daniel Browett was the actual recorder of the conference mentioned in this chapter. The quote from Elder Woodruff's journal is verbatim.

According to the personal history of James Robins, on file with the Daughters of the Utah Pioneers, "James was baptized there [Apperley] in October 1840 by Elder Robert Harris."

75

December 1840

A CHEERY FIRE IN THE hearth warmed the interior of the Gadfield Elm chapel. Outside, a cold rain splattered the building, with expectations it would turn to snow. The disagreeable weather would keep the anti-Mormon ruffians away today.

Daniel Browett surveyed a room full of church members who were considering emigration to America with a company under his direction. Everyone was dressed in Sunday best. He was in a jovial mood, partly because it was a week before Christmas, partly because his mother and sister were going with him, and partly because the embarkation date was getting close. Members of the Twelve had arranged for a ship called the *Echo* to leave Liverpool in mid-February. It appeared that around a hundred saints, most of them from the three-county area of Hereford, Gloucester, and Worcester would be on board.

Ann Eagles was not in a jovial mood. All her life she prided herself on her ability to make decisions. As she sat on the third row of the church pews

Daniel had help make, with Bobby and Hannah sitting to her left, and James, Nancy, Henry, Katherine, Elias, and Jane, sitting on her right, she was still undecided leaving England. Deep inside, she had never been happier in her life. She remembered time and time again the words Elder Woodruff had told her the night she listened to him teach the gospel: *You will find the teaching of this church will square with the teachings of the New Testament, and it is the only church you can say that about.* It was true. She was at peace with the gospel and the plan of salvation.

Whether or not to go to America was another matter. Hannah, Nancy, and Henry were leaving England but her two oldest sons, George and William, were not. Elias and Jane, both in their teens, would do what their mother would do. Sitting there in her best black wool coat still wrapped around her aging body, hiding what had been her husband's favorite blue crepe evening dress, Ann's mind desperately sought for an answer. Part of her wanted a new life in America, too. But George and William had given her a half dozen grandchildren already. If she went to Nauvoo she would never see them again. Then again, Hannah had given her mother three grandchildren already, with another on the way. If she didn't go on the Echo, she would never see them again, either. She prayed that Daniel Browett might say something in his remarks that would help her make up her mind.

The whole festive gathering, in Daniel's view, seemed like a dream. Several things came vividly to his mind: Elder Woodruff and his mission to the United Brethren. How each person in the chapel had become converted to the church. How each life had been changed. The miracle of Bobby's conversion. The conversion of Martha, his mother, and Hannah's mother. Henry's marriage to Katherine Hill. What it would be like living in Nauvoo with the Prophet Joseph Smith. Building a temple. Owning land. Enjoying basic freedoms guaranteed by the United States Constitution.

Daniel sensed that the meeting itself represented the stark contrast between the world and membership in the church. He could not recall a time when a group of people smiled more, laughed more, and glistened with the Spirit of Christ. He contrasted the gathering to parties he had attended with Bobby and Squire Hastings, the drinking, the smoking, and the worldly conversation. Tonight there was indeed a festive mood, but it was tempered with quiet dignity.

Spreading his notes before him, Daniel prepared to speak and entertain questions: Cost of the voyage for adults, two pounds seventeen shillings six demies. Cost for children, nineteen shillings three demies. Port of embarkation, New Orleans. During of trip across the Atlantic, expected to be four or five weeks. Change to a steamboat in New Orleans. Ten more days up the Mississippi to New Orleans.

Daniel scanned his audience again, his eyes misting. "I thank Elder Woodruff and the other members of the Twelve for the confidence they have shown in calling me to this special responsibility to take a company of the Saints to America."

With her arms locked with those of Martha and Rebecca, Elizabeth took her lower lip in her teeth, feeling grateful for her husband's leadership qualities: Trusted lay preacher in the United Brethren congregation. One of the first converts of Wilford Woodruff. Conference clerk. District president. And now president of a company of Saints bound for Nauvoo.

Daniel's smile was infectious. "It appears that more than a hundred saints will be on board the ship. The brethren organize each company with a leadership of seven men. Under their direction, and after much deliberation and prayer, I have chosen six assistants."

There was a hushed murmur in the crowd.

Daniel named John Cheese, John Ellison, Robert Harris, William Jenkins, James Lavender, and David Wilding. They stood.

"All those of you who can sustain myself and these brethren as your presidency during the trip, please manifest by raising your right hand."

Every hand went up except that of Henry Eagles. His recommend for the voyage had been approved by Brigham Young, based on Daniel's approval.

Daniel frowned. *Please Henry, no trouble today.* His voice turned shaky. "Are there any opposed? Manifest by the same sign."

Henry sat as a piece of stone, his expression hostile. He laughed inwardly, knowing the distress he was causing. *I'm not a member. Why should I vote either way?* His hand did not go up.

Daniel breathed a sigh of relief.

Temporarily distracted by Henry's non-vote, Hannah clutched the arm of her husband. It was no mistake that Daniel had addressed his brother-in-law as "Robert" instead of "Bobby." He had received instructions to do so. Robert Harris, Jr. had changed his life. He was no longer Bobby the pugilist, or Bobby the butcher. He was Robert the dedicated Mormon, a man who would wear the name of his father the rest of his life.

Daniel took a deep breath and began his remarks. "Brothers and Sisters, it will be the goal of the seven men you have sustained to get you safely to Nauvoo, Illinois, United States of America. We hope to arrive there in time for you to acquire farm ground and building lots, and to get crops in and gardens planted."

Robert closed his eyes and wondered what it would be like to actually own land. He could see himself behind a team of horses, turning over the prairie sod. Cutting trees, hewing logs, building a log home. No one to take his farm or his home away.

Speaking with confidence now, Daniel continued. "Elder Brigham Young and the other brethren have established a shipping agency at Liverpool. They have secured group passage rates that are far less expensive than if you negotiated them yourselves. Of course that is for steerage passage, including your baggage." He outlined the cost.

"You are responsible for your own provisions, bedding and cooking utensils. We will help you organize into groups for cooking and eating. You will need to be in Liverpool no later than Saturday, February thirteenth. If you arrive early you are responsible for your own lodging. If you have relatives or friends in the Liverpool area, please arrange to stay with them until you can board the ship. You are also responsible for your travel from here to Liverpool. Rail passage is available from any of our large cities such as Worcester or Gloucester."

Daniel glanced at his notes, paused, and said, "Let me take your questions."

"Why are we going to New Orleans instead of New York City?" one quickly asked, pointing out what he thought might be a glaring discrepancy.

"The brethren have determined that it is much cheaper to go through New Orleans than New York. That's why we are leaving in February. That way we can avoid the heat and sickness of the summer climate in New Orleans. We should be going up the Mississippi in April, when the weather is favorable. We will charter a steamboat when we get there which reduces the overall cost to all of us, just as it has reduced our costs to charter the ship in Liverpool."

"But isn't it treacherous to cross the Atlantic in the winter?" Levi Roberts queried.

The eyes of Ann Eagles widened. *Treacherous?* The word sounded foreboding. She made a frightful face.

Daniel's answer did little to salve her concerns. "Yes, but ships are departing almost daily. Only a few have any problems."

Ann's face remained sullen, hard, and puzzled. *A few? What if our ship is one of the few?*

"What is Liverpool like?" John Cox asked.

"I have just returned from Liverpool. Until that trip I had never been there. I suspect that none of you have ever been there. The church is using Liverpool because it is centrally located between Great Britain and Ireland. There are many converts from Ireland as well who are emigrating. A few may be on our ship – we don't know how many yet. Certainly there will be at least two hundred non-members on board as well.

"The Liverpool harbor has channels that are easily navigable because it is situated just a few miles up the Mersey Estuary from the Irish Sea and Liverpool Bay. Liverpool is also a day's sail nearer in distance to America than is London. The city itself has crowded docks and fireproof warehouses. You'll see ships of every nation. There are two hundred thousand people who live there, many of them at poverty's extreme. I am to caution you to be on the lookout for those who would steal from you. Be careful, brothers and sisters. It is a city of contrasts – a haven of churches but a home of brothels – the super rich and the super poor. It is overcrowded, rambunctious and tough."

"What can you tell us about money?" a voice in the back asked.

"Sovereigns are more profitable than silver or any other money in emigrating to America. When we get there, beware of American paper money. Banks in America are breaking almost daily."

Hannah was not concerned much about money tonight. Rather, she was feeling self-conscious because of a bulging stomach. Hannah had come to the meeting in an oversized and modified wool day dress, covered with a dull gray shawl. All night she surveyed the chapel for another woman who might be in a family way, but could see none. As she listened to the questions and answers, she decided to save her questions for later so that she could ask them in private. Would the ship make her seasick? Would it be dangerous for her unborn child? There was a likelihood that her child would be born during the trip, especially if the voyage took longer than expected. How would her three children fare? How many other children were going?

Despite her outward display of happiness, Hannah had deep regrets about leaving England. If her mother did not go, it was doubtful she would every see her again. Same for Elias, Jane, and her other brothers and their families. As she had contemplated the matter, a scripture came to mind. *Therefore shall a man leave his father and his mother, and shall cleave unto his wife: and they shall be one flesh.* Her and Robert were determined to go. She knew it was the right thing to do, but knowing it still did not make it easy.

For another hour Daniel answered questions about a variety of subjects: baggage limitations, how to pack, what food to take, cooking onboard, rumors of unscrupulous sailors, disease prevention, lack of doctors.

Elizabeth thought of her Aristotle book, her lack of experience, and began dreading circumstances during the voyage that she might be needed.

After the question-answer period, people gathered in clusters to discuss what they heard. Ann Eagles found herself clinging to Hannah's arm, listening to small talk among Robert and his friends. Levi Roberts and John Cox would be on the *Echo*. Edward Phillips and William Pitt planned on emigrating later, after they saved more money. John Davis, who would marry Mary Ann Weston in four more days, on Joseph Smith's birthday, was delaying a decision until he felt he had his mother's approval.

Her own family was another matter, and Ann was in a quandary. Robert and Hannah, and James and Nancy, were emigrating. So were Henry and his new wife, Katherine. But George and William were not members, worked at the dairy, and had not desire to go to Nauvoo. She counted the grandchildren she would be leaving behind. Then she counted the grandchildren that would be leaving on the *Echo*. And the ones that would be born in the future, some in England, some in America.

Cluster conversations continued well into the next hour. Finally, Hannah asked her mother the inevitable question: "Well, Mama, what do you think? Are you going with us?"

Ann had heard only one thing all night that helped her. Saturday,

February thirteenth. That's the day everyone who was going on the *Echo* was supposed to be in Liverpool. If she paid a small deposit for herself and her two youngest children, Elias and Jane, it would not be much of a loss if she did not get it back.

"I may as well pay my deposit," Ann said with a reluctant sigh.

"Mama!" Hannah screamed. "You're going with us!"

Ann merely acknowledged Hannah's reaction with a warm smile, then reached inside her purse and looked for Daniel to tell him the news.

A FINAL WORD

Daniel Browett, Elizabeth Browett, Robert (Bobby) Harris and Hannah Maria Eagles Harris are real characters. Just as portrayed, they lived in Gloucestershire when Elder Wilford Woodruff went on a mission to England in 1840. The majority of the other characters are real as well.

Although a traditional family history portrays Bobby as a pugilist, there is no evidence that he was a contender for the British heavyweight championship. He likely participated in boxing at local fairs only, and probably was an ordinary fighter. Otherwise, the story you have read is based on a true story.

Volume two of this series will find the main characters on a ship, headed out of Liverpool for New Orleans. It will chronicle their dangerous trip across the Atlantic, their trip on a steamboat up the Mississippi River to Nauvoo, and their first years in the Mormon settlement.

ABOUT THE AUTHOR

Darryl Harris received his B.A. degree in communications from Brigham Young University in 1966, after attending Idaho State University. He was graduated from Marsh Valley High School in 1959 and was raised in the small Idaho communities of McCammon and Arimo.

After being employed by the *Deseret News* in Salt lake City and the *Post-Register* in idaho Falls, and Evans Advertising Agency in Salt Lake City, he began his own business, Harris Publishing, Inc.1, in Idaho Falls in 1971. The firm has seventy-five employees and it publishes twelve different magazines, many of them national. Some of them are: *SnoWest, SledHeads, Houseboat, Pontoon & Deck Boat, Riverjet, Potato Grower, The Sugar Producer, Mountain West Turf,* and *Idaho Falls.*

His church callings have included bishop, counselor in a bishopric, mission president (Korea Seoul), stake mission president, and area public communications director (Southeast Idaho). He and his wife continue to reside in Idaho Falls. They have five children and fourteen grandchildren.